Bob ~pherd is a security advisor and author of the *Sunday*
Tin   p Ten Bestseller *The Circuit: An ex-SAS Soldier's True*
Acc   : *of One of the Most Powerful and Secretive Industries*
Spau   *d by the War on Terror*. A 20-year veteran of Britain's
elite   cial Air Service with more than a decade and a half of
priva   ecurity work to his credit, Bob has successfully negotiated   ome of the most dangerous places on earth as both a
soldie   and private citizen. Shepherd is a regular media
comm   ator on security issues and has appeared on *CNN*
Intern ional, *BBC One*, *BBC World* and *BBC Radio*. He also
share: s insights on hostile environments through his weekly
blog,   w.bobshepherdauthor.com

The
Infidel

Bob Shepherd

with M. P. Sabga

SIMON &
SCHUSTER

London · New York · Sydney · Toronto

A CBS COMPANY

First published in Great Britain by Simon & Schuster UK Ltd, 2010
A CBS COMPANY

1 3 5 7 9 10 8 6 4 2

Simon & Schuster UK Ltd
1st Floor
222 Gray's Inn Road
London WC1X 8HB

www.simonandschuster.co.uk

Simon & Schuster Australia
Sydney

A CIP catalogue record for this book
is available from the British Library.

Trade Paperback ISBN 978-1-84737-775-3
Hardback ISBN 978-0-85720-058-7

Printed in the UK by CPI Mackays, Chatham ME5 8TD

To Margaret Moth

Camerawoman
1951-2010

Your eye was fearless, your talent boundless
and your love of life – infinite.

Prologue

Kabul 2008

The cursor ticked impatiently. Rudy glared at it. To think he'd once regarded a blank computer screen as the height of enticement; a siren beckoning him to write stories that would reveal buried truths and maybe, if he worked hard enough, influence the war in Afghanistan. Two years in Kabul had put paid to that.

Most nights, Rudy would be out drinking with the rest of the city's disillusioned expats. But it was a bank holiday back home. All the domestic correspondents covering Westminster and the Royal Family had hauled their pampered arses to the Cotswolds leaving entire swathes of column inches to fill. Rudy's editor in London wanted a thousand words from him no later than 8 p.m. The mandate, as always, was broad yet stiflingly narrow. 'Whatever strikes your fancy, dear boy. Readers adore you. Just keep giving them what they want.'

Rudy checked his watch. His deadline was less than an hour away. There was no excuse, really. He could write the entire story without leaving his office. The news wires had furnished him with plenty of raw material; facts, figures, quotes he could credit to 'senior officials'. All he had to do was plug the information into his template of rotating names, dates and death tolls and cap it with a punchy lead.

He scanned the detritus of his desk. Among the spiral note-books, ballpoint pens, yellowed papers, computer gear and communications equipment stood a half-emptied bottle of his favourite tipple: The Famous Grouse. Several generous pours of the blended Scotch had failed to produce anything by way of copy. He was reaching for another when a box stashed behind a pile of old notebooks caught his eye. Rudy unearthed it and wiped the dust from the label: Cragganmore 29 Year Old. The extravagant single malt had been sitting there untouched for what seemed like donkey's years.

Rudy shrugged and uncorked the bottle. The peaty fumes circled his head like a cavalry charging to the rescue. He decanted the amber liquid into a tumbler and raised it to his mouth. Out of nowhere, a screaming pain flared up in his right buttock. He'd been sitting at his desk for so long the entire right side of his body had frozen stiff. His left side, meanwhile, was so hot his skin had practically blistered. It was one of the many drawbacks of being posted to a shithole. Like most foreign offices in Kabul, Rudy's was heated by wood-burning stoves and powered by a large diesel generator. In the winter months, his office was like the moon: one side lit and warmed by fire, the other plunged into cold darkness.

Rudy threw the Scotch into his mouth and funnelled it down his throat. Agony slowly dissolved into relief as a wave of warmth silenced his old injury. Now he was ready to work. He poised his hands over the keyboard and let fly.

COALITION BLASTED
OVER CIVILIAN DEATHS

BY Rudy Lipkingard
Correspondent, Kabul

KABUL, 23 March –
Three Afghan civilians were
killed and dozens wounded after
being caught in crossfire between
NATO forces and suspected
Taliban insurgents.

He sat back and read his opening line, imagining his editor's reaction. '*Are you taking the piss?*' No one gave a fuck about dead Afghans. Rudy knew that. Readers barely raised an eyebrow any more when British soldiers were killed, unless of course, several died in a single day. The last time he had written about a lone British military death in Afghanistan, the story was slashed from five hundred words to fifty and buried in a news round-up.

Rudy reviewed his lead again, searching for ways to make it appeal to both his editor and the legions of faceless, nameless readers he allegedly informed. The words 'goodies and baddies' whipped through his mind like a tornado, dredging up clichés and sensationalist turns of phrase that would boost circulation numbers. Rudy positioned his hands over the keyboard ready to strike once more.

'Sir, come in, sir, over,' crackled a voice.

Rudy slumped back in his chair. 'Bugger . . . bugger . . .' he muttered as he grabbed a radio from his desk.

'Sir, come in, sir, over,' repeated the voice. It was Haroon, his head of security. By this time of night the Afghan was usually tucked up on a wooden slab in his guardhouse hugging his AK-47 like a teddy.

'What is it, Haroon?' said Rudy into the radio.

'Sir, there is a beggar at the gate, over.'

'Get rid of him,' said Rudy. 'And for God's sake don't give

him anything to eat or drink or he'll come round again.'

'Sir, the beggar says he know you, over.'

Rudy rolled his eyes. Haroon should have known better than to bother him with this. News bureaus in Kabul attracted every conceivable sort of person: aid workers seeking coverage of do-gooder projects; disgruntled Afghan officials selling stories of corruption 'at the highest levels of government'; musicians raising funds for cultural tours of Europe; shady business types plugging Afghanistan as an 'exciting investment opportunity'; so-called 'reformed radicals' offering to disclose the exact hiding place of Osama bin Laden – for a fee; locals with a marginal grip of English looking for work as translators; and beggars of every ilk, from able-bodied men to children disfigured by their parents to earn the family bread.

'You may find this difficult to fathom, Haroon, but I'm not in the habit of befriending beggars,' said Rudy.

'Sir, I do not understand, sir, over.'

'Just get rid of him, Haroon,' Rudy snapped.

'Sir, he is English man. He say he will not leave until he see you, over.'

An English beggar in Kabul? Jaded as he was, even Rudy was intrigued. 'Keep him there. I'll be right out.'

Wazir Akbar Khan was a magnet for vagrants. Though aspects of the neighbourhood resembled poorer areas of Kabul – no street lights, unpaved roads, open sewage ditches – there were ample features advertising its affluence: industrial-sized generators that cost more to run for a single day than most Afghans earned in a month; wooden guardhouses plonked outside fortified gates, and, of course, Kabul's most ubiquitous status symbol – Toyota 4x4s.

The night sky was clear and an icy wind lashed Rudy's face

as he stepped into the courtyard. Haroon was waiting for him,
a torch pointed down at his feet. Rudy could just make out the
tails of the guard's beige cotton shalwar kameez peeking out
from beneath a thin, black coat.

'It's bloody cold out here,' Rudy complained.

Haroon shone the torch on his employer. 'Sir.'

Rudy recoiled. 'Not in my eyes, Haroon.'

'Sorry, sir.' Haroon pointed the torch back toward the ground
and beckoned Rudy to follow him. The light bounced along a
cobbled walkway, swept over an iron gate and stopped on a sliding partition. Inside the small opening Rudy could see a filthy
grey turban and a disfigured hand raised to resist the intrusive
glare. Rudy took the torch from Haroon and aimed it indirectly
at the figure. The hand lowered and a face took form: sunken,
heavily bearded, punctuated by jaundiced, dark eyes. Rudy
adjusted the light to reveal more of the stranger. The man looked
as if he'd been ripped to pieces and stuck back together with
little regard for the original form. His shoulders caved inward
and one sloped a few inches lower than the other. His legs
appeared to buckle, as if they couldn't support the weight of his
torso. His clothes – a stained shalwar kameez and a woollen
vest – had been torn and mended many times over. Despite the
bitter cold, the stranger wore flimsy sandals slipped over socks.

Had he not lived in Kabul for so long, Rudy might have been
moved by such a pitiful sight. But the stranger was no different
from thousands of other down-and-out Afghans wandering the
streets in search of handouts. 'This man isn't English,' Rudy
declared.

A voice rose up from the other side of the gate. 'You're damn
right I'm not English.' The belligerent accent was instantly rec-
ognizable – Scottish. Rudy was stunned. 'Let me see your face,'
the stranger demanded. His voice was powerful, as if he were

channelling someone younger and stronger.

Rudy stepped back and held the torch under his chin. 'Rudy Lipkingard,' said the stranger. 'I bet you never thought you'd see me again.'

Rudy turned the light back on the beggar and studied him closely. There was an echo of familiarity in the face, a heaviness in the brow that clawed at the memory.

'Remember giving us this, you ambitious little twat?' The beggar shoved a business card through the partition. Rudy took it. The paper was worn as thin as tissue, the ink barely legible but it was definitely one of his. He must have passed out hundreds like it around Kabul. 'I've come back,' said the man. His voice grew heavy with emotion. 'I've come back. I've come back.'

Rudy nodded to his guard. 'Haroon.'

'Yes, sir.'

'Open the gate.'

Rudy showed the stranger to his office and offered him a chair beside the wood-burning stove. In the warmth of the fire, the man appeared to melt into a heap of rags. He smelled horrendous, like sour milk. 'Give me a minute to chase the chill from my bones,' said the stranger. 'The cold in this damn country would have killed William Wallace.' The man pawed his thighs as he took in his surroundings, his expression alternating between weariness and wonder, like he'd stumbled upon a lost civilization after a harrowing journey. His eyes settled on the treasure on Rudy's desk – the bottle of Cragganmore.

Rudy moved swiftly to head off a needless waste. He reached for the Famous Grouse. 'May I offer you a drink?'

'Saving the Cragganmore for your posh guests?' asked the stranger.

Rudy stiffened.

'Don't worry, mate,' said the man. 'I used to be like you – a pretentious git. Not any more, mind. After what I've been through, I wouldn't trade a dram of the Grouse for a whole bottle of your precious Cragganmore.'

Rudy poured the man a drink and let him enjoy a pull before engaging him. 'So,' said Rudy. 'What can I do for you?'

'Do for me?' said the stranger, still savouring the whisky on his tongue. 'I gave you the greatest story of your career, mate.'

The greatest story of your career, mate. The words were familiar but Rudy couldn't connect them to a time or place. He scrutinized the stranger again. 'I'm sorry, I didn't catch your name.'

The stranger's eyes narrowed with insult. 'My name? My bloody name? Are you taking the piss?'

'I'm sorry,' said Rudy. 'I, I . . .'

The stranger rose and slammed his glass on the desk. 'You wanker!'

The furious response was unexpected. Rudy feared he had unwittingly taken in a lame animal only to discover it was rabid. He tried to calm his guest. 'There's no need to get upset.'

The irate Scot bent over and unravelled an old, blood-caked bandage from his ankle. The layers of putrid cloth fell to the ground, revealing a shiny, metal object. Rudy's heart skipped a beat. *My God*, he thought. *It's a gun!* Rudy reached for his radio to call Haroon. Before he could grab it, the stranger rose and extended the object toward his host. It was a stainless-steel digital camera. Rudy heaved a sigh of relief. 'Go on then,' said the stranger, 'take a look at what's on it.'

Rudy plugged the camera into his computer. The hard drive hummed as, one by one, pictures populated the screen. There were dozens of them, snapshots of scenes more incredible than anything Rudy had ever seen in Afghanistan. When they finished rendering, the stranger clicked on the first picture in the series. 'Maybe this will jar your memory.'

The screen filled with the image of two men dressed in Afghan clothing: one pale, stern and ginger, the other olive-skinned with dark Mediterranean eyes framed by thick, black brows. Suddenly it all came flooding back to Rudy – the meeting on the Jalalabad road, the story he'd abandoned, the men he'd given up on. 'Now do you remember me?' asked the stranger.

Rudy blinked in disbelief. The shell of a human being standing before him was one of Afghanistan's most wanted fugitives.

Chapter 1

Kabul 2006

The 4x4 was fully loaded and ready to go. Two steel containers – one filled with a dozen 9mm pistols, the other extra magazines, ammo and cleaning kits – lay hidden in the boot underneath a blanket. John Patterson and his team were seated in their usual positions: John at the wheel; his fellow Scot, Dusty Miller, beside him; and their Afghan translator Haider in the rear. Resting on the floor were three black canvas bags, each concealing an AK-47 short made ready with a round in the spout.

'Mr Patterson.' The faux awfully, awfully voice was muffled by layers of steel and glass. 'Mr Patterson!'

Dusty checked his side mirror. Simon Hampson was waddling toward them, his rounded face glistening with sweat.

'What do you think he wants?' asked Dusty.

John turned the key in the ignition. 'I don't really care.'

The sound of the revving engine forced Simon to move faster. His stubby legs struggled to move his heavy-set body to the front of the 4x4 before it pulled out. 'Don't you dare leave this compound!' Simon planted his hands on the bonnet, an act of respite he tried to mask as an ultimatum.

Haider watched Simon with the cool reserve he'd once

ascribed to the British but had come to claim as his own. Flashing a superior smile – the only fault line in a contiguous swathe of thoughtfully groomed stubble – the green-eyed Afghan spoke. 'I believe Simon fancies himself to be – how do you say – a superhuman? superhero?'

'Close,' said Dusty, 'but I think the word you're looking for is super-twat.'

Haider smiled. 'I do not believe he intends to move.'

'Then we'll have to drive over the top of him,' said John.

Dusty cocked his head to one side and assessed the obstacle. 'Think we have enough horsepower to clear the fat bastard?'

Simon waved a finger at the windscreen. 'Mr Patterson, I *order* you to dismount that vehicle immediately!' As soon as the words left his mouth Simon realized he'd miscalculated – badly. John's thousand-yard stare retracted and locked on his position. A wave of dread rolled over Simon as the vehicle door swung open and John climbed down. He closed in on Simon's position.

'Am I wearing a uniform?' said John, his Angus brogue pacing each step.

Simon tried to conceal his mounting panic. 'What are you on about?'

John continued his advance. 'Are you wearing a uniform?'

Scenarios all involving physical pain swooped through Simon's head. His body tilted back, bracing for a blow. 'You're talking nonsense, man.'

John stopped one foot short of Simon and squared up to him. Standing face to face, the two men looked as if they belonged to different centuries. Simon was a poster child of modern excess, a corpulent body disfigured by decades of inactivity, a face swollen with entitlement. John, by contrast, personified discipline and hard work. Bands of muscle, the kind forged through years of physical taxation, ringed his forearms. His blue eyes were embedded in whites yellowed by overexposure to sunlight. The clearest evidence of his age, however, was a yawning crease etched into his forehead. The rest of his face was hidden beneath a flaming red beard that belied his forty-eight years.

John raised his chin. 'Well, seeing as you're not in uniform and I'm not wearing one, why are you acting like we're still in the military?'

Terrified, Simon retreated to the instincts of class. 'Have you no respect for someone who once held the Queen's commission, Mr Patterson?'

'I didn't have much respect for them when I was in uniform,' said John. 'We're all civilians now. Don't call me "Mr Patterson". The name is John.'

The sting of the insult was tempered by Simon's relief at having been spared a beating. He proceeded cautiously. 'I am well aware that we are no longer in Her Majesty's services. Mr' – he stopped and corrected himself – 'John, but we are employees of ShieldGroup and as such we are expected to adhere to the *modus operandi*, if you will. Now, it has come to my attention that not only did you disregard a request from SOCA to reinstate two of your students, but you sent a report to Pete Mitchell in London defending your actions – *in unnecessary detail*, I might add. You can't just ignore SOCA. They're our client. They tell us what to do, not the other way around. Had you cleared all of this through me first, a gross misunderstanding could have been avoided.'

John dismissed Simon's protest with a smirk.

'I am ShieldGroup's in-country manager for Afghanistan,' Simon puffed. 'I need to be informed of all matters pertaining to our operations here, especially those that could impact on us negatively.'

John's face hardened. 'I don't answer to you.'

'You can't ignore the chain of command simply because you share a history with someone. You're a fixed-term contractor with ShieldGroup. Mr Mitchell is a director of this company. He does not have time to indulge your conspiracy theories. Remember your place Mr' – again, Simon caught himself – 'John.'

'I don't know what your little spies in London have been telling you, but whatever passes between me and Pete Mitchell is none of your damn business.' John shoved his finger in Simon's spongy chest. 'So if you know what's good for you, you'll wind your neck in and let me get on with my job.'

Simon smiled snidely. 'You haven't a clue how corporations work, have you?'

John turned and walked away.

The growing distance buoyed Simon's confidence. 'Typical SAS hubris,' he called after John. 'You think those three letters make you invincible but they don't. The SAS counts for nothing in the real world, do you hear me? Nothing!'

Chapter 2

The Afghan officers quietly jockeyed for seats on the reviewing stand. They moved in fits and starts; as if sharing space was a totally alien concept. The least civilized looking of the group, a tall, beefy character with an unruly grey beard, gold epaulettes and a knitted white skullcap was the first to mark his territory. Two younger men – each wearing long black robes with matching turbans – remained standing like sentries on either side of him.

Rudy recorded the scene in his notebook. *25 June 2006. KMTC. 7.30 a.m. An Afghan General flanked by men who appear to be two Taliban.*

The young journalist paused to take in the rest of his surroundings. The Kabul Military Training Centre was buzzing with activity. Soldiers dashed about, taking advantage of the low morning sun, mindful that by midday, the soaring temperature would turn even the lightest of tasks into a test of endurance. The dominant uniforms were Afghan – green surplus, hand-me-down combats from Western nations – with a spattering of NATO forces thrown in for good measure; Americans in digitally patterned beige and grey; Brits in low-tech two-toned brown; Italians in smartly tailored, crotch-hugging camouflage. The camp itself was comprised of low concrete buildings grouped around a large stone garden. Old Soviet tanks and nineteenth century British cannons – relics of failed foreign occupations – lined the enclosure. The camp's current inhabitants had also made their distinct, albeit conflicting marks. A mosque perched on a hillock twenty feet above the garden stood as testament to Islamic Afghanistan's triumph over the infidel Soviets – or *kafirs* as they were called locally. Less pious were the blackened, concrete shells of bombed-out buildings, souvenirs of the brutal civil war that swept the Taliban to power and the American-led campaign that drove them out.

Rudy catalogued each detail like a detective combing a crime scene. Great stories, he believed, came about through serendipitous moments of glory or by peeling back seemingly innocuous features to find the truth buried within. The first report of his new posting – an Afghan National Army graduation – clearly fell into the latter category. Rudy was part of a press junket of ten journalists invited by ISAF – the NATO-led International Security Assistance Force – and the Afghan Ministry of Defence. He had hoped for something more exclusive if not exciting for his inaugural dispatch. Rudy dreamed of emulating his role model, John Simpson, the BBC correspondent who 'liberated' Kabul with the Northern Alliance in 2001. The prospect of becoming the print world's John Simpson was the deciding factor for Rudy when he accepted the three-year 'hardship' assignment. Afghanistan, unlike domestic beats, not only gave him a chance to report stories that would enlighten readers, it could also earn him something which every journalist secretly craved – star status.

As expected, the Afghan National Army graduation was highly orchestrated. Rudy and the rest of Kabul's international press corps were plied with food and drink and led to the parade ground for five-minute one-on-one interviews with an ISAF spokesperson. The narrow time windows were tactical, sufficient for getting the facts, prohibitive toward anything probing. But Rudy, brimming with enthusiasm, wasn't prepared to capitulate so easily.

A well-manicured hand reached out toward him. 'Thank you for coming this morning,' said the equally polished voice.

Rudy shielded his eyes to assess his interviewee. The spokesperson looked every inch the dashing NATO officer: tall, well-groomed, temples tinged with enough grey to convey authority. 'Thank you for inviting me, sir,' said Rudy. 'Could I get your full name and title please?'

'Lieutenant Colonel James Pilkington Howard, Public Affairs Officer to the Commander of ISAF Forces, Afghanistan.' Rudy scribbled as Howard spoke. 'I would prefer it, however, if you would refer to me in your article anonymously. "Senior officer" seems to do the trick.'

'Is that for security reasons, sir?' asked Rudy.

Howard dismissed the notion with a wave of his hand. 'Not at all. More of a gesture of humility on my part. What you're about to see is the result of the commander's efforts and those of his counterparts in the Afghan MoD. I am loath to assume credit for what is rightfully their work.'

'I understand,' said Rudy. 'So tell me, how many recruits are graduating today?'

'Roughly a thousand soldiers give or take. A typical Afghan National Army battalion, or *kandak* as it's known in Dari,' said Howard.

'Can you tell me about the training they've received?'

'Every ANA recruit undergoes ten weeks of basic combat skills and infantry training here at the KMTC.'

'Who trains them?' Rudy asked.

'ANA officers overseen by ISAF mentors, primarily American, British, Canadian and French,' Howard explained.

'So who has ultimate authority then?' Rudy pressed. 'The ANA or ISAF?'

Howard laced his fingers together. 'What takes place here is best described as a partnership. The ANA and ISAF are united in achieving the same goal – bringing security and stability to the new Afghanistan.' Howard unfurled his fingers and looked directly at Rudy. 'That unity starts here.'

Rudy bristled at the stilted tagline, no doubt dangled in the hope he would devour it now and regurgitate it later in his copy. He hated being treated like a trained seal. 'So what exactly is the role of the ANA? Is it to supplement ISAF's operations in Afghanistan?'

'The long-term goal', said Howard, 'is to build an Afghan army that will stand and fight on its own.'

Rudy saw an opening. 'How then would you respond to reports of high AWOL and desertion rates among ANA recruits?'

Howard appeared unfazed by the fact that Rudy had done his homework. 'When one endeavours to build an institution from the ground up, a few setbacks are to be expected. It's taken four years to bring the ANA from nought to twenty thousand troops. Now that we have a strong foundation in place, we hope to bring that total to seventy thousand over the next two years.'

'What's the rush?' asked Rudy. 'Is ISAF looking for a quick exit from Afghanistan?'

'No,' Howard insisted. 'This is not about accelerating timetables. What we're doing is gradually shifting the burden of security from ISAF to the Afghans.'

Rudy kept digging. 'Where will these new recruits be deployed?'

'Throughout Afghanistan. Foreign expeditions are not on the cards at present.' Howard smiled cheerily.

The stab at humour only fed Rudy's intuitive dislike of the man. Howard didn't fidget or display a single nervous tick. He was far too smooth to be trusted. 'Is Helmund Province "on the cards"?'

'Helmund is currently in a transition period,' said Howard 'I'm not at liberty to comment on operations there.'

'Why not?' countered Rudy. 'You do represent ISAF.'

'Yes, but command of the southern Afghan provinces won't officially pass to ISAF until next month,' Howard explained.

'I'm afraid I don't follow,' said Rudy. 'British forces are deploying to Helmund. If ISAF's not in charge of them then who is?'

Howard flashed the patient but condescending expression of onc accustomed to tutoring the less informed. 'Yes, well, it can be rather confusing. Presently, there are two military missions working in parallel to stabilize Afghanistan; Operation Enduring Freedom which is a US-led operation and ISAF which is overseen by NATO. US troops under the command of Operation Enduring Freedom have been operating in Helmund since 2002. If all goes according to schedule, however, roughly three thousand British troops under ISAF's command should replace US forces in Helmund by the end of next month. Does that clarify the situation for you or do you require further explanation?'

Rudy detected a note of derision in Howard's impeccably polite delivery. Bastard. 'Are the Brits being sent to Helmund because the Americans are failing there?' he asked.

It was a loaded question. But Howard's face remained placid. 'Failure has nothing to do with it. The deployment of British troops to Helmund is part of the planned expansion of ISAF's area of responsibility. In that respect, it is important to bear in mind that Operation Enduring Freedom was focused on rooting out remnants of al-Qaeda and Taliban in Helmund. Now that that objective has been addressed, the British mission will focus on supporting aid efforts already under way there; hence their designation as PRTs.'

'PRTs?' enquired Rudy.

'Provincial Reconstruction Teams,' said Howard. 'PRTs execute development projects for maximum impact: building roads, bridges, schools; things aimed at winning hearts and minds.' As he spoke, an Afghan military brass band began tuning its instruments. An ear-splitting cacophony of hoots, slides and shrieks filled the air. 'I'm terribly sorry,' said Howard, 'but the ceremony will start soon and some of your colleagues in the press corps are waiting to speak with me.'

Rudy reckoned he could have an hour alone with Howard and he'd still walk away with nothing. If his story were to stand out from the rest, he'd have to interview another official connected to the day's proceedings, someone unaccustomed to dealing with the press. He quickly searched the faces on the reviewing stand. 'I appreciate your time, Lieutenant Colonel Howard. Before I go, do you think it would be possible to interview one of the ANA officers?'

'I'm sure that could be arranged,' replied Howard.

Rudy pointed to the grey-bearded Afghan general and his turbaned entourage. 'What about that gentleman there?'

Howard bowed his head before answering. *A crack in his facade?* Rudy wondered. 'Ah yes. General Ustad Rasul. The professor,' said Howard.

'Professor?' asked Rudy.

'Ustad. It's Arabic for professor,' Howard explained.

'What's the story with the chaps in black turbans?' asked Rudy. 'They look like Taliban.'

A note of disapproval grazed Howard's cut-glass voice.

'Those gentlemen are General Rasul's nephews.'

'Forgive my lack of political correctness,' said Rudy. 'I'm new to Afghanistan.'

'It's a very common misperception,' said Howard. 'If we judged every man in Afghanistan by the colour of his turban I'm certain we'd see more enemies than friends here.'

'Well, I would be most grateful if you could introduce me to General Rasul,' said Rudy.

'Of course,' said Howard. 'Come and find me after the ceremony.'

Chapter 3

The drive from ShieldGroup's compound to the KMTC was a six-mile straight shot along the Jalalabad Road, a deeply pocked, dual carriageway where sleek 4x4s, unsteady lorries, rusty cars, donkey carts and beaten-up bicycles brawled for space. Travelling the road was the automotive equivalent of bare-knuckle boxing. Speed limits didn't exist, hit-and-runs were common and drivers were expected to punch through any opening they could find – even if it meant crossing the dirt median and steering against oncoming traffic. Indicating was for weaklings.

John kept his eyes peeled as he turned out of the ShieldGroup compound and into the chaos. Despite having made the journey hundreds of times, he refused to be lulled into a false sense of security. The odds of dying in an accident on the Jalalabad Road were high. The odds of getting whacked by an insurgent were even higher. IEDs, improvised explosive devices, initiated with wires or detonated remotely; suicide bombers wearing explosive vests; truck bombs driven into targets; all had been deployed on the Jalalabad Road to deadly effect. And for good reason. As the only vehicle route east out of Kabul, it was heavily trafficked by NATO forces, Afghan military and police, diplomatic convoys and Western aid workers; rich pickings for insurgents. The road's design also lent itself brilliantly to ambush. Deep sewage

ditches bordered both sides, making off-road evasion impossible.
If pursued, vehicles had no room to manoeuvre.

Should trouble strike, confrontation was practically inevitable;
hence why John and his team always kept vehicle weapons close
to hand: AK-47 shorts with armour piercing rounds, compact
enough to handle in a confined space but powerful enough to
punch through metal and take out an assailant. The pistols in the
back of the 4x4 were for their students.

John dodged and weaved his way through the traffic, past
rows of wood and corrugated tin shacks selling clothing, food
and household items. Visually he swept the Third World strip
malls, picking out elements an untrained eye would dismiss as
insignificant. A donkey cart with a bundle of rags tied on top.
Did it conceal explosives? His surveillance shifted to the road
ahead. An oncoming truck was driving toward them erratically.
A suicide bomber? Everywhere John looked, he saw potential
attackers.

In any other profession, such boundless paranoia would be
disabling. In the commercial security world it was an asset –
until it became inconvenient that is. After all, ShieldGroup
hadn't hired John for his easy-going personality. Tough, uncom-
promising and fiercely proud of his working-class Arbroath
roots, John didn't suffer fools, especially those in authority.
Most managers found him a right pain in the arse. But on the
open market, his mix of skills was virtually without peer. An
eighteen year veteran of 22 SAS Regiment, John had done it all:
high-profile operations; boat troop staff sergeant; chief instructor on training wing for SAS selection; assault and sniper team
commander for the Regiment's counter-terror wing; and two
tours with 14 Int, the military's elite covert surveillance unit.
Security firms didn't call John Patterson when they had a
vacancy to fill, they called him when they had a deal to close.

John was just the sort of ace in the hole ShieldGroup needed to win the contract with the Serious Organized Crime Agency – SOCA, Britain's answer to the FBI. The brand-new agency was looking to outsource a task that could make or break its nascent reputation: training the CNPA, the Counter Narcotics Police of Afghanistan. Interest in the CNPA was high throughout Whitehall. The Home Office wanted to show something was being done to stem the flow of cheap Afghan heroin on British streets. The Foreign Office, having failed dismally in its efforts to spearhead international counter-narcotics initiatives in Afghanistan, was hoping the CNPA would claw back some respectability for it. But of all the government ministries, none had a bigger stake in the CNPA's success than the Ministry of Defence. Not only was revenue from Afghanistan's illegal drugs trade funding the country's growing insurgency, but also if a parallel could be drawn between Britain's Afghan policies and reducing drugs crime back home it could go a long way towards justifying the continued commitment of British troops to an increasingly unpopular conflict. If anyone doubted how high the stakes were, they only had to look at the bottom line. Of the hundreds of millions of pounds Britain had pledged toward Afghan reconstruction, more than two-thirds had been ear-marked for anti-drugs initiatives.

Pete Mitchell knew John would impress SOCA – and pour his heart and soul into the job. Mitch was ex-Regiment and one of the few non-commissioned lads to make it big on Civvy Street. To sweeten the deal, he allowed John to bypass ShieldGroup's middle-management bullshit on all matters relating to the contract including the selection of his support team.

Dusty Miller was John's first choice as co-instructor. A fellow Scot, Dusty had passed the gruelling SAS selection under John's watchful eye before moving on to Air Troop. Determined to get his sharpest recruit back under his wing, John had Dusty cross-decked to Boat Troop for a year-long rotation. The pair bonded so thoroughly that the younger Scot left the Regiment after only six years to follow John into the commercial security world. The fact that it paid better than the army didn't hurt either. Haider, meanwhile, had been chief translator for an embassy in Kabul where John had been head of Close Protection. John knew exactly what to expect from both men. With Dusty, he got a bright lad with excellent skills whose Glaswegian humour and toughness made him excellent company. With Haider, he got a top-flight translator fluent in Dari, Pashto, Farsi, Arabic, Russian, and, most importantly – English.

For over a year, John and Dusty worked tirelessly to perfect the training programme: developing scenarios, creating drills, making the classroom work engaging. Meanwhile Haider proved to be a brilliant translator capable of deciphering the most obscure Afghan dialects. The trio had a ball working together and took pride in the fact that their students left fully prepared to operate in an insurgent-rich environment. But for all its professionalism, there was an element of the CNPA programme that threatened to undo all the good work being done, a recurring problem John and his team were powerless to correct. Some of the students who showed up were clearly not up to scratch. Some were so crippled by old war wounds that they couldn't kneel or grip a weapon properly. It was disturbing – and telling. SOCA was supposed to vet each recruit thoroughly before sending them to Kabul for training. If the agency was failing to weed out candidates with obvious physical defects, who else were they letting through?

John had sent a string of emails warning SOCA and Mitch that more scrutiny was needed. Nothing was done and the inevitable happened. The latest batch of students from Nuristan province had included two highly suspicious characters. John had dismissed them immediately. When it was discovered the two men were nephews of a powerful Afghan general, SOCA had ordered John to reinstate them. He'd refused.

Dusty flipped down the passenger visor, partially obscuring John's view.

'What are you doing?' asked John.

Dusty twisted the cap off a tube of sunscreen. 'You want some?'

John rolled his eyes. 'Air Troop mincer. Are you going to tie a sweater around your shoulders too?' He started laughing.

'Fuck off,' Dusty protested. 'Once. I did that once.'

'I can't remember, was it yellow? No wait,' said John. 'Pink.'

The well-worn jab rolled off Dusty. He squeezed a thick line of white lotion onto his fingertips and rubbed it into his forehead. 'Pointless you having some anyway,' he said. 'You're already full of wrinkles, you Boat Troop minger.'

The banter tapered as they approached the final and most treacherous leg of their journey, the turn-off for the KMTC. The team's vigilance kicked into high gear. Groups of off-duty soldiers and Afghan civilians waiting for minivans to ferry them into Kabul lined the north shoulder of the road directly outside the camp. It was a hell of a place for a bus stop. An insurgent could nest there for hours waiting to strike. Dusty and Haider scanned the crowd for telltale signs of suicide bombers – excessive sweating, mumbling of prayers, lack of body hair from ritual cleansing – while John looked for an opening in the traffic.

Chapter 4

Lines of freshly trained ANA recruits stood to attention under the glaring sun, waiting for their graduation to commence. The brass band struck up a tune more suited to conjuring a cobra from a basket than inspiring a military procession. The Afghan Colour Guard kicked into action. Holding the national flag and a regimental standard aloft, the veterans of what were now bi-monthly ceremonies marched the length of the parade ground and came to a halt.

The band transitioned to a new melody. The front row of recruits filed forward, arms and legs flailing in an unsynchro-nized goosestep. Mismatched boots kicked out as they circled the edge of the square. The passing faces echoed the lack of cohesion. Some were clean-shaven, some sported thick mous-taches while others were heavily bearded.

Lieutenant Colonel Howard viewed the spectacle with the detached expression he'd cultivated since his own graduation from Sandhurst. Beneath his unfathomable facade, however, a cauldron of emotions stewed: disbelief, anger but most of all, disgust – with the proceedings as much as himself.

Howard looked at the journalists he'd charmed so effectively just minutes before. They were huddled together at the far end of the square, wilting in the heat as they observed the ceremony with lifeless eyes. Did any of them possess the acumen or even the desire to recognize the truth literally paraded in front of their faces? NATO couldn't teach the Afghans how to march together let alone how to stand and fight on their own.

No one, of course, would raise the point or its troubling implications. But it wouldn't be that way for ever. Howard knew that someday, with the benefit of hindsight, Britain's fourth estate would claim it had known all along that the Afghan experiment was destined to fail. Journalists would write stories – the more ambitious among them books – naming and shaming those responsible. That's why Howard asked not to be named in the press. He didn't want future generations having written records of his involvement in such a tragic fiasco.

Howard hadn't always held the mission in such contempt. A Guards officer and former SAS Troop Commander, he relished front-line postings. They were infinitely more appealing than manning a press desk back in London. He'd shipped out to Afghanistan, confident he understood the scope of the task awaiting the general he served. The commander of ISAF faced formidable challenges: difficult fighting terrain, a growing insurgency and a pressing need for more boots on the ground. But every campaign had its obstacles and Howard, like many officers of his rank, was sanguine about its prospects. His arrival in country only validated his optimism. Kabul was a boom town. Signs of progress were everywhere: construction cranes dotted the skyline, the ancient streets teemed with local shoppers sifting through tables of imported goods. There were even establishments catering to sophisticated consumers: private clubs where a weary officer could enjoy a Cuban cigar and a fine whisky.

Then everything Howard believed about his mission, his profession and even his country was shattered. It wasn't an act of violence that had decimated his convictions. A chance meeting had quietly sown the seeds of Howard's inner destruction. He hadn't seen his former military mentor for years. Like a student returning from university, Howard was eager to demonstrate how much he'd accomplished since they'd served together. He boasted about Afghanistan's bright future and his role in shaping it. Then his mentor asked the question that would alter Howard's life irrevocably. '*Do you have any idea what's even happening in Afghanistan?*'

Chapter 5

John pressed his credentials against the windscreen. A quick glance by the soldiers on duty and he was waved through. As usual, the first checkpoint of the KMTC was cleared with no effort. He drove through one hundred yards of concrete chicane to the second checkpoint, a sliding fence bordered by blast walls. Any threats overlooked by the guards at the front gate were supposed to be caught here.

Two soldiers ducked out of a guardhouse. John and Dusty observed their movements closely. From a distance, the two Afghans looked like twins: dark moustaches and beards, ill-fitting uniforms belted at the waist, scuffed black boots and brand-new AK-47s. It was only when they got within spitting distance that any distinguishing characteristics could be deciphered: black kohl lining the eyes of one, orange nail varnish on the hands of the other.

'I give them five seconds,' said Dusty.

'Four,' said John.

'You're on.' Dusty and John watched as the two Afghans set to work. The soldier with black-rimmed eyes used a long mirror to check underneath the chassis of their 4x4 while the other lifted the bonnet.

'One thousand and one, one thousand and two . . .' Dusty counted.

'They're taking their time today,' said John.

'. . . one thousand and three, one thousand and four . . .' Dusty continued. The bonnet slammed shut and the soldier with the painted fingernails walked back to the guardhouse.

'Kettle must have already boiled,' John quipped.

'Bastard,' said Dusty. 'Where's the other one?'

John pointed straight ahead. The other soldier had completed his search and was in the process of pulling back the sliding barrier. 'Told you they wouldn't make it to five seconds.' John turned around. 'Haider, how many Guinnesses do you reckon Dusty owes me?'

Haider looked as if he'd been asked the question many times. 'I have lost count.'

The gate slid open and John pressed the accelerator. 'Let's see if you live long enough to collect them,' said Dusty. He looked down at the soldier as they drove past. 'An insurgent could strap a fifty-pound bomb to each axle and that fanny wouldn't catch it.'

A queue had formed ahead of the camp's third and final checkpoint, a gate controlled by a metal bar lowered and lifted manually. Two black Suburbans with US diplomatic markings idled ahead of it. On the other side, an Afghan soldier wrestled a large cloth sack from a group of children – two girls and a boy dressed in brightly embroidered garments.

Dusty gestured at the Suburbans. 'Fucking VIPs. No wonder there's a hold-up.'

'I believe there is a graduation this morning,' said Haider.

'Again?' said Dusty. 'They just had one a few weeks ago. Bloody sausage machine this place is.'

A second Afghan soldier carrying a metal detector walked out of the guardhouse. He swept the device over the confiscated cloth sack. A shrill alarm sounded. Suddenly, the doors of the

Suburbans flew open. Half a dozen men dressed in matching black T-shirts and body armour poured out. They were all armed with M4 carbines. The personal weapon of choice for US Special Forces was also a favourite of private security contractors working for American government contracts in Afghanistan.

The Afghan guards dived for cover as the security team charged the children. 'Down on the ground! Get the fuck down now!' screamed the team leader, a muscle-bound man with a goatee beard and wraparound sunglasses. He grabbed the boy by the scruff of his neck and threw him to the ground. 'Get your fucking head down now!' He pointed his weapon directly at the girls. 'You too,' he barked. The girls froze in terror. The team leader shouted more aggressively. 'Don't make me fucking touch a female. I don't want some crazy mullah slapping a fatwa on my ass. Get down there now with your fucking brother or cousin or whoever the fuck he is!' He motioned to the ground with the barrel of his rifle. The girls dropped to their knees and lowered themselves until all three children were lying face-down in the dirt with M4s trained on the backs of their heads.

John's eyes narrowed angrily as he kicked open his door. 'Fucking bastard,' he said. Dusty and Haider were right behind him.

The team leader raised his rifle when he saw John approach. 'Get the fuck back in your vehicle!'

John stopped and placed his hands flat on his legs, the most non-aggressive stance he could assume short of lying down spreadeagled. 'What threat am I to you?' he asked.

The team leader held his weapon steady. 'I said, get the fuck back to your vehicle now!'

'This is an Afghan training camp. You have no right to tell us what to do here.' John gestured toward the children; the little boy's trousers were stained with wet. 'And you definitely have no right to bully a bunch of defenceless kids. That wee laddie's so scared he's pissed himself.'

'Defenceless kids my ass,' said the team leader. 'There's an IED in that bag. Don't be fooled by these little shits. They're fucking insurgents.'

'You won't mind then if I take a look?' said John.

'Take a look at what?' said the team leader.

'The IED,' said John. 'I'm demolitions trained.'

The team leader lowered his rifle. 'If you're fool enough, be my guest.' He jerked his chin. 'But do it over there.'

John ignored him, picked up the sack and shook it vigorously. The security team eyed each other nervously as a chorus of clinking metal sounded. 'Hear that?' said John. He untied the bag, rummaged inside it and pulled out a handful of objects. 'Brass bullet casings,' he said, tipping his hand. The casings fell to the ground like golden rain.

'Looks like you lads got your knickers in a twist over nothing,' smirked Dusty.

John kept dropping casings, mocking the team with each noisy fistful.

The team leader grew defensive. 'Well a bunch of kids lugging around a bag full of bullet casings can't be up to no good.'

John threw the bag to the ground. 'What they're up to is feeding their families,' he hissed. 'These kids are Kutchi. They scour the firing ranges for bullet casings to sell on as scrap.'

The team leader smiled at his cohorts. 'I've had plenty of kutchi and it ain't never looked like that.' The schoolboy humour spawned a wave of chuckles.

'You thick wankers,' John blustered. 'The Kutchi are nomads. They were wandering through Afghanistan long before any of us got here and they'll be doing it long after we're gone.

Not everyone outside your armoured Suburban is the enemy, you know. Treating innocent children like terrorists, acting like you fucking own the place – all you're doing is turning people against the Coalition. Al-Qaeda should have you on their fucking payroll.'

'You best mind that tongue of yours,' said the team leader.

'What the fuck are you going to do about it?' John walked over to the children. They were still lying on the ground, trembling.

'Stay away from my prisoner,' the team leader warned.

John helped the boy to his feet. The child's dirty face was streaked with fat wet tears that pooled in a long, black scar running the length of his jaw. 'Apologize to this laddie and give him ten dollars,' said John.

The team leader aimed his M4 at John again. 'Back off now or I swear I'll Mozambique you, motherfucker!'

John pounced. Before the team leader could react, the angry Scot grabbed the barrel of the M4, flipped it and smashed the butt into his face. The team leader fell to the ground like a wounded stag. John stood over him, daring the rest of the security team to respond. Unsure of how to react, they lifted their rifles to the firing position. Threatening calls collided as they screamed over one another: 'Back off, motherfucker!' 'Move away! Move away!' 'Blink, motherfucker, and you die in the dark!'

'Fellas,' said Dusty, trying to interject an element of calm. 'Fellas!' He finally managed to hold their attention. 'I think we all need to take a deep breath here.'

The security team looked at each other, waiting for someone to take command of the situation. A young man with an Eye of Providence tattooed on his forearm stepped into the breach. 'Who the fuck are you anyway?'

'We're security contractors, just like you lot,' said Dusty. 'We're here to check in with Range Control, that's all.'

'What's your friend's fucking problem?' asked the tattooed man.

John opened his mouth to speak. Dusty stopped him. 'He's Scottish,' said Dusty, as if that explained everything.

The tattooed man looked John up and down. 'Well, Braveheart here can suck my dick.'

John lunged but this time Dusty blocked him. The younger Scot restrained John with one hand while he reached into his pocket with the other. He pulled out a twenty-dollar bill and handed it to Haider. 'Be a mate and give this to those kids.'

Haider took the money and walked over to the boy. The child was still sobbing. Haider folded the money in the boy's hand and pointed to John and Dusty. The boy wiped away his tears and smiled at his defenders.

Chapter 6

The recruits finished their lap of the parade square and settled into two straight lines. They continued to march in place while an ANA officer walked up and down, inspecting their ranks. After two passes, the officer barked orders in Dari. The recruits fanned out along either side of a long table draped in the black, red and green colours of the Afghan flag. Prayerbooks paired with AK-47s were dispersed like place settings along it. The recruits put one hand on the prayerbooks – there weren't enough for everyone, so some were forced to double up – and pledged their loyalty to the new Afghanistan. When they finished, the entire *kandak* cheered. '*Allahu Akbar!*' '*Allahu Akbar!*'

Howard wondered if any of them had the faintest idea what they'd signed up for. It wasn't that he pitied the young recruits. He couldn't give a fig what happened to them. Howard's curiosity was strictly a function of envy. He resented the soldiers' innocence as only a man who'd lost his could. If only he had ignored John Patterson's words. But he couldn't. Pride had compelled Howard to defend his position to his mentor.

'*Do you have any idea what's even happening in Afghanistan?*' asked John.

'*Of course,*' bristled Howard. '*I'm a staff officer.*'

'*So tell me,*' said John. '*Are we winning the war or are we losing it?*'

'*We're winning of course.*'

'No,' said John. '*We're losing it, mate.*'

Until then, Howard had never even thought to question ISAF's rosy weekly dispatches. But John's words forced him to peel back the layers of propaganda. Howard re-read every press release ISAF had ever produced. Buried among the stories of reconstruction efforts, humanitarian aid and local cooperation a disturbing, undeniable trend emerged. NATO casualties in Afghanistan had been rising steadily every year since the invasion. The West wasn't winning the war. Not by a long shot.

Once his eyes were opened, Howard could find no respite. Even the bubble of Kabul was pricked. The capital's so-called prosperity – the new buildings, the shops, the drinking clubs that had so impressed him – they weren't signs of progress at all. They were islands of consumption funded by stolen donor money to service Afghanistan's new elite: a mafia created and supported by the Coalition he so dutifully served. As Howard quickly discovered, the country's Western-backed strongmen were a clever lot. They understood that a veneer of credibility was essential for keeping their coffers filled. The criminals hid behind any number of titles: MP, judge, cabinet minister. But the most morally reprehensible, in Howard's view, were the men he dealt with most closely: Afghanistan's Ministry of Defence, NATO's partners. Embezzlement and extortion of foreign funds were misdemeanour offences in the Afghan MoD. Most generals were still active warlords. Many had a hand in the country's opium trade. Some maintained ties with militant groups.

NATO's generals and the Western politicians dictating its policies turned a blind eye. Prevailing wisdom held that if relations with the Afghan MoD broke down, NATO troops could end up policing the country indefinitely. Preserving the

NATO–Afghan alliance was deemed paramount. But no matter how many times Howard weighed the benefits, the costs of maintaining the partnership didn't add up. Individually, Afghanistan's generals may have kept a tight rein on their fiefdoms but, collectively, they had no authority. They couldn't even take credit for Kabul's relative stability. That distinction belonged to the 20,000 ISAF troops stationed in and around the capital.

The freshly minted ANA soldiers left to receive their new assignments – postings that would cast them far from the security of their villages and provinces. The policy was designed to bolster Afghanistan's central government by weakening tribal bonds. Howard had once thought the policy genius. Now, he saw it for what it was: textbook Western hypocrisy. Because for all its talk of unity and cooperation, the truth was NATO was no more united than Afghanistan's warring ethnicities. 'Local' interests always trumped broader strategy, hence why so many NATO countries refused to deploy their troops to dangerous areas. Indeed, Howard's own identity was intractably tribal. How often had he fantasized about resigning his commission and exposing the farce he helped to perpetuate? But doing so would betray Her Majesty's Services. He'd be labelled a traitor and cast out of the British military – his tribe.

The next wave of recruits set off. General Rasul's nephews bowed to their uncle and left the stand. Their departure gave Howard the green light to leave as well. Rather than take the shortest path directly in front of the Afghan officers, he plotted a route that would not disturb their view. As he walked above and around, Howard felt like a man drowning in his own complicity. He longed for an event to rescue him from his impotence, a drama to cast a sheen of dignity on his pathetic collusion. Sudden, noble exits, however, were for heroes. And

Howard could find none of those in Afghanistan, just villains, pawns and accomplices.

John slammed the steering wheel. 'Why the fuck did you do that?'

Dusty met John's anger with his own. 'Do what?'

'Give in to those wankers. The idea was to make them pay,' grumbled John.

Dusty gritted his teeth. 'If I decide to do something off my own back, it's nothing to do with you.'

John visually swept the parking lot as they drove past. 'Like hell it isn't. You made us all look a right bunch of fannies, digging into your own pocket like that.'

Dusty moved his head in an exaggerated arc. 'The way you were going on, you'd have got us all killed – including the kids. Those fuckers were itching to unload a magazine into someone.'

'It never would have come to that,' John argued. 'Tossers like that act all big and tough but at the end of the day it's all piss and wind. Isn't it, Haider?'

'This is between you and me,' said Dusty. 'Keep him out of this.'

'According to you, I was about to get us all killed so I think Haider should have his say,' John shot back.

Dusty turned around to face Haider, his expression warning to tread cautiously. 'OK then, Haider. What do you say?'

Haider spoke dispassionately, as if he were conducting a post-mortem. 'The actions of those men most certainly dishonoured those children. In my village, such an offence would not go unpunished.'

'There you go,' said John, his tone implying he'd won the argument. 'It's a matter of honour.'

'Well, this isn't Haider's fucking village,' Dusty countered.

'There's no honour in Kabul. Security teams can do whatever they want here and get away with it.'

John threw the 4x4 into reverse and backed into a parking spot outside a five-storey structure sandwiched between the KMTC headquarters and the parade square. He checked his watch when he got out of the vehicle. 8.15 a.m. 'We're running behind. I was hoping to get a shoot-in ourselves before the students get here.'

Dusty was still fuming. 'You nearly got your morning shoot-in back there.'

'Oh don't go on,' said John. Dusty folded his arms and leaned against the 4x4. 'Are you coming or what?'

'You go on with your mate,' said Dusty, referring to Haider. 'I'll keep watch over the vehicle.'

John turned, then reconsidered. 'Are you sure?' he asked.

Dusty nodded – his way of accepting the peace offering. 'I'm sure.'

An Afghan soldier emerged from behind a corner. John caught sight of him over Dusty's shoulder. 'I've seen that lad before,' said John. 'I don't like the look of him.'

Dusty turned around. 'Him? He's looking for work as a translator.' Haider appeared offended. 'Don't worry. I told him we already have one.'

'Then why's he watching us?' John pulled Dusty aside. 'Does he have business with you?'

'Of course not,' said Dusty.

'This sideline of yours could get us both fired,' John warned.

Dusty grew defensive. 'It was only the one time. I told you.' John didn't look convinced. 'I mean it,' said Dusty. 'I'm finished with all that.'

John committed the Afghan's face to memory. 'OK then. We'll be inside.' John disappeared with Haider into the building.

When they were gone, Dusty waved the soldier over. 'What you got for us, mate?'

'You late,' said the Afghan. 'You say eight o'clock.'

'Couldn't be helped,' said Dusty. 'Go on then. I don't have all day.'

The Afghan un-cinched a small cloth sack and poured the contents into his hand. 'Beads,' he said. 'Lapis. Very, very old. I give you very good price.'

Dusty examined the small blue objects. 'I've seen ones just like these for sale on Chicken Street. Made in India.'

'No made in India,' the Afghan insisted. 'Ancient artefact. Genuine lapis from Badakshan.'

'My clientele are quite discerning,' said Dusty. 'If these are fakes, they'll know it.'

'Of course,' said the Afghan. 'That is why I sell you the best. Always the best.'

Dusty looked sceptically at the Afghan. 'How much?'

'Today, I give you special price. Just for you,' smiled the Afghan.

'How much?' Dusty repeated.

The Afghan made great show of mental calculations. 'Three hundred dollar US,' he declared.

'Fifty,' said Dusty.

The Afghan's face melted into mock horror. 'No, no, no,' he said. 'I sell for fifty, I lose money. Two hundred dollar US. My best price, just for you.'

'Seventy-five,' said Dusty. 'I don't have time to keep haggling. That's my final offer take it or leave it.'

The Afghan sucked in his lower lip before nodding. 'OK.'

John and Haider walked down a bare corridor to an unmarked office. Three men dressed in Afghan uniforms were seated inside. They were all smoking and drinking small glasses of green tea. Two desks, a filing cabinet and a white marker board were the room's only furnishings. The humble set-up was misleading. Range Control coordinated what was arguably the most fought over piece of real estate in the Afghan capital – the KMTC live-fire ranges. Thirty-odd square miles of open land surrounded by bald mountains, 'the ranges' as they were known were used to run drills using live ammunition. Practically everyone toting a weapon in Kabul wanted time on them and the pecking order was ruthless. American troops always had first refusal, followed by ISAF, then ANA troops and, finally, commercial security teams. With all the big-footing and bribing, John always insisted on confirming his sessions in person at least two hours ahead of time.

John knocked on the door before entering. 'Good morning,' he said. The normally gregarious Afghan officer in charge buried his head in some papers. John and Haider knew immediately that something was wrong. They checked the white board: ShieldGroup had been erased from the 10 a.m. slot.

'Why are we off the board?' asked John.

Haider translated the question. The officer in charge shrugged his shoulders and mumbled a few words in Dari.

'He was told ShieldGroup is prohibited from using the ranges,' said Haider.

'On whose orders?' asked John.

Haider translated again. 'A general from the Ministry of Defence.'

'I want a name,' John insisted.

Haider asked the question. The officer shook his head. John addressed the officer directly. 'I've been coming here for over a year. I've never been anything but respectful towards you and now you won't give me a name? Where's your honour?'

Haider translated. The officer's proud expression dissolved as he answered.

'He said he would like to tell you but he cannot. If he does, he will lose his job,' said Haider. 'His entire family depends on him.'

John knew the officer wasn't exaggerating. In fact, losing his job was probably the very least that would happen if he betrayed an Afghan general.

Chapter 7

Haider waited until they were outside the building before uttering a word. 'It must be General Rasul.'

'I know,' said John.

'You realize he will prevent us from using the ranges until his nephews are reinstated into the training course,' said Haider.

'We're off the ranges then because I'm not budging,' said John.

Dusty straightened up as John and Haider approached. 'What happened in there?'

'We're banned,' said John.

'What do you mean, banned?' said Dusty.

'No access to the ranges until further notice,' said John.

'The order came personally from General Rasul,' Haider added.

'Bloody hell,' said Dusty. 'Don't tell me it's those two little twats. I say we go find them right now and sort this out.'

John considered the idea. 'No,' he said. 'SOCA's not getting off the hook that easily. They were the ones who let Rasul's nephews on the course; they can damn well sort this mess.'

'Excuse me.' A slim, youthful man waving a notebook and pen jogged towards them.

John and Haider ducked into the vehicle leaving Dusty to deal with the interloper.

'I overheard you mention General Rasul. I'm a journalist you see, and I was hoping to get an interview with the general this morning but the chap who promised to arrange it seems to have vanished.'

Dusty raised an eyebrow. 'Rasul? Were you meeting him here?'

'The general is at the graduation ceremony. I'd approach him directly but I'm afraid he won't see me without his entourage present.'

'His entourage?' Dusty said.

'Two tall fellows in black turbans. They just left a few minutes ago.'

Dusty processed the information. 'Sorry. Can't help you, mate.' He opened the passenger door and climbed in.

'My name is Rudy – Rudy Lipkingard.' Rudy shoved a business card in Dusty's hand. 'I write for a newspaper.'

Dusty read the card and handed it to John for inspection. 'A journalist, eh? Well, I've got a story for you,' said Dusty.

Rudy's eyes lit up.

'If men like me and my mates were in charge of British policy in Afghanistan instead of the fannies back in Whitehall, this war would be won already. Now fuck off.' Dusty slammed the door in Rudy's face.

John sped off. 'As soon as we get back to the compound I'm calling a meeting with SOCA,' he said. 'What was that bloke banging on about?'

'Are you ready for this,' said Dusty. 'He wanted an introduction to General Rasul.'

'You're fucking kidding me,' said John.

'I'll do you one better than that,' Dusty continued. 'According to that journalist bloke, Rasul had an entourage here with him this morning – "tall fellows in black turbans".'

Dusty checked the passenger rear-view mirror, a standard procedure so ingrained it was second nature to him. 'Haider,' he said, craning his neck. 'Do us a favour and move over.'

Haider slid his body from the centre of the back seat to the right side. Dusty angled the mirror to take full advantage of the view through the rear window. In the far right corner he saw it clearly, a Toyota Land Cruiser with blacked-out windows and no registration plate. It was trailing twenty yards behind them. 'We've got a tail,' said Dusty.

John kept both hands on the steering wheel as he assessed the Toyota himself. There was nothing overtly suspicious about it. The model was popular with Afghan generals. The fact that this one appeared to be leaving the KMTC at the same time as them could very well be a coincidence. But John wasn't prepared to stake his life on it. He pulled over ahead of the camp's exit and waited for the Toyota to pass them. Dusty and Haider needed no explanation of his actions; they didn't trust coincidences either.

A cloud of fine dirt sprayed the windscreen as John merged with the flow of traffic on the Jalalabad Road. He cast his gaze out along the highway. Three hundred yards ahead he spotted a Toyota identical to the one they'd seen. It was stopped on the side of the road. The dust around the vehicle hadn't settled, indicating that it had just pulled over.

'Eyes on that 4x4 on the right,' said John. He held his speed steady as he manoeuvred closer to the shoulder. He didn't want the Toyota to know it was being watched. For the same reason, Dusty adjusted his mirror to observe the vehicle covertly as they passed.

John overtook the Toyota in less than a second. The passenger window was rolled down. He caught a glimpse of a black turban through it.

'Two up, no sign of weapons,' said Dusty.

'Did you recognize any of them?' asked John.

'The nephews.' Dusty turned to John. 'I'm sure of it.'

As they spoke, the Toyota pulled back onto the road and resumed its course. The timing was too neat to be random. The nephews were deliberately tailing them.

The Toyota was five vehicles behind and now driving erratically. John weighed up their options. He could try and outrun it. But that would only delay the inevitable confrontation. The nephews were obviously looking for a fight. Right now John had them in his sights. The next time, he might not see them coming.

'If those fellas want to take us on, I say we get it done and dusted,' said John.

'I agree,' said Dusty.

'As do I,' said Haider.

The Jalalabad Road roundabout offered a chance to test the nephews' resolve. John knew from experience that some men will only attack when they have the element of surprise. If they lose it, they back down. John wanted to force the nephews to show their hand. 'I'm going to pull around to the outside of the roundabout, turn right and do a box. If they follow, get ready for a hit.'

Two hundred yards ahead of the roundabout, a bottleneck formed. Vehicles slowed as four lanes of traffic converged on a space designed for two. Rather than follow the flow, John inched their 4x4 towards the outer edge of the roundabout, like a fish swimming sideways. He checked his mirror: the Toyota was carving the same conspicuous path. The nephews had to know by now that John was on to them.

At the first turn-off, John broke free and floored it. Dusty and Haider grabbed their canvas bags, pulled out two AK-47 shorts and placed their thumbs on the safety catches to be ready to switch from 'safe' to 'fire'. The weapons were already cocked and locked.

'Keep it down and out of sight until you're ready to fire,' Dusty said to Haider.

Haider nodded.

John searched for ways to increase their advantage. If they stayed on the main road, the Toyota would either engage them from the rear or pull up on their left side – the driver's side in Afghanistan. John was no Hollywood action hero; he couldn't drive and return fire at the same time. And Dusty would have to shoot past him if they were attacked on the left. The best possible scenario would be for Dusty and Haider to have a direct line of fire. John needed to force the Toyota into a contact right flank. An upcoming block of Soviet built flats – the Microrian complex – offered their best prospect. It was ideal – concrete buildings laid out on a grid road system with no blind alleys or cul-de-sacs.

The wheels screeched as John took a sharp right into the complex. The Toyota skidded and spun out as it nearly missed the turn. Dusty and Haider lifted their AKs to the ready but kept them below the level of the windows so as not to allow the nephews a view of their firepower.

'You see even a hint of a weapon and you let them have it,' said Dusty.

'Stand by,' ordered John. He swerved to the left and hit the brakes. As the Toyota pulled level with them, Dusty caught sight of a rifle coming into the aim.

The crack of high velocity rounds mixed with shattering glass as Dusty and Haider discharged several rounds right through the windows at their attackers. The Toyota hurled forward fifty feet, jumped a kerb and slammed into the wall of a building.

The thud sounded like an incoming mortar. The passenger door of the Toyota flung open on impact. A bloodied torso came tumbling out.

Dusty and Haider quickly changed magazines while John checked his mirrors: there were no other vehicles behind them. The nephews it appeared had acted alone.

The Microrian residents spilled out of their apartments like rats escaping a flooded sewer. Women in burkas unleashed high-pitched screams. Children started shouting and throwing stones. John knew they needed to get out of there quickly, but not until they were certain both nephews were dead. He swung past the wreckage, searching for signs of movement. The front end of the vehicle was crushed. The driver's head had smashed through the windscreen, splattering blood, flesh and skull across the wall of the building. Making a positive ID on the fly was impossible. More remained of the man who'd fallen out of the passenger side. His upper body had been shredded by bullets but his face was still eerily intact. There was no doubting his identity. The man was a nephew of General Ustad Rasul.

Chapter 8

'They were al-Qaeda.' John stared at the slack-jawed faces sitting across the table from him. It's not as if they were learning this for the first time. His post-incident report had been distributed to everyone present: Ian Hunt from SOCA, Simon Hampson and a representative from ISAF, Lieutenant Colonel James Pilkington Howard. 'Do I have to say it again?'

Simon looked to the men on either side of him before answering. 'You're taking tremendous liberties. What evidence do you have that General Rasul's nephews were, as you claim, associated with al-Qaeda?'

John kept his cool. He'd been waiting three days to deliver his debrief. It should have taken place the night of the incident but ShieldGroup HQ had sent word to hold off until Mitch could get there from London. He never made it. John figured it was all a stalling tactic to give ShieldGroup and SOCA time to cover their collective arses. James Howard's presence only confirmed his suspicions. No one wanted the uncomfortable truth to come out. But no amount of flannel could hide it – not this time. John had a paper trail a mile long documenting ShieldGroup's and SOCA's failures. 'Everyone in Kabul knows Ustad Rasul is Hizb-i-Islami and so were his nephews,' said John.

Ian leaned forward. He looked lost. 'I'm sorry but what does that have to do with al-Qaeda?'

John wasn't surprised. Ian didn't have a clue about Afghanistan. Never once in the past year had John seen SOCA's top man leave his heavily fortified Kabul office. The fact that Ian had ventured out to ShieldGroup's compound could only mean one thing: SOCA were shitting themselves. 'Hizb-i-Islami is a militant Islamic faction led by Gulbuddin Hekmatyar, a Pashtun warlord,' John explained. 'The Yanks loved him during the Soviet occupation. They designed the stinger missile specifically for Hekmatyar's fighters.'

Simon sighed. 'And what, pray tell, does that have to do with anything now?'

John didn't bite. 'I won't go into the history of Hekmatyar's shifting alliances. What matters now is that Hizb-i-Islami supports Osama bin Laden. They're basically al-Qaeda in Afghanistan.'

'That's an oversimplification.' Simon's tone was defensive. 'Many Hizb-i-Islami commanders support President Karzai, including General Ustad Rasul.' He turned to Ian. 'It is also worth noting that Rasul is a respected scholar. He's a university professor.'

John nodded. 'And that makes him trustworthy? I bet you never even heard of Hizb-i-Islami or Ustad Rasul until we kicked his nephews out of the CNPA programme. What have you been doing for the past three days, Simon? Scouring the Internet looking for bits of information to make ShieldGroup and SOCA look less incompetent?' John addressed Ian. 'Rasul is a professor of Islamic studies. His speciality is finding passages in the Koran to justify waging jihad. Whose side do you think he's on?'

'Just because someone studies the Koran doesn't make them the enemy.' Simon smiled knowingly at the ISAF rep. 'Rasul is an ANA general. He's on our side.'

'It's all filthy politics,' said John. 'Putting Rasul in the

Ministry of Defence was the only way Karzai could secure the Nuristani vote. And Rasul's happy to be there because now he doesn't have to worry about Afghan troops interfering with his smuggling business.'

'What smuggling business?' asked Ian.

'Rasul's boys traffic all sorts over the border to Pakistan,' said John. 'Lumber, jewels, drugs.'

Ian looked offended as if John's words were a personal attack on him. 'We all know the Afghan government has its share of corruption, but that's a very serious charge.'

'Are you joking? Karzai's own brother is a drugs trafficker.' John shook his head. 'SOCA may do a fine job back home, Ian, but this isn't Manchester airport or Dover docks. You're operating in a deeply entrenched insurgency. No offence, but you're way out of your depth here. And don't play dumb when it comes to Karzai's ministers and generals running drugs over the border. It's just easier for you to focus on the scumballs at the bottom, that's all.'

Simon stood and pointed an accusing finger at John. 'You're out of line, Mr Patterson!'

John sat back and laughed. 'Stop showing off for the client, you prat.'

Ian assumed the role of peacemaker. 'Gentlemen, gentlemen. Let's try to focus on the issue at hand.' Simon sat back down as Ian continued. 'John, I'm still not clear on how you determined that General Rasul's nephews were associated with Hizb-i-Islami.'

'It's all there in my report,' John maintained.

Ian flipped through the bound document resting on the table in front of him. 'I'm sorry but I read this report in its entirety. It made no mention of Hizb-i-Islami or General Rasul's alleged association with them.'

John sat up and eyed the report suspiciously. 'Mind if I take a look at that?'

Ian slid the document across the table to John. The title explained it all.

KABUL 25-06-06
Contact between ShieldGroup Employees & Afghan
  Civilians
Prepared: 28-06-06 by Simon Hampson
Job Title: In-Country Manager Afghanistan,
  ShieldGroup Int'l

John glared at Simon and threw the report down on the table. 'I didn't write this.'

Simon scooped it up and clung to it like a piece of rare parchment. 'This is an official ShieldGroup document.'

'It's total crap.' John spoke directly to Ian. 'Since this tosser is too scared to tell you what really happened, I'll do it. It was my translator, Haider, who fingered those lads as Hizb-i-Islami.'

Ian's eyes moved from John, to Simon and back again. 'Let me make sure I understand you correctly. Your actions were based entirely on the opinion of a single Afghan translator?'

'Haider is from Nuristan, Rasul's territory,' said John. 'He knows the players there. Rasul's nephews were boasting to him during one of the tea breaks about their involvement with Hizb-i-Islami. What more confirmation do you need?'

'Informed as it may be, Haider's opinion is not irrefutable proof,' said Simon. 'And what do you know of Haider really? He could have been fanning the flames of some ancient ethnic dispute for all you know.'

John wanted to grab Simon by the neck and pin him to the wall. 'You have some nerve questioning Haider's integrity. I'd trust him with my life, which is more than any man can say for you.' John turned to Ian. 'And let's not lose sight of the real issue here – namely your agency's failure to properly vet the CNPA recruits.'

Ian cleared his throat. 'For the record, I don't actually go on the ground. But I assure you my people do everything in their power to perform background checks on all the CNPA candidates. You must understand that the security situation outside Kabul sometimes prevents them from travelling to the provinces to perform those checks directly. They're doing the best they can in a very challenging situation.'

'Their best is shite,' said John. 'Your people have a history of not vetting recruits properly and I've got stacks of emails to prove it. And seeing as we're all speaking on the record here, whether you're in the field or not, when the people you manage make mistakes, it's on your shoulders.'

Ian grew defensive. 'You are failing to appreciate the big picture.'

'Fuck the big picture,' said John. 'There's no whitewashing what's happened here. SOCA recruited two al-Qaeda for a training programme funded by British taxpayers. Your agency isn't fit for purpose.'

'It is not your place to say whether we're fit . . .' Ian interrupted.

'Like hell it isn't . . .' shot back John.

Ian talked over him. '. . . for purpose. All of us sitting at this table are here at the invitation of the Afghan government . . .'

'Give me a fucking break . . .' laughed John.

Ian's voice grew louder. '. . . and the Afghan government has questions, valid questions, about what happened to General Rasul's nephews.'

Suddenly, John realized what was really going on. He should

have seen it coming. How could he have been so blind! He leaned back and masked his revelation with a calm, steady tone. 'What kind of questions?'

Ian's expression turned from indignation to smugness. 'Well for one, they'd like to know what you and your team were doing at the KMTC the morning of the incident.'

'We were checking in with Range Control,' said John. 'We had a session booked.'

'Range Control has no record of a ShieldGroup booking,' said Ian.

'Rasul had us bumped. Ask the officer in charge of Range Control. He can confirm it,' replied John.

'The officer in charge doesn't recall a booking either,' said Ian.

John sat up. 'What are you implying?'

'The implication is that you and your team were looking for Rasul's nephews with the aim of provoking a confrontation,' said Ian.

'Bollocks,' said John.

'There's also the question of your vehicle,' Ian continued. 'It's been inspected and there are no incoming bullet holes. One would conclude therefore that you were the aggressors, not General Rasul's nephews.'

John stared coldly at Ian. The SOCA bureaucrat was grey from sitting in his office for weeks on end. He reminded John of a mushroom. 'Have you ever been in a contact?'

The question clearly made Ian uncomfortable. 'I don't see how that has anything to do with . . .'

John cut him off before he could finish. 'We got the drop on the nephews, Ian. We whacked them before they whacked us.'

'So you admit that you fired first,' Simon interrupted.

'You're damn right we fired first. We were fighting for our

lives!' John slammed his fist on the table. The sound reverberated throughout the room. His eyes filled with scorn. 'SOCA dropped me and my team right in the shit and if you're not willing to admit it, I'll have a talk with the British ambassador and let him know how your agency is *really* performing in Afghanistan.'

Simon turned white. 'There's no need to trouble the ambassador . . .'

'Shut up,' said John. 'You're so far up the client's arse . . .'

'The ambassador is powerless at this stage of the process.' The voice descended on the conversation like the eye of a storm. It was Lieutenant Colonel Howard's first contribution to the meeting.

John studied Howard's face. 'How so?'

'Because it's gone beyond him. This is an ISAF matter now.' Howard looked John directly in the eye. 'May I speak candidly?'

'I don't know,' said John. 'Can you?'

Howard swallowed the insult and carried on. 'You are right about General Rasul and his deal with Karzai. It is indeed filthy politics. Be that as it may, Rasul is a powerful member of the Afghan Ministry of Defence. ISAF needs his support. We are simply not in a position to alienate him by ignoring his concerns. I beg you to bear in mind however that our intention is to humour him which is very different from giving him exactly what he wants. Granted, I have not seen a copy of your original report . . .' Howard looked pointedly at Simon, '. . . but rest assured that based on the evidence we have seen thus far, it is ISAF's position that you and your team believed you were acting in self-defence.'

'We did act in self-defence. Full stop,' insisted John.

Howard thumbed through a copy of the sanitized report.

'One thing I would like to get clarification on. Did you or did you not discharge a weapon during the contact?'

'I was driving,' said John.

Howard folded his hands on the table. 'Is there anything else you would like to contribute at this time?'

John shook his head.

'Then I believe I speak for everyone here when I say you have certainly given us much to think about. That will be all for now, thank you.'

John stood up to leave.

'Mr Patterson,' said Simon. 'Hand in your weapons and stay in the compound.'

John didn't dignify Simon's order with a response.

The men at the table waited for John's footsteps to recede before speaking. 'The opinion of a single translator – he's got nothing. Nothing at all,' said Ian.

'Of course he's got nothing,' Simon added. 'I never under-stood why everyone is so in awe of ex-SAS. They're no better than anyone else.'

'I served with the Regiment for two years,' said Howard. The words fell like a hammer. 'John Patterson was my troop staff sergeant. You underestimate him at your peril.'

Simon tried to recover from his gaffe. 'As ShieldGroup's senior manager in Afghanistan, I want you to know that we are prepared to cooperate fully with ISAF on this matter.'

Howard ignored Simon. 'What is SOCA's official position on all of this?' he asked Ian.

Ian gestured toward the report on the table. 'It's all there in black and white. General Rasul's nephews were dismissed from the CNPA training course due to physical disabilities.'

'And the contact on the Jalalabad Road?' said Howard.

Ian smiled. 'We'll defer to ISAF on the matter.'

'How convenient for you,' said Howard. 'It is ISAF's position that the contact was the result of an unfortunate misunderstanding between two groups of civilians and is therefore not a military matter. ISAF regards this as an internal Afghan affair. The Afghan authorities will prosecute the matter as they see fit.'

'What about Patterson and his men? Do you think they'll go quietly when the Afghans come to arrest them?' said Ian. 'They'll be bleating their story to every journalist in Kabul.'

'It would benefit no one, least of all John Patterson and his team, to alert the press. Doing so would only force the Afghans to make examples of them. I'm sure all parties concerned will agree that this matter is best dealt with quietly,' said Howard. 'And John Patterson didn't discharge a weapon. I will personally urge the Afghans to be lenient with him. With any luck, this will all blow over in a matter of weeks.'

'What about Patterson's family?' said Ian. 'They could make a lot of noise.'

Simon shrugged off the concern. 'Patterson was in the ranks. Working class. Whatever family he has isn't bright enough to make waves.'

Howard stepped in to defend his old mentor. 'John Patterson has no family – not any more.'

'What about his co-instructor?' Ian grabbed the report and read from it. 'This Malcolm Miller?'

'I think he's divorced. Definitely no children – or at least any he'll own up to,' said Simon. 'No one will miss him.'

'And the translator?' asked Ian.

Simon laughed. 'Who's going to take the word of a raghead?'

Chapter 9

The only sound in the room was the hum of fluorescent lights. Dusty lay on his cot, a Bergen slouched at his feet. Haider sat at a desk, half-heartedly studying a magazine. Neither of them had said a word since the discovery.

A blast of cool air tumbled in as John opened the door. His expression said what Dusty and Haider already knew. They were all condemned men.

'We're being stitched-up. Big time,' said John. 'They didn't say it but I'd bet my mortgage they're handing us over to Rasul.'

Dusty sat up and emptied the contents of his Bergen onto the cot. 'I've sifted through this five times in the past hour. My passport's gone, mate.'

John eyed the debris on the blanket. 'When?'

'Maybe when I was in the cookhouse. I can't be sure,' said Dusty. 'Have you seen yours lately?'

'No. But if yours is gone I bet they got their hands on mine too.' John looked at Haider. 'You have to leave Kabul at first light. We'll help you get a vehicle. Then Dusty and I will head to the airport. I'm sure we can bribe our way onto a plane without passports.'

'I'm afraid not, my friend,' said Haider. 'I just phoned one of my contacts at the airport. Security was issued photographs of us with instructions to arrest on sight.'

John quickly formulated an alternative plan. 'Then we'll go to Kandahar and fly out of there.'

Haider shook his head. 'Kandahar will have received the same orders. Flying out of Afghanistan is not possible.'

'We're proper fucked, mate,' said Dusty.

'Then we'll drive,' said John. 'We'll head to Jalalabad and cross at Torkham into Pakistan.'

'There is only one road to Jalalabad,' Haider reminded him. 'You will be caught before you get there.'

'Fuck it,' said Dusty. 'We'll travel off road, make our way through the Khyber Pass, go to Islamabad and knock on the door of our embassy. Let's see if *those* fuckers are as eager to screw us as this lot here.'

'Your throats will be cut.' Haider put his hand to his chest. 'My friends, I have learned much from you. But now you must listen to me. No white man can travel through the Khyber Pass unescorted and live.'

'I'd rather take my chances than rot in some stinking Kabul jail,' said Dusty.

'I agree,' said John. 'The Khyber Pass is our only option.'

'Wait!' Haider stood up. 'You must think.'

'There's nothing to think about,' said Dusty. 'We're not going to jail.'

'If you stay in Kabul, yes, jail is a certainty,' said Haider. 'But Kabul is not what matters in Afghanistan.'

'What are you suggesting?' asked John.

Haider raised his chin. 'I'm suggesting there is another way.'

Chapter 10

It started with a flicker, a hint of artificial light tearing the canvas of a magnificent dawn. The flashes quickened until two circles took shape; high beams that grew larger and more menacing as the car thundered up the road. It was the only vehicle heading out of Kabul. John and Dusty were certain it was coming for them.

John tracked the advancing vehicle from the passenger seat. He turned to Haider. 'You should get going.'

Haider's hands were glued to the steering wheel. 'I will wait here with you.'

'The sun's rising,' said John. 'You should have left a half-hour ago. There's no point hanging around here. It will only complicate matters.'

'Loyalty is not complicated,' said Haider. 'I will stay by your side as long as I can.'

Dusty interrupted from the back seat. 'If you want to be a fucking hero, keep yourself out of the shit. If you get caught you're worse than useless to us.'

'He's right,' said John. 'Everything hinges on you getting to Dogrum safely.'

Haider weighed his instinct to remain against the logic of John's argument. 'Very well.'

John and Dusty climbed out of the vehicle. Haider rolled

down the window to speak to them. 'Are you absolutely certain you do not want me to wait here with you?'

'I don't want them lumping you in with us any more than you already are,' said John. 'Get moving and don't forget, when you've gone as far as you can by road, burn out the vehicle. If it's tracked back to ShieldGroup it could blow your location before you've had a chance to get everything in place.'

Haider summoned a smile. 'Are you daft? I'm selling it.'

John grinned. It was probably the last time they'd see each other and Haider was cracking jokes. 'I put a white phosphorous grenade in the glove compartment. When you're ready, pull the pin, throw it on the seat and close the door.'

'If all goes well, I should reach Dogrum in a few days. I will be expecting you in three weeks – perhaps a month. It is difficult to tell with your guides. I gave them half the money now. They'll get the rest when you are delivered safely,' said Haider.

'You're sure they'll know who we are?' asked John.

'They will know you,' Haider assured him. 'Are you certain you do not want to know their identities?'

'No,' said John. 'If for some reason we don't link up with them, better we never knew.'

'Do you have the coordinates for Dogrum just in case?' asked Haider.

John checked his GPS. 'Got them.'

'I am sure you will not need them,' said Haider. 'Your guides will look after you as I would.'

'Well then, we have no fucking chance, do we,' laughed Dusty.

Haider took John's hand. 'Good luck, my friend,' he said, pulling John in to kiss him on both cheeks. He waved to Dusty. 'Inshallah, we shall meet again soon.'

Haider drove off leaving the two Scots by the side of the

road. Nearly nine hours had passed since they'd decided to do a runner. At first, Haider's suggestion seemed nothing short of complete madness – travel to Nuristan to his native village of Dogrum and argue their innocence before a *jirga* – a traditional council of elders. Who would care what a bunch of old men from Nuristan had to say about anything? But Haider was adamant that no official in Kabul, not even President Karzai, had the authority to overturn the ruling of a provincial council. In Afghanistan, a *jirga*'s decision was final.

If John and Dusty could clear their names in Nuristan, Rasul couldn't lay a finger on them. At least that was the theory. In practice, things could turn out quite differently. The pair had many factors against them, not the least of which was their ethnicity. As a native, Haider had a decent shot at winning over a group of Nuristani elders but the odds of two Scots sidelining a powerful local like Ustad Rasul seemed incredibly remote. Race aside, there was also the question of getting to Nuristan. The distance from Kabul to Dogrum was approximately one hundred and fifty miles as the crow flies. Back home, John and Dusty could walk that distance in a week or less. But Nuristan and its neighbouring provinces harboured some of the most inaccessible and hostile terrain on the planet: soaring sheer-faced mountains, deep valleys cut by wide, fast-flowing rivers, dirt tracks no wider than a man's hand. Roads were practically non-existent and most villages could only be accessed on foot or by air. Even high-tech tools of warfare had found their limits in Nuristan. The landscape was riddled with overhangs and caves unreadable by satellites or pilot-less drones. The area was so impregnable Osama bin Laden was rumoured to be hiding there.

John and Dusty had considered driving part of the way. But they ruled it out for fear of getting caught at a checkpoint. As a local, Haider wouldn't raise an eyebrow provided he was travelling alone. John and Dusty, on the other hand, were *Western* fugitives. Many Afghans would arrest them out of sheer pleasure. They'd be identified, detained and sent back to Kabul, if not executed on the spot. That left one option for getting to Nuristan. They'd have to hoof it.

The morning air crept through the cuffs of John's trousers and circled his legs. Both he and Dusty had dressed to blend in with the local guides Haider had arranged for them: long tan shalwar kameezes, grey waistcoats, tan shawls draped over their shoulders and grey turbans circling their heads. The only Western articles that remained were confined to their backs – their Bergens – and their feet: lace-up leather hiking boots with heavy rubber soles. Sandals would have been less conspicuous, but their pampered Western feet would never survive walking a mile in an Afghan's shoes, let alone a hundred.

The sun crested above the mountains, casting an orange hue over the summits. John ran his eyes along the blushing peaks. His last trip up a mountain had ended his military career. What ending would he meet this time around? He adjusted the straps of his Bergen. It'd been years since he'd shouldered the weight of a full pack and his muscles rebelled. He embraced the pain as an old soldier would a trusted mate. Nothing on his person was dispensable. He and Dusty had helped themselves to only essential items from the ShieldGroup stores: ten days' worth of British army rations; military maps of Afghanistan; binoculars; head torches; night vision sights; infrared glow sticks; handheld Global Positioning Systems; low-tech Silva compasses (for when satellites were inaccessible); spare batteries; duct tape; bungee cords; collapsible shovels; medical packs; Gortex bivvy bags; cold weather gear; Leatherman pocket knives and 1,500 US dollars – all the cash they could lay their hands on at such short notice.

Weapons rounded out their kit. Both men opted for 9mm pistols with four extra magazines each. When it came to rifles, however, the pair couldn't agree. Against John's advice, Dusty had grabbed a Heckler & Koch 5.56mm, the Bentley of automatic rifles. John stuck with his trusted AK-47 short. Not as flash as the Heckler & Koch but, he argued, more easily re-supplied with extra rounds, magazines and spare parts in the wilds of Afghanistan. The AK was also dependable. You could neglect it for years and it would still fire. The 5.56 was like a high maintenance woman – it would only put out with constant attention.

Everything was in order for their long trek to Nuristan. But John and Dusty couldn't leave Kabul without attending to one last, crucial item. They needed a witness; someone to tell their side of the story in case they didn't return.

The advancing car pulled over twenty yards from the two Scots. A gangly young man stepped out of the passenger side. Rudy examined the odd-looking pair. 'Mr Miller?' he asked.

'It's Dusty.' He kneeled down, unzipped a small pouch secured to his ankle and pulled out a camera.

John regarded the item with irritation. 'I thought we were only bringing essentials?'

'Documentation is essential,' Dusty countered. He handed the camera to Rudy. 'Do us a favour, mate.' The journalist hesitated. 'It's not bloody rocket science. Just point and press the button.'

Rudy framed the two Scots from the waist up and snapped. 'I was very intrigued by your phone call last night,' he said, handing the camera back to Dusty.

Dusty inspected the image on the external viewfinder. 'Not bad.' He showed it to John, who nodded with approval.

Rudy cleared his throat. 'I hate to interrupt, but I assume you didn't ask me here just to take your picture?'

'Keep your knickers on.' Dusty put away the camera, reached into his waistcoat and pulled out a bound report. He tossed it to the impatient journalist. Rudy read the cover page.

KABUL 25-06-06
The Ambush of ShieldGroup's CNPA training team by
   Hizb-i-Islami militants
Prepared: 25-06-06 by John Patterson
Job Title: Director of CNPA Training, ShieldGroup Int'l.

Rudy's eyes widened with delight. 'What is this?'

Dusty raised his chin. '*That* is the greatest story of your career, mate.'

Chapter 11

The vehicle was armoured. The windows were closed and protocol dictated they couldn't be opened. There was no escaping General Ustad Rasul's toxic odour, an overpowering blend of cheap cologne, spicy food, old sweat and rotten flatulence. It smothered everything in the confined space. Lieutenant Colonel Howard tried breathing through his mouth, but it only added another level of discomfort to his already besieged senses. A sour film of faecal matter coated his tongue. *How appropriate*, he thought. *I'm literally eating Rasul's shit.* But eat shit he must if John Patterson and his men were to be delivered unharmed to jail as promised instead of driven to the outskirts of Kabul tortured, eviscerated and left for the vultures. The possibility was not in the least bit remote. Before adopting the fig leaf of 'general', Ustad Rasul was known by another moniker: 'The Killer of Kamdesh'. His litany of atrocities included crucifying his enemies by nailing them to trees.

Having been deprived of the opportunity to exact revenge on the spot, Rasul had settled for turning the arrests into a spectacle. No less than seven vehicles had been pressed into service. Four 4x4s filled with armed Afghan police flanked by two Hummers mounted with heavy machine guns. Tucked safely in the middle of the convoy was the general's level B6/7 armoured Toyota – a gift from NATO. It was enough firepower to take on three platoons let alone three men. Howard dearly hoped the overkill would only be for show. He'd made clear to Simon Hampson that John and his team were to be fully briefed about their impending incarceration and given assurances that everything was being done to secure their quick release. Still, Howard knew there was every possibility his instructions would be ignored. Simon Hampson was exactly the type to exploit the situation to take a man like John Patterson down a peg or two. Howard had lain awake the night before imagining it. John and his men would be dragged from their quarters disoriented and half asleep, thrown to the ground, handcuffed and abused. Howard knew John would never take such treatment lying down. He would come out swinging – maybe even at Rasul himself. If that happened, the affair could drag on indefinitely.

The arrest party pulled into the ShieldGroup compound at 5.30 a.m. as planned. Simon Hampson was waiting for them at the entrance. His fat face was ashen.

The two outlaws crouched in a patch of dead ground, watching the traffic. They should have been well clear of the city limits by now, but the meeting with Rudy had started late and gone on longer than expected. Fucking journalists. John had allocated three minutes for Rudy; more than enough time to hand over a report. But he hadn't bargained on all the damn questions. Rudy just wouldn't shut up. 'What are you doing in Afghanistan . . . Why can't you tell me where you're going . . .?' Blah, blah, blah. Rudy had banged on for close to twenty minutes; enough to throw their entire plan.

John and Dusty should have rendezvoused with their local guides just after sunrise. The RV was on the Jalalabad Road approximately half a mile east of the Kabul Gate. If the guides had grown impatient and left, John and Dusty were in the shit. They stood little chance of getting past the Kabul Gate by themselves and there was no getting round it. A manned checkpoint positioned on a stone bridge crossing the Kabul river, the Gate was bordered by a mountain on one side and a deep gorge on the other.

John kept a lookout for police while Dusty observed the checkpoint through his binos. A line of vehicles: three trucks and a minibus were stopped on the far side of the bridge. A rock slide had made the road impassable. Local men, eight by Dusty's count, were shifting the debris while a police officer directed the operation from atop a large boulder. Ahead of the bridge, a lone truck and driver waited patiently for the all-clear.

Dusty handed the binos to John. 'Any ideas?'

John assessed the situation. They couldn't stay put and they couldn't return to Kabul. That left one realistic option; they had to get through the Kabul Gate on their own. John recalled a rule he drilled into all of his students. '"If" and "maybe" have no part in a successful operation. Base your actions on facts only.' John tucked his words away and hatched a plan loaded with assumptions: if they paid the driver of the truck ahead of the bridge, maybe they could hitch a ride with him. If they hid their Bergens in the wheel wells, maybe the police wouldn't see them. If they covered their faces with their shawls, maybe no one would notice they were Westerners. If they were stopped, maybe they could avoid questioning by pitching in with the clean-up operation.

The police were absorbed with bossing everyone about and seemed to take no notice of the two men walking toward them. 'I bet we could sneak right past those lads,' said Dusty hopefully. Suddenly, the policeman in charge pulled the radio from his belt. He held it to his ear and looked in the direction of the two Scots. John turned around. A convoy was coming up the road. It was roughly two miles away. Great plumes of dust swirled in its wake. John reckoned there were six maybe seven vehicles. 'Something tells me that's for us.'

Dusty looked at the convoy and back at the bridge. The policeman was yelling at the civilians, hounding them to work faster. 'What do you want to do?'

John reached beneath the folds of his shawl for his AK. 'We'll fight our way through the gate. You commandeer a vehicle. I'll take care of the police.'

'Mr John? Mr John?' The voice called to them from the side of the road.

The boy attached to it had appeared from nowhere. He was wearing a tattered jumper, dirty trousers and a round embroidered hat. As soon as John saw the black scar on the child's face, it clicked – the Kutchi boy from the KMTC. The child pointed to himself. 'Rafar,' he said. He waved John and Dusty over. 'Come, come,' he said. 'Come now. Hurry, hurry.'

Rafar stepped off the road and vanished. John and Dusty hurried after him. To their great relief they found Rafar scrambling down a dirt track that was undetectable from the road. They followed him down, over slippery patches of fine gravel to the riverbank. The slim slice of earth dead-ended beneath the Kabul Gate. Angry water gushed from the mountain base and ran straight for twenty yards before tumbling down a steep gorge. Beneath the bridge, the sound of the waterfall was near deafening.

The grinding of heavy vehicle brakes screeched overhead. The convoy was stopping. John and Dusty scanned the wall of rock to one side of them. It was sheer and slick with heavy moss. There was no way to scale up or along it. They searched the head of the waterfall for a crossing; a shallow pool or row of stones they could walk over. There was none, only water churning violently. They could go no further.

The sound of metal slamming into metal rumbled the air. An object dropped from above. John and Dusty recognized it before it disappeared beneath the frothing white water: a .50 calibre machine gun; Dushka, Russian-made. A much larger black object slammed down on top of it. It was a Hummer. Stifled screams came from inside the vehicle. Palms of hands pounded the bulletproof windows in vain. John and Dusty could see the terror in the drowning Afghans' eyes as the cab disappeared beneath the water's surface.

'Come, come,' Rafar called. The boy bent over and disappeared into the side of the mountain. At last John and Dusty saw it – a narrow opening concealed within the folds of the rock. Rafar was leading them into a tunnel.

Chapter 12

John and Dusty secured their head torches and followed their young guide into the darkness. The interior of the tunnel was much wider than its opening suggested: eight feet high and six feet wide – big enough for a man or large animal to walk through. The thin beams from the torches illuminated patches of the structure: stone walls and a vaulted ceiling like those found in a covered bazaar. John guessed they were in one of the Silk Gorge tunnels; an ancient network extending from the Afghan capital all the way to Jalalabad in the east. Built by spice traders to protect themselves and their cargo from thieves stalking the Silk Road, the tunnels were now used to smuggle opium, insurgents and explosives into the Afghan capital.

Rafar darted forward like a fearless tadpole oblivious to any potential dangers blighting his pond. John and Dusty, by contrast, were on high alert. Militants and drugs traffickers were known to booby-trap tunnels to scare away rivals and the authorities. If they struck a tripwire or stepped on a pressure plate the blast could send the walls caving in on top of them, unless their bodies absorbed the brunt of the shock directly, in which case they'd either be dismembered or have their insides pummelled to mush. There were also natural disasters to consider – flooding or the walls collapsing from wear and tear.

*

It was a full-on pile-up. Rasul's convoy had gone round the
waiting traffic and over the bridge so quickly that by the time
anyone realized the road was blocked, it was too late to stop.
The lead Hummer had slammed into a boulder and spun
around before colliding with one of the 4x4s and skidding off
the bridge. Two of the 4x4s were overturned. Wounded policemen had crawled out of the wreckage. Some were able to sit up.
Others were too injured. No one was helping them. The able-
bodied were too busy trying to free the passengers in the
armoured Toyota. It was pinned between the second Hummer
and the mountain.

After a few false starts, the Hummer was shifted. The doors
of the Toyota were severely damaged. When they wouldn't
budge, the police called for a crowbar. At first, they tried
pounding the bulletproof windows. When that proved futile,
one of them tried prising the door open. He was joined by
another man and another until three sets of hands were on the
crowbar. With red faces and muscles straining they finally managed to open the heavy armoured door.

Two policemen pulled General Rasul out of the vehicle. He
had a large cut on the side of his head and his grey beard was
matted with blood. When the police were certain the general
could stand on his own, they returned to the truck to rescue the
remaining passengers. Alone and disoriented, Rasul looked at
his injured escorts. He singled out one of them: a young man
with a haemorrhaging gash on his thigh. Rasul started shouting.
The injured man struggled to get to his feet but lost his balance
and fell over. Disgusted, the general un-holstered his pistol.

Lieutenant Colonel Howard was freed by the police just as
Rasul pulled the trigger. The bullet went right through the
injured man's head, splitting it like a melon.

Chapter 13

John and Dusty threw their Bergens through an opening and crawled out of the tunnel on hands and knees. Fuzzy discs of colour – red, green and orange – clouded their vision as their eyes readjusted to daylight. A group of people came into focus. It was an entire Kutchi family: four adults and six children including Rafar. The family had a menagerie of livestock in tow: two camels laden with patchwork bundles, several donkeys, a small herd of goats and two large white fluffy dogs. The adult men were dressed like typical Afghans. But the woman and girls had nothing in common with the blue ghosts roaming the streets of Kabul in burkas. They were clad in eye-catching colours, their dresses a mix of vibrant reds, blues and fuchsias. Some were hemmed with silver coins that chimed as they moved. Headscarves embellished with bold prints scattered over deep-green and saffron-yellow backgrounds partially covered their faces. Layers of coloured metallic bangles adorned their arms from elbow to wrist.

The oldest-looking member of the family – a man with white hair and a matching beard – stepped forward. 'Javid,' he said, pressing his hand to his chest. Before John and Dusty could return the gesture, Javid picked up both of their Bergens. The two Scots marvelled at the old man's strength.

John reached for the packs. 'We've got them.'

Javid ignored him and walked the Bergens over to a donkey. The beast had two wooden crates strapped to its sides. Javid dropped a pack in each and covered them with thick blankets. He then placed two shallow boxes containing a litter of baby goats on top and secured them with rope netting. Black and white furry heads poked out from between the holes, bleating. John and Dusty nodded to each other approvingly. It would take a very sharp eye indeed to spot two Westerners among these nomads.

The tawny landscape around Kabul gave way to patches of lush earth. Save a few words exchanged in hushed tones, John and Dusty followed the Kutchi silently, studying their actions and rituals, searching for hidden cultural lines that could trip them up. Some boundaries they already knew not to cross, such as those surrounding women. John and Dusty were careful to maintain a respectful distance from them at all times. Conservative and insular, the Kutchi were fiercely protective of their females. The patriarchal structure was most apparent on the roads. The men always walked at the front of the caravan with the camels while the women and children followed behind with the donkeys and goats. When they approached a tunnel, however, the order of march reversed – the men and camels would fall back allowing the women and donkeys to take the lead.

An hour before sundown the caravan stopped in a fertile valley outside a small village of mud-brick buildings. John and Dusty had been walking for eleven hours straight; their hosts even longer. But rest was still a long way off. The women and girls led the donkeys to the village to collect fresh water while the men pitched camp. The large patchwork bundles were untied from the camels and unfurled on the ground. As the cloths unrolled, each section expelled a tent component: ropes, wooden poles, metal stakes. Working in pairs – a man and boy each – the Kutchi tied the ropes to the poles and laid the patchwork cloth over the top. The poles were then lifted and the ropes pulled taut until a dwelling twenty feet by ten feet and roughly eight feet high at its apex took shape. The structure was secured with metal stakes which the men drove into the earth using rocks gathered from the valley floor.

In less than thirty minutes, the tent was up and ready. John and Dusty meanwhile, assembled their own accommodation. Feeding wire loops through one end of their bivvy bags, they constructed two one-man tents, which they positioned thirty yards from their hosts' camp.

As dusk fell, the women returned. The older ones led the donkeys, now laden with plastic containers of fresh water. The girls trailed behind, balancing bundles of brushwood on their heads. They dropped their wares and quickly set about domesticating the family dwelling, laying rugs, decanting water into beautiful earthen pitchers and lighting a fire.

The smell of meat stewing wafted over from the Kutchi camp. John and Dusty felt like kids with their noses pressed against a sweet-shop window. All they had to look forward to were British army boil-in-the-bags – sausage and beans and Irish stew. They were about to tuck into them when Rafar came running over. 'My father say you come eat with us.'

The women looked on approvingly as John and Dusty tucked into goat stew sweetened with raisins. They ate greedily, shoving huge spoonfuls into their mouths. The food was basic but immensely satisfying: warm and filling – exactly what their bodies craved after a day of physical exertion. When they finished, Javid and Rafar sat down beside them.

Javid uttered a few sentences in Pashto. 'My father ask you want more?' said Rafar.

'Tell your father we've eaten well,' said John. 'And we thank him for his generosity.'

Rafar translated the answer.

'Where did you learn to speak English, little mate?' asked Dusty.

Rafar smiled proudly. 'Kabul and Peshawar,' he said. 'Aid worker mans teach me. I speak English too good, no?'

'Like a posh wee lord,' said Dusty. 'Do you think your English is good enough to explain how you plan on getting us to Dogrum?'

Rafar put the question to his father. Javid picked up a thin piece of brushwood lying next to the fire. Using the ground as his canvas, he fashioned a basic map of Afghanistan's eastern provinces. Javid spoke as he moved the stick from the bottom of the map to the top. Rafar translated. 'We here,' Rafar pointed to a dot on the left. He moved his finger to the right toward what looked like the border with Pakistan. 'Two day time, we stop to graze animal. Next, we go up.' Rafar walked his fingers as he talked. 'Gogamunda, Sorobi, Shamaket. In one week time, we in Mehtarlam. We stop to graze animal. Must let animal graze every four day. One week time pass and we in Nungarack. Then Vaigal, then Dogrum.' Rafar smiled proudly.

John and Dusty studied the dirt map. 'Will there be many tunnels?' asked John.

'We walk in tunnel until we reach high mountain,' said Rafar. 'High mountain tunnel too dangerous. Too much water. Too much bomb.'

'There could be bombs in the other tunnels as well, mate,' said Dusty.

Rafar repeated the statement to his father. Javid shook his head no and answered. 'My father say no worry. We know all tunnel where bomb sleep. We also know where bomb sleep in ground.'

John and Dusty exchanged glances. 'Sleeping bombs can move,' said John.

Rafar relayed the concern to Javid. The elder Kutchi responded sceptically. 'My father ask how can bomb sleep in ground move?'

John reached for the brushwood Javid had used to draw the map. 'May I,' he said. He carved two burrows in the dirt. 'Say this is a road. One you've travelled many times.' John made two marks to the right of the lines. 'These are bombs – landmines buried three metres off the road. Now, let's say there's a very harsh winter and lots of snow falls in the mountains.' John drew a series of vertical zigzags. 'The snow melts and flows down the mountain over the ground where the bombs are sleeping. The water moves the ground and the bombs along with it. So now, instead of sleeping three metres off the road the bombs are lying on the road.'

Rafar explained the scenario to his father, referencing John's illustration.

'Father ask if sleeping bomb can move in tunnel?'

'It's possible,' said John. 'But unlikely. Most bombs laid in tunnels are attached to a thin piece of wire. We call them booby traps.' John held up the stick. 'What you need to do is get a stick about this long, only thinner, more flexible; maybe a reed or a piece of plastic. Place the stick between your thumb and forefinger and hold it in front of you as you walk,' John demonstrated. 'Keep it waist height with the end just an inch or so off the ground. This way, you'll feel the wire with the stick instead of running into it with your legs and setting off the bomb.'

Javid took the stick from John and examined it while his son explained.

'Tell your father, if he likes, Dusty and I will go into the tunnels first from now on.'

Rafar relayed the offer to Javid. 'My father say thank you. Is most kind.'

Javid spoke again and got up to leave. 'My father say we must sleep now. Many day walk ahead.'

'Please, tell your father we are both grateful for his hospitality,' said John.

Javid bowed to his guests and disappeared into his tent. Rafar lingered.

'Hey, little mate,' said Dusty. 'Why do the women and donkeys always go first into the tunnels?'

Rafar shrugged his shoulders. 'Camel is worth more than woman and donkey.'

John chuckled quietly as the boy left to join his family. 'Cheeky little git.'

Dusty picked up the stick and threw it on the fire. 'I think he was serious.'

Chapter 14

The Elbow Room Restaurant and Bar was Kabul's most popular international watering hole. Open every day for lunch and dinner, the eclectic menu ticked all the comfort food boxes from vegetarian chilli to imported club steaks served to order at nineteen US dollars a pop. The real draw for homesick foreigners though was the drinks: cocktails, spirits and beers served in flagrant violation of Afghanistan's strict anti-alcohol laws.

Fridays were the Elbow Room's busiest day of the week; the Muslim day of rest when an English breakfast buffet replete with bacon and pork sausages – Islam's forbidden meat – drew hordes of Westerners nursing hangovers. There were no spaces left in the parking lot when Rudy's driver pulled up. It'd been overtaken by 4x4s from the embassies around town. An Afghan attendant directed them back to the main road, where, he assured them, the Elbow Room's own local guards would keep watch over their vehicle.

Rudy walked down a long narrow alley and through the door at the end. Kabul's monotone streets dissolved as he found himself enveloped by apple, emerald and sea greens. The palette cast a sickly glow over the security men tucking into plates of unlimited food washed down with five-dollar cans of lager and ale.

Rudy had no idea what Simon Hampson looked like. A twenty-dollar gratuity to the barman soon solved that problem.

Apparently, Simon was a regular. 'Lounge,' said the barman. 'Teenaged prostitute named Ping on his arm.'

Simon didn't acknowledge the journalist hovering over the plush sofa. He was too distracted by Ping's underaged neck which he groped with greasy fingers.

'Excuse me, Mr Hampson,' Rudy interrupted.

Simon looked up. He freed his hand from Ping to take a pull from a bottle of lager. 'Do I know you?' he asked, swallowing his words along with his beer.

'My name is Rudy Lipkingard. I'm a journalist. I left several messages with your office regarding an interview.'

Simon cocked his head, as if he were searching his memory. 'Doesn't ring a bell, I'm afraid.'

'Odd,' said Rudy. 'Your HR department in London assured me they had passed my messages on to you. As did the PR representative they eventually referred me to. Chap named Verdi. Big City firm. Charges by the hour.'

Simon sank back into the sofa. His enormous gut poured over his belt. 'I have no idea what London gets up to.'

Rudy looked pointedly at Ping. 'And I'll bet your London office has no idea what *you* get up to here.'

Simon's expression turned indignant. 'If you're implying there's something untoward with the young lady, you're mistaken. Miss Ping is my secretary.'

Rudy knew Simon was squirming and kept the pressure up. 'I have no doubt she's a valuable member of your staff. As are all the prostitutes you employ, I'm sure.'

Simon's pretence evaporated. He jerked his head at Ping. 'Leave us,' he ordered. The girl obeyed. He turned his full attention to Rudy. 'Listen, you little turd. I don't know who you are or what you're up to, but I have friends in Kabul. Powerful friends. Don't fuck with me.'

Rudy sat down next to Simon. He wiped the air with his hand as if imagining a headline. '"Respected Security Manager is Notorious Kabul Pimp."' He smiled at Simon. 'Cracking story, don't you think?'

Simon didn't answer immediately. He took another long pull of lager and sank into the sofa as if nothing in the universe could touch him. 'What is it you're after? Money? Is that it? Are you thinking to blackmail me, you little shit? Well, I suggest you reconsider. Sully my good name and I'll take legal action against you and whatever rag it is you write for.'

The blustering couldn't hide the panic in Simon's eyes. 'And you'll have no shortage of libel lawyers queuing to take your money,' said Rudy. 'Not that you'll have much left after you are deported from Afghanistan, sacked and discredited.'

Simon wrapped both hands around the lager bottle. They were trembling. 'How much then?'

'I don't want your damn money,' said Rudy.

'Then what the hell are you after, man?' said Simon.

Rudy let Simon sweat it out a few more seconds. 'I want to talk about the 25th of June.'

Simon shook his head. 'I haven't the faintest clue what you're talking about.'

'Let me refresh your memory,' said Rudy. 'There was a fire-fight between employees of ShieldGroup and two al-Qaeda operatives recruited by the Serious Organized Crime Agency to train as Afghan counter-narcotics police. Ring a bell?'

Simon was visibly unnerved by the extent of Rudy's knowledge. 'Why are you bothering me? You should be talking to SOCA.'

'I did,' said Rudy. 'They said they couldn't comment on the affair. National security.'

'You've got your answer then,' said Simon. 'Piss off.'

'But I still have so many questions.' Rudy moved closer to Simon, physically hemming him in. 'Tell me what you know about John Patterson.'

'Patterson?' Simon smirked. 'I'll tell you about John Patterson. He's dangerous; not right in the head. Everyone knows it. The Afghan authorities are dying to get their hands on him and his sidekick, Malcolm Miller. Those two are the most wanted men in the country right now. More than bin Laden even.'

'Can I quote you on that?' said Rudy.

Simon's face turned white. 'No, you cannot fucking quote me. Anything I say to you is strictly off the record. If you're so damned interested in what happened on the 25th of June I suggest you request a copy of ShieldGroup's report on the incident. It will answer all your questions.'

'Slight problem there I'm afraid,' said Rudy. 'Your PR flak informed me that while ShieldGroup is more than happy to share its quarterly and annual financial reports, internal company documents may contain – how did he put it? – ah yes, *proprietary* information which could undermine ShieldGroup's competitive standing in the security industry should it be made public. Of course, I would try and petition SOCA through Freedom of Information, but that could take years and I don't want to wait that long. So unless someone in a position of authority at ShieldGroup is willing to speak to me – *on* the record – regarding the events of the 25th of June, I'll have no other option than to investigate and write about whatever ShieldGroup misdeeds I can confirm right now, such as the in-country manager for Afghanistan running a local brothel staffed by Chinese sex-slaves.'

Simon started perspiring. 'You don't want to waste your time on me. I'm no one. You have no idea what's at stake here – not for me personally,' he added hurriedly. 'I'm talking about the company. Big money, just the sort of thing you journalists love to write about.'

Rudy milked more information. 'What kind of big money?'

'The biggest there is,' said Simon. 'Military contracts.'

'The SAS,' said Rudy.

'No,' said Simon. 'But that's a good place to start digging.'

'You're being too cryptic, Mr Hampson. If you want me to go away, you're going to have to give me a name.'

Simon fidgeted. 'For Christ's sake, man, I've laid it all out on the table for you. Soaking wet and naked on a silver platter.'

Rudy kept pressing. 'A name, Mr Hampson. Someone in a position of authority who can comment.'

Simon crumbled. 'Pete Mitchell.'

'Who is he?' Rudy demanded.

'ShieldGroup director. Ex-SAS, Military Cross,' said Simon. 'That enough for you to go on, or will you be requiring a photograph and a postcode?'

'The name is quite sufficient,' said Rudy. 'Will this Pete Mitchell be able to tell me about the 25th of June?'

Simon took another shaky pull of beer. 'He can tell you about everything – including John Patterson.'

Chapter 15

The sound of helicopter blades clubbing the air echoed throughout the mountain pass. John and Dusty searched the skies behind
them. A black insect-like Apache bolted out from between two
peaks, dropped down to the valley floor and swept back up, past
the winding mountain road they were walking with the Kutchi.
No sooner had the gunship disappeared over a northern ridge
than a Chinook followed on its heels. The airborne taxi was far
less agile than its smaller, swifter counterpart, plodding along at
a steady altitude. The helicopters were probably flying as a team;
the Chinook ferrying troops and equipment, the Apache travelling ahead, scouting for potential hazards.

'What's the Coalition doing this far north?' said Dusty.

'Don't know,' said John. 'I bet you they're hunting al-Qaeda.'

'Lucky bastards.' Dusty elbowed John. 'Remember when
you'd give your right arm for an operation like that?'

John didn't have to stretch his memory. The sight of soldiers
heading out on operations always filled him with longing. It had
done since he'd left the Regiment. It wasn't just the adrenalin
rush or the chance to test his skills that he missed. John didn't
even resent retiring two years shy of collecting his full pension.
What he yearned for was more powerful than money and more
satisfying than glory – John wanted to be part of an elite group
again.

Most civilians had no idea what that really meant. To them, 'elite' was a throwaway word, a label for flash cars, big houses and designer dogs. John wanted no part of that world. He couldn't stand people who acquired things just to impress others. That's why he felt so at home in the SAS. It was built on individuals who couldn't give a toss what others thought of them. Regiment lads were steeped in self-belief. It was the only place where John ever felt he truly belonged. He reckoned that's why he never managed to adjust to life on Civvy Street. You couldn't show an ounce of initiative in the civilian world without some manager shitting all over it. Self-reliance terrified the weak.

For years, John felt like a castaway marooned on a desert island. But as he watched the Chinook fly out of sight, he realized his sense of isolation was receding. Something else, a new emotion, was taking hold of him. John first sensed it near the lakes of Sorobi. The days of walking had expelled the pollutants of Kabul from his lungs, allowing them to deliver more oxygen to his muscles. His arms and legs were growing more powerful; like they used to be. His mind was strengthening as well. Afghanistan's rugged, wild landscape had reinvigorated John's senses. He couldn't remember when he'd last been so sharp, so in tune with the world around him. For the first time in a decade, John wasn't regretting his past or dreading his future. He was living in the moment. He was free.

John doubted even his guides could appreciate what he was feeling. The Kutchi had no yardstick to measure their liberty by. From cradle to grave, they were completely self-sufficient. No one recorded their births or deaths. No passports tracked their movements. No files were kept to remind everyone of their weakest, darkest moments. They weren't slaves to monthly mortgage payments or hounded for National Insurance contributions. They would never suffer the indignities of selling their labour to survive. The Kutchi simply existed as they had for centuries, wandering from India to Iran over borders they had never recognized nor ever would.

The sound of gears grinding travelled up from the valley floor. Javid raised his hand and the caravan came to a halt. John and Dusty took cover behind a low stone safety barrier. They peered over the wall with their binos. An open-cab truck carrying six ANA soldiers with AKs strapped to their backs was driving up the mountain.

John and Dusty followed the truck's progress as it wound its way higher. The soldiers seemed to be in no hurry and the road demanded concentration. Carved down one side of the mountain, it resembled a string of coiled sausages. The fat sections could just accommodate two passing vehicles; the slim areas, one small truck. Every bend was blind, every turn a hairpin. No signs warned travellers to exercise caution but there was no need. Each missing section of safety barrier bore testament to a vehicle which had lost control and plunged to the valley below.

The soldiers stopped two levels down from the caravan; a six-hundred-yards line of sight; double that distance on foot. They dismounted from their truck and took up positions on either side of the road. Three of the soldiers remained standing while the others huddled beneath blankets.

'Why did they stop?' Dusty whispered.

'I'm not sure,' said John. He waved Javid over. Rafar followed behind. John handed the elder Kutchi his binoculars. He spoke in a whisper while Rafar translated. 'Why have the soldiers stopped?'

Javid spoke. 'My father say soldiers look for people,' said Rafar.

'Could they be looking for us?' asked Dusty.

Rafar put the question to his father. 'My father say no. Many soldier run away from army. Soldiers look for runaway soldier. Not you.'

'Tell your father we can't risk getting caught,' said John. 'It would be dangerous for us and for all of you. You go ahead. We'll stay here until the soldiers leave and catch up with you later.'

Rafar relayed the plan to his father. Javid rejected it. 'My father say is too dangerous. Soldiers stay too long time. Many bandit come with night. You come with us. Is no problem.'

John looked for a path to take them all down the mountain out of view of the soldiers. The vertical drops between road levels were steep. The rock was soft shale. Maintaining a foothold on such an incline would be difficult under the best of circumstances. The only alternative route John could identify was a narrow, twisting goat track. But it led up the mountain, not down. 'Tell your father we respect what he says but we can take care of ourselves. Go ahead and we'll find you when the soldiers have gone.'

Rafar conveyed John's words to his father. Javid accepted the plan but Rafar wouldn't have it. The boy started pleading. The back and forth between father and son grew increasingly animated, punctuated by hushed hisses and thrashing hands. When it concluded, Rafar turned to John. The child's smile was so broad his face could barely hold it. 'Mr John,' said Rafar. 'You no need stay here. There is other way down mountain. I show you.'

'What other way?' asked John.

Rafar pointed to the goat track. 'Other side of mountain. There is tunnel.'

John looked at the mountainside, then back at Javid. The old man's face was taut with concern. 'Is the tunnel dangerous, Rafar?'

Rafar toed the dirt and shook his head no.

John pointed to the goat track. Drawing on his limited knowledge of Pashto the elder Scot spoke directly to Javid. 'Khatir?' he asked. *Danger?*

'Der, der,' said Javid. *Very, very.* The old man spoke rapidly.

When he finished, John looked down at Rafar. 'Tell us what your father said. All of it.'

Rafar finally confessed that the tunnel flooded regularly. It was so dangerous, the Kutchi had a name for it – the tunnel of tombs.

Chapter 16

Lieutenant Colonel Howard lifted the demitasse cup to his mouth and sipped the piping hot liquid. It slid down his tongue like liquid velvet; just the right balance of acidity and no stray grinds. He'd grown so used to the overpriced, unpalatable sludge served up in London that he'd forgotten what a proper espresso should taste like. At least NATO had got something right in Afghanistan. Giving the Italians a cafe at ISAF HQ was an inspired decision.

'Pinky!'

Howard shuddered at the nasal greeting. Only one person on earth reduced his name to that crass contraction: Howard's US Army counterpart Lieutenant Colonel Walter Raleigh. The two met bi-monthly, ostensibly to ensure that the NATO-led and American-led missions in Afghanistan weren't sending mixed messages. Unofficially, the meetings were used to pass informal communications between their respective generals. They weren't scheduled to talk for another week at least.

Raleigh delivered a blow between Howard's shoulders. 'How ya doin', old chap? Top of the morning to ya.' Tired English idioms were Raleigh's idea of diplomacy. It didn't seem to occur to him that his good-natured effort was damned annoying. 'Want some company?'

It was the last thing Howard desired. But Raleigh's intrusion, like his greeting, was too heavy-handed to be random. This was no casual visit. Howard nodded at an empty chair. 'Please,' he said.

Raleigh deposited his muscular frame on the wooden seat. He was a mountain of a man, broad and tall with close-cropped hair shorn at sheer angles. 'What cha drinkin'?' he asked.

An Italian waiter cum soldier walked over to the table. 'Espresso,' said Howard. 'They make an awfully good one here.'

Raleigh thumped his chest. 'I never put caffeine in the temple, my friend.' He turned to the waiter. 'Good morning. You got any decaf?'

'No,' replied the waiter curtly.

The abruptness failed to penetrate Raleigh's cheerfulness. 'You got any clear pop like a Sprite or anything like that?' he asked.

'No,' said the waiter.

Howard stepped in. 'Please bring the lieutenant colonel a Fanta. Lemon. Thank you.'

The waiter left to fill the order. 'Good thing you're here or I'd die of thirst,' said Raleigh.

'So,' said Howard. 'To what do I owe this unexpected visit, Walter?'

Raleigh paused to repress his natural exuberance. 'I was hoping to have a word with you. Between friends.'

Howard felt ill at ease with the suggested intimacy. 'You want to discuss something of a personal nature?'

Raleigh considered his response. 'Let me put it this way. Some questions are better asked and answered in a casual setting. It's . . . less embarrassing.'

Howard felt more put off than intrigued. 'What kind of questions?'

The waiter returned with a Fanta, a napkin and an empty glass which he placed on the table. 'Much obliged,' said Raleigh. He circled the rim of the soda can with the napkin. 'I'm not sure how to say this so I'll just come right out with it. I was wondering whether or not you've had any luck locating those two nationals of yours. The ones who flew the coop.'

Howard's inner cauldron spiked. The ShieldGroup incident was privileged information, not to mention a strictly British–Afghan affair. Why the hell were the Yanks interested? 'This is ISAF,' said Howard. 'Many nations are represented here. Could you be more specific?'

Raleigh pulled the tab from his Fanta and drank directly from the can. 'Come off it, Pinky. I guess I shouldn't have blurted it out like that. But don't you think you're being a little touchy. I mean, if those boys were soldiers, that'd be one thing. But they're private security contractors. Hell, it's not like American contractors are saints.'

'What is your point, exactly?' asked Howard.

'The point is shitstorms happen all the time in Afghanistan. It's raining on you now but it could pour on us tomorrow.' Howard could feel his dislike of the American tipping into full-blown hatred. 'I didn't come here on a high horse to lecture you, Pinky. We just want to get a read on the situation. So please, tell me – are you close to finding those boys or not?'

Howard considered whether to hide behind protocol. He could say he was not at liberty to discuss the matter outside official channels. But that would only move the enquiry out of his sphere of influence, something he was keen to avoid. 'The short answer is no, we haven't been able to locate them.'

'Do you have any idea where they might be holed up?' asked Raleigh.

'As I said, we haven't been able to locate them.'

'Hmmm,' Raleigh grumbled. 'That could be a problem for us.'

'I fail to see how it is *your* problem at all,' said Howard.

Raleigh took another gulp of soda. 'You know Enduring Freedom is making a big push north-east.' He stopped to stifle a belch. 'Kunar . . . *Nuristan* . . .' Raleigh waited for Howard to respond. 'Come on, Pinky. Do I have to spell it out for you?'

'Yes. You do,' replied Howard.

Raleigh dropped his voice to a whisper. 'Your nationals pissed off General Rasul. Royally. The Pentagon wants four forward operating bases up and running in the Kunar–Nuristan corridor before fall. Now we can do that without General Rasul's backing but you know as well as I do that he can make a lot of trouble for our boys up there. Rasul sees no difference between your troops and our troops. All Westerners are the same in his eyes. And I don't mean to sound insensitive, but we don't want to see American blood spilled because some Afghan warlord has a beef with a couple of Brits.'

Howard's cauldron boiled over. A deep crack erupted down the centre of his forehead. 'I would beg you to keep in mind that the British wouldn't be here were it not for America's "beef" as you put it with Osama bin Laden. Don't you dare presume to take the moral high ground, Walter. Not when British soldiers are dying fighting what everyone knows is America's war.'

The outburst humbled the strapping American. 'I'm sorry,' said Raleigh. 'It was never my intention to diminish the British contribution to Afghanistan. I for one can assure you that the United States of America deeply appreciates everything the British have done and continue to do to help eradicate the scourge of terrorism . . .'

The words sounded contrived but Howard knew they were sincere. He regretted having squandered a rare display of emotion on someone as hopeless as Raleigh. He wasn't a bad chap deep down. Like so many Americans, Raleigh was programmed to believe that the enemies of the United States were a threat to all free nations.

'. . . and I personally value the special friendship between our two great nations,' Raleigh continued. 'So, please accept my apologies.'

The line in Howard's forehead receded. 'The matter is forgotten,' he said. 'And if General Rasul becomes a problem for you, you have my word we will do what we can from our end to help smooth things over, though I'm afraid he's not terribly receptive to us at present.'

'Actually,' said Raleigh, 'there is something you can do and by you, I mean ISAF. But that's a discussion best left to a higher pay grade.'

Tempted as he was to let their superiors deal with the problem, Howard was loath to be blindsided again. 'What did you have in mind, Walter. Between friends?'

Raleigh leaned in. 'General Rasul has made it clear that he expects any American presence in Nuristan to – how can I say this tactfully – have an economic as well as military impact. Bottom line is, we can send our Special Forces into the mountains to hunt al-Qaeda so long as we got regular troops in the villages working on development projects.'

'Why do you need ISAF's help?' asked Howard. 'Enduring Freedom runs its own PRTs.'

'Manpower, my friend. Enduring Freedom doesn't have enough troops in theatre to supply PRTs in Kunar–Nuristan. Not with the way things are going in Iraq. We were hoping ISAF could shift some of our boys operating under its command.'

'Hoping?' said Howard sceptically.

'We don't want to strong-arm anyone,' said Raleigh. 'Hell, we know NATO's got its hands tied with so many ISAF nations refusing to deploy to hard areas. Goddamn potted plants.'

'What timetable did you have in mind?' asked Howard.

'ASAP,' said Raleigh. 'Within the next two weeks.'

'Impossible,' said Howard.

'Hey, unless you locate your boys and smooth things over with General Rasul, we don't have another option.'

'We can't snap our fingers and re-deploy troops on a whim,' said Howard. 'We have to consider the impact on our overall operation.'

Raleigh finished the rest of his soda and laid the can down on the table. 'Like I said, Pinky. We don't *want* to strong-arm anyone.'

Chapter 17

'I good guide. I help you,' Rafar insisted.

'No,' said John. He and Dusty were losing patience. They'd agreed with Javid that Rafar would lead them to the tunnel and then return to the caravan. But the boy refused to go. John knelt down to bring himself eye level with his young guide. 'Your father is waiting for you. We'll be fine.'

Rafar folded his arms defiantly. 'I stay here. You need me.'

'I can't allow that,' said John. 'You're still a child—'

Rafar stomped his foot. 'I not child!'

The words and actions unearthed a long buried memory in John: blond hair and a small voice insisting *I'm not a baby*. 'What if the soldiers make trouble for your sisters?' said John. 'You need to protect them.'

'Soldiers not make trouble for sisters,' said Rafar. 'They too ugly.'

John stood up. 'Enough is enough now. We gave our word to your father.' Rafar swayed back and forth. John was well acquainted with the childish stalling tactic. He pulled his trump card. 'You dishonour me by disobeying,' he said.

Rafar had no comeback. 'You make big mistake,' he said.

John placed his hands on Rafar's shoulders. 'Go on now. We'll be fine. I promise.'

'Wait!' said Rafar. The boy removed his jumper. He grabbed

a section with his teeth and tore two red strips from the garment. 'For face,' he said handing it to John. 'I see you soonest, inshallah.'

John waited for Rafar to vanish over the ridge. When he was certain the boy wouldn't return, he fixed his head torch and poked his head through the tunnel opening. A blast of ammonia hit him like a closed fist. John switched on the light. A cluster of bats flew toward him. He pulled back, narrowly avoiding the creatures as they bolted out of the tunnel. He stuck his head back in and looked down. The light from the torch bounced off the floor. It was covered with water. John tilted his chin up. The ground ran level for twenty yards then dipped sharply. Into what he could only imagine. He twisted around to inspect the roof. Rows of bats – hundreds of them, lined the ceiling. It explained why Rafar had given them cloth to cover their faces. The tunnel was plastered in bat shit.

John ducked out. 'I'll go first.'

'Like hell,' said Dusty.

'Come on,' said John. 'Age before beauty.'

'Your eyes are shot,' Dusty countered. 'If that tunnel is mined you won't see a wire until you've tripped it.'

John grabbed a loose stone and threw it through the entrance. A faint plunking sound followed. 'There's at least five inches of water in there. If there's a booby trap, we'll feel it before we see it.'

Dusty put on his head torch and looked through the entrance. Rings emanated from where the stone had landed. He pulled his head out again. 'Rafar said everyone knows this tunnel floods, right?'

'So what?' asked John.

'So it's reasonable to assume that if anyone did lay a mine in there, they'd put it high against the wall. I'm going first,' said Dusty.

John shook his head. 'You're way wide of the mark.'

'Explosives pack less of a punch when they're detonated underwater,' said Dusty. 'Everyone knows that.'

'Really,' said John. 'You served with the most elite Regiment of the best military in the world. You think a drug-runner high on opium or a pimple-faced insurgent knows as much about demolitions as you? I'll bet you all the Guinness you owe me that if there is a booby trap in there it's planted low.'

Dusty thought about it. 'Don't just stand there. Get a move on, old man.'

John hit the water and began his descent. He walked with his head down and shoulders stooped, a long flexible stick pressed between his thumb and forefinger feeling for tension wires – just as he'd shown the Kutchi over the campfire. Dusty trailed five yards behind him, rifle at the ready, looking ahead and behind for other travellers or signs of structural weakness. The tunnel was in a hell of a state. Sections of wall had crumbled away, depositing debris on the floor. Water dripped from the ceiling and welled up from below, feeding the foul, excrement-slicked stream washing over their feet. The whole thing looked like it could give way at any second. For all they knew, part of it may have already collapsed.

The air grew more stagnant the deeper they travelled. The smell of bat shit grew unbearable. Their eyes watered uncontrollably from the toxic fumes. The onslaught eventually migrated to John's stomach. He tried to stave it off, but his body convulsed. He leaned over and vomited.

'Are you all right, mate?' asked Dusty.

John cleared his throat and spat out a ball of thick, bitter phlegm. 'Brilliant,' he said.

The going was agonizingly slow. The floor was pocked with holes; some small enough to catch a foot and twist an ankle, others so deep they could swallow a leg to the knee. Every three hundred to five hundred metres, a shaft of natural light followed by a whiff of fresh air would hold out the promise of an end in sight. But it was just a break in the long tunnel network, an exit leading to another entrance and more darkness beyond.

'Hold on a second,' said Dusty.

John straightened up. A bolt of pain shot through his neck. They'd been at it for hours. He could compartmentalize his discomfort as long as he was concentrating on avoiding a big bang. As soon as his focus was pulled, however, his body would complain. 'What is it?'

Dusty nodded toward the path ahead. 'Up there.'

John pushed the nagging ache to the back of his mind. They were up against a major obstruction, a mound of earth and rocks piled practically to the ceiling. The only opening was a small gap in the far right corner just big enough for a man to squeeze through.

'I don't like the look of that one bit,' said Dusty.

John agreed. There was something unnatural about the way the rubble had fallen. It looked like an ambush, a ruse to force someone through the narrow opening. John turned around to speak to Dusty. The sudden movement caused his lower back to spasm. He tried to straighten it but that only made his muscles rebel even more. 'Give us a second,' John winced. He dropped to his knees and curled his right arm under his torso. Using his left arm as a fulcrum, he rolled onto his back and slowly lowered his feet to the floor.

Dusty snickered. 'Fucking geriatric. You should be using a Zimmer frame to check for booby traps.'

'I'll show you who's a geriatric when I get this back sorted.' John kicked his feet out. Three successive pops sounded as his spine released. He rolled onto his stomach and pushed himself up.

'Do you want to turn back?' asked Dusty.

'Do you?'

'No.'

'Then let's get moving.'

Dusty stopped him. 'Why don't I go first this time? Give you a chance to relax your back for a wee while.'

'I'm still point man on this operation. Stand back.' John re-assumed his mine-detecting position and advanced slowly toward the rock pile. When he reached the obstruction, he inspected it thoroughly before attempting to crawl through it. Wedging his foot into the wall, he secured his stance and peered through the opening. He scanned the walls and ceiling for trip-wires. Satisfied it was clear, John wedged his body through the hole and lowered himself down the other side. 'Fucking hell!' he cried.

Dusty called to him. 'Did you throw your back out again?'

'No,' said John. 'There's a booby trap.'

'What kind?' asked Dusty.

John paused. 'I'm not sure.'

'A wire? A pressure plate? What is it?' asked Dusty.

'I don't know,' said John. 'It's hard to tell.'

Dusty rolled his eyes. 'How fucking blind are you?'

John looked at the headless corpse floating in the water. 'The damn thing's already gone off.'

Body parts and pieces of uniform were strewn everywhere. John took stock of the carnage: a severed leg, a hand, a boot with a foot inside. He identified the remains of four torsos. One of them was lying face-down on top of an AK-47. The water on the floor of the cave was still stained with blood and the corpses were only slightly bloated. John reckoned the victims had died within the last two to three days.

Dusty crawled through the gap in the mound. 'Who are they?'

'ANA,' said John. 'Look at the uniforms – or what's left of them.'

Dusty crouched down and inspected the wall. 'Flash burns and shrapnel pocks. I bet it was a fragmentation mine.' He stood up and looked down on the pool of rotting flesh. 'None of these bastards stood a chance.'

'I think there were survivors.' John nodded at the rubble. 'An explosion would have brought this wall down. Someone built it after the fact.' He pointed to the corpse lying on the AK-47. 'That body's booby-trapped.'

'Are you sure?' said Dusty. 'Not that I'm suggesting we test the theory.'

'By my count, there are four casualties,' John explained. 'But I only see one weapon. Someone carried three away and left that one behind as bait.'

'Think they were deserters?' asked Dusty.

'Who knows,' said John. 'But if the survivors bothered to lay a trap here there are bound to be more up ahead. Let's get moving.'

With his stick leading the way, John stepped delicately between the corpses and forged ahead. A hundred yards later a thin beam of sunlight greeted him around a sloping bend. John had to fight the urge to run toward it. The water in the tunnel picked up speed as the incline grew steeper. John kept the stick immersed, allowing the end to bend with the force of the water. He continued to walk methodically, feeling for any changes in pressure. Suddenly, there it was – the dreaded tension of a wire pulled taut. He dropped to his knees and adjusted his head torch. It took a few seconds but he finally saw it: a thin line strung eight inches above the water. John followed it with his eyes. The wire was pegged to the wall on his right. The other end was tied to a chunky cylinder the size of a soda can. It was a classic fragmentation mine.

John studied the booby trap, trying to determine whether it was detonated by tension or tension release. If it was tension, he could disarm it simply by cutting the wire. But if it was tension release, severing the wire would trigger the explosion.

John waited for Dusty to catch up. 'What do you make of this?' Dusty crouched and inched his body toward John's. 'I'd really like to disarm this thing,' said John.

Dusty examined the mine. He was just as stumped. 'I say we mark it and leave it alone.'

John handed Dusty the stick. 'I'll do it. You go on.'

Dusty took the stick and stepped over the wire, taking care not to catch it on the cuffs of his trousers. He walked to the end of the tunnel. Before he exited, he called back to John. 'All clear!'

John took the piece of red cloth Rafar had given him and tied it gently around the wire. It was the best he could do to warn others who may follow. His task complete, John stepped over the wire and walked towards the light.

He found Dusty sitting on the gentle grade of a foothill, his face turned up to the sun. John sat down beside him. 'Any sign of the Kutchi?' he asked.

Dusty raised his arm and pointed forward. In the distance, John could see a thin line of white smoke drifting skyward. He took out his binos. Javid and the caravan had pitched camp a couple of miles ahead.

'We should get going. They'll be waiting for us,' said John.

The weary pair rose to their feet. Suddenly, a faint voice called from behind. It was coming from inside the tunnel. John and Dusty looked at each other – alarmed. The voice kept calling. 'Mr John! Mr John!'

Chapter 18

Rudy clicked the send button and smiled. Another story filed ahead of deadline. His editor in London had to be impressed. Not only was he producing enough copy for three correspondents, his dispatches were streaks ahead of the competition. Most reporters in Afghanistan rehashed the same three stories again and again: soldiers who died in combat, soldiers doing good deeds and the opium trade. Rudy couldn't understand it. There was so much else going on. Like the feature he'd just finished on how far women had come since the days of the Taliban. Rudy's story centred on Aqalla, a fourteen-year-old, illiterate child bride who'd poured boiling water on her genitals to stop her husband from raping her every night. Aqalla desperately wanted to get an education. When Rudy asked her doctor how likely that would be, he was stunned to learn that not only was Aqalla's dream impossible, it was illegal. The Afghan parliament had passed a law barring married women from attending school.

How that story managed to fly under the radar of the Western press corps, Rudy couldn't fathom. And it wasn't the only one. He'd written features on the plight of Afghan orphans (who knew adoption was forbidden in Islam?), Kabul's booming kidnap-for-ransom trade and of course, the Afghan National Army.

With so many stories locked and ready for print, Rudy could get stuck into the juicy tip he'd prised from Simon Hampson. He opened his web browser and typed the words 'Pete Mitchell ShieldGroup' into the search engine. The search produced just one news item.

SAS HERO HITS PAYDIRT

LONDON 10 December 2004 –

An ex-SAS hero bagged himself a £5 million windfall after selling his security training firm to ShieldGroup International. Pete Mitchell MC founded Ajax Ltd. in 2003 to train private security contractors working in Iraq and Afghanistan.

'There is growing demand for security professionals worldwide,' said David Verdi, spokesperson for ShieldGroup. 'Acquiring Ajax not only ensures that ShieldGroup's clients will continue to receive the highest standards of service from the industry's most elite professionals, it will also position the company to take greater advantage of the expanding market for security sector reform in post-conflict areas.'

ShieldGroup International is a listed company. The firm currently has operations in Iraq with plans to expand into Afghanistan next year.

The item seemed straightforward. But Rudy had a hunch all the high-minded terms spouted by the PR flak masked a deeper agenda. What exactly was 'security sector reform in post-conflict areas'? He ran a search. The answer was buried in a think tank policy paper published online. '. . . *rebuilding national police and military . . . in Iraq, Afghanistan, and other post-conflict areas.*'

Typical think-tank rubbish written by wonks whose experience of Afghanistan was probably gleaned entirely through second-hand sources. If they'd bothered to actually visit Afghanistan, they'd know that the country was knee-deep in conflict. Flannelling aside, at least Rudy had established ShieldGroup's main motive for buying Pete Mitchell's company: it gave them a ready-made security training unit rather than having to build one from scratch. But how much money could there be in training the CNPA, the Counter Narcotics Police of Afghanistan? Was it really enough for ShieldGroup to throw John Patterson and his team to the wolves?

Rudy searched the papers on his desk for the notebook he'd used during his meeting with Simon Hampson. Scribbled in caps at the bottom of a page were the words *MILITARY CONTRACTS*. Was ShieldGroup positioning itself to take over training of the Afghan military? Rudy Googled 'ANA ShieldGroup'. The search yielded nothing. It made sense. Outsourcing ANA training would be virtually impossible; every NATO partner with a soldier in Afghanistan would insist one of their national companies get the job.

Rudy checked his notes again. What was he missing? He grabbed John Patterson's report and flipped through it. The names of the major players leapt off the pages . . . ShieldGroup . . . SOCA . . . CNPA. ShieldGroup . . . SOCA . . . CNPA. What was the connection with military contracts? Rudy drew a graph linking the three actors together. ShieldGroup was awarded a contract from SOCA to train the CNPA. That would mean that technically, the Afghan Government wasn't ShieldGroup's direct employer, it was the British government.

'Of course!' Rudy whispered excitedly. He typed: 'ShieldGroup Training UK Military'. The search engine redirected him to a page buried on the UK Parliament website.

Memorandum From ShieldGroup
International. June 2006

The Role of Private Military and Security
Companies in Delivering Force Readiness.

1. Introduction

This paper is submitted to the Defence
Committee Inquiry for the purpose of describing
how PMSCs (Private Military and Security
Companies) could help deliver force readiness
in a cost effective and efficient manner. The
UK Armed Forces are currently experiencing
manpower issues driven by extensive
operational commitments. Due to the need to
constantly train new recruits, skilled Armed
Forces personnel are being diverted from
military duties into areas which could be
effectively outsourced to the private sector.

ShieldGroup International has a proven
capability in hostile environment preparedness
initiatives, having effectively trained

Afghanistan's Counter Narcotics Police on
behalf of SOCA. The Serious Organized Crime
Agency can attest to ShieldGroup's
professionalism and high standards.
ShieldGroup maintains a database of qualified,
vetted instructors, many of whom have Special
Forces backgrounds.

Rudy couldn't believe it. Fuck the ANA. ShieldGroup wanted
to train the entire British military! A deal like that could potentially be worth billions. Compounded over decades, it was a
licence to print money. And the company had positioned itself
perfectly with SOCA. No wonder Patterson and his men had
been thrown under the bus. If SOCA were hit with a scandal
over its operations in Afghanistan, everything ShieldGroup was
working towards would come crashing down.

But why had Simon Hampson put him onto Pete Mitchell
specifically? Rudy opened his email and punched in his editor's
address. *Onto something potentially huge*, he wrote. *I need to
extend my home leave in London by at least a week to investigate. More soon. – RL.*

Chapter 19

The screams shattered the tranquil night. John covered his ears but it didn't help. The sounds had already left an imprint. They ricocheted through his mind as he debated whether to interfere. As an outsider, he had no right to judge Javid's methods. But the rationalizations rang hollow when faced with the cries of a child in distress.

John and Dusty couldn't believe it when Rafar had come skipping out of the tunnel waving the red strip of cloth John had used to mark the booby trap. *Mr John! Mr John! I find for you!* Though relieved to see the boy had come through unharmed, John was concerned over how Javid would react. Would he blame the two Scots for his son's disobedience?

Javid hadn't said a word to John or Dusty. All his anger was directed at Rafar. But this was no garden variety corporal punishment – a few slaps around the head and neck. Javid was pounding the shit out of his son. The boy's every wail, his every sob, pierced John's heart like a dagger.

'I can't just sit here and listen to this,' said John.

'Mind your own business,' Dusty warned him.

John slid out of his bivvy bag and looked at the Kutchi tent. The evening fire had reduced to embers, lending a haunting aura to Rafar's howls. 'He wouldn't be in trouble if it weren't for us.'

'Bollocks,' said Dusty. 'Rafar brought this on himself.'

John shoved Dusty with his hand. 'How can you just lie there like nothing is happening? Javid treats his animals more humanely.'

Dusty sat up. 'What do you suggest I do? Go over there and lecture Javid on how to raise his son? If I'd pulled something like that when I was a wee lad my old man would have beaten me senseless.'

'Mine too,' said John. 'All the more reason we should do something.'

'Do you want to get to Nuristan or not?' asked Dusty.

The question threw John. 'What are you on about?'

'Do you even begin to appreciate what happened today?' said Dusty. 'We had maybe what, a one in ten chance of getting through that tunnel alive? I was pulling skills out of my arse I haven't used since the Regiment. The fact that I'm sitting here now with you arguing is pretty fucking incredible, mate. I'm starting to think we might actually pull this fucker off. That is, if you get your priorities straight.'

John was insulted. 'Don't worry,' he said defensively. 'We'll pull it off.'

'Not if you drop us in the shit. Javid already thinks we're more trouble than we're worth,' said Dusty.

'You don't know that,' said John.

'Of course he does,' Dusty countered. 'We're nothing more than a business transaction to him and if the numbers don't add up, he'll leave us stranded on some mountainside and not think twice about it.'

'You're wrong,' said John. 'Javid gave his word to Haider. Honour matters here. Men give their lives to defend it. So I say we do the honourable thing and go over there and try to reason with Javid.'

Dusty pursed his lips, like he was holding back.

'Go on,' said John. 'Spit it out.'

Dusty looked him directly in the eye. 'You may not care whether or not you live or die, but I for one plan on getting out of this thing alive.'

The words reopened an old wound. John felt sick. He never expected Dusty of all people to bring *that* up.

Dusty shook his head apologetically. 'I'm sorry, mate. I didn't . . .' another howl rang out from the Kutchi camp. 'All that noise is getting to me too I guess.'

'Forget it,' said John. 'You're right. I should mind my own business.' The beating sounds subsided momentarily, only to resume with greater fury. Another soul-destroying scream followed. John slid back into his bivvy bag and stared blankly at the sky.

Chapter 20

Three waves of earth rose and dipped toward the horizon; each representing a day's travel around a mountain and through a valley. Thirty miles in the distance, eighteen-thousand-feet peaks ruled the sky. Rising majestically from a ring of clouds, they looked temptingly close, a fatal distraction in a landscape that required absolute awareness. Javid had warned everyone to remain cautious over the next few days. The trail they were following was beset with dangers both natural and man-made. Landslides, earthquakes, landmines and bandits had all visited the area. A single dirt path – a taupe current in a sea of undulating brown – was the only way through it.

The women swayed unconsciously to the rhythm of the ambling livestock. Ahead of them, Javid and the other Kutchi men led the way up a footpath. Dusty and John were twenty yards behind the caravan, Dusty watching the rear, John guiding the donkey as he kept an eye forward. The track narrowed as it ascended, ploughing its way through barren dunes and past rocky outcrops until it delivered the caravan to a whisper-thin slice of earth six hundred feet above the valley floor. Millions of shards of grey and beige shale covered the area. Boulders weighing tons rested carelessly on the sloping ground, daring to be disturbed. John looked down on the canyon they'd climbed out of that morning. He could see how the river running through it

had deepened the gorge over millennia. Cliffs fifty feet high rose
on either side of the water. Suspended within them were cave
entrances carved by melting snows cascading down the mountains. The black holes looked like grotesque drama masks. John
imagined they were spectators; this one slating his efforts,
another cheering him on. The invented audience stayed with
him until the spell was broken by Rafar. The boy was running
to deliver a message from his father.

'Mr John! Mr John!' the young Kutchi called.

John pulled back the reins of the donkey. 'What is it?'

Rafar was as cheerful as ever. Javid's brutal punishment had
failed to dent the child's affection for the two Scots. 'You must
prepare for rain,' he said breathlessly.

John looked at the sky. The weather was exceptionally mild
given the altitude; clear skies, light breeze. 'You're sure?'

'My father say rain come soon,' said Rafar. 'He send warning. Rain make ground too thick.'

Dusty looked at John and then the boy. 'Thick? I don't
follow.'

Rafar searched for another word. 'Thick.' He lifted his feet
one after the other, like he was stomping grapes. 'Thick
ground.'

'Ahh,' said Dusty. 'You mean muddy.'

'Mud-dee,' Rafar committed the new word to memory.

'Thanks for the heads up, little mate,' said Dusty.

'RAFAR!' Javid called sharply. The older Kutchi waved to his
son from the front of the caravan. Rafar's face fell as he ran to
rejoin his father.

Dusty and John dug out their waterproofs from their buried
Bergens: three-quarter-length Gortex anoraks with hoods. Any
concerns they had at being identified as foreigners by passing
aircraft were quickly put to rest by a line of black clouds rolling

in from the east. They swept over the distant peaks, growing
angrier as they curled across the sky. Any pilot patrolling the
area would stay well clear of the weather front.

Minutes later, the heavens opened with biblical rage. Hard,
fast, rain – the likes of which John hadn't seen since the jungles
of South East Asia – hammered the earth. Sheets of water ran
down his face, obscuring his vision. The sound of water pelting
his jacket filled his ears. John turned his attention to the ground
underfoot. The parched earth couldn't absorb the volume of
rain. Giant droplets bounced off the shale and dispersed once
more. Impromptu waterfalls formed along re-entrants lining the
slopes above the footpath. It was only a matter of time before
part of the trail washed away. But Javid kept pressing ahead.
John weighed whether to risk alienating his guide by stating the
obvious – to keep walking through the storm was madness.

A thump sounded ahead. John and Dusty stopped. A gust of
air rushed past their legs. The two Scots knew immediately it
wasn't natural. It was overpressure from an explosion. But
where did it come from? The ground shook, spooking the livestock. The camels and donkeys reared up, the dogs ran in
circles, barking. The Kutchi looked alarmed as they tried to
control the terrified animals. John and Dusty wanted to get up
front to determine the source and location of the blast. But they
had their own donkey to contend with. John kept a firm hold
on the reins while Dusty helped bring the beast under control.
The din of animals and rain was broken again, this time by a
series of successive bangs.

'Mines!' John shouted. He handed the reins to Dusty. 'The
rain must have triggered them. I'll go warn the others!'
Suddenly, the earth began to tremble violently. The Kutchi
screamed as the ground beneath their feet turned to liquid. John
froze in horror as the swathe of earth where the caravan stood

sloughed off the mountain like a piece of dead skin. Rocks and boulders tumbled down, feeding a stream of flowing debris. It churned and crushed the Kutchi and their animals, dragging them under before hurling what remained over the side of the cliff and into the valley below. John reached out his hand in vain, looking for signs of life he could pluck from the moving rubble.

Dusty dropped the reins and slapped the donkey on its hindquarters, sending it down the mountain. He grabbed John with both hands. 'You can't help them!' he cried. 'We have to save ourselves!' The ground was still shaking as the two men backtracked down the disappearing trail. Bursts of adrenalin fed John's heart, stretching the minutes into hours. A hundred feet from the valley floor, they found a cave entrance. They jumped through it and kept moving, crawling deeper and deeper inside until the sound of nature's wrath was silenced by absolute darkness.

Chapter 21

John and Dusty emerged from the cave traumatized by what they had witnessed. The aftermath shook them further still. An entire side of the mountain was gone: cliffs, boulders, the path people had travelled for centuries had all vanished. In the valley below, a hill of debris dammed the once mighty river. The altered landscape filled John with humility. It had taken minutes for nature to tear down what had been built over millions of years. For a man whose identity was inexorably tied to mastering his surroundings, it was an unwelcome reminder of how truly powerless he was.

'I don't suppose you see the donkey?' asked Dusty.

The immediate needs of survival overtook any larger questions in John's head. Being stranded in the wilds of Afghanistan with no guides and no kit would strain the capacity of even the most resourceful survivalists. They needed their Bergens. The shell-shocked pair made their way toward the earthen dam where the remains of the caravan lay. They found their donkey drinking from a pool of muddied water. The animal was uninjured and still carrying its load.

They secured the donkey and set about searching for survivors, a task both men agreed was probably pointless. The landslide had mowed down everything in its path. Tufts of fur, pieces of cloth, and lumps of flesh – animal and human –

peppered the ground around them. A hand protruding from the rubble caught John's eye. He bent over and pulled it. The earth released it without a fight. The limb was all that remained of its owner. Similar deceptions lay elsewhere: feet, arms and legs torn from bodies pummelled to oblivion.

'Over here!' Dusty cried. He started digging the earth furiously. 'A body!'

'Can you ID it?' John called.

'I'm not sure,' Dusty panted, 'it could be Rafar.'

John rushed over to help. Dusty had uncovered a section of leg from thigh to calf. John scraped away more dirt to reveal a foot. The sandal was missing and the ankle was twisted around backward. Further up, Dusty excavated more – a torso, a shoulder. John recognized the sweater. Rafar's! The positive ID added greater urgency to their task. The pair worked quickly, peeling back layers of the earthen coffin until the boy lay uncovered in the foetal position.

John shoved two fingers into Rafar's neck while Dusty checked the boy's mouth for blockages. 'Can you find a pulse?' asked Dusty.

'Shhh,' John hissed. He moved his fingers in a circle. He felt one, the rhythm light and thready. 'He's alive but in distress. How's his airway?'

'Clear.' Dusty placed his hand flat on the boy's cheek. 'He's cold as a stone. If we don't get him warmed up soon, he'll go down with hypothermia.'

A light tremor shook the ground. John shielded Rafar's body with his own until the movement subsided. 'Let's get him back to the cave before we're all buried. Grab hold of his legs.'

The two men rolled Rafar onto his back. He was in worse shape than they had initially realized. There was a large T-shaped gash on the boy's forehead and a piece of shale embedded in his side. There was very little blood where the large piece of rock had entered the body, an ominous sign.

Back in the cave, John and Dusty improvised an A&E. They layered their bivvy bags to form a single, cushioned bed and placed the child on top of it. John cut-off Rafar's wet clothes and wrapped him in a dry blanket while Dusty got the medical pack ready. The nylon roll contained field dressings, fracture straps, alcohol wipes, a suture kit, syringes and vials of morphine and antibiotics. They lit a fire and put water on to boil both to clean the child's wounds and to prepare hot liquids to warm him. As they waited for the water to heat, they decided how best to tackle Rafar's injuries.

Dusty inspected the piece of rock lodged in Rafar's side. It had penetrated just below the ribcage at a forty-five degree angle. 'It's in there deep,' he said clinically. 'All we can do is clean the area until we can get him to a hospital. If we try to remove it here, he could bleed out.'

'A hospital?' said John. 'Out here? Are you taking the piss?'

Dusty remained detached. 'If we remove that rock now it could worsen any internal bleeding. And there's no way of knowing how many of his organs have been damaged.'

Dusty's tone only fuelled John's emotion. 'If we wait and do nothing he'll die for sure. We need to be aggressive. It's his best shot,' John pleaded.

Dusty studied the wound again and nodded. 'OK then. We'll do it your way. He's got a lower tib and fib fracture. We'll set that and sew up his head best we can while he's out, but we'll have to wait until he comes to before removing the rock.'

'He'll be in agony,' said John.

'We'll need to know how his body reacts to the procedure. It's not like we have monitors here. We need him awake,' said Dusty.

John conceded and the two men set about tending to Rafar's minor injuries. Starting with the fracture, they manipulated his ankle back into place and cleaned his legs with cooled, boiled water. They then padded the hollows with spare items of dry clothing and secured the limbs together with fracture straps; one wrapped above and below the break; the others around his thighs, and above and below the knees.

They then moved on to Rafar's head wound. Dusty started by cleaning the gash with a damp bandage.

'How bad is it?' asked John

Dusty dabbed the wound as he spoke. 'It looks superficial. But it's messy. There's a lot of swelling.'

'You'd better do the suturing then,' said John.

Dusty stopped what he was doing. 'You do it. I'll make an arse of it.'

'Don't be daft,' said John. 'You're the medic here. When was your last medical attachment?'

'Two years before I left the Regiment,' said Dusty.

'Where?' asked John.

'A&E Birmingham,' said Dusty.

John shoved the suture kit at Dusty. 'Birmingham has a children's wing.'

Dusty refused to take it. 'What if I scar him for life?'

'He's already full of scars.' John pressed the kit into Dusty's hand. 'One more isn't going to make a difference.'

Reluctantly, Dusty pulled out a horseshoe-shaped needle pre-threaded with silk. He removed the sterile sleeve and assessed his young patient. The colour was beginning to return to Rafar's face. Dusty got to work quickly – he didn't want the boy regaining consciousness mid-suture. Starting at the outer edges of the wound, he sewed the ragged skin together until the gash was closed.

John cradled Rafar as he came to. 'Rafar? Rafar?'

The boy's eyes flickered. 'Mr John . . .' he moaned.

'Save your strength.' John dipped a bottle cap into a mug of warm, sugary tea and tipped it into Rafar's mouth. 'Sip this slowly,' he said. 'It will make you feel better.'

The child swallowed the capful of sweet liquid. 'There was bomb.' Rafar kept speaking between sips of tea. 'Camel step on bomb. Big boom. I come warn you. Then ground move.'

'It was a landslide,' said John. 'You're lucky to be alive.'

'My father?' asked Rafar. 'Where my father?'

John and Dusty looked at each other. 'You're injured, little mate,' said Dusty. 'You've got a rock stuck in your side. We're going to have to take it out.'

John stroked the boy's hair. 'It's going to hurt but you need to stay awake. You can't go back to sleep. It's for your own good. Do you understand?' The frightened child nodded. 'Good,' said John. 'You're very brave. Before we start, we'll have to clean the wound. Are you ready?'

John held Rafar's shoulders. The child howled as Dusty swabbed the skin around the point of entry. The boy's distress cut right through John. 'Is the area sterile?' he asked impatiently.

'As sterile as it's going to get in this environment,' said Dusty.

John wound a piece of bandage around a stick and held it over Rafar's head. The boy's eyes welled with tears. He was terrified. 'I'm going to put this in your mouth,' said John. 'As soon as you feel pain, you bite down on it as hard as you can. You understand?'

Rafar tried to put on a brave face. 'Yes, Mr John.'

John placed the stick between Rafar's teeth. 'It's very important you don't move until we get the rock out of you. We'll be fast. Just keep biting down on the stick.' John slid over next to Dusty and nodded. Dusty placed his hands on either side of the entry point and pressed down. John grabbed the exposed piece of rock and pulled it out in one swift movement. His heart sank when he saw the exhumed sliver of shale. It was like a hunting knife – eight inches long with jagged edges.

Blood began pouring from Rafar's side. Dusty applied pressure with a field dressing. Rafar yelped through clenched jaws. John removed the stick. 'It's all over,' he said, kissing Rafar's face. 'You're very brave.'

John continued to comfort the boy while Dusty dealt with the haemorrhage. He applied a fresh dressing to the wound and examined the old bandage. His face dropped.

'What's wrong?' asked John.

Dusty sniffed the blood-soaked dressing. His expression turned grave. 'He's bleeding internally. His bowel's perforated.' Dusty passed the bandage to John.

John held it under his nose. The foul scent confirmed Dusty's grim diagnosis. Rafar's abdominal cavity was filling with blood and human waste. Without emergency surgery, he'd die.

'There's nothing more we can do for him,' Dusty whispered.

John's mind raced. If Rafar was strong enough to survive the landslide, surely he could pull through this. There had to be a way to help him.

Dusty grabbed a vial and syringe from the medical pack.

'What are you doing?' John asked.

Dusty plunged the needle into the vial. The syringe filled with clear liquid. 'Giving him morphine to ease his pain.'

'Are you off your head?' John hissed. 'You give him morphine now and he'll die. He needs antibiotics.'

Dusty held the loaded syringe over the child. 'He needs to be made comfortable. He's beyond antibiotics.'

John seized Dusty's wrist. 'Don't be so quick to stick him in the ground. We can save him still.'

Dusty kept his cool. 'How?'

John's eyes darted back and forth as his mind groped for a viable plan. 'We'll find a village. We'll leave him with the locals. They'll get him to hospital . . .'

'You said yourself there's probably not a hospital out here.' Dusty lifted John's hand away. 'He won't survive the night.'

John sprang to his feet. 'We need to move now then.' He started gathering kit together. 'We'll make a stretcher . . .'

The furious packing strained Dusty's reserve. 'Think for a second, will you? We can't just walk into a village in broad daylight. We're bloody fugitives.'

'We'll slip in and out without anyone noticing,' said John as he rolled up the medical bag. 'Rafar won't talk.'

'He doesn't have to.' Dusty snatched the medical pack from John's hands. 'Look at him. Fracture straps, sutures, field dressings. The Afghans will know that foreigners have been working on him – foreigners with access to military medical kit. It won't take long to put two and two together. If there was a half a chance to save his life, I'd say to hell with it and take the risk. But there isn't.' Dusty pressed the syringe in John's palm. 'Let's just ease his pain.'

John stared at the syringe. He shifted his gaze to Rafar's face. The boy was clearly in agony. John kneeled beside the child. 'I'm going to give you some medicine,' he said softly. 'It will make you feel better.' John tapped Rafar's arm and waited for a vein to surface. He slid the syringe underneath the boy's skin and poised his thumb over the plunger. John looked into Rafar's eyes one last time before they shut for ever. Their innocence bore into John's soul, reviving old memories. John told himself he was doing what was best. But at the critical moment, logic abandoned him. John withdrew the needle and squirted the morphine out onto the floor of the cave.

Dusty shook his head.

'He'll get through this,' said John. 'I know it.'

The hours passed. Dusty slept while John lay awake next to Rafar. He cradled the child all night, stroking his hair. The following morning John awoke to the sound of birds singing. He couldn't remember falling asleep. He checked on Rafar. The boy's eyes were closed and his face was peaceful. John laid his hand on the boy's chest. It was still. Rafar was dead.

Chapter 22

The email response from Rudy's editor was abrupt. *You're paid to cover events in Afghanistan, NOT England. If there's something of interest here, I'll assign a domestic correspondent to investigate. Your request for extended home leave is denied. – LJ.*

Rudy wasn't about to hand over his scoop to some fat-arsed domestic reporter. So instead of spending his first precious home leave in his favourite pub regaling old friends with tales of derring-do in dangerous places, Rudy was pounding the pavements of the King's Road hoping to ambush Pete Mitchell.

Rudy knew Chelsea well. He'd spent more nights than he could remember there pulling girls and blowing his wages in trendy bars. But his old stomping ground now held wonders anew. The cleavage on display was a feast for his hungry eyes. Having been deprived of the female form in Kabul, even the headless, legless mannequins modelling lacy women's lingerie in shop windows were a cause to leer. Other details previously obscured by the familiar also caught his attention. Rudy used to think London was dirty but it was a bloody microchip factory compared to Kabul's lead-fumed, shit-infested streets. Noises leapt out at him too. For weeks his ears had been bombarded by the loud hum of generator motors. In their absence, he found himself enjoying sounds he'd once taken for granted: the comforting rumble of a black cab engine; the squeak of a red bus slowing down; the click of women's heels on concrete pavements.

Not every rediscovery was a delight though. Rudy had never realized before how ostentatiously excessive London truly was. Kabul's affluent were rarely seen. They barricaded themselves behind heavily guarded compounds and armoured vehicles to conceal their wealth from potential kidnappers. Chelsea's toffs, sloanies and nouveau riche on the other hand, thought nothing of sauntering down the street with their riches on display. Men's jacket cuffs yawned like wizard sleeves, advertising expensive watches and bespoke working buttons. Women with waxy botoxed features teetered about in high heels with bright-red soles; a designer trademark intended to draw attention. Every emaciated wrist was adorned with an expensive handbag. From head to toe, the bodies screamed what the tongues were no doubt dying to say: *I've got shedloads of money. Envy me.*

Rudy stepped off the King's Road into Wellington Square. Grand Georgian terraces – architectural reminders of glory days passed – wrapped around the manicured lawn. He found an empty bench with a direct view of number 40: the unmarked headquarters of ShieldGroup International. He pretended to read a paper and waited for Pete Mitchell to appear, an imprecise exercise given that Rudy had no idea what the man looked like. The only image that existed of Mitchell was a blacked-out, bereted silhouette. Still, Rudy was confident something would distinguish the former elite soldier from the toffs parading in and out of number 40. Mitchell was from the ranks – a non-officer and working-class roots had a nasty habit of pushing through even the most polished veneers.

After twenty minutes, a man in velvet loafers and rolled shirt-sleeves descended the steps. The shoes couldn't hide what the flesh on the forearm betrayed. 'Pete? Pete Mitchell?' Rudy said it as if he were an old acquaintance.

The man stopped. 'Who's asking?'

Rudy studied the man more closely. He was rather unremarkable: average height, average build, thinning hair, pudgy middle. He smelled like stale cigarettes. It was difficult to believe such a man could have served with the likes of John Patterson. But the three-word response confirmed Rudy's suspicions. England's middle and upper classes would never dream of admitting they didn't recognize someone. 'There's no use denying it.' Rudy pointedly looked at the faded outline on the man's forearm – a crowned parachute with wings, the insignia of the Parachute Regiment. The image had been lasered off. 'Officers don't have tattoos, so unless ShieldGroup has another SAS hero-in-residence, I'm guessing it's you, Mr Mitchell.'

Mitchell's hand swooped down on Rudy's crotch. The young journalist's entire body ignited with pain. 'What do you want?' Mitchell growled. 'Tell me or I swear your bollocks will be lying in the gutter.'

Rudy's heart raced, his breathing was short and shallow. He danced on his toes, trying to speak. 'I want to talk to you about . . .' he squeaked.

Mitchell squeezed harder. 'About what?'

'. . . John Patterson.'

Chapter 23

'It's a dead end.' Dusty ripped the night-vision goggles off his face. 'Another set of batteries wasted. We keep going like this and we'll be well fucked.'

John left Dusty to his rant and studied the area with naked eyes. The moon and stars were bright but he knew the light was misleading. The long shadows stretching across the landscape masked how truly unforgiving it was. He looked at the mountains towering on either side of them. They rose from the ground like ancient earth gods guarding their passage. John switched on his night sights. Curtains fell on his peripheral vision as his eyes channelled into a monocular view. The soft shadows regrouped into sharp corners of pixelated green, transforming the protective mountain-gods into angry gatekeepers. John looked ahead. He and Dusty were just yards from a cliff edge. They couldn't go forward and they couldn't go left or right. It was indeed a dead end. John switched off his sights. 'It'll be light in two hours. We can go back to camp, collect the donkey and search for another route before sun-up; get a head start on tomorrow night.'

Dusty stuffed his goggles into the top flap of his Bergen. 'If you want to try, go ahead. That's me for tonight.'

'What do you mean, that's you for tonight?' said John. 'We're not out for an evening stroll in the park. We've just lost an entire night walking up a blind alley. We need to make up for it now.'

'We're not in the Regiment any more,' Dusty huffed. 'You're not in charge of me.'

John tried to reason with Dusty. 'You had six years in the Regiment. I had eighteen. That gives me three times the skills and three times more experience than you. It makes sense that I'm team leader.'

Dusty shouldered his Bergen. 'So you're the team leader of the two of us eh? Tell you what then, mate. Can I be the 2 I/C?'

John got the message, he didn't push it any more. Forcing the issue would only spark a nasty argument and by the time it was decided the sun would be up. The pair backtracked along their fruitless route, their spirits more destitute than ever. Losing the Kutchi had been more than just an emotional blow. The practical difficulties of getting on without local guides were proving almost impossible to overcome. Without Javid and his family as cover, John and Dusty couldn't travel in broad daylight. The two Scots spent their days in caves and cliff faces, sleeping rough, waiting for nightfall. When the sun disappeared, they'd tie up the donkey and head out on foot with their Bergens. Using their night vision aids sparingly to conserve batteries, the two men would study the contours of the earth, searching for crossing points through the mountains. They stayed off tracks that might lead to villages and religiously avoided roads where passing vehicles might spot them. Such discipline didn't make their task any easier. It was one thing to walk from point A to B in a straight line and quite another to leg it over uncharted, labyrinthine terrain. John and Dusty were literally feeling their way through the dark. They'd wander up valleys that would seem full of promise, only to run smack into sheer drops. Four times they'd stumbled across bottlenecks still mined from the

Soviet occupation. And then there were the mountains – peaks so imposing that Sir Edmund Hillary himself would feel challenged.

At first, they took the setbacks in their stride. But sixteen days of hard routine with little progress to show for it was doing their heads in. They were constantly bickering. If Dusty wanted to cache the Bergens, John would insist they take their packs with them. If John wanted to ford a river, Dusty would dismiss it as too dangerous. They couldn't agree on anything and the proximity of their destination only added to their sense of frustration. According to the counter on John's GPS, they were thirty miles from Dogrum. At their current rate, it would take more than two months to get there. Their bodies, not to mention their food supplics, would never last the course.

Back at camp, John savoured two disciplined spoonfuls of boil-in-the-bag. When he finished, he sealed it up and tucked the remainder away in his Bergen. He watched disapprovingly as Dusty tucked into his greedily. 'How many ration packs do you have left?'

Dusty spoke with his mouth full. 'One.'

John counted the packs in his Bergen. 'You should have three and a half. I told you to pace yourself.'

Dusty licked the last precious morsels of food from the bag. 'Well, pardon me, Mr Dalai-fucking-Lama, but not all of us can live off fresh air.' He crumpled the empty ration pack and looked around – his expression suggested he was far from sated. He pointed to the donkey grazing behind John. 'Tell me again why you insist on keeping that animal alive.'

'In case one of us gets injured,' said John.

'Every time we have to come back to collect him, he slows us down,' Dusty argued. 'And I'm hungry.'

John stroked the donkey's nose. 'Don't talk that way in front of Hamish.'

'Hamish?' Dusty stood up. 'Fucking Hamish?'

'It's a good Scots name,' said John.

'That's not the point!' Dusty threw the empty pack down. 'No wonder you won't let me kill it. You've gone and named the bloody thing!'

'I haven't ruled out the idea,' said John. 'If we're desperate, I'll slaughter Hamish myself. But we haven't reached that point yet. So stop your moaning.'

'I'm hungry,' said Dusty.

'What is your problem?' said John. 'When I was your age, I could go three weeks straight on hard routine. This should be a piece of piss for you.'

'Fuck hard routine,' said Dusty. 'Either we shoot Hamish – listen to me, now you've got me saying it – either we kill that animal or I swear I will find a village and steal one even if it blows our cover.'

John let go of the donkey. 'OK then,' he said. 'Shoot Hamish. Carve him up. Have yourself a feast. If you need me I'll be over there – enjoying my fresh air.' John jumped up on a boulder. Dusty pulled his pistol from his waistband and aimed it at the donkey's head. He stopped and lowered the weapon.

'What are you waiting for?' said John.

Dusty made a great show of releasing the magazine on the weapon and checking it. 'I'm trying to do this as humanely as possible.'

'By taking your time?' John taunted. 'That's fucking humane.'

Dusty lifted the pistol and aimed once more. He operated the trigger halfway, lifted his head and refocused. Four head bobs later, he gave up. He couldn't bring himself to shoot the donkey. 'Fuck,' he muttered, flicking the safety on.

John jumped down from the boulder. 'Guess you're not *that* hungry then.'

The crack pushed Dusty to breaking point. He tucked his pistol back in his trousers, ran at John and tackled him. 'You had to go and name it!' he said, slamming his fist into John's jaw.

John grabbed Dusty's shoulders and head-butted him. Dusty stumbled back, blood gushing from his nose and mouth. John swung around and wrestled him into a headlock.

Dusty hacked up a wad of blood and spat it out. 'Come on then, old man, show us what you've got.'

John shoved two fingers in Dusty's nostrils and pulled. Dusty howled. 'Dirty bastard!'

John looked up suddenly. His fingers were still hooked into Dusty's nose. 'Did you hear that?' he panted.

'Hear what?' Dusty wheezed.

A light tinkling sounded from behind the boulder. Seconds later, the source of the noise appeared. A goat with a tiny brass bell tied around its neck.

Chapter 24

The server behind the counter danced his fingers over the cash register. 'Would you like any fries with that?'

'No,' said Pete Mitchell. 'Just the coffees.'

While Mitchell paid for the order, Rudy looked for an empty table. The place was packed with smartly dressed clientele tucking into meals of greasy burgers washed down with spring water. Not the usual scene one would expect at a McDonald's. Then again, this McDonald's was on the King's Road. 'Are you sure you want to talk here?' Rudy asked.

'Not posh enough for you?' said Mitchell.

'There are a lot of business people,' said Rudy. 'They could hear us.'

'Follow me.' Mitchell grabbed the coffees and led Rudy down a staircase. As soon as they reached the bottom, Rudy realized there was nothing to worry about. Upmarket customers didn't frequent the underbelly of the fast food outlet. It was a receptacle for Chelsea's undesirables: Polish builders, Filipino housekeepers and other non-English-speaking workers who kept the neighbourhood clean and functioning. It was the golden arches version of the *Titanic* – first-class passengers up top, riff-raff down below.

Mitchell slid into a corner booth and peeled the lid off his coffee. 'So, you know John Patterson.'

Rudy settled carefully into the seat opposite. 'Yes, yes I do,' he said, adjusting himself. His testicles were still on fire.

'You're lying,' said Mitchell. 'John would never talk to a reporter.'

Rudy sipped his coffee sparingly. He was hoping for a long conversation. 'Apparently he had good reason to bend that rule.'

'Stop mincing around and tell me what you want,' Mitchell demanded.

Determined to keep control of the conversation, Rudy refused to let Mitchell set the pace. 'How would you describe John Patterson – professionally?'

'John Patterson is a legend,' said Mitchell. 'His military record was flawless.'

'And his work in the private sector?' asked Rudy.

Mitchell stared hard at Rudy, sizing him up. 'You know nothing, mate.' He rose to leave.

'I know what happened on the Jalalabad Road,' said Rudy. 'The shoot-out between Patterson's team and two Afghans.'

The details stopped Mitchell in his tracks. 'If you've come here to dig up dirt on Patterson, you're on a hiding to nowhere. Fuck you and your witch-hunt. A scumball like you isn't fit to lick John Patterson's boots.'

The character defence threw Rudy. Why would Pete Mitchell of all people say good things about ShieldGroup's fall guy? Rudy suspected a red herring. 'What can you tell me about that incident?'

'John Patterson made a judgement call in a very tough situation,' said Mitchell.

'Why did you leave him in Afghanistan? You had plenty of time to bring him and Malcolm Miller back to the UK,' said Rudy.

'I did want to bring them home,' Mitchell insisted. 'I fought like a dog for three days to make it happen. But it wasn't ShieldGroup's call.'

'Whose was it then?' Rudy pressed. 'Who was so keen to keep them in Kabul?'

Mitchell paused. 'How much do you know about the contact?'

'I've seen the report,' said Rudy.

Mitchell paused again. 'What exactly did it say about the civilians involved?'

Rudy knew he was being tested. He dropped the bombshell. 'That they were Hizb-i-Islami terrorists who support al-Qaeda.'

Mitchell buried his head in his hands.

'I know a great deal, Mr Mitchell,' said Rudy. 'I know SOCA fucked up and recruited two al-Qaeda to train with the CNPA. And instead of holding your client to account, ShieldGroup sold out John Patterson and his team to protect its bottom line.'

Mitchell froze. 'Sold him out?'

'Spare me the righteous indignation. I looked into your dealings with ShieldGroup,' said Rudy. 'You're an unusual story, Mr Mitchell. Not many SAS squaddies go on to become successful entrepreneurs. How much did ShieldGroup pay for your company? Five million pounds?' Rudy dropped the figure like an indictment. 'Quite a payday for a start-up that had only been in business for little over a year.'

'I got lucky,' said Mitchell. 'ShieldGroup wanted a training service. My little company specialized in training security professionals for hostile environments. It was all above board. And it has nothing to do with John Patterson.'

'I'm not so sure.' Rudy rolled his coffee cup between his hands, like he was warming up for a kill. 'When ShieldGroup bought you out, was it an all-cash deal?'

'What difference does it make?' asked Mitchell.

'A great deal,' said Rudy. 'If ShieldGroup put five million pounds directly into your pocket, it really doesn't matter to you what happens to the company in the long run. Your financial future is secure. If the company paid you partially in stock, however, your fortunes are linked directly to ShieldGroup's performance. Seeing as you stayed on as a director after the deal was made, I think it's safe to assume you're a millionaire on paper only.'

Mitchell clenched his jaw. 'You're lucky I don't launch you through that wall. I don't know what rubbish you've got in your head—'

'It's not in my head.' Rudy unfolded his newspaper. Tucked inside was a copy of ShieldGroup's memorandum outlining its plans to train the British military. 'It's a matter of public record.'

Mitchell examined the paper. 'I don't understand.'

'Don't play dumb, Mr Mitchell. A child could connect the dots. Two years ago, ShieldGroup saw the writing on the wall. With Iraq and Afghanistan sucking up more and more soldiers, it knew it was only a matter of time before the government outsourced British military training to the private sector. So ShieldGroup bought your firm and used the acquisition to land a high-profile training contract with a major government agency – SOCA. All was going swimmingly until your man on the ground, John Patterson, uncovered gross negligence on the part of the client. But instead of fixing the problem, SOCA buried its head in the sand and the situation came to blows on the Jalalabad Road. You could have moved John Patterson and his team out of Afghanistan immediately. Instead, you handed them over to the Afghans and struck a deal with SOCA: we'll cover up your mistakes and in return you back our bid to train Britain's armed forces.'

Mitchell shook his head. 'I don't know what to say.'

'Why don't you start with an on the record comment,' Rudy suggested. 'You can tell me in your own words why you sold out John Patterson.'

'You still don't get it, do you?' said Mitchell. 'I would never do anything to harm John Patterson. All I've ever done is try to protect him. My history with him proves it.'

'You're lying,' said Rudy.

Mitchell looked Rudy directly in the eye. 'If it weren't for me, John Patterson would be dead right now.'

Chapter 25

John sharpened his knife on a stone, wiped the blade clean and cut the skin from the goat's carcass. 'How's that smoker coming?'

Dusty laid some twigs in a fire well positioned at one end of a shallow trench. At the other, a four-foot-high teepee-shaped structure fashioned from sticks waited to receive strips of animal flesh for smoking. 'Ten minutes,' he said. 'I just need to fix a couple of shelves and find some stones to cover this trench over.'

'It's risky having a fire going after sun-up,' John warned.

'If we don't get that goat cooked up soon it'll be maggot food,' said Dusty.

John nodded in agreement, though in truth he could have waited. It didn't make sense to draw attention to their position. But Dusty needed to get his way this time. Another big bust-up and they might really do damage to each other. 'I'll cut some big chunks to roast straightaway,' said John. 'We'll cold smoke the rest. After we eat, I'll sort your nose if you want.' It was the closest John had come to an apology.

'You think I'd let you near this face?' Dusty nodded to the donkey. 'Can you believe this guy, Hamish?'

John kept butchering while Dusty finished assembling the smoker. 'Remember that night exercise we did together at

Sennybridge Training Area?' said John. 'The parachute infil-
tration; you busted your nose on your knee when you landed?'

'What about it?' said Dusty, fitting shelves woven from flexible sticks into the teepee.

John draped thin strips of goat flesh over the shelves. 'I was
having a brew with the other lads when you walked over to us
holding your nose. *I need a medic. I need a medic,*' he chuckled.

Dusty laid stones over the trench. 'Fat lot of sympathy I got
from you. You said, "You are a medic, you wanker."' The two
Scots laughed heartily at the shared memory.

The fire was burning full tilt with a goat leg roasting on top.
John sliced off a chunk and offered it to Dusty. 'You have the
first piece,' he said.

Dusty took the steaming meat. 'Are you sure?'

'Go on,' said John. Dusty tore into it. 'Is it good?'

'It's a little bland,' said Dusty, still chewing. He took another
bite to stave off his hunger and jumped up. 'I've got just the
thing for this,' he said, rummaging through his Bergen. He
pulled out a small plastic tub filled with white packets.

'What do you have there?' asked John.

Dusty ripped open a packet and sprinkled the contents on the
meat. 'Curry powder.' He held it out to John. 'Want some?'

John shook his head. 'I thought we agreed; essential kit only
on this trip.'

'Curry's an essential,' said Dusty. 'It's a staple of the British
diet.'

John reached for Dusty's Bergen. 'No wonder you've been
moaning for the past two weeks. Your bloody Bergen's a stone
heavier than mine.' Before Dusty could object, John started
pulling things from the pack. 'One boil-in-the-bag – OK.

Clothes – OK. Medical supplies – OK. Extra 5.56 magazines – I still think you should have gone with the AK but OK. Wait, wait, what do we have here?' John pulled out a tube of sun-block and a pair of sunglasses.

'Sun damage,' said Dusty.

'Mincer,' said John. 'You know you couldn't wear sunglasses when I joined the Army.'

'Sorry, granddad, but I'm not ending up as blind as you,' said Dusty.

John reached inside the Bergen again and pulled out a small cloth bag. He shook it. 'What's in here?'

Dusty skipped a beat before answering. 'Weights for a fishing line.'

'Good thinking,' said John. He plunged his hand back in the Bergen. 'What the hell?' He pulled out a silver flask.

'Come on, mate,' said Dusty.

John unscrewed the cap and sniffed. 'This is a Muslim country. Do you know what the locals in Dogrum would do to us if we brought alcohol into their village?'

'They won't find it,' said Dusty. 'Hell, you didn't even know I had it until now, so calm down. It's just a wee nip of Scotch.'

'A wee nip, ay? Well, I guess you won't miss it then.' John tilted the flask to pour it out.

Dusty was horrified. 'What are you doing?'

'What you should have done before we left Kabul,' said John.

Dusty wrestled the bottle from John. 'Are you off your head? This is a single malt.'

'I haven't survived landslides and tunnels to be done in by a few ounces of whisky,' said John.

Dusty put his nose over the flask and inhaled. 'Pouring this out would be a sin against Scotland. You may as well piss on the Saltire.'

'Oh get off your high horse,' said John. 'Acting like a Rupert with your posh whisky. Like you'd know the difference between that and something sold in a Tesco 3 for 2.'

Dusty took a pull from the flask. 'Oh, you're wrong, my friend. It's like all the beauty of the Highlands dancing on your tongue. Heaven on earth, this is.'

'Wonderful.' John was annoyed. 'Get drunk. You'll be of real use to us then.'

'Stop acting like my fucking fath . . .' Dusty caught himself. An ancient pain welled in John's eyes. 'Sorry, mate. I wasn't thinking.'

John sliced a piece of meat from the leg bone and shoved it into his mouth. He tasted nothing.

Chapter 26

The women were dressed for action: tits pouring out of low-cut tops; thighs squeezed into tight miniskirts. They prowled the High Street in packs, outnumbering their male prey five to one. Not that the odds would increase Rudy's chances of pulling. These women weren't interested in meeting just any bloke. Like Rudy, they'd come to Hereford for one reason only – to find an SAS soldier.

Hereford's status as SAS HQ had been the MoD's worst-kept secret since 1980: when an SAS anti-terror team was broadcast live abseiling down the front of the Iranian Embassy in London. Before the daring raid, few people knew the Regiment even existed, let alone where it was based. Once the cat was out of the bag, however, the public couldn't get enough of the elite soldiers in black. Some SAS men cashed-in on the phenomenon. A few wrote best-selling tell-alls revealing the Regiment's operational secrets. One in particular was always on the telly, lending his voice to documentaries or popping up on the News with his face blacked out. The anonymity spawned a host of imitators. Nearly every pub in Britain had a sad regular who claimed he was 'the second man on the balcony' at the Iranian Embassy.

Getting flannelled by a fantasist was definitely a possibility in Hereford as well. But Rudy was desperate. He'd exhausted every resource he knew of to get information on John

Patterson's past. He'd even put in a call to the SAS adjutant in Hereford only to have the phone put down on him. When it came to SAS soldiers – even retired ones – public records didn't exist.

Rudy trolled the High Street looking for watering holes that might cater to the Regiment. Trendy wine bars; free houses; chain pubs; nothing grabbed him. His reporter's instincts kicked in when he eyed a queue of women outside a nightclub; *flies to honey*, he thought.

The booming bass notes coming from inside the club shook the pavement. Rudy cut to the front of the line and tried to enter. Two bouncers blocked his way. Husky, hard and bald, they looked like father and son: one just out of teens, the other on the wrong side of fifty. 'Where do you think you're going?' asked the older man.

Rudy smiled politely. 'I was just wondering – do ladies drink free tonight.'

'Not on a Saturday,' said the bouncer. 'Back of the queue.'

'I don't suppose you could tell me if SAS men drink here?' Rudy asked.

The two bouncers exchanged glances. 'I don't suppose I could,' said the older one.

Rudy interpreted the response as a signal to furnish more incentive. He reached into his wallet and produced a twenty-pound note. 'I'm a journalist.'

The bouncer tucked the money in his pocket and nodded to his younger colleague. 'Keep an eye on things while I help the gentleman here.'

The bouncer led Rudy down an alley. The narrow passage-way stank of stale piss and fresh vomit. 'Is there a side entrance?' asked Rudy. The bouncer turned around and grinned broadly. A sinking feeling took hold of Rudy. 'Maybe I should just go and wait in the queue with the others.' The bouncer lifted Rudy by the jacket and slammed him against the wall. Rudy's head throbbed with pain. 'I'm sorry,' he stammered. 'If I offended you . . .'

The bouncer grabbed Rudy's jaw and turned it violently. 'Shut up,' he growled. He stuck his face right in Rudy's. 'No one around here ever refers to the Regiment by those three letters you used back there, you hear me. The Regiment doesn't need the attention.'

'Forgive me,' said Rudy. 'I didn't realize you were one of them.'

The bouncer released him. Rudy almost collapsed when his feet touched the ground. 'I'm not,' said the bouncer. 'But I've known the lads since the 1970s. I've played rugby with them, boxed with them, and I still drink with them. They had a nice peaceful life here until you journalists fucked it for everyone. So don't go sticking your nose where it doesn't belong.'

Rudy's knees trembled. He adjusted his jacket. 'I understand. Can I go now?'

The bouncer blocked Rudy with his arm. 'I'll be phoning the other doormen around Hereford. If I find you sneaking around town again, you'll get the good news.'

Rudy ran back up the alley and ducked into a wine bar. He ordered three fingers of Scotch to steady his nerves. His hands were still shaking as he threw his money down on the bar. A man sidled up next to him. He looked intimidating, like the bouncer, only younger with a full head of hair and a nose pushed to the side of his face.

'You're not from here,' the man observed. A broad grin revealed a chipped front tooth. 'You follow rugby at all?'

Had it happened anywhere else, Rudy would assume he was

being propositioned. But whatever the odds were of wandering into Hereford's only gay bar he wasn't going to stick around and find out. He downed his drink in one gulp and left.

Rudy bowed his head and walked briskly along the cobblestoned street. The whisky diffused throughout his system. His fear abated as a comforting numbness washed over him. Rudy found a seat underneath a street lamp and processed the events that had brought him to this point. He'd been so single-minded in getting his story that it never occurred to him that it might be hazardous to his health. Within a span of three days he'd had his testicles crushed and narrowly avoided a beating. And he was in Britain. If so-called 'civilized' chaps like Pete Mitchell were prepared to tear lumps off him just for asking a few questions, what would the Afghans do to him? For the first time in his short career, Rudy had to ask himself a question most journalists never face. Was he ready to put his life on the line for a story?

Rudy pulled out his reporter's notebook and flipped through the pages from his conversation with Pete Mitchell. In the last line, he'd written the question that had brought him to Hereford: *Patterson's past? SOCA-ShieldGroup Smear Campaign?* He looked up from the page. A sign in an upmarket off-licence called to him like a beacon. Rudy put his notebook away and walked into it.

An old shopkeeper greeted him from behind the counter. 'Good evening, sir. How may I be of service?'

Rudy examined the bottles of whisky behind the cash register. 'What's your most expensive Scotch?'

The shopkeeper reached for the top shelf and pulled down an expensive-looking box. 'I've got a sublime Cragganmore single malt twenty-nine-year-old.'

'How much?'

The shopkeeper tilted the box to reveal a triple-digit price tag. Rudy didn't hesitate. 'I'll take it,' he said.

The old man wrapped the whisky in sheets of white tissue paper. 'You're not planning on drinking this straight away, are you?'

'Not yet,' said Rudy. 'It's incentive.'

The shopkeeper slid the mummified package into a bag. 'Incentive for what, if you don't mind me asking?'

Rudy took the bag. 'To find the truth.'

Chapter 27

John fed a piece of brushwood to the fire and checked the position of the sun. 'Is your kit together?'

Dusty sat against a rock, sucking a strip of smoked goat. 'It won't be dark for a few hours yet. Anyway my kit's always together. Part of the game, isn't it?'

'I know,' said John. 'But I want to get moving as soon as possible. We've already lost two days.'

Dusty gnawed the meat jerky. 'We would have lost more if we hadn't taken a break. I was getting a bad case of crotch rot from all the weight I dropped.'

John was surprised Dusty had kept the condition under wraps. They'd both seen patrols sidelined by soldiers who'd let their thighs rub raw before speaking up. 'Why didn't you tell me? We could have stopped – or at least taken a tactical dhobi.'

'I hate wading through rivers with my kit on,' said Dusty. 'Besides, our rations were running out. I figured it was either chafe or go hungry.'

'You're sure you're fit enough to travel?' asked John. 'We can lie up another day if you need to.'

'Shh.' Dusty sat up. 'Did you hear that?'

John tuned his ears to their surroundings. The only sounds he could detect were the crackling of the fire and the wind whistling through the valley below. 'Hear what?'

'Deaf git.' Dusty scanned the valley floor. 'There,' he said, pointing. Two motorbikes were driving up a dry riverbed. 'I'd know the sound of those engines anywhere. 250cc. Probably Chinese-made.'

John kicked dirt over the fire.

'What are you doing?' asked Dusty.

'Putting this out before they see it,' said John. 'I'm in no mood for a drama.'

'You wouldn't know an opportunity if it bit you on the arse, would you? With those motorbikes we could reach Dogrum tonight. This is the break we've been waiting for.' Dusty ran to an open patch of high ground and waved his arms.

'You think they're just going to give us those motorbikes?' said John.

Dusty kept waving. 'We'll trade Hamish for them.'

'A donkey for two motorbikes?' said John.

'We've got money,' said Dusty. 'We'll work something out.'

John looked at the motorbikes through his binos. The drivers were Afghan. One of them had an AK slung over his shoulder. 'They're armed.'

'So are we,' said Dusty. 'Just stay out of the way and let me handle it.'

A few minutes later, the Afghans pulled up. They were in their early to mid-twenties with thick bushy beards and dark eyes. Dusty held his hands up to show them he was unarmed. 'Hey there, lads. Don't suppose either of you speak English?' The two men eyed Dusty silently. Their faces were hard and expressionless. 'Your mo-tor-bikes,' said Dusty, punching each syllable in the hope of breaking through the language barrier. He pointed to Hamish. 'We trade donkey for motorbikes. Do you understand?'

The two Afghans exchanged glances and cut their engines.

The unarmed one dismounted and brushed past Dusty to have a closer look at the animal.

Dusty romanced his live merchandise. 'It's a fine beast,' he said, curling his arm. 'Very strong.'

The Afghan inspected the animal's hooves, hindquarters and ears. When he finished, he looked at his armed companion and shook his head no.

The armed Afghan spoke to Dusty. 'You have money? US dollar?'

Dusty smiled. 'Excellent. You do speak English.' He glanced at John as if to say *told you so*. 'What would you say to one hundred dollars for each motorbike.'

The armed Afghan spoke to his companion in Pashto.

John spoke up. 'I think they're insulted.'

'Shut up and let me do the haggling.' Dusty spoke to the armed man again. 'One hundred dollars for each motorbike and we'll give you the donkey for free.'

The two Afghans smiled greedily. The armed one spoke. 'You rich enough to buy motorbikes, you rich enough to rob!' The unarmed Afghan pulled a concealed knife from his clothing and waved it in front of Dusty. His companion aimed his AK at John.

The two Scots raised their arms, looking more disappointed than frightened. 'Come on now, lads,' said Dusty. 'Surely we can engage in a transaction that will leave everyone satisfied.'

The Afghan with the AK dismounted his motorbike and kicked over Dusty's Bergen. He searched the pack with his free hand, tossing aside food, clothing and medical supplies. When he found the small sack, he untied it with his teeth and tipped it upside down. Blue lapis beads spilled onto the ground.

John looked angrily at Dusty. 'Crotch rot wasn't the only thing you kept from me. You said you were finished smuggling antiques.'

'Can we discuss this later?' Dusty said guiltily.

'Fishing weights my arse,' said John.

The Afghans were too consumed by their find to notice the squabbling Scots. The one with the knife gathered up the beads and pressed his blade to John's throat.

'Money!' he demanded.

John looked at Dusty. 'You heard the man. Hand it over.'

Dusty unfastened the pouch strapped to his ankle, pulled out his camera and laid it on a rock. He reached in again and produced a wad of dollars. The Afghan withdrew his knife from John's neck and snatched the money from Dusty's hand. He walked over to his companion and started counting the haul.

'Offer to take their picture,' said John.

'What?' said Dusty. 'Why?'

'Just do it,' said John.

Dusty picked up his camera. The sudden movement startled the Afghans. They stopped counting. The younger Scot held up the camera. 'Your picture,' he said. 'Let me take it.'

Before they could object, Dusty snapped the photograph. The Afghan with the AK swung his rifle between the two Scots. 'What should I do now?' said Dusty.

'Show them the bloody thing,' said John.

Dusty held his hands up and walked slowly toward the Afghans. He extended the camera to them and pointed to the external viewfinder. 'Look here,' he said. The two Afghans stared at their own image – mesmerized.

Four rapid cracks ripped the air. The two Afghans collapsed on top of each other, blood draining from the double taps to their heads. Dusty stepped away from the bodies and looked at John.

'*Let me do the haggling*,' John mocked as he tucked his pistol back into his trousers.

*

Dusty stepped over the dead men to the motorbikes. He unscrewed the fuel cap on one, looked inside and gave the bike a shake. 'There's half a tank of petrol, maybe three-quarters. That should be enough to get us to Dogrum.' He checked the fuel tank on the other bike and gave John the thumbs up. 'We're in business.'

'Stop grinning and help me bury these lads.' John got his collapsible shovel out while Dusty marked a six foot by two foot rectangle in the dirt.

John looked at Dusty's outline and shook his head critically.

'What now?' Dusty moaned.

'You lay a body in there and the head will end up pointing north or south,' said John.

'Let's just get them in the ground and get going,' said Dusty.

'We need to cover our tracks,' said John. 'Bury them like that and you may as well place a big crucifix on top. Their faces need to point toward Mecca.' Dusty re-plotted the rectangle, found his shovel and got to work.

Once the Afghan thieves were imprisoned for all eternity, the two Scots set about modifying the motorbikes to ride at night. John popped the infrared filters off their torches and taped them to the headlights, making sure to leave no parts exposed. The adjustment would allow them to see with their night sights while remaining invisible to the naked eye. Dusty prepped the tail lights in a similar fashion, blacking them out with tape and fastening two infrared glowsticks on top.

When they finished, John and Dusty turned their attention to Hamish. Their last connection with the Kutchi had exhausted its usefulness. Dusty cut down the crates that had concealed their Bergens so well, while John slid the reins from the donkey's head. 'Good luck, Hamish,' he said. 'Go find yourself a nice village somewhere.'

They strapped their Bergens to their motorbikes with bungee cords and prepared to descend into the pitch-black valley with John, the less skilled rider, in the lead. John put on his night-vision goggles, cranked the accelerator and raised his feet. The bike jerked forward. His Bergen shifted, throwing him off balance. He managed to right the bike before it skidded out from under him. John planted his feet back on the ground. Dusty re-secured the Bergen for him and gave the bungee cord a tug. 'That should hold now.'

'Any advice before I give this another go?' asked John.

'Yeah,' said Dusty. 'Don't fall off.'

John twisted the accelerator – gently this time – and lifted his feet once more. The motorbike purred as it carried him down into the valley. Cruising along the hard surface of the dry riverbed, John felt exhilarated. The wind in his hair, the video-game like quality of speeding through a landscape using night-vision aids; it reminded him of Scud-hunting in an open-topped Pinky during the First Gulf War. The joyride turned to drudgery however when they started climbing. The rocky landscape was incredibly difficult to negotiate. John constantly had to dismount and push his way past obstacles. Every time he was forced to hoof it, Dusty would turn it into an opportunity to show off his superior technique. He'd pull ahead, rock the bike onto the front tyre and swing the back end around 180 degrees to look down on his lagging companion.

Four hours of watching Dusty pirouette had strained John's patience to breaking point. He cut the engine and took off his night sights.

Dusty twirled around to face him. 'You need a break?'

John swung his leg over the back of his bike and stood with his knees partially bent. 'I can't feel my balls.'

'You've got to stop slamming your arse down on the seat

every time you hit a bump.' Dusty slid his night-vision goggles onto the top of his head and pulled out his GPS.

'Another night of this and I'll be a eunuch,' John complained.

Dusty checked their position. 'There won't be another night,' he said. 'We're here.'

'Here?' John looked into the darkness. 'Are you sure this is the valley?'

'According to my readings,' said Dusty.

John pulled out his GPS. 'You may be good on a bike,' he said, waiting for a satellite to register their position, 'but you're shite at navigation.' The countdown lit up the screen. But Dusty was right. They were a thousand metres from the latitude and longitude Haider had given them back in Kabul. John put his night sights back on. 'Where the hell is Dogrum then?'

Dusty and John scanned the area for man-made structures – anything that would indicate human settlement. There was nothing. They decided to rest up and try again at sunrise. But daybreak shed no light on Dogrum's location. All they could see in the mist-filled valley was uninterrupted, primordial wilderness: an angry river slicing through a deep canyon; dense patches of undulating green; a waterfall; bushy-topped trees twenty and thirty feet tall; jagged cliffs climbing toward peaks that vanished into clouds.

John and Dusty drove onto a track paralleling the river. The route meandered up the side of a mountain and disappeared around a bend. They rode along it, moving in and out of low-hanging clouds. As they approached the bend, the fog lifted to reveal a narrow cascade of water flowing from a re-entrant. It fell in a graceful arc down into the valley. They climbed off their bikes and walked them through the passageway. The water spat at them as they passed, covering them in icy droplets. When they emerged on the other side – their faces shiny and wet – they were astounded by what they saw: livestock grazing on terraced steps carved into the earth. Civilization! The cultivated land ran from a high ridge down to the edge of the canyon. A powerful waterfall tumbling over a mountain fed the river hundreds of feet below. A rope bridge connected the farmland to a village on the other side of the gorge. It was like something out of a storybook – a cluster of buildings floating above a shelf of earth less than twelve feet wide. A crumbling stone wall wrapped the slender plateau like a pair of embracing arms.

Examining the village through their binos, they could see there were roughly twenty buildings – two-storey flat-topped structures with stone foundations and walls fashioned from logs and mortar. The rectangular dwellings linked and overlapped like Lego stacked at odd angles. Those nearest the plateau had latticed open-air balconies overhanging the canyon. As the buildings ascended, each flat roof provided a courtyard and walkway for the one above. A man could climb from the bottom of the village to the top without his feet ever touching the ground.

'I can't believe we didn't see this before.' John looked back to the head of the valley. 'It was right in our line of sight.'

Dusty kept observing through his binos. 'Makes you feel for the Yanks. They're looking in caves for bin Laden. He's probably living over there in a two-up two-down.'

'Well, whoever built this place didn't want to be found.' John searched the village. There were no men visible, only women gathering water from a well and walking it up to the houses. Their dress was modest: long sleeves, ankle-length skirts, veils covering their hair. Unlike the Kutchi, the clothes were muted – greys and beiges with an occasional burst of colour. A scarlet red veil draped elegantly over the head of one woman caught John's eye. Her face was beautiful: high cheekbones, strong jaw, full lips, green eyes. The headscarf contrasted sharply with the child at the woman's knee: a little girl with pale skin and curly blonde hair. John was instantly captivated.

Dusty tucked away his binos. 'Think it's Dogrum?'

John emerged from his trance. 'If it is, they're expecting a family of Kutchi to roll up, not two Westerners travelling alone. I don't want to scare those women. Let's move slowly, see how they react to us.'

Dusty climbed onto his motorbike. 'I hope Haider's an early riser.'

Dusty led the way down the track and along the fields. The clouds thickened again, threatening rain. When they reached the rope bridge, the pair stood astride their bikes, trying to determine how much weight the structure could tolerate. The ropes were frayed and some of the planks lining the bottom were missing.

'We need to take this one at a time,' said Dusty. 'I'll go first.' Dusty inched his bike onto the bridge and bounced up and down to test its resilience. Satisfied it could take the weight, he gently twisted the accelerator and headed across.

John listened to the boards skipping underneath Dusty's tyres. A crack suddenly disrupted the rhythm. It sounded like thunder. John hadn't seen any lightning. He looked back at the fields. They were still.

Dusty reached the other side and gave the OK sign. Lacking Dusty's delicate touch with the accelerator, John dismounted his motorbike and pushed it along. He looked down between the planks as he walked. The ravine was dark and menacing, like the jaws of a crocodile opening for a kill. Another crack rumbled the air. This time, John knew it wasn't thunder.

Instinctively, he hit the deck. A single green tracer round burst out of the village and flew over his head, snapping a suspension rope. Flashes of green and the crack and thump of high velocity rounds erupted from the fields. The village responded with more bullets. John and Dusty were caught in crossfire.

Chapter 28

John dropped the bike and sprinted across the bridge. Dusty covered him as he ran. When he reached the other side, John ran past Dusty and jumped over the low stone wall encircling the plateau. Dusty dived in behind him.

An RPG round slammed into the houses above. The sound of women and children screaming and men shouting commands in foreign tongues echoed overhead.

'Haider didn't mention they'd have a welcoming party for us,' said Dusty. 'Whose side are we on then?'

More rifle fire erupted from the village. Ribbons of green tracer rounds streaked across the sky. They weren't aiming at John and Dusty. The villagers were targeting the fighters on the other side of the bridge. 'Whoever's in the field started this,' John panted. 'I'd like to get eyes on them.'

Dusty took his binos from his waistcoat, twisted them in half and handed one of the sights to John. Armed with a monocular each, the pair assessed the warring parties. As far as they could tell, the villagers had four rifles and no other weapons to defend themselves. John saw two of the faces taking aim from the edge of a balcony; they were light-skinned – just like Haider, but with full beards. The fighters in the fields were much better armed. They had at least a dozen weapons including an RPG launcher stationed in the middle terrace and a heavy machine gun positioned up top. John tried to catch a glimpse of their faces but the smoke from battle kept obstructing his view.

Despite the advantage in firepower, the field fighters couldn't get the upper hand. After twenty minutes of non-stop fighting, there was a sudden break in the action. The smoke started to dissipate. John took advantage of the clearing to study the terraces. Through his monocular, he saw a man reloading an RPG. The fighter had a pampered haughtiness about him. It was a distinct feature, one John had seen before. He searched his memory, recalling places and people he'd encountered over the years. His mind honed in on a desert location on the eve of the First Gulf War. John dropped his monocular and looked at Dusty. 'It's a fucking Saudi,' he declared.

Dusty looked through his monocular. 'Where?'

'The RPG position,' said John.

Dusty moved his line of sight down and left. 'Are you sure?'

'He's Saudi all right.' John slapped Dusty's shoulder. 'That's it then. We're fighting for the villagers.'

'I'll fight for whoever you want,' said Dusty. 'As long as we're on the same side.'

The rifle fire from the village grew more sporadic. 'They're running low on ammo,' said John. 'We need to move fast or they'll be overrun.'

'How are you for ammo?' asked Dusty.

John felt underneath his waistcoat. 'I've got four full mags. Do you have any smoke grenades?'

'No,' said Dusty.

John looked at his abandoned motorbike. It was still lying on its side in the middle of the bridge. His Bergen was tied to the back of it. 'Do you have something I can use as a run bag?'

Dusty unfastened the pouch from his ankle, emptied it and gave it to John.

John slid the nylon bag up his arm. 'I've got two smoke grenades in my Bergen. Cover me. Wait for my signal to advance.'

Dusty nodded. 'Who do you want to take out first: the machine-gunner or the Saudi with the RPG?'

John put his rifle in his right hand, grabbed his knife with the other and held it in the attack position. 'The Saudi.' John dived back over the wall and rolled onto his stomach. Bullets cracked overhead as he combat-crawled onto the bridge. He tried to move quickly, but his feet and knees kept falling between the gaps in the wooden planks. One of the field fighters charged down from the terraces. He was wearing an Arab *shamag* – something you'd never see on an Afghan. The foreign fighter aimed his rifle at John. 'To hell with it,' John muttered. He sprang to his feet and ran to the motorbike with his knife raised. In one fluid motion, he swooped down on his Bergen and slashed the bungee cord to free it. A bullet ricocheted off the motorbike frame and another raced past his ear as he retrieved the grenades from the pack. Unable to determine which direction either round had come from, John fell to his stomach and aimed his AK toward the fields. Through his rifle sight, he saw the man with the *shamag* collapsed on the lower terrace. John looked behind him. Dusty was up on one knee, the barrel of his 5.56 still raised from having just shot dead the foreign fighter.

John ran to the far side of the bridge, took up a covering position and waved to Dusty. Firing and manoeuvring, the two Scots pepper-potted their way up the terraces toward the centre. The machine-gunner on the top tier sprayed the ground around them with bullets. John pulled the pin from a smoke grenade and threw it in front of the RPG position. A loud pop sounded as the canister released dense orange smoke. 'Change of plan!' John yelled. 'I'll take out the machine-gunner. You hold down the RPG!' John ran through the smoke and took aim at the top terrace. A white skullcap surfaced from a blanket of green. John aimed three inches below it and fired. The round ripped through the gunner's face, spraying flesh and skull everywhere. Through his sight, John saw another fighter rushing to the aid of his fallen comrade. John killed him with a fast and accurate double tap to the torso.

The remaining fighters on the upper terraces came charging out of their positions. 'Two o'clock!' John shouted. He and Dusty fired four shots in rapid succession. Three of the fighters collapsed. Panicked, those left alive scattered. 'I've got them!' John shouted 'You hold down the RPG!' Dusty laid down suppressing fire on the RPG position while John pursued the three renegade fighters. Two were running along the ridgeline. The grain stalks were high and grabbed John's legs as he pursued them. One of the fighters stopped to reload. John kept moving as he raised his rifle and fired. The round caught the fighter in the shoulder and spun him around. The wounded man's companion made the fatal mistake of looking back. John stopped, aimed and shot the man dead. He ran to the wounded fighter and finished him off with a round to the body. The man's skin was light and his features were Afghan – a Nuristani among the foreign fighters.

Dropping his empty magazine and replacing it with a full one as he ran, John chased the third fighter down the terraces to the edge of the canyon. Trapped with nowhere to flee, the fighter swung his rifle around and fired on automatic until his ammo was spent. John easily evaded the sloppy bursts.

The game was over. The fighter threw down his rifle, raised his arms to heaven and cried with defiant jubilance: '*Allahu Akbar!*' John took in the man's features. Like the fighter manning the RPG, this one was Saudi too. 'You think you're going to paradise, fucker?' said John. The foreign fighter tore open his shirt, inviting John to shoot him. John lowered his rifle and spat. 'You don't deserve a warrior's death.'

Several rounds came screaming out of the village. The fighter fell backward over the edge of the cliff and into the gorge below. He'd been shot in the back.

Victorious cries rang out from the bridge. John looked. A group of light-haired men – villagers – were cheering and waving their rifles victoriously. They'd come down from their rooftops to help drive back the invaders. John waved to them. 'Get over here, lads!' He ran to Dusty who'd been holding down the RPG position single-handedly. 'How many are left?' John shouted.

Dusty didn't look up from his sight. 'Three.' He fired a shot. 'Make that two.'

'No bother,' said John. Dusty looked behind him. The villagers were running toward them with guns aloft.

'Typical Afghans,' said Dusty. 'Never on time.'

John knelt on one knee and searched for the remaining fighters. 'Three o'clock,' he said.

'I see him,' said Dusty.

The pair fired simultaneously and the target dropped. There was only one fighter remaining: the Saudi with the RPG. John signalled to the villagers. 'He's all yours, lads!' The four Nuristanis stormed the RPG position. A last, furious burst of gunfire erupted. Smoke filled the air as angry screams drowned out the cries of the dying. Then, as quickly as it started, the fighting stopped. The four villagers emerged from the smoke, their clothes and faces splattered with the blood of their enemy. One smiled broadly and opened his arms to embrace the two Scots. John did a double-take. 'Haider?'

Chapter 29

'I just need a few more days,' Rudy pleaded.

Lucinda was unmoved. 'Far better correspondents than you have attempted far cleverer ploys to extend their home leave. Your flight leaves Heathrow tonight. Be on it.'

'Ploy!' Rudy stood up and pulled down the collar of his shirt. 'These bruises are real, Lucinda. Decorum prevents me from showing you the other injuries I've sustained on this story.'

Lucinda smiled lasciviously. 'You wouldn't be the first man to drop his trousers in this office.' Rudy shuddered at the thought. Lucinda was well past her prime, if indeed she'd ever had one. Her thick waist poured over the top of her skirt and her hair was dyed a scary circus-clown orange. A kinder demeanour would normally gloss over such common, middle-aged cracks. But Lucinda was like an old house a cowboy builder had fixed up to sell. There was no hiding her structural damage. 'You've shown a great deal of pluck, dear boy,' she continued, 'but from where I'm sitting, you have no story. Our readers don't care about private security companies. It has no bearing on their lives.'

Rudy bit his tongue. How could an editor of a major British newspaper be so editorially short-sighted? Granted, Lucinda was known to make correspondents fight for their stories, but this one had genuine merit. 'With all due respect, that may have been the case a few years ago but not now. Private security is a multi-billion-pound business. And most of those billions come straight from the public coffers. I honestly believe that this story would have enormous appeal to our readers. It has everything: corruption, abuse of taxpayer funds, fraud, cover-ups.'

Lucinda's eyes glazed over. 'It's not sexy. Our readers have certain expectations. It's not rocket science, dear boy. Just put your ego aside and focus on what interests the public, not you personally.'

'I care deeply about the public interest,' Rudy insisted. 'And if you'd bothered to read even half the stories I've filed from Kabul, you'd know that.'

'Ah, now I understand.' Lucinda grew even more condescending. 'I thought you knew better. You think the public interest and what interests the public are one and the same.' She waved her finger back and forth. 'No, no, no. What our readers want is something all together different. They want distraction, something to take their minds off their dreary little lives.' She looked at Rudy and pouted. 'Don't take it so hard. I was concerned I may have made a mistake sending you to Kabul. Now that you've learned the first secret of the craft, you'll write something worth printing. I'm sure of it.'

The comment was like an open-handed smack. Rudy worked from sun-up to sundown getting original stories for that bitch. 'What's wrong with the stories I've sent you, Lucinda?'

Lucinda sighed. 'No one wants to open a newspaper and read about a teenager scalding her private bits. People think of Afghanistan in simple terms – goodies and baddies. British soldiers – goodies; Taliban – baddies. Goodies, baddies, goodies, baddies.' She circled her finger like a schoolteacher. 'Come, say it with me – goodies, baddies—'

Rudy refused to degrade himself by playing along. 'The story I'm working on has all of that.'

Lucinda wound in her finger. 'Then tell it to me in those terms.'

Rudy swallowed his pride. 'Well . . . the baddies are a private security company, ShieldGroup, and their client, SOCA. The goodie is a whistle-blower named John Patterson. That's why I need more time here. I'm trying to gather more background information on him.'

Lucinda rose from her chair and walked to the front of her desk. She picked up a paper and read it as if it urgently required her undivided attention. A long silence ensued but Rudy knew better than to be the first to break it. Lucinda was testing him, trying to make him beg. Fuck her.

Lucinda put down the paper and continued the conversation as if no time had passed. 'Tell me more about your whistle-blower.'

'He was in charge of training Afghan counter-narcotics police recruited by SOCA,' said Rudy. 'According to him, SOCA unwittingly allowed two Afghan insurgents to infiltrate the programme.'

'Hmm.' Lucinda looked sceptical. 'It sounds rather high level. How did *you* learn about this?'

Rudy hadn't mentioned the ShieldGroup report to Lucinda – at least not yet. If he let her in on it too soon, she'd bring in her newsroom pets to verify its authenticity and then instead of having the scoop of a lifetime, Rudy would end up being the third name in a shared byline. 'Interviews with Patterson,' he said.

Lucinda wasn't buying it. 'Either you're a very lucky journalist or you've been duped by a fantasist. This Patterson character, did he claim to be descended from the Romanovs as well?'

Rudy wanted to grab the loose skin on Lucinda's chin and strangle her with it. 'Patterson's legitimate.'

'Then why are you having so much trouble finding information on him?' asked Lucinda.

'He's ex-SAS,' said Rudy. 'There's nothing on him in the public domain.'

Lucinda's demeanour changed instantly. 'SAS?' she said. 'Good heavens, dear boy, you buried the lead.'

Rudy smiled. He'd cracked it. 'May I have those extra days now?'

Lucinda flourished her hands. 'No, no, no. We can't leave Kabul unattended. Not with a war on. But no worries. I'll get you the help you need.' Rudy started to speak but Lucinda shushed him. She picked up her phone and stabbed the speed dial. 'Could you be a dear and come to my office?' Lucinda never spoke that way to subordinates. 'You *are* a darling.'

The hairs on the back of Rudy's neck went stiff. Lucinda reserved that saccharine voice for only two people at the newspaper – the publisher and the resident . . .

A man wearing a grey pin-striped suit and silk cravat knocked on Lucinda's door. No journalist in the Western hemisphere dressed that way. 'Thank you for coming so quickly,' Lucinda cooed. 'Rudy, surely you know Harry Boaz. Our special correspondent to the Ministry of Defence?'

Of course Rudy knew Harry. But he was no correspondent – special or otherwise. Harry was the newspaper's resident spook.

Chapter 30

Haider plunged his hands into a bucket and rubbed them together. Dried blood lifted from his skin, staining the water. Dusty watched it change from light pink to deep red. His gaze shifted to Haider's now heavily bearded face. Back in Kabul, Haider had always worn Western clothing and kept his beard clipped. His appearance was as tempered as his behaviour. Dusty couldn't get over the transformation. He never imagined that a bloodthirsty warrior lurked beneath that mild-mannered disguise.

'This is the second time our village has been attacked in as many weeks,' said Haider. He called to a young boy in a dialect Dusty had never heard him speak before.

'What language is that?' asked Dusty.

Haider splashed his face. 'Kamviri,' he smiled. 'It is the language of the Kom, my people.'

The boy brought two buckets of water over and gave one each to John and Dusty. John plunged his face into the water, pulled it out and shook it. Drops flew from his red beard. 'Do you know who's targeting you?' he asked.

'Hizb-i-Islami.' Haider barked another order in Kamviri. The boy whisked the buckets away.

The two Scots exchanged looks. 'Because of what happened with Rasul's nephews?' asked John.

'No,' said Haider. 'The Rasul clan has agreed to a *jirga*. The attacks on Dogrum have nothing to do with what happened in Kabul. We were attacked because of the Americans.'

'I don't follow,' said Dusty. 'What do the Yanks have to do with Dogrum?'

'A few weeks ago, the Americans built a military base near Kamdesh – the capital of this district,' Haider explained.

'We saw two helis flying north a few weeks back,' John offered. 'An Apache and a Chinook. We figured they were hunting al-Qaeda.'

'Yes,' Haider confirmed, 'but the Americans aren't just fighting al-Qaeda with aircraft and guns. They hope to buy the loyalty of the Nuristani people with good deeds. American soldiers came here asking if we'd like a micro-hydro station to electrify Dogrum. We declined and asked them not to return but the insurgents must have seen them come here. The attacks are a warning . . .'

John finished the thought. 'Do business with the Yanks and you're dead.'

'Precisely,' said Haider. 'Instead of driving al-Qaeda out of Nuristan, the Americans have driven them down from the mountains and into our villages.' Haider bowed his head. 'The first attack came at night. We were unprepared. My brother was killed. He left behind a wife and a child.'

John placed his hand on Haider's shoulder. 'I am truly sorry for your loss.'

Haider patted John's hand and composed himself. 'But today, we were victorious, thanks to you, my friends.'

John smiled humbly. 'It wasn't all down to us. You and the other men fought bravely today. I'm sure your brother would have been proud.'

John waited for Dusty to add a compliment. But Dusty had

more questions. 'How soon were you attacked after the Yanks
came here?'

Haider thought about it. 'Five days,' he said.

'And after that,' asked Dusty. 'Did the Yanks visit Dogrum
again after the first attack?'

'No,' said Haider.

'So why would Hizb-i-Islami attack you a second time?' said
Dusty.

'The Americans are visiting many villages in the district. As
long as they continue, we will be vulnerable,' said Haider.

Dusty shook his head. 'I don't know, Haider. How can you
be sure Rasul wasn't behind the second attack – if not both of
them?'

'I told you,' said Haider. 'Rasul's clan has agreed to a *jirga*.'

'They could have changed their minds,' said Dusty.

'If they did not want to allow the *jirga* to decide our differences, the Rasuls would have withheld their consent,' Haider
explained. 'To go back on their word now and launch an attack
would be dishonourable.'

Dusty scoffed. 'You trust General Rasul to keep his word?'

'If we were at war with the Rasuls, I would have reservations,' said Haider. 'But right now our people are at peace.'

'What do you mean *right now*?' asked Dusty.

'Rasul and his nephews are Kshto. My people are Kom,' said
Haider. 'Kom and Kshto have fought many wars over the centuries. The last one ended eight years ago when the main Kshto
village in this district was burnt to the ground. Many Kshto
fled north to Barg-i-Matal – an area controlled by Hizb-i-
Islami. That is when the Rasuls joined them. They were
nothing before that. Now Ustad Rasul sits in the Ministry of
Defence.'

'So it makes even more sense that what happened here this

morning was General Rasul and the rest of Kshto getting their own back,' said Dusty. 'Don't pin it on the Yanks.'

'No,' Haider insisted. 'The Kstho do not tell Hizb-i-Islami what to do and who to attack. You must understand how Hizb-i-Islami operate. They are not, as they claim, holy warriors. They are whores who fight for whoever throws money at them. When the Soviets were in Afghanistan, that was the United States. Now that the Americans are here, it is al-Qaeda and al-Qaeda, as you know, is controlled by Saudis and Pakistanis. Their agenda is not to fight the Kom but to drive the Americans and the Coalition out of Nuristan. That is why Dogrum was attacked. There is no other reason.'

'No offence,' said Dusty. 'But it sure sounds like a tribal pissing match to me.'

'Or maybe al-Qaeda and Hizb-i-Islami are deliberately trying to stir the shit,' John offered. 'If the Kom and Kshto are at each other's throats again, it makes it that much harder for the Yanks to get a foothold in Nuristan. Think about it: if the Americans strike a deal with one tribe, they automatically make an enemy of another. It's like trying to plug holes in a dyke – one is sealed and another one springs open.'

'I have not considered that possibility but I would not rule it out,' said Haider. 'The same tactic was used during the Soviet occupation.' He placed his arm around John. 'Come, my friends. The Majlis is eager to meet Dogrum's saviours.'

Haider escorted them to a grand balcony overlooking the canyon. Buttressed by tree trunks set at thirty degree angles to the rock face, the structure looked like it was suspended in mid-air. As they wound their way up, Haider gave some background on the Majlis. The Malek, or leader, he explained, was always appointed, while the other council members were elected by popular vote (men only, John assumed). Haider made it clear that not just anyone could stand for office. In addition to being morally upright, virtuous and God-fearing, Majlis members also had to be literate. As Haider waxed on about religious and academic qualifications, John was struck by how different the Afghan was on his home turf. Back in Kabul, Haider was usually tight-lipped and reserved. He rarely mentioned Dogrum, let alone its customs. Watching him lecture with such passion, John realized how immensely proud the Nuristani was of his people and their traditions. Dogrum brought out the best in him.

Three men – one old, two young – sat cross-legged on threadbare carpets, waiting to receive them. Haider introduced the oldest first: Anvar, the Malek of Dogrum. Anvar was a hard-looking character with a cracked face, bald head and a long beard dyed henna orange. His status was designated by a geometric insignia woven into the sleeve of his robe which he wore over a traditional shalwar kameez. Haider described Anvar as a living legend. The old man had fought the Soviets at close quarters during the 1980s – and had the scars to prove it. As Haider spoke, Anvar peeled back his kameez to reveal a raised, jagged mark left by a Russian bayonet.

The next man Haider introduced was Baidullah – 'the most educated man in Kamdesh district', he boasted. Baidullah looked the part with his round, gentle face that wrinkled when he smiled. Haider explained that Baidullah had studied at a madrassa – religious school – in Pakistan and hoped to study Islamic law at al-Azar University in Cairo one day.

The third member of the Majlis was Daud, oldest son of the previous Malek of Dogrum and Anvar's nephew. The fact that Daud hadn't succeeded his father as Malek was no reflection on the young man's character, Haider explained. 'Daud was an infant when his father died fighting the Russians.'

'Was he out in the fields with us this morning?' asked John.

'Yes.' Haider grabbed Daud's shoulder. 'He is most anxious to distinguish himself in battle. If Daud is to succeed Anvar as Malek one day, he must prove he has the courage and acumen to lead.'

Anvar motioned to John and Dusty to join them. Unaccustomed to sitting cross-legged, John struggled to bring one knee flush with the floor. When the two Scots settled down, Anvar rang a bell. A boy came to the balcony carrying a large platter filled with cheese, bread, dried fruit and nuts and small glasses of green tea.

Haider asked John and Dusty to help themselves. 'It is customary for guests to eat first,' he explained.

Dusty reached toward the platter with his left hand. John stopped him and muttered under his breath. 'Don't make an arse of it.'

Dusty withdrew his left hand and reached with his right. John got stuck in as well. The sharp cheese, fresh bread and strong, sweet tea were a welcome break from boil-in-the-bags and goat jerky. Only when they'd had their fill did Haider and the Majlis eat.

'So,' said Dusty. 'Tell us more about this *jirga*. When does it start?'

Haider washed down a mouthful of food with his tea. 'The *jirga* will be held in Kamdesh village, a day's walk from here.'

'So two days at the earliest then,' said Dusty.

'Perhaps,' said Haider. 'There are still some details to agree first.'

Dusty looked unsettled. 'The whole reason we came here was for a *jirga*, mate. Don't tell us it could all go tits up.'

Haider tore a piece of flatbread and grabbed a piece of cheese with it. 'This is Nuristan, not London. You cannot rush the process,' he said. 'Before the *jirga* can take place, the *zamanat* must be agreed. It is a payment submitted by us and the other party in advance of the proceedings.'

'Like bail?' asked John. 'To make sure everyone shows up?'

'No,' said Haider. 'As I explained, once someone agrees to allow the *jirga* to settle a dispute, there is no going back. A Nuristani's word is his life. The *zamanat* is to guarantee that both parties abide by the *jirga*'s decision. If a party is found guilty, their *zamanat* is awarded to the injured. If a party is found innocent and the other party refuses to accept the *jirga*'s decision, their *zamanat* is not returned.'

'So if we're found innocent and the Rasuls don't accept it, do we get their money?' asked Dusty.

'If that were to happen, the Rasuls' *zamanat* would not come to us. It would be distributed to the community,' said Haider. 'Fines here are not intended to enrich individuals, they are intended to benefit everyone.'

John mentally inventoried their cash and possessions. 'How big a payment will we have to make upfront then?'

Haider put the question to Anvar. He translated as the old man spoke. 'When blood has been spilled, the *zamanat* is quite dear: fifty even seventy-five head of cattle is not unheard of.'

'We don't have cattle,' said Dusty.

'Most parties will agree to an equal payment in cash,' said Haider.

'So if the *jirga* finds us guilty . . .' Dusty looked hopefully at John. '. . . we'll just hand our money over to the Rasuls and that's it. We're even?'

Haider again put the question to Anvar. He translated as the old man spoke. 'If the *jirga* believes we murdered Rasul's nephews in cold blood, it will order our execution. An eye for an eye. If they so wish, the Rasul clan can demand money instead of our heads. The *zamanat* may be enough to appease them, but in cases of murder, the injured party can demand more. We call such payments *deiyat*.'

'We've got a word for that too,' said Dusty. 'Blood money.'

Chapter 31

Harry lifted his glass and inspected it. His expression soured. 'They forgot the mint. What beastly establishment serves Pimm's without fresh mint?' He lowered the glass and peered into it as if it were a crystal ball. 'And what on earth is that?' He fished a limp cucumber spear from the drink. 'I've never seen such a poor specimen of *cucumis sativus*.'

'Not used to flying commercial are you?' Rudy's observation was anything but casual. Highlighting Harry's privileged status was his way of stating *I am a real journalist and you are an errand boy who trades access for influence.* Rudy nursed his Famous Grouse. 'Next time you order a drink in an airport terminal, you may want to stick with something served neat.'

'Right you are, my good man. Right you are.' Harry took a cautious sip of his Pimm's. 'So, you're having trouble finding information on someone,' he began. 'John Patterson was the name I believe?'

Rudy put on his poker face. Harry hadn't hauled his arse out to Heathrow to help him with his story. He was there to pump Rudy for information and stick him on a plane. 'I appreciate the offer but Lucinda's concerns are premature. I'm having minor difficulties with one small aspect of my story but to be honest

I've hardly exhausted all channels. There's really no reason for you to get involved – not at this stage anyway.'

Harry tilted his chin. 'Lucinda told me you're basing your investigation on a report?'

Rudy held his expression and didn't react. Lucinda hadn't a clue about the ShieldGroup report. But clearly someone had told Harry about it. Rudy wondered what channels the information had gone through. Did SOCA raise the alarm? Or had some ex-general or MP on ShieldGroup's board of directors phoned a crony to put a stop to the story? Rudy's heart leapt with glee. He was obviously onto something huge! 'I have several sources,' he said nonchalantly. 'Like any good journalist.'

Harry stirred his drink. 'If you're worried I'll steal your thunder, allow me to assuage your fears. The story is one hundred per cent yours. I give you my word, I won't go crying to Lucinda for a byline.'

'We both know you've been at this game a long time.' Rudy intended the sentence to carry a double meaning. 'Any concerns I have are not unreasonable.'

Harry sat back in his seat. 'You shouldn't be so reluctant to accept help from a colleague. It doesn't have to end in tears, you know. Collaborations can benefit both parties in unexpected ways.' He folded his hands and made a steeple with his fingers. 'For example, what if I could help secure you an embedded assignment with British troops in Helmund?'

Rudy could literally feel his mouth water. The queue for embeds with troops in Helmund was a mile long. The MoD kept a list of preferred correspondents and news organizations that could jump it. Rudy's name wasn't on it. 'I've applied with the MoD.'

'This is exactly the kind of thing I'm talking about.' Harry sat up. 'I'll phone some contacts and see what can be done to expedite your request.'

'That won't be necessary,' Rudy insisted.

'Don't be so proud,' said Harry. 'This is how things get done.' He took another sip of his drink and grimaced. 'Private security contractors,' he announced, as if they'd been discussing the topic for hours. 'I remember a time when we didn't refer to them in such politically correct terms. We called them what they are. Mercenaries. Remember that ghastly business with Mark Thatcher in Equatorial Guinea?'

'The failed coup,' said Rudy. 'If you ask me, the prat should be rotting in an African jail.'

'It's really quite extraordinary if you think about it,' Harry mused. 'A century ago, such exploits would be regarded as the routine business of Empire. Now it's vilified. It does make ripping good copy, though.'

Rudy couldn't stomach Harry's attempts to sound like a genuine newsman. 'So you admire mercenaries, then?'

'It's not a question of admiration. Our armed forces are stretched to capacity and with defence budgets under siege, well, the situation will only get worse. If Britain is to remain a first-class military power, the considerable resources of the private sector must be tapped.'

'You sound like a lobbyist,' Rudy observed. Harry chortled. Clearly, he was not insulted by the remark. 'There's just one flaw in your argument,' Rudy continued. 'A rather critical one, I might add. Outsourcing military jobs doesn't save money, it merely shifts it from the public domain into private hands. If defence budgets are really under siege, wouldn't it make more sense for Britain to rein in its ambitions?'

Harry pushed his drink aside. 'The British are a terribly civilized people. Our distaste for mercenaries is great. But our distaste for irrelevance is even greater. If we are to remain a global power, we must project military force overseas as and when required. The military can no longer do that alone. It must be supplemented. For better or worse, mercenaries are now vital to our national interest. Besides, what harm is there in shifting non-combat roles to private security contractors? As Lady Thatcher showed us all, privatization is good value for money.'

'Only if the private sector does the job as well as the military would,' Rudy countered. 'And where does it stop? How much of our armed forces are we going to privatize? The way things are going – will we even have a British military in ten years' time? Or will it be armies of private mercenaries controlled by multi-national corporations?'

'You make it all sound so conspiratorial,' said Harry. 'But the only difference between a traditional army and its modern corporate counterpart is the titles of the managers. One is led by generals, the other by CEOs.'

'What about accountability?' said Rudy. 'The state keeps the army in check. But private security companies are unregulated. No one holds them to account when things go wrong.'

'When individual mercenaries commit crimes, they should be punished.' Harry sounded like a government paper. 'The industry sees it that way as well. They are keen to demonstrate they are capable of self-policing, just like the military.'

'But what if the problem isn't individual mercenaries?' said Rudy. 'What if the problem is the whole structure? Private security companies don't exist for the national good, after all. They exist to turn a profit.'

'One can endlessly speculate,' said Harry. 'But the fact remains that private security companies have become, for better or worse, a necessary appendage of our armed forces.'

'Here's a thought,' said Rudy. 'What if the British Army withdrew from Iraq and Afghanistan? Then there wouldn't be a need for private security companies.'

Harry plonked the cucumber spear back in the drink. 'That, my good man, would serve no one's interests.'

Chapter 32

The door creaked open and a pair of tiny feet shuffled across the floor. John lay still on his side, pretending to be asleep. He remained motionless as his senses tracked the boy's progress; the hollow clunking of logs being loaded into the wood-burning stove; a match strike; a whiff of sulphur followed by a sudden burst of warmth. John waited for the feet to depart and the door to close. When he was certain the boy was gone, John sat up and checked to make sure Dusty was still asleep.

Creeping carefully past the stove, John made his way to the only window in the tiny, second-storey, single-room dwelling. He put his head above the parapet and waited. The sun wasn't up but the village women were already awake, gathering water from the village well, collecting fire wood, tending the fields and milking cattle. As John had discovered already, women were the workhorses of Dogrum. All the men did was count their herds, talk politics and fight – poorly.

John's eyes darted from one figure to another, searching for hints of colour. A woman walked across the bridge. She was carrying a hurricane lamp in one hand and a bucket in the other. John's heart skipped a beat when he caught sight of the red veil adorning her head. He shifted his eyes: left, then right and left once more for good measure. He needed to make sure no one was watching him watch her.

He knew his behaviour broke all the rules but John couldn't help himself. Since he'd first spied the woman and her blonde child through his binoculars, he could scarcely think of anything else. It wasn't lust. John was drawn to the pair by something much deeper – a desire to turn back time.

The woman emptied the bucket of milk into a pitcher and disappeared into her house. She reappeared a minute later balancing a tray on her head. Moving gracefully, the heavy tray becoming an appendage of her tall, elegant body she made her way up to the rooftops. John basked in her every detail: the sad green eyes, the shiny black plaits peeking out from beneath her veil, the little blonde-haired girl never more than two feet from her knee. For the past week, the woman and her daughter had laid breakfast outside John and Dusty's door. And every morning, John rose early hoping to catch a glimpse of her. So far, she hadn't noticed him – which he knew was probably for the best.

John lowered his head beneath the sill as she neared. He waited to hear the rattle of the tray hitting the ground before stealing one final glance. He raised his head again. Instead of a face turned demurely away, John was stunned to discover a pair of shocked green eyes staring back at him.

'What time is it?'

John ducked his head below the window and turned his back to the wall. 'Just gone five,' he said.

Dusty sat up and rubbed his eyes. 'Good. Breakfast should be here.'

John retrieved the tray from outside. The woman was long gone. He swept the rooftops to see if she was lingering. If only they had locked eyes a moment longer – then he would have a clearer idea of what lay behind hers.

It was the usual generous spread: glasses of sweet tea with a pot of extra sugar, a pitcher of warm goats' milk, fresh bread, cheese wrapped in cloth and an assortment of fruit both fresh and dried from the village orchards. John tore a piece of bread from a flat loaf and inhaled. 'I could get used to this, you know.'

Dusty joined him at the squat table. All the furniture in the room including the chairs had sawed off legs. It was like living in a reception classroom. Dusty tucked up his knees and reached for a glass of tea. He sipped the Afghan drink and frowned. 'What I wouldn't give for a mug of builder's brew. This shite is like liquid tablet.'

John tried the tea for himself and smiled. It was indeed reminiscent of his favourite Scottish confection. 'I'm telling you, Dogrum has everything we need: food, comfortable beds . . .'

'There are no mattresses,' Dusty pointed out.

John fanned his hands before the tray. 'But the rest of the service is five star. We're living like kings here.'

Dusty cut open a pomegranate and handed half of it to John. 'Well, don't get too used to it because one way or another we'll be out of here soon.'

John waved the fruit away. 'You have it. I know they're your favourite.'

'Go on,' said Dusty. 'This could be our last decent meal – ever.'

John took the half globe and picked the red seeds from the white pith. 'Do you have any regrets?'

Dusty held the pomegranate above his mouth and squeezed. 'About what?' he said, his mouth filling with juice.

'About coming here,' said John.

Dusty swallowed and looked at John. 'Who dares wins – right? Fuck ShieldGroup, fuck SOCA, fuck Rasul and his fucking nephews and fuck those old bastards in Kamdesh if they find us guilty tomorrow.'

The *jirga* was set to take place in thirty-six hours. John, Dusty, Haider and the Majlis were leaving for Kamdesh that morning. They were travelling light: weapons, basic kit, water, some food and their *zamanat*. As anticipated, the guarantee for Haider and the two Scots was steep – seventy-five head of cattle. John and Dusty's portion, fifty cattle, equalled $1,500 – all the money they had.

After breakfast, John and Dusty headed down to the bridge. The Majlis were already there ready to go. Anvar, the old Malek, was sat atop a donkey, a round woollen flat-topped pakol covering his shiny bald head. The educated Baidullah and young Daud were standing beside him.

Twenty minutes later, there was still no sign of Haider. The Afghans in the party seemed unbothered by the delay but John was concerned. Haider was as punctual as a German rail operator. Finally, Haider emerged from his house – but he wasn't alone. Two people were following him. John recognized the pair instantly: the woman in the red veil and her daughter. A sickening thought suddenly occurred to John. Had he been watching Haider's wife?

The woman threw herself at Haider's feet, tears streaming from her eyes. Haider kicked her away and left her and the child weeping on the ground. He was visibly agitated when he joined the others on the bridge. John was anxious to hear Haider's explanation of what had just happened. But no excuses were offered. Haider didn't even apologize for making everyone wait. John had no choice but to respect his silence.

Haider quickly got down to business. He briefed John and Dusty again about the day's journey. The first leg was the most difficult in terms of terrain – three hours uphill through dense woodland. The second leg was less challenging physically but far more dangerous. They had to travel along the LanDay Sin

Road, the MSR – main supply route – for the US base in
Kamdesh. 'Before we had to worry about bandits,' Haider
explained. 'Now, we must worry about insurgents as well.'

The party climbed to the top of the terraced fields and down
the other side of the ridge. An animal track circled around a
foothill before delivering them to the base of a high mountain.
As they ascended through an ancient oak forest, wildlife stalked
the ground and the canopy overhead; a flying squirrel jumping
from branch to branch, a musk deer bolting through the under-
brush; an Ibex scraping its scythe-shaped horns against a tree
trunk. The animal noises tapered away the higher they climbed
until the earthy smell of deciduous vegetation gave way to clean
scented pines.

All morning John tried to shake the image of the woman in
the red veil falling at Haider's feet. But he couldn't get it out of
his head. He was angry with Haider for treating her so callously
and himself for caring. John tried to separate and contain his
feelings, but the more he tried, the more jumbled they became.
His desire to know what the woman was thinking when she'd
caught him looking at her only compounded the confusion. Was
she surprised by John's brazenness? Scared? Outraged? Or did
her shocked expression mask a mutual curiosity? Had he caught
her looking at him?

By nine thousand feet John's emotional skirmishes evaporated
as the stress of altitude took over. He felt nauseous and light-
headed. A week of sitting idle in Dogrum, eating unpasteurized
cheese and drinking unpurified water had left him poorly prepared for mountain climbing. John felt so ill, he feared he might
have to ask his fellow travellers to stop and rest. Luckily, Anvar
saved him from embarrassment by suggesting it first.

The old man climbed down from his donkey and stretched
his legs. He cast his aged eyes over the valleys below and spoke.

'Anvar is telling us he killed many Russians in those valleys,' said Haider.

'Really,' said John. 'We'd be honoured if he could tell us more about those times.' Haider put the question to Anvar. The old man was more than happy to oblige.

Haider translated as Anvar told the story of how he became a Mujahideen. 'In the month of Capricorn in the year 1358: 1979 to the infidel, the Russians came to Afghanistan with their tanks and their bombs . . .' he began. 'At first, they left us alone. Then one day, the Russians came to Dogrum. They rounded up all the young men and took us away. Back then I was a lion with a proud full beard and thick hair. Those bastards sheared me like a spring lamb.' He swept his wrinkled hand over his bald head, '. . . then they threw me in a cell along with a hundred others, all of us plucked like chickens. The conditions in the Russian prison were terrible. The Russians treated us worse than animals. The days were unbearable but the nights were worse. The Russian guards would take prisoners away for interrogation. The men they took never returned. The Russians killed them all in cold blood. We could hear them from our cell, screaming for mercy. After a score of days, those of us left alive all swore on the Koran that if we escaped, we would start a revolution and drive the infidel out of our lands. And by God's infinite grace and wisdom, we did. Ten of us escaped the Russian prison. Allah guided us to the mountains to fight alongside our Mujahid brothers. For months we fought in the same clothes we had worn in prison. We fought until they turned to rags. But did we care for our own comfort? We did not! We were fighting for our freedom. We were fighting for the glory of Allah. My brother-in-law Mohammed, Daud's father, was martyred in Kunar. So was the son of a doctor from Mirdesh, a man named Ali. Dozens of Kom men died heroically in battle.'

The old man bowed his head as he remembered his fallen comrades.

'In the West, we were told that Hizb-i-Islami drove the Soviets out of Afghanistan. But listening to you, Malek, it sounds like they have taken credit for your bravery,' John said tactfully.

Anvar's old face filled with resentment. 'Lies,' he said through Haider. 'Propaganda. Hizb-i-Islami say it was they who began the jihad against the Soviets. But they did not. It was the Kom people. We are the true Mujahideen. Hizb-i-Islami used our revolution to line their own pockets. They went to Pakistan asking for weapons to fight the Russians. The Pakistanis gave them bullets – good bullets, but Hizb-i-Islami never sent them to us. They sold them and kept the money and then sent us cheap bullets half filled with gunpowder.' Anvar shook his head. 'The smoke from those bullets would give away our positions and the Russians would shoot back with mortars and grenades. Many Mujahideen were martyred this way. But, we still won many battles.' The memory of victory invigorated the old man. He raised his finger to the sky. 'We kept fighting until by the grace of Allah the Russian infidel was driven from our land for all eternity!'

John drew strength from Anvar's tale. If the old man could hump it in those hills for months on end with crap ammo and one change of clothes, John could work through a tiny bout of altitude sickness. His nausea subsided.

The group made their way down the other side of the mountain to the LanDay Sin Road. They followed the MSR for half a mile before moving up onto a track which paralleled it. Every twenty minutes or so, the sound of low-revving engines straining in first or second gear would sound behind them. John and Dusty would peer out from behind the curtain of trees and look down on the road thirty feet below. Most of the vehicles were civilian 'jinglies': flatbed trucks with rows of brass chains strung along the chassis to ward off evil spirits. But a fair amount was US military – Humvees ferrying troops to and from the base near Kamdesh. The two Scots couldn't believe how vulnerable the military convoys were to attack. Fully armoured vehicles were too heavy for the Yanks to transport up to Nuristan by helicopter, so the troops were making do with partially armoured Hummers. Travelling at low speeds, the convoys inevitably announced their presence miles before they came into view. Insurgents had all the time in the world to get IEDs into position and detonate them.

The clanging of brass chains signalled the approach of local vehicles. They were travelling west toward Kamdesh. Dusty looked at them through his binos. 'Three trucks,' he said.

'Civilian?' asked John.

Dusty confirmed with a nod of his head. 'Not sure what they're transporting though. Everything's in sea containers.'

They waited for the convoy to move up the road before resuming their journey. Suddenly, the bang of a rocket leaving a launcher and the slam of a missile hitting its target rumbled across the valley. Screeching brakes and metal crunching metal followed. John and Dusty whipped out their binos. One of the flatbed trucks was lying on its side with thick, black smoke billowing from a hole blown through its sea container.

A group of men armed with RPGs and AKs came dashing out of the tree line. Splitting themselves into groups, they rounded up the truck drivers and forced them to their knees by the side of the road.

'What is happening?' Haider whispered.

'The convoy was attacked,' said John. 'It could be insurgents. It could be bandits. I'm not sure.'

Dusty scanned the forest for more armed men while John kept watch on the road. The assailants moved from driver to driver, patting them down and confiscating their wallets and mobile phones. One of them gathered up the phones and checked them individually.

'They took the drivers' mobiles,' said John. 'I think they're using them to gather intelligence.' One of the armed men pulled a knife from his waistcoat and paced back and forth in front of the kneeling men. The drivers were shaking. The man with the knife clearly revelled in their fear. He stopped in front of the middle driver and gestured to two of his armed companions. They seized the driver and lifted the trembling man to his feet. The man with the knife pressed his blade to the driver's jugular.

'Looks like one of the drivers is going to get it,' said John. Dusty turned his binos on the scene.

Sweat streamed down the driver's face. His lips were moving rapidly – perhaps in prayer. The man with the knife lifted his right elbow, preparing to drag the blade across the driver's neck. At the final moment, he grabbed the driver's jaw and shoved it to one side exposing an ear. The driver let out a blood-curdling scream as his ear was slowly sliced from his head. His assailant prolonged the torture as long as possible, dragging the blade back and forth like a saw. When he finished, the driver cupped his head with his hand and fell to the ground, his fingers unable to contain the red deluge. The knife wielder threw the severed ear onto the smoking truck and moved on to the next driver.

Dusty winced with disgust. 'Bloody animals.'

'May I take a look?' Haider asked.

Dusty handed his binos over. 'They are not bandits,' said Haider. 'They are insurgents. The trucks were carrying supplies to the US military base. Those drivers are lucky. Today the insurgents take ears. Next time, it will be heads.'

Haider explained the situation to Anvar, Baidullah and Daud. Daud spoke. Haider answered him forcefully.

'What's the matter?' asked John.

'Daud believes we should intervene,' said Haider. 'I told him it is not necessary. The insurgents do not intend to kill the drivers, only to warn them.'

The sound of another driver howling reverberated through the pass. 'Tell him we'd all love to take those fuckers out, but they've got us outgunned and we don't know the area,' said John.

'I agree,' said Dusty. 'They're scum but let's not lose our cool.'

Haider relayed the Scots' position to Daud. It only fed the restless Nuristani's hunger for battle. Daud grew more insistent.

'Tell him to shut up before he gives away our position,' said John.

Daggers flew from Daud's eyes. He raised his voice in protest. It was enough to prompt Anvar to intervene. A few words from the old man and Daud shut up. The Malek of Dogrum had delivered the final verdict. This was not their fight.

Chapter 33

Lieutenant Colonel Howard clicked the folder labelled *Press Releases ISAF Casualties*. Two sub-files appeared on the screen: *Non-Hostile Death Notices* and *Hostile Death Notices*. Howard opened the folder titled 'hostile death notices'. His inner cauldron simmered as he counted the number of documents inside. At the start of June, the folder had contained only one – a template. He opened it and printed a hard copy.

Template 1

ISAF service member killed in southern Afghanistan

KABUL, Afghanistan (date) – An International
Security Assistance Force service member was killed
during a hostile incident in southern Afghanistan.

'My sincere condolences to the family of this brave
service member,' said (insert name). 'This ISAF
soldier was fighting for a safe and secure Afghanistan.
We will always remember his sacrifice.'

It is ISAF policy not to release the nationality of any casualty prior to the relevant national authority doing so. Next of kin have been notified.

Template 2

ISAF service member killed in eastern Afghanistan

KABUL, Afghanistan (date) – An International Security Assistance Force service member was killed during a hostile incident in eastern Afghanistan.

'I offer my condolences to the family of this brave service member,' said (insert name). 'We will always remember the sacrifices of our service members as we continue to support the people of Afghanistan.'

It is ISAF policy not to release the nationality of any casualty prior to the relevant national authority doing so. Next of kin have been notified.

The sound of spitting ink cartridges was interrupted by knuckles rapping on the door. 'Hey there, Pinky.'

Howard breathed deeply and reminded himself that the annoying nickname was a term of endearment. 'Walter,' he smiled. 'Right on time as always. Please do come in.'

Raleigh took a seat on a leather sofa positioned under a window. 'You got that letter for me?'

'Just printed it off.' Howard handed the document to him.

'Much obliged,' said Raleigh, donning a pair of reading glasses. He quickly read Howard's handiwork. 'You Brits sure have a way with words. I could never write anything half this good. Mind if I change the quotes to make them sound more American?'

'Do whatever you like,' said Howard. 'I would caution you, though, to be sure to rotate the templates regularly. One would not want to appear . . . callous after all.'

'Thanks for the warning.' Raleigh removed his reading glasses and sighed. 'You know, I try to write something unique and heartfelt for every soldier who dies, but sometimes you just run out of ways to say I'm sorry. Remember the situation we had last year in Kunar?'

'I vaguely recall it,' said Howard.

'Four Navy SEALS got pinned down on a mountaintop by insurgents. Sixteen soldiers – eight SEALS and eight Special Aviation Ops – were sent in to extract them. It all went to rat shit. Their chopper got shot down and by the time the dust cleared there were nineteen soldiers dead. Nineteen obituaries in one day. Can you imagine?'

Howard counted the hostile death notices crowding his computer. He turned the screen to Raleigh. 'I've written eleven press releases for British soldiers since June. All of them were killed in action in Helmund.'

Raleigh nodded respectfully. 'Your boys are in it up to their necks there.'

The trite comment nourished Howard's simmering anger. He walked out from behind his desk and looked his American counterpart in the eye. 'They need reinforcements, Walter.'

Raleigh bowed his head and raised his hands. 'That's way above my grade. And yours too I might add.'

'Forget our pay grades for the moment,' Howard said calmly. 'Let's say, hypothetically, it was within our power to influence policy. It's become abundantly clear that the situation in Helmund is far worse than anyone anticipated. If the Coalition is to have any hope of securing the province, it must triple, or even better – quadruple the amount of troops there immediately.'

Raleigh played along. 'I'm not saying that I agree or disagree with that statement. But the fact is, boots on the ground are a precious commodity, Pinky.'

'All the more reason the Coalition should use the ones we have in theatre to better effect,' Howard countered.

Raleigh's eyes slanted. 'I get the feeling you aren't talking hypothetically any more. What are you after?'

Howard paused. The silence was strategic. He was hoping it would lend greater weight to his request. 'Lobby your superiors. Tell them they need to suspend operations in the north-east provinces and redeploy troops to Helmund.'

Raleigh shook his head back and forth. 'You are living in a fantasy world because there ain't no way that will happen.'

'It won't if we all remain silent.' Howard appealed to Raleigh's reason. 'What is the point of having troops in the Kunar–Nuristan corridor when the Taliban have regrouped in Helmund and Kandahar? That's where the fight is, Walter. Mark my words, this war will be won or lost in the south. The Coalition needs to focus all of its energies there now.'

'Try telling it to the Pentagon,' said Raleigh. 'Or didn't you get the memo? We're all about the hearts and minds right now. That's why our FOBs in Kunar–Nuristan are doing PRTs instead of fighting. Which reminds me, our mutual friend General Rasul is busting our balls to make him governor of the whole goddamn province.'

Howard felt a burning in the pit of his stomach. 'Don't tell me you'll bow to such an outrageous demand?'

'It depends. There are a lot of Afghans who don't want it to happen. Rasul isn't exactly lacking in the enemies department you know,' said Raleigh. 'But if Washington thinks it will help win the war, believe me, it won't be long before we're all calling him Governor Rasul.'

The fire in Howard's gut grew more intense. 'How can the US possibly support Rasul's ambitions?'

Raleigh jerked back. 'I thought you'd be psyched. If Rasul becomes governor, he won't be your problem any more. Governors deal directly with Karzai and Karzai deals directly with us. ISAF can wash its hands of the old bastard.'

'I admit, from a purely selfish perspective, it is appealing,' said Howard. 'But making Rasul more powerful is in none of our interests. He's a warlord for heaven's sake.'

'Everyone in Afghanistan has skeletons in their closet, Pinky. In fact the more skeletons they got, the more we need them onside. If Rasul cooperates with us, then Nuristan is ours.'

'Do you really think a man like Rasul will help you achieve your objectives?' Howard could no longer contain his anger. His reserve abandoned him. 'The United States has learned nothing from Helmund. My God, man, it wasn't the British who allowed the province to fall to pieces. You Yanks were all so bloody convinced that the great healing powers of democracy would win everyone over that it never occurred to you that you might actually have to fight to win this war. Do you know how many US troops were in Helmund before the British took over?'

Raleigh lowered his eyes. 'I won't deny we could have done more.'

'Three hundred,' Howard blasted. 'Three hundred soldiers to police an area the size of Wales. And that went on for four years, Walter. Four years you gave the Taliban to regroup and rearm.' Howard picked up a pen clicked it rapidly and threw it down on his desk. He ran his hands down his face but the stain of rage was too deep to wipe away. 'And you wonder why our lads are *up to their necks* as you put it.'

Raleigh didn't respond immediately. He looked terribly wounded by Howard's words. 'You know, Pinky. I'm not stupid.'

'I never accused you of lacking intelligence, Walter.'

'Come on,' said Raleigh. 'Just say it. You think I'm thick as fuck.'

Once again, Howard regretted his loss of control. No good ever came from showing emotion. 'It was not my intention to attack you personally.'

'I deserve it.' Howard wasn't sure how to interpret Raleigh's statement. Americans were so rarely self-deprecating. 'You don't have to lecture me about how we fucked up in Helmund,' Raleigh continued. 'Or how we're fucking everything up still. But there's nothing I can do about it, Pinky. In case you haven't noticed, I'm not paid to think. I'm paid to toe the line. My orders are to stay on message. And right now that message is things in Afghanistan are just fine, thank you very much.' Howard raised his hands like an evangelical preacher delivering a sermon. 'Praise be to God, Lord Jesus we're winning the war, hallelujah!'

The theatrics dissolved the tension between the two men. Howard felt strangely moved by his counterpart's candour. 'You're not the only person in this room guilty of complicity,' Howard murmured.

The confession emboldened Raleigh further still. 'I don't know if I ever told you this, Pinky, but my daddy fought in Vietnam. He wasn't an officer, mind. Daddy was a grunt – a fightin' man. He used to tell me that the only people who had a say in the way that war was fought were politicians and CIA spooks. The boys on the ground had no voice. So I thought that if I went to college and joined up as an officer, I could maybe keep history from repeating itself. And look what I've become: another yes man following orders handed down by suits in Washington who care more about opinion polls than the lives of their men and women in uniform. Politicians have no clue about long-term objectives. They think this war is about one thing and one thing only – hunting bin Laden. I swear if I hear the words "high value target" come out of one more snot-nosed congressman's mouth, I'll lose it. I got patrols stuck on mountaintops for weeks at a time going black on food and water while they search for a needle in a haystack. They get no support; hell, they aren't even trained to fight a guerrilla war. But our generals keep sending them on a wild goose chase so they can tell the politicians back home that we're hot on the trail.' Raleigh looked out the window. 'If I had half the courage my daddy had I'd quit over this bullshit.'

Howard was speechless. He had no idea that the burden he shouldered silently was shared by someone else. 'I have considered that very option more times than I can count, Walter. But, inevitably, I find myself asking what good would come from it?'

'I hear you,' said Raleigh. 'Who gives a fuck if a lieutenant colonel resigns. But I have to believe that God wouldn't have brought me here unless I was meant to do something good. One day, his purpose will reveal itself.'

The turn toward spirituality snapped the frail bond between the two officers. Whatever faith Howard had possessed was lost. 'How do you keep yourself sane in the meantime?'

Raleigh held up the death announcements. 'I do my job.'

Chapter 34

The Great Hall in Kamdesh dwarfed every other building in the humble provincial capital. Thirty-odd men dressed in traditional clothing, turbans and pakols gathered outside the elaborately carved wooden doorway, waiting for the *jirga* to begin. The crowd parted for an old man with a long white beard and knitted white skullcap. 'It is the mullah,' said Haider. 'The most senior religious figure in the valley.' The door opened with great ceremony and the mullah went inside, followed by the local Maleks and their respective Majlis. The opposing parties were the last to enter: the plaintiffs, four men dressed in black turbans and robes representing General Rasul's clan and, finally, the defendants.

Anvar disappeared into the Great Hall accompanied by Daud and Baidullah. 'Are you ready, my friends?' Haider asked. John and Dusty nodded in the affirmative. Their expressions suggested otherwise. 'Do not be nervous,' Haider assured them. 'Nowhere in the world will you find a court of law as honest and incorruptible as the *jirga*. No man is considered lesser than another here. All are equal. It is, in the words of the West, a true democracy.' Haider placed a hand on each of their backs. 'Have faith,' he said.

Inside the Great Hall was one enormous room with no dividing walls. Hand-woven, thick-piled carpets covered the floor.

Pillows wrapped in hand-stitched red and blue kilims lined the perimeter. The most striking feature though was the carvings adorning the wooden support beams – flowering curls of calligraphy, parallel rows of perfectly symmetrical pin wheels, intricate geometrical designs. John nodded to a vertical swathe of Arabic script etched into the lintel above the doorway. 'What does it say?'

'Do not veil the truth with falsehood, nor conceal the truth knowingly,' said Haider.

'Is that an old Nuristani proverb?' asked John.

'It is from Koran.' Haider pointed to the other verses around the room. 'All of these are from Koran. It is a symbol of our willing submission to Allah, the one true God.'

Dusty whispered to John. 'It's a bloody sharia court.'

Haider overheard him. 'It is not a sharia court. The ways of the *jirga* date back to when my people lived in darkness, as pagans worshipping idols. We converted to Islam only a hundred years ago. That is where the name Nuristan comes from. It literally means land of light.'

Boys entered the Great Hall carrying trays laden with tea, fruit and nuts. The various Majlis staked their patches and sat down to eat. The groups did not interact with one another. There was no pumping of hands, man hugs, flying kisses or other hollow gestures. Contact was limited to dignified nods and the rare smile. John canvassed the faces, looking for flashes of contempt and other signs of long-simmering hatred. It was there – but it was tempered by mutual respect. John felt instantly at home. It was just like being on a rugby pitch.

The mullah called for silence. The voices died and he launched into a brief speech. As he spoke, Haider translated. 'The mullah is welcoming everyone to the *jirga* and inviting the Maleks to share news of their villages.'

'News?' asked Dusty. 'What does that have to do with us?'

'It is not connected with our case,' Haider explained. 'We do not have television or satellite telephones here. There is very little communication between the villages. This is an opportunity to share information.'

As the Maleks spoke, Haider offered a running commentary of their remarks. They all opened with variations of the same greeting. 'Peace be upon you, mullah . . . God is great . . . may he bless this *jirga* and all who gather here . . . it is a great honour to represent the noble village of . . . we will respect the findings of this great and honourable *jirga* . . .' The news items from the villages were more compelling. Apparently, Dogrum wasn't the only one that had been attacked in recent weeks. Report after report painted a picture of a valley under siege. The Malek of Kamdesh described a battle between insurgents and US forces stationed near his village. 'The insurgents in the mountains fired a rocket into the American base. The Americans responded by firing their big gun at the insurgents.' John took 'big gun' to mean some form of artillery piece. 'The insurgents ran to our village for protection,' the Malek continued. 'We told them to leave but they threatened to cut our throats and rape our women if we did not give them asylum. The cowards commandeered a house with a family inside. The family tried to flee, but there was not enough time. An American helicopter flew over and fired at it. A thousand bullets it unleashed; like fingers of fire reaching down from the sky. The Americans killed the insurgents but the family was hurt as well. Several were wounded and one died, may God favour him.'

There were also stories of retribution for cooperating with US forces. One Malek described the fate of an elder who had agreed to allow US troops to train a police force for his village.

'Three days after signing the contract with the Americans our Malek was kidnapped. His body was found near the Pakistan border with a note pinned to his clothing. "Don't work with Americans or this will happen to you!"'

When it was Anvar's turn to speak, the mood grew more intense. John had no way of knowing whether it was the old man's standing in the valley or the fact that he had two foreigners with him; but everyone appeared intensely inter-ested in what Anvar had to say. He began with a detailed account of the first attack on Dogrum. 'We tried to defend ourselves against the insurgents but we were unsuccessful. They had many Kalashnikovs and their knowledge of the bat-tlefield was very advanced.' A lone tear streamed down Anvar's face as he lowered his chin and listed the dead. Then, like a stage actor with an audience hanging on his every word, he paused, shook off his sorrow and raised his head. 'But Allah in his merciful wisdom sent us two saviours.' He pointed to John and Dusty.

The room erupted in whispers. A member of Rasul's clan – a ferocious-looking character with an eyepatch and a brass dagger slung around his waist swamped the din with an angry tirade. His rant was riddled with the words 'kafir', 'Gishmoni' and 'Imra'. The majority of the room appeared to agree with him. Haider chose not to translate the outburst, but John and Dusty knew it couldn't be good.

'What's he saying?' asked John.

'He is a donkey,' said Haider, as if the one-eyed man's com-ments weren't worth relaying.

'Why does he keep repeating the word "kafir"?' asked Dusty.

'Kafir are non-believers,' Haider said quickly. 'Infidel.'

'So he's talking about us.' Dusty gave John a worried look. 'Who are Imra and Gishmoni?'

'Imra, Gish and Moni,' Haider corrected. 'They are pagan gods: Imra, the god of creation, Moni, his deputy and Gish, the god of war.'

Dusty's eyes simmered with suspicion. 'I thought this was the land of bloody light.'

Haider dismissed his concerns. 'His exact words were "These men are not saviours. They are infidel demons; Gish and Moni sent by the devil Imra to destroy our people and steal our souls."'

Dusty turned to John. 'We're fucked.'

'Do not place any importance on this fool,' Haider insisted. 'He is all piss and wind as you would say. Besides, it sounds much worse in English.'

'It sounds pretty fucking bad in your language too,' Dusty hissed.

The mullah called for silence. The one-eyed man ceased talking and Anvar continued his story. 'The insurgents came again at dawn; this time armed with rockets as well as Kalashnikovs. Dogrum fought bravely but again we were overwhelmed. We prayed to Allah to intervene, to pluck victory from the jaws of defeat. And Allah in his mercy answered our prayers.' Anvar described how John and Dusty swept through the fields, picking off insurgents one by one. He made great show of the fact that the two Scots left the last kill – the final glory – to the fighters of Dogrum. 'They fought not like two men but twenty,' said Anvar. 'With Allah as my witness I declare these men are not like other infidel. They are great warriors sent by Allah to save Dogrum!'

This time, instead of objections, Anvar's words were greeted with nods of approval. Others followed and soon a wave of unvoiced endorsement swept the room. The representatives of Rasul's clan clearly sensed the sentiment turning against them.

When Anvar sat down, they asked the mullah to call the murder trial to order immediately.

The mullah agreed to hear the case without delay. He called for the submission of *zamanat*. John and Dusty handed Haider their 1,500 dollars which he gave to Anvar along with a promissory note for his share; twenty-five cattle – almost a third of Dogrum's total herd. Before handing the money to the mullah, Anvar invited Rasul's clan to count it – a formality, Haider explained that was rarely acted upon. The room was collectively shocked when Rasul's clan took up the offer. 'Who are they to question our integrity?' Haider muttered.

As Rasul's clan divided the bills into piles, Haider explained again how the guarantee worked. 'The *zamanat* binds both parties to the *rogha-jura* – the final decision of the *jirga*. If a party withdraws from the process for any reason, they forfeit their payment and it will be used to fund a project to benefit the whole community.'

'Didn't you say that if we're found guilty Rasul's clan not only gets to keep our money but can demand more?' Dusty's tone implied his faith in the process was dwindling fast.

Haider turned his palms up. 'Inshallah, the *jirga* will find us innocent.'

'They better bloody well find us innocent or it won't be the Rasuls taking your head from your shoulders, mate,' said Dusty.

John shushed him. 'If the *jirga* finds us guilty, the *zamanat* should be enough. Fifteen hundred dollars and twenty-five cattle is a king's ransom here.'

The money was counted and given to the mullah. The Rasul clan then submitted their *zamanat*. It was modest by comparison – a note promising thirty head of cattle, just nine hundred dollars' worth. 'No double standard there,' Dusty said sarcastically. John shushed him again.

The mullah took the Rasuls' payment and invited them to argue their case. The one-eyed man with the dagger spoke on behalf of the clan. Thin on facts, his testimony was designed to play on the emotions of all assembled. 'How proud we were of our two sons when they were given the great honour of fighting the scourge of the poppy,' he began.

Haider editorialized as he translated. 'Who does that donkey think he is fooling? Everyone knows the Rasuls control the opium trade through Nuristan.'

The one-eyed man continued. 'When our sons left to receive their training in Kabul, they carried the hopes of all the Kshto people on their shoulders.' The man denied that Rasul's nephews had any ties with Hizb-i-Islami or any other militant group. 'They were honest men, proud Kshto and loyal Nuristanis. Their only desire was to bring peace and prosperity to this land. Their hearts were pure.' He pointed to Haider. 'But this Kom man's heart is dark and filled with evil. He works with the infidel. His purse is fat with their money. He cares not for the Nuristani people. He wants only for himself and as Allah says, he who wants only for himself is a bad person destined for hell. His greed is proof that his heart is not pure. It burns with the hatred of old blood feuds – wars that have driven so many of my people from this valley. By the grace of Allah, we have learned to live peacefully with our Kom brothers. But not everyone wishes peace. This Kom man saw an opportunity to dishonour the sons of Kshto.' The one-eyed man switched his focus to John and Dusty. 'The infidel were complicit in his treachery. They expelled our sons from their studies without cause and spat in the face of all Kshto.' The man circled the room; joining his one good eye with everyone's as he passed. 'The treacherous troublemaker and his infidel accomplices will tell you they are innocent. They will tell you that they killed our sons in self-defence. But you must ask yourselves – who started this battle? In word and deed our sons were attacked first. They had no choice but to defend their honour and that of our people by confronting this Kom and his infidel masters.' The man stopped and raised a finger toward heaven. 'Allah demands justice. I ask this great and noble *jirga* to do Allah's will. Give us blood for blood, lest the feud between our tribes ignite once again to the detriment of all.'

The one-eyed man sat down. Whispers engulfed the room once more. John didn't need a translator to tell him what they were saying. Everyone's face was pinched with concern. Not surprising since the argument they'd just heard carried an implicit warning: find the infidel guilty or there will be war.

Anvar did his best to repair the damage. Speaking on behalf of Haider, John and Dusty, he presented the facts to the *jirga*: from the nephews' confessed involvement in Hizb-i-Islami to the shoot-out on the Jalalabad Road. His manner was confident and his argument persuasive. 'I urge this noble and honourable *jirga* to trust in Allah's wisdom. There was no deliberate act of murder. The deaths in question were the result of self-defence, a right which Allah bestows on honest men.' He finished by asking the *jirga* to remain steadfast and courageous. 'Do not be intimidated by threats of war and discord,' he warned. 'It is man who made us Kom and Kshto, not Allah. And it is only by his grace that our tribes have laid their differences to rest. If another blood feud ensnares our two peoples, it will not be Allah's will but the will of Kshto agitators and their Hizb-i-Islami masters who wish to profit from our quarrels.'

When Anvar finished, the mullah asked the two parties to wait outside the Great Hall while the *jirga* made its decision. The deliberations continued for the rest of the day. Later that afternoon, the *jirga* adjourned without rendering a verdict.

The sun sank, taking John and Dusty's hopes with it. The two Scots ate sparingly and bedded down for a sleepless night. 'If they thought we were innocent, they would have said so by now,' said Dusty.

John motioned to Haider. He was lying beside them, snoring. 'It can't be all that hopeless,' John whispered. 'Look at him, sleeping like a baby.'

'That's because he thinks there's a life after this one.' Dusty lifted his head and stared hard at Haider. 'Do you think he was telling the truth?'

John was swift to respond. 'Yes.' His answer was emphatic. 'I think Haider believes the *jirga* will be fair to us.'

Dusty lowered his head. 'I mean about Rasul's nephews. Do you think Haider lied about them being Hizb-i-Islami?'

John was taken aback. 'Why would he do that?'

'Maybe that one-eyed fucker was right,' said Dusty. 'Maybe Haider was using us to stick it to his old enemies.'

'Don't be ridiculous,' said John. 'He wouldn't screw us like that. Haider's our mate.'

'Is he?' said Dusty. 'Look at him. He's nothing like he was in Kabul.'

John refused to indulge Dusty's accusations. 'Haider would have been way better off without us here. He could have left us back in Kabul, you know.'

'Maybe he had another reason for bringing us here,' Dusty countered.

'Like what?' John challenged.

Dusty searched for an explanation. 'I don't know,' he mumbled.

'I think the stress is fucking with your head,' said John. 'Haider's put his reputation and possibly his life on the line to try and save our arses. You should be thanking him, not questioning his motives.'

Dusty was far from chastised. 'I'll thank him when we're found innocent.'

By morning, John and Dusty were resigned to their fate. Like condemned men eating a last meal, they spent their final hours doing what they enjoyed most – taking the piss out of each other. 'If anyone's bloody Imra it's me,' said Dusty.

'Are you hell,' said John. 'Imra's the god of creation. All you're good at is shooting and blowing shit up.'

'No one called either of you Imra,' Haider interrupted. 'It was Gish and Moni. And it is not wise to keep repeating those names,' he warned. 'It offends Allah.'

Dusty looked at Haider and burst out laughing.

Haider was indignant. 'You dare mock our beliefs?'

Dusty answered with more laughter. John made a half-hearted attempt to quiet him. 'Come on now.' He turned to Haider. 'He's just having a laugh.'

Haider looked at John earnestly. 'You are a great warrior and a great friend. Allah knows this. You must believe he will protect us.'

Later that morning, they received word that the *jirga* had made its decision. The parties were called to the Great Hall. The air inside it was thick with bad breath and body odour. It reeked of discord. 'Are you prepared to abide by the findings of this *jirga*?' asked the mullah.

'We are,' said Anvar.

'We are,' said Rasul's people.

'Prepare for reconciliation,' said the mullah.

John and Dusty raised their chins, determined to meet death fearlessly.

'It is the *rogha-jura*,' said the mullah, 'that no murder was committed.'

Rasul's clan erupted in protest. John and Dusty froze with disbelief. Haider grabbed John and hugged him. '*Allahu akbar!*' he said.

'Silence!' called the mullah. The room settled down. 'No murder was committed but it is also the ruling of this *jirga* that an offence has been committed and the defendants must pay.'

Dusty clenched his fists. 'Here comes the stitch-up,' he said.

'The honour of the Rasul family has been tarnished by the acts of the defendants,' the mullah declared. 'It is the ruling of this *jirga* that the defendants must pay a fine in the amount of one hundred cattle.'

The fine hit John like a wrecking ball. Their *zamanat* wouldn't cover it all. 'Tell them we've given them all the money we have,' he said to Haider.

The blood drained from Haider's face. 'This is highly unusual,' he said.

'They don't want our money,' Dusty hissed. 'They want our heads. The bastards are just being back-handed about it.'

Haider spoke to Anvar. The old man addressed the mullah. 'The fine is unreasonable. Surely the *zamanat* should be enough?' Anvar reasoned. 'The foreigners have no possessions and they have no more money to offer.'

The leader of the Rasul clan spoke. 'If they lack money and cattle they must pay with blood.'

Anvar appealed to the mullah. 'Honour is precious but these men should not be made to pay with their lives.'

'The decision of the *jirga* is final,' said the mullah. 'The debt must be settled. We must have harmony between Kom and Kshto.'

The one-eyed man unsheathed his dagger. 'We demand retribution for the honour of our slain kinsmen and for all Kshto!'

Anvar raised a hand to the one-eyed man. 'Withdraw your

blade,' he commanded, conjuring a voice from his days on the battlefield. John was awestruck by the old warrior's presence. 'The village of Dogrum will pay the additional fine – twenty-five cattle. The debt is settled.'

Rasul's clan baulked at the suggestion. 'Your village is poor. You would let your people starve to protect the infidel? You are not fit to be Malek!' They beseeched the mullah. 'The fine must benefit the community, not destroy it. It is not acceptable that the infidel walk free while Dogrum's children go hungry. The infidel must pay with their lives.'

The mullah held up his hand to quiet the Rasuls. He addressed Anvar. 'They are correct. Your village cannot suffer to save these men. If blood is the only way to settle the debt, then that is how it must be.'

Anvar looked at John and Dusty. Suddenly, the old man's eyes ignited. 'Our village will not suffer, Mullah. On the contrary, by repaying their debt to us, the foreigners will make Dogrum stronger.'

The one-eyed man mocked the suggestion. 'How can the infidel repay you without resorting to banditry?'

Anvar bowed respectfully to the Mullah. 'The foreigners are rich with knowledge. They can teach us many things.'

The one-eyed man spat on the floor. 'The infidels' knowledge is corrupt and worthless.'

The Mullah silenced him. 'What can these men teach you that would equal twenty-five head of cattle?'

'What they know is worth a thousand head of cattle,' Anvar declared. Whispers circled the room once more. Anvar revelled in it. He raised his finger and pointed to the two Scots. 'They will teach us how to defend ourselves.'

Chapter 35

Dogrum's weapons and ammunition were laid out on Anvar's balcony, awaiting inspection. John and Dusty inventoried the pathetic arsenal: four Russian Makarov pistols, four rusting AK-47s with old empty magazines, ten newer AKs with fifty magazines – most of them depleted as well; one Russian RPD light machine gun with a single 200 round belt, and one RPG-7 launcher with no rounds.

John turned to Haider. 'Are you sure this is everything?'

'Yes,' said Haider.

Dusty picked up a Makarov, put the safety catch on and removed the magazine. He opened the slide and looked inside the chamber. 'The firing pin's sticking out.' He threw the weapon down. 'That's one for the decommissioned pile.'

Anvar was offended by Dusty's cavalier treatment of the pistol. He protested from his perch on a cushion. The old man looked terribly frail. The journey to Kamdesh and the strain of the *jirga* had aged him ten years.

'What's his problem?' asked Dusty.

'You treated that weapon as if it were garbage,' said Haider.

Dusty was unapologetic. 'Tell Anvar if the firing pin is protruding and a round is chambered the pistol could fire accidentally. It's not safe to use.'

'Don't lecture me on the consequences of a faulty firing pin,' said Haider. 'It does not excuse your lack of respect.'

'Wind your neck in,' said Dusty.

John inserted himself between the pair. 'He's just trying to be thorough,' he assured Haider. John pulled Dusty aside. 'Try to be more sensitive, will you?'

Dusty examined the remaining pistols. One by one, he rejected them. 'They're all rubbish. You can forget about teaching pistol work.'

'Could you explain the situation to Anvar?' John asked Haider.

The old man took the news badly. 'Anvar says those pistols have been proven in battle.' Haider adjusted his voice, indicating he was now speaking for himself. 'You must understand that pistols are highly prized among our people. They are a symbol of status.'

John appreciated the concern. 'Please tell Anvar we have no doubts these pistols have served Dogrum well in the past. But they have become very dangerous. You're lucky your fighters haven't accidentally shot themselves or each other. If they want to carry them for show, I'll allow it. But they are no longer fit for battle.'

Haider put the proposal to Anvar. The old man accepted John's terms.

John and Dusty moved on to the AKs. Dusty stood over the newer rifles reclaimed from the insurgents who attacked Dogrum. 'These are in fine nick.' He gestured to the four beaten-up AKs and then at John. 'Those look in worse shape than you,' he joked.

John kneeled down, picked up one of the older rifles and moved the safety catch to safe. 'Don't judge a book by its cover,' he said. Holding the weapon firmly with his right hand, John wrapped his left hand around the magazine, gripped the front with his fingers and flipped the magazine release catch with his thumb. The magazine clung to its housing, indicating it had not been properly maintained.

'Stuck is it?' Dusty taunted.

John wrestled the magazine out and passed it over his shoulder to Dusty. 'Shut up and check that, will you?' While Dusty emptied and stripped the magazine, John made the AK safe for further inspection. He flicked the safety catch down one click to automatic, rolled the rifle to the right and cocked it. A bullet kicked out of the chamber and fell into his hand. 'How's that magazine?'

Dusty held up a thin piece of zigzagged metal. 'The spring's shot.' He turned to Haider. 'Have you had many stoppages with these weapons?'

'Yes,' Haider confirmed.

'Have you lot ever bothered to empty the magazines?' Dusty asked.

Haider translated the question for Anvar. The old man grinned. 'According to Anvar, they have been emptied many times into the enemies of our people.'

Dusty smiled despite himself. 'I mean apart from that?'

The old man shook his head no.

Dusty walked over to Anvar and showed him the spring. 'See how long this is?' He tugged the ends. 'See how loose? The tension is shot. That's what happens when you keep the magazines loaded all the time. If the springs don't get a chance to expand once in a while they forget how and stop working.' Anvar took the spring from Dusty and examined it.

'We can make do without the old magazines,' said John. 'I don't know what we're going to do about ammo though.'

'By my count we have nine full magazines for fourteen AKs,' said Dusty.

John flipped the AK in his hands and looked down the barrel. 'Make that thirteen.' He waved Haider over and invited him to have a look. 'See those pock marks? The barrel's practically shot through.' John laid the AK next to the decommissioned pistols and magazines. 'How the hell are we supposed to train twenty-odd fighters when we can't even arm them all?'

Haider explained the situation to Anvar. 'Our fighters will share weapons,' the old man declared.

'This isn't the ANA.' John rubbed the back of his neck. 'Does Dogrum have any cash set aside or valuables to sell? Anything to buy more weapons and ammo?'

'There is nothing,' said Haider. 'Our most valuable assets were cattle and we barely have enough left to provide milk, let alone meat for the winter.'

Dusty spoke to John. 'Could I have a word with you?' He looked at Haider. 'Alone?' He waited for Haider to join Anvar at the far end of the balcony before continuing. 'What are you doing?'

'We need more weapons and ammo if we're going to train these people right,' said John.

'Even if we had money for new weapons, the clock is ticking.' Dusty nodded to the mountains in the distance. 'I don't know about you, but meat or no meat, I'm not keen on getting snowed in here for the winter. Let's just work with what we have, train these lads up with dry drills and get the hell back to civilization.'

John wouldn't have it. 'These people put everything on the line for us. We can't just play at teaching them how to defend themselves. They need proper weapons and live-fire exercises.'

'I want to do right by them too. But the situation is what it is. There's no point in drawing it out,' said Dusty.

'The only thing the insurgents have over this village is

firepower,' John insisted. 'If we don't have enough weapons we'll make more. We never had enough kit in the Regiment. Hell, during the First Gulf War we were making Claymores out of ice-cream cartons and dockyard confetti. We can do the same here with plastic containers and petrol.'

Dusty ticked off the flaws in John's plan. 'We've got no det cord, no cable and no way of initiating them. Look around, mate. This place is stuck in the Dark Ages.'

John walked to the edge of the balcony. Looking down past the bridge into the deep, rocky ravine, he catalogued Dogrum's raw materials: wood, ropes, rocks, boulders, animal skins, plastic containers and a few scraps of metal. If the situation called for slingshots and catapults, he'd be sorted. As much as John hated to admit it, Dusty was right. The only thing that had changed in Dogrum since the Middle Ages were the foreigners trying to control it.

John looked longingly at the weapons taken from the insurgents. If only he could get his hands on more of them. Then Dogrum's fighters would be unstoppable. His eyes suddenly lit up. 'Where did these weapons come from?' he asked.

Haider stood. 'The insurgents.'

'No, I mean where in Nuristan?' said John. 'Didn't you say that Hizb-i-Islami had a training camp up north somewhere?'

'Near Barg-i-matal,' said Haider.

John grew more excited. 'Can you find out where it is – exactly?'

'Of course,' said Haider. 'There are no secrets in Afghanistan.'

'Hold on a minute,' Dusty interrupted. 'I don't think I like where this is headed.'

John took his fervour down a notch. 'If you have a better idea, I'm all ears.'

Dusty pursed his lips. He had nothing.

John egged him on. 'Come on,' he said. 'It'll be good fun. Besides, we're both low on ammo ourselves.'

Dusty shook his head. 'No way, no way, no way can we pull it off.'

'What other choice do we have?' John argued. 'We'll do a recce first to see if it's achievable, OK?'

Haider was baffled. 'What do you intend to do?' he asked.

'What every Regiment lad since the Second World War has done when he can't get the weapons he needs,' said John. 'We'll steal them.'

Marching recruits, whining instruments, and an international assembly of disinterested officers; it was for all intents and purposes a carbon copy of the ANA graduation ceremony Rudy had covered ten weeks earlier. But there was a subtle difference in his perception this time around, something amiss with the soldiers circling the parade square he hadn't noticed before.

It wasn't just the ceremony. Rudy's encounters in London had opened his eyes to many things. Admittedly, Pete Mitchell did make him question his reporter's instincts. But the revelation that Harry had been made aware of the ShieldGroup report dispelled any doubts in Rudy's mind. There was definitely a concerted effort afoot to discredit John Patterson and bury his story.

Rudy searched the reviewing stand for the now infamous white skullcap and grey beard of General Rasul. It was harder to pick him out of a crowd without his turbaned bookends. This time around, though, Rudy wasn't leaving without an interview.

'Sorry to keep you waiting,' said Lieutenant Colonel Howard.

Rudy pumped Howard's hand. 'Thank you for seeing me again.'

'Not at all,' said Howard. 'I'm here to answer your questions. Fire away.'

'Actually, sir, I was hoping to speak with a representative from the Afghan Ministry of Defence,' said Rudy. 'You never did make good on the offer you made the last time I was here.'

Howard's expression remained affable. 'I'm terribly sorry, but I speak with so many members of the press. If I did fail to follow through on something, I do hope you will accept my sincerest apologies.'

'Water under the bridge,' said Rudy. 'You promised to introduce me to General Ustad Rasul.'

'Sadly, General Rasul is not here today.' Howard craned his neck toward the reviewing stand. 'But we do have several high-level Afghan officers in attendance. One of them attended university in England. His English is excellent. Shall I introduce you?'

Rudy didn't know why, but he got the distinct feeling Lieutenant Colonel Howard was trying to put him off Rasul. 'I've been trying to contact General Rasul for several days but the Afghan MoD is – well, useless, frankly. They rarely pick up the phone and when I do manage to leave a message, no one returns my calls.'

'Communications among Afghans, especially those in positions of authority, can be, rather, how shall I say – familial? You'd have better luck going through a family contact: sons, brother, cousins – even distant ones. Do you have a local fixer?'

'Couldn't you help me cut through the red tape?' Rudy asked.

'I could,' said Howard, 'but, between you and me, General Rasul may not be with the Afghan MoD for much longer.'

Rudy perked up. 'Has something happened?' he asked. 'Has ISAF had a falling out with the general?'

'Far from it.' Howard looked around. 'Speaking strictly off the record – President Karzai is considering appointing General Rasul Governor of Nuristan. It could happen very soon. Are you sure I can't introduce you to someone here now?'

'Thank you for the offer, but I'm afraid my story involves an aspect of the ANA which General Rasul is most qualified to comment on,' said Rudy.

'Very well then.' Howard extended his hand. 'If you change your mind, you know where to find me.'

'Will do, sir.' Rudy hovered on the edge of the parade square, dissecting his conversation with Howard. Was the lieutenant colonel being helpful by pointing out there were better Afghans to interview? Or did he want to keep Rudy away from General Rasul? The 'off the record' comment was so completely out of character. NATO officers didn't engage in rumour-mongering – not with members of the press. Then, it clicked. If a low-level spook like Harry knew about the ShieldGroup report, a middle-ranking British officer stationed in Afghanistan would surely know about it as well. After all, General Rasul worked closely with ISAF. Was NATO trying to cover up the story too?

The uneven columns of graduating recruits stumbled past. Two collided with each other and fell over. Rudy took out his notebook and scribbled. '*Graduation day. ANA troops can't march together. How will they fight together?*'

Chapter 36

The Hizb-i-Islami training camp was a three-day walk from Dogrum; two and a half if done hard. Haider was right. There were no secrets in Afghanistan. He'd simply sent word to the surrounding Kom villages asking if anyone knew where to find it. News filtered back that a group of brothers had spent a month with the insurgents in early spring – before Hizb-i-Islami started attacking the Kom valley. Haider struck a deal with the brothers. If they would escort a party from Dogrum to the Hizb-i-Islami training camp – once for a close target recce and then a second time to steal weapons – they could keep a share of the spoils.

Dusty had serious reservations about the plan. 'You said Hizb-i-Islami were enemies of the Kom. And now you're telling us these lads trained with them?'

'The brothers are from a poor Kom village,' Haider explained. 'They were lured to Hizb-i-Islami by the promise of money, not ideology. The insurgents never paid them, so they came home.'

Dusty turned to John. 'He's lined up a bunch of mercenaries to lead us to a hornets' nest.'

John shrugged. 'What do you think people called us when we were working for ShieldGroup?'

'It's not the same and you know it,' said Dusty.

John spoke to Haider. 'Did the brothers give you their word?'

'Yes,' said Haider. 'I trust them,' he added.

'Then that's good enough for me,' said John.

They met the brothers at sunrise at a predetermined RV high in the mountains overlooking Dogrum. They found the young men wrestling beneath a cluster of pine trees. The brothers' shared physical features – pale freckled skin, straight eyebrows, ginger flecked hair, long faces and angular noses – swamped their individual attributes. Two had blue eyes. The rest were a muddy kaleidoscope of greenish brown.

Sweating and smiling, they exuded the type of playful confidence John possessed as a young soldier on selection; a pure audacity untouched by loss. He liked them straightaway. One of the brothers stepped forward and bowed respectfully. 'Ehsaan,' he said. He tapped his brothers on the shoulders as he introduced them: 'Moakam, Ali, Usman, Sarwar, Ghazi, Muzaffar.'

Tongue-tied by the names, John dubbed the brothers *The Magnificent Seven*. He asked if he could inspect their weapons. Each brother had a Chinese-made AK exactly like the ones taken from the insurgents who'd attacked Dogrum. 'Did you get these from the camp?' he asked through Haider.

Ehsaan explained that Hizb-i-Islami had given them all rifles, but there were other weapons in the camp including RPGs.

'Did they teach you how to use RPGs?' John asked.

Ehsaan shook his head no. 'Kshto and foreign fighters got to train with explosives, rockets and pistols. The Kom were given rifles only, nothing else.'

'Do you know how many weapons they have stored in the camp?' John asked. 'Or what kind of ammunition they have?'

Ehsaan apologized. 'Everything was kept in a locked building,' he explained. 'Only the foreign instructors had a key.'

John told Ehsaan not to worry. 'That's what the recce is for.'
He briefed the brothers on their mission and objectives. 'I know
you won't cheat us because you all look like Scotsmen,' John
began. 'And that, by the way, is the highest compliment I know
of. We will not engage the enemy on this mission. Our purpose
now is to gather intelligence. We will stay out of sight of the
enemy. We will watch them from a distance. We will study their
routines and assess their capabilities.'

When John finished, Ehsaan spoke. 'He asks, when will they
fight?' said Haider.

John spoke directly to the young man. 'If our mission is successful – never.' The Magnificent Seven looked disappointed.
John stepped back and lifted his AK above his head. 'I have
fought many battles,' he declared. 'And I have defeated many
enemies – some with a rifle . . .' John lowered his weapon and
looked each brother in the eye, '. . . but my greatest victories
have come without firing a shot. That is the difference between
a good warrior and a great warrior.'

The Magnificent Seven accepted John's words as if he were
a prophet. Dusty whispered over John's shoulder. 'I think
they're actually buying that crap you fed them.'

John was indignant. 'I meant every word of it.'

Dusty pointed downhill. 'See that canyon? We'll have to walk
around it if that fat head of yours gets any bigger.'

The Magnificent Seven led them down the mountain,
through pine, ash and walnut forests to the banks of a wide,
rapidly flowing river. They spent the rest of the day following
the water, helping each other over slippery rock faces and
searching for animal tracks that offered a better footing.
Occasionally, the riverbank would open onto carpets of green
grass and the group would stop to share food and stories. The
Magnificent Seven loved hearing about John's exploits. He in

turn was fascinated by their lives. The brothers were the most sheltered men he'd ever met. They had never seen a movie, never eaten in a restaurant, never taken a ride on an aeroplane or train. Lifts and escalators were practically beyond their comprehension.

'What is the purpose of moving steps?' Ehsaan asked through Haider. 'Can your people not walk properly?'

When John described skyscrapers, the brothers looked at the mountains, trying to imagine man-made structures in their place. John assured them the tallest buildings in the world were no match for the Hindu Kush.

Dusty's attempts at conversation weren't as successful. The brothers seemed to regard him as less important and therefore less interesting than John. Dusty did make some headway when he asked if the brothers knew any Western music. Despite their isolated upbringing, all of them had heard of Michael Jackson and could recite the chorus to 'Billie Jean'. When Dusty tried to build on the connection by describing dance clubs in his native Glasgow, the cultural divide proved too wide to bridge. 'We have heard that the West has public houses where men drink alcohol,' said Ehsaan. 'Is there such a place in your village of Glasgow?'

When the topic turned to geo-politics, the Magnificent Seven weren't nearly as naive. The Hizb-i-Islami training camp had put them in contact with foreign fighters from all over the globe: native and British-born Pakistanis; Saudis and other disgruntled Gulf Arabs; Russian-speaking Uzbeks; Chechens; Uighurs from western China. The brothers claimed that despite the shared bond of Islam, relations among the fighters were far from brotherly. The Nuristanis – especially the Kom and Kshto – distrusted each other completely. The foreign fighters all thought each other inferior. Some refused to fight alongside different ethnicities or travel beyond Nuristan to wage jihad in other areas of Afghanistan. 'It sounds like NATO,' John told them.

Shortly before nightfall, the group set up camp in an orchard a hundred yards from the river. John was concerned they might upset the landowners but Haider assured him no offence would be taken so long as they didn't pick the fruit.

Dusty grabbed the branch of a pomegranate tree and shook it, releasing a red globe. 'What if it's fallen off the tree?'

'If you take so much as a twig it is considered theft,' said Haider.

Dusty kicked the fruit away, stripped off his clothes and stomped toward the river. 'This fucking country,' he muttered.

Dusty's swim quickly turned into a spectacle. Unaccustomed to seeing other men naked – even from the waist up – the brothers were fascinated by the younger Scot's lack of modesty. They stared at him, pointing and commenting as if he were an animal in captivity. When John joined Dusty for a wash, the brothers' behaviour grew even more intrusive. One by one they waded into the river until John was completely surrounded.

Dusty called to John from outside the circle. 'Wait till you try and take a dump. They'll be wiping your arse for you.'

'At my age, I'm not far off it,' John called back.

After dinner, John divided Haider and the brothers into pairs and assigned each a guard shift for the evening. 'Do you trust them not to fall asleep?' asked Dusty.

'No,' said John.

'I'll take the first shift,' Dusty offered.

John settled into his bivvy bag, tucked a folded jumper under his head and slid his pistol underneath it. He positioned his AK to his right side, ready to respond to an attack at a moment's notice. As he fell asleep, his thoughts drifted back to his days in the Regiment operating in the jungles of South East Asia. One night in particular stood out – he was awoken by a weight bearing down on his chest. John thought it was an enemy soldier sneaking up to cut his throat but when he opened his eyes he discovered it was nothing more than a harmless civet cat that had crawled into his basha looking for a warm place to sleep. That was the thing about the wilderness. Everything seemed hostile at first.

The image of the flea-bitten cat had just faded when John was rattled awake.

'You're up, mate,' Dusty whispered.

Though his four hours of sleep had felt more like four minutes, John didn't moan or complain. Without so much as a yawn, he holstered his pistol, rolled up his bivvy bag and joined Haider and Ehsaan down by the riverbank.

'Did you get enough sleep?' asked Haider.

'I'm fine,' said John. 'How are the lads holding up?'

'The brothers are strong.' Haider nodded at Ehsaan. The oldest of the brothers was standing twenty feet away, his rifle poised for action. 'You need not worry about them. They want to impress you.'

'Hardly,' said John. 'Did you see the way they were all over me in the river? They don't think I can look after myself, let alone them.'

'They surrounded you because they fear losing you.' Haider turned his face to John's. 'You are the leader they have been waiting for.'

John smiled uncomfortably. 'Don't be daft.'

Haider gestured to Ehsaan again. 'Think about who has ruled Afghanistan during his lifetime: foreigners, charlatans, puppets. He is desperate for true leadership. He craves it more than food, more than water – more than air.'

'I'm not a leader,' said John.

'But you are,' Haider insisted. 'The brothers asked me if they could come and train with us in Dogrum. I told them I would ask you.'

'It's not up to me,' said John. 'Anvar is Malek. It's his decision.'

'Anvar will agree to whatever you want.' Haider placed his hand on John's shoulder. 'Anvar sees there is greatness in you, just as the brothers do.'

Unaccustomed to compliments, John wasn't sure how to respond. In the Regiment, competence wasn't celebrated, it was expected. The only feedback he'd ever received for a job well done were nit-picking criticisms by officers. It was the same in the civilian world; all John had got was grief from incompetent managers who were threatened by his ability. 'I'm just an ordinary bloke with a set of skills that happen to be of some value here. Believe me, back home, I am nothing special.'

'You are too humble,' said Haider. 'The SAS is revered the world over.'

'Well, it isn't revered back home,' said John. 'I get the same pension as an army cook.'

'Then your country is run by fools.' Haider raised his face to the stars. 'I do not believe our friendship is an accident. I believe Allah brought us together. That is why I had no fear to stand before the *jirga* with you. I have not told you this before, but I feel I can do so now. My family begged me to distance myself from you. "Do not ally yourself with the infidel," they warned. But I told them that to deny you would be to deny the will of Allah.'

John ignored the religious overtones and focused on Haider's reference to family. With the exception of his brother's death, Haider had never spoken of them. John immediately thought of the woman in the red veil. He'd assumed she was related to Haider, but the question of how was too delicate a subject to raise.

Now, at long last, he had an opening. 'I remember how upset your family was the morning we left for Kamdesh.'

Haider sighed. 'Do not interpret Roshanak's actions harshly. She is a woman. She is weak and I am all she has left.' John nodded. He hoped his body language would convey the question he was bursting to ask: *Who is Roshanak to you?* 'When she married my brother, she became my sister,' Haider continued. 'Now that he is gone, may Allah take mercy on him, it is my duty to take care of her.'

The news hit John like a blast of oxygen. *Roshanak was not Haider's wife!* The connection he felt with her was not forbidden. But was it real? He fished for more details. 'Her concerns for your safety are understandable.'

'More than you know.' Haider sighed. 'I fear she will never find another husband.'

The obvious follow-up – *why?* – risked sounding too intrusive. 'She must have loved your brother very much,' John commented.

'You are sentimental,' said Haider. 'Roshanak's heart is neither here nor there. She is twenty-four – very, very old for a bride. No man will take her. And she has no sons to look after her.'

John thought of the little blonde girl who was always with Roshanak. 'Your brother had no children?'

'Allah took his sons. His only surviving child is Shams – a daughter. The name means sunshine.' Haider's expression grew weary. 'Shams is delightful but she will need a dowry for marriage.' Haider stopped himself. 'I should not complain. A man without responsibility is a man without purpose. Family is a blessing.'

John shared the sentiment more than Haider could know.

*

The next day, the group climbed high into the mountains where glaciers covered the ground all year. The terrain was barren. Great gusts of wind swept through the open spaces, pushing the group from behind or forcing them to tilt into it depending on its direction. Unseen and unpredictable, it was nature at its most intimidating. The Magnificent Seven kept closing around John like a human flak jacket to shield him from the elements. Their lack of concern for their own safety made him admire them all the more. If John could turn anyone into top-flight soldiers, it was these lads.

As they traversed the last stretch of desolate landscape, John caught a strong whiff of musk. His mind rewound to the recently excavated memory of the civet cat that had climbed into his basha. He stopped and put his finger to his lips, the universal signal for silence. 'Do you smell that?' he whispered.

Haider and Dusty both inhaled. John followed with a deep breath of his own. Though less pronounced than before, the scent of musk was unmistakable. 'I swear I smell cat piss.' John searched for the source. He saw something moving fifty yards downhill from their position, near the tree line. A smoky-white animal with grey markings emerged from the background. It was slinking gracefully toward the forest. John's eyes softened with wonder. 'Is that a snow leopard?'

Dusty and Haider looked in the same direction as John. 'Where?' asked Dusty.

'On the edge of the wood. It's stunning,' John marvelled.

'I don't see it, mate,' said Dusty.

Haider's eyes darted back and forth, searching. 'When my grandfather was young, he saw a snow leopard. No one in my village has seen one since. I thought they had all gone from Afghanistan.'

The big cat arched its back and looked over its shoulders. For a brief moment, its fierce grey eyes connected with John's. The leopard opened its mouth. John waited for the great roar that would finally betray the beast's location to all. But the cry was mute. The leopard turned and leapt into the trees.

Haider was still searching in vain. 'Where is it?'

John watched the rare cat disappear into the forest. 'Forget it,' he said. 'It's gone.'

As they made their way down the mountain, John thought he saw hints of the animal's smoky white fur. But the leopard never materialized again. Even its scent had vanished. By the next morning, John was wondering whether the creature had really existed.

Chapter 37

The soldiers looked like they'd seen death and cheated it. Howard recognized the platoon's uniforms: Canadian Light Infantry. One soldier was busy stripping the barrel of a 7.62mm general purpose machine gun. The rest were transferring equipment from a Mercedes G Wagon into a wooden shed thrown up beside the public affairs office. The shack was overflow accommodation for ISAF troops taking off from Bagram airbase, the main US military hub outside Kabul.

An Army major emerged from the PAO's office. His doughy body and round spectacles suggested he was a pen-pusher. He looked more solicitor than soldier. When the troops took no notice of him, the officer stopped and cleared his throat. The infantrymen put down their gear and stood to attention. 'Have you forgotten how to salute?' said the officer, winding up for an extended reprimand. The major began ticking off one pedantic infraction after another: filthy boots, facial stubble, no head dress.

Howard's cauldron stewed. He couldn't countenance bullies, least of all officers with an unearned sense of entitlement. His thoughts harkened back to an inky sky over Hereford.

It was 6 a.m. the dead of winter. Young Captain Howard, fearing he'd be late for his first trip with 22 SAS Regiment, had set two alarms that morning to make sure he and his troop left on time. He found six of his eight men waiting for him at the camp's quadrangle, their para bags packed for a diving course with the Royal Navy. Howard laid his para bag beside theirs and nodded like he belonged there.

Like other officers who'd passed SAS selection, Howard believed it was not only his right, but his destiny to command a regimental squadron. The two-year posting with Boat Troop was a natural progression for someone with his breeding and background.

'Good morning, lads.' His cheerful tone was sprinkled with a light dusting of arrogance. 'I'm glad to see some of you are punctual. Any sign of the other two?' The troopers looked at one another. It was clear they were in possession of information to which Howard wasn't privy. Before he could press them for an explanation, two canvas-topped Land Rovers pulled up and out climbed his missing men.

'You lads all met the Rupert?' asked John.

Howard was riled by the generic label. But if that was the way his troop staff sergeant wanted to play it, so be it. 'Yes, staff. We've met.'

John frowned at the young captain. 'You're in the Regiment now, not the Guards. There are no ranks or last names here. I'm John, you're James. Got it?'

Howard was lost for words. No soldier had ever spoken to him like that. It just wasn't the done thing. 'Very well then . . . John.' He looked at Dusty. 'And by what name would you care to be known.'

'This is Dusty,' said John. 'He's on a cross-deck from Air Troop at my request. Say hi to the new Rupert, Dusty.'

'Hi, new Rupert,' Dusty deadpanned.

The other troopers smirked. John cut their fun short. 'The heaters are blasting so no whingeing about the cold. Load your gear and let's get moving. James, you're with me.'

Howard climbed into the front passenger seat of John's Land Rover. The heater was going full throttle but it did little to ward off the icy wind seeping in from the canvas top, not to mention the chill from his troop staff sergeant. Two troopers stuffed their para bags in the rear and climbed over the tailgate to their seats. 'Everybody in?' asked John. 'Got all your gear?'

'Would you like me to drive?' Howard offered. Officers never chauffeured the lower ranks. Howard reasoned his magnanimous gesture would more than compensate for his less than stellar start with John that morning.

'Do you know how to get to where we're going?' asked John.

Howard looked at him askance. 'We have maps, don't we?'

John put the vehicle into gear. 'I'll take that as a no.'

Somewhere in the Herefordshire countryside, Howard was roused by a sharp shove to the shoulder. 'Wake up, James,' said John.

Howard sat up. John looked very disappointed with him. 'Terribly sorry,' said Howard. 'Bit of a late night I'm afraid.'

The excuse didn't impress John. 'No one sleeps during vehicle moves. It doesn't matter if we're operational or driving down to the south coast of England. When we move, all eyes are open.'

Howard felt he was overreacting. 'It wasn't as if I was driving.'

'You're in the SAS now,' John snapped. 'You're part of a team. If all three of you fall asleep and then I fall asleep at the wheel, where would we be?'

For the second time that morning, Howard had been lambasted by a subordinate. Perhaps it was some sort of initiation ritual meant to provoke him. He refused to be led. 'I appreciate your candour, staff.'

'Don't fucking staff me.' John's tone wasn't nasty – just impatient. 'That's the last time I'm telling you.'

The troopers sneered. 'Typical fucking Rupert, here for two years,' said one.

'Extra fucking baggage,' remarked the other. The trooper looked in the wheel well. 'Speaking of extra baggage – one, two, three . . . hey John. Is your kit back here?'

'Yeah, mate,' said John.

'Well, I only count three bags,' said the trooper.

'James?' said John. 'Where's your para bag?'

This time, Howard knew he'd done nothing wrong. 'I carried my para bag personally from my quarters this morning. It was in the quadrangle ready to be loaded on the Land Rover.'

John steered into a lay-by. 'Everybody out,' he said. 'You too, James.' The second Land Rover pulled in behind them. John rapped on the driver's window. 'How many para bags do you lads have?'

Dusty flashed a wily grin. 'Four,' he said.

John banged his hand on the side of the Land Rover. 'Get out.'

Everyone gathered around John. 'There are no secrets here so, James, I'm going to debrief you in front of the team. Now, you did two things wrong this morning. The second was to nod off before we were through the camp gates. The first thing you did wrong was leave your gear behind. This isn't the Guards, James. There's no "bat man" to polish your boots, clean your kit and wipe your arse. You're responsible for your own gear and that includes loading it. You might think I'm coming down on you hard because you're a Rupert, but I'm not. What if we weren't going down south for an exercise? What if we were about to parachute off the back of a C-130 into the sea on a live operation? Everyone new to the Regiment is on a learning curve – a steep one.' John addressed the group. 'That's why we help each other out and learn from each other's mistakes. On that note . . .' he turned to Dusty . . . 'You knew James left his para bag back at camp. You would have seen it in your headlights when you pulled out after us. How do you think it would look if we turned up at the Navy with one man kitless?'

'We would have looked a right bunch of wankers,' Dusty admitted.

'That's right.' John addressed the other troopers. 'James is one of us now. The next time any of you get it into your heads to stitch up the new Rupert, think twice because you could stitch us all up.'

It was baptism by fire but Howard was converted. From that day on, military rank meant nothing to him. Leading men was not a God-given right. It was a privilege to be earned. John Patterson had made an indelible impression.

'That's enough, major,' Howard called.

The blustering officer turned around. His face reddened when he realized he was out-ranked. Howard addressed the badgered Canadians. 'Where are you flying off to?'

One of the infantrymen stepped forward. 'Kandahar, sir.'

Howard looked at the other dishevelled troopers. 'It appears as if you've already been on ops,' he said.

'Yes, sir,' the soldier confirmed. 'We've been on thirty-six hours straight, south-west of Kabul. We got into a contact on our way here too.'

Howard nodded. 'How are your lads?'

'They're just tired,' said the soldier. 'No casualties.'

Howard turned to the major. 'These men are deploying to one of the hardest areas of the country. I think you would agree they have more important things to do right now than shine their boots.' The major had no come back. Howard addressed the troopers once more. 'Try and rest while you can. And all the very best while you're down in Kandahar.' The soldiers saluted Howard. 'I should be saluting all of you,' he said.

Having put the major in his place, Howard entered the public affairs building. He found Walter Raleigh's office at the end of the corridor. The strapping American seemed genuinely pleased to see him. 'Pinky! What the hell are you doing here?'

Howard's reply was less exuberant. 'I was hoping to have a word with you, Walter.'

'I was just about to go grab some lunch if you want to come with me,' said Raleigh. 'We got everything here: pizza? burgers?'

Howard loathed American fast food. 'I'm more of a bangers and mash man, myself.'

Raleigh raised an eyebrow. 'Some advice, Pinky. I might know that you're talking about sausages but some of the female troops around here might not take too kindly to the reference.'

'I'm afraid I don't follow you,' said Howard.

'Bangers.' Raleigh cupped his hands like he was holding two melons. 'In American, that's how men describe a woman's, um, you know . . . their breasts.'

Howard never ceased to marvel at how Yanks and Brits could speak the same language and yet not understand each other. 'Bagram's culinary wonders will have to wait, I'm afraid. I need to discuss a matter that requires a certain level of discretion.'

Raleigh invited Howard into his office and closed the door. The American leaned on the edge of his desk. 'If this is about freeing up troops for Helmund, you're S-O-L.' Howard didn't recognize the acronym. 'Shit-out-of-luck,' Raleigh explained. 'In case you've been living in a cave somewhere, the Pentagon is gearing up for a major surge in Iraq. I'm fighting tooth and nail to hang on to the soldiers I already have.'

'I know about the Iraq surge,' said Howard. 'Please do let us know when Washington remembers it's committed to fighting a war in Afghanistan as well.'

'You're preaching to the choir, Pinky.'

'I know, Walter. In any event, I'm not here to discuss Helmund. It's more of a personal matter,' Raleigh's face brightened with anticipation. 'Two days ago, a British reporter came to see me. He wanted me to arrange an interview with General Rasul.'

Raleigh pondered the implications. 'Do you think his request had something to do with your two missing nationals?'

'It's hard to say,' said Howard. 'I told him about Rasul's impending governorship . . .'

Raleigh's face tightened like a screw. 'Aw, hell, Pinky. That wasn't meant to be leaked.'

'. . . strictly off the record,' Howard added hastily. 'I offered to put him in touch with another Afghan general, but he insisted Rasul was the most qualified person to comment on his story.'

'Sounds fishy,' said Raleigh. 'You know if the press gets wind of what happened with your nationals and Rasul's nephews, you'll have an all-mighty mess on your hands.'

'The mess isn't my primary concern,' said Howard. 'I'm more worried about the two missing men. With Rasul as powerful as he is, he'll make examples of them if the story hits the headlines. And with so much at stake in Afghanistan right now it's doubtful the British government will go out on any sort of limb to save them.'

'Those boys are fucked all right.' Raleigh raised his chin. 'Just out of curiosity – why do you care so much? Who are they to you?'

Howard inhaled deeply. He had hoped to keep his relationship with John and Dusty under wraps. Revealing it was the price he'd have to pay to secure Raleigh's cooperation. 'I served with them in the SAS.'

Raleigh nodded. 'Brothers,' he said, as if the word were sacred. 'How can I help?'

'I want to throw this reporter off the scent. Give him something else to focus on while I try to locate the missing men,' said Howard.

'What did you have in mind?' asked Raleigh.

'Military embeds are proving popular with the press corps. This reporter should get word any day now that he'll be deploying with a British unit to Helmund Province. That will occupy him for the next week or two but I'm worried about what he may get up to after that. If you could arrange an embed for him with US forces, it would buy me more time.'

'He's print right? Not TV?' asked Raleigh.

'Correct,' said Howard.

'It shouldn't be too hard to set up then. The Dod doesn't care one way or another with print reporters. It's the TV guys they're worried about,' said Raleigh.

'How very strange,' Howard observed.

'Do the math, Pinky. Newspapers are read by thousands. TV is watched by millions,' said Raleigh. 'So, what's the fella's name?'

'Lipkingard,' said Howard. 'Rudy Lipkingard.'

Chapter 38

The 4x4 slammed into a pothole, whiplashing Rudy forward, then back.

'Are you OK, sir?' asked Haroon.

Rudy grabbed his neck. 'I'm fine. Why the bloody hell is it taking so long.'

'Too many cars,' said Haroon.

Rudy looked past Haroon's head through the windscreen. Traffic was bumper to bumper on the main road. He searched for possible rat runs through side streets. But the entrances were all blocked by concrete barriers and armed guards who'd only allow residents through. It was madness. Not only were the roadblocks unnecessary, they exacerbated Kabul's already dysfunctional road system. Rudy's office was less than a mile away and he'd been in the car for forty-five minutes.

'Is there another way we can go?' asked Rudy. Haroon spoke with the driver. The two Afghans exchanged rapid sentences in Pashtun, peppered by the occasional English word – 'petrol . . . mobile'. The insertion of the intelligible made the conversation even less comprehensible to Rudy. 'Can we drive around this?' he asked.

'Yes,' said Haroon. 'But we need more petrol.'

Rudy checked the time. 'We'll walk to the general's house. Tell the driver to refuel and meet us back here.'

Rudy climbed out of the vehicle and waited for Haroon to
deliver the instructions to the driver. His head of security was
proving useful in all sorts of ways. When NATO and the
Afghan MoD turned out to be dead ends to General Rasul,
Rudy took to heart Lieutenant Colonel Howard's advice about
accessing Afghanistan's power brokers. He gathered his local
staff and asked if anyone had a family member close to Rasul.
It turned out Haroon had a cousin who worked security at the
general's private residence in Sherpur, Kabul's newest and
wealthiest neighbourhood. One phone call and Rudy had his
interview. If Afghanistan's machinery was tribal, family blood
was the grease that kept it humming along.

Haroon nodded to a set of guards policing a concrete barrier.
'I speak to them. Please, sir, you wait here.'

Rudy studied the pink and blue domes rising from behind the
barrier. It was early evening and the waning sun was thick with
pollution. The filtered light softened the pastel mounds, lending
them an almost impressionistic quality. Rudy imagined what the
area must have looked like before its metamorphosis. Prior to
the US-led invasion, Sherpur was nothing more than a col-
lection of squatter huts and an old army barracks. But the
wasteland was in a prime location near all the major embassies.
The warlords in Karzai's government saw an opportunity. They
tore down the barracks, razed the huts and divided the land
among themselves.

The plots were rumoured to have gone for well-below market
value. When it came to building on them, however, Sherpur's
residents were in competition to spare no expense. Financed by
siphoned aid money or the country's opium trade, the compounds were said to be as corrupt as they were opulent. The
word *narcotechture* was often used to describe them. But like
any good journalist, Rudy was inclined to withhold judgement

until he could see it first-hand. Jealousy and class warfare were, after all, an inevitable by-product of progress. And real estate development often had positive knock-on effects, trickle-downs in the form of improved infrastructure and creeping gentrification.

The concrete barriers parted and Rudy and Haroon stepped onto the most valuable real estate in Kabul. The houses were enormous: Disneyfied Taj Mahals with embellishments drawn from every imaginable influence, Ionic and Corinthian columns, Islamic mosaic tiles, balconies encased in ultra-modern green and pink perspex. It was like someone had inhaled a copy of *Architecture through the Ages* and sneezed it out.

When it came to infrastructure, however, Sherpur turned out to be no more evolved than the rest of Kabul. The streets were muddy, rutted and bordered by open ditches filled with rubbish and foul green sludge. No power or phone lines crisscrossed the neighbourhood. Boys dressed in rags pushed wheelbarrows filled with fruit, phone cards and plastic bags from one compound to another. They sold their goods – and no doubt, their bodies – to the battalions of local security guards protecting the residences. The rumours were indeed true. Sherpur was a fortress that benefited no one but the powerful men inhabiting it. Rudy wondered what ordinary Afghans must have thought each time a new dome was added to its skyline. Did it give them something to aspire to? Or did the ostentatious displays generate resentment? Rudy recalled a statistic he'd read. Half a million people in Kabul were homeless or living in makeshift accommodation. He took out his notebook and wrote: *A stain of ostentation on a tapestry of social ills.*

Rasul's compound was the last on the street. Like its neighbours, it was a concrete ode to all things tasteless. The perimeter of the property was surrounded by an eight-foot-high breeze-block wall crowned with loops of silvery razor wire. The front of the property was reinforced by half-a-dozen concrete barriers six feet high and twelve feet long. A wrought-iron gate inset with Islamic inscriptions and patrolled by five armed guards was the only way in and out of the property.

One of the guards walked up to Haroon and embraced him. The two exchanged kisses on both cheeks. 'My cousin,' Haroon explained.

The cousin barked a few orders and the gates opened onto a paved driveway that curved around a landscaped courtyard with a working fountain in the middle. The water feature was the height of luxury in a country that had suffered years of drought.

A handful of guards surrounded Rudy and Haroon. One of the men stepped forward, smiled and patted them down for weapons. The young journalist made a mental note of the tight security. Rasul's home was better protected than the KMTC.

After they'd been searched – twice – Rudy and Haroon were escorted to Rasul's front door and asked to remove their shoes. They stripped down to their socks and stepped inside. The front hallway was cavernous, a double-height ceiling towering over a polished marble floor. It looked more like a palace than a private residence.

A man wearing a long black robe and black turban descended a sweeping staircase adorned with gilt balustrades. He introduced himself through Haroon as General Rasul's private secretary. The secretary explained that the general was running late and asked them to wait in an adjoining room until he returned from his 'very important state business'.

The waiting room was even more posh than the hallway. The marble floors were covered with silk rugs that must have cost

five thousand dollars a piece. A large picture window overlooking the driveway was draped in green and gold brocade
curtains that spilled onto the floor in shimmering pools. Instead
of plastic chairs or overstuffed cushions – seating typically
found in Afghan homes – Rasul's guests were treated to a
leather sofa and matching end chairs.

Rudy settled into a chair and observed the private army
assembled in Rasul's driveway. Clearly, he didn't want to piss
off the general but he didn't want the interview to be a waste of
time either. Rudy's mind ticked over. He needed to order his
questions so that any difficult ones seemed like a natural exten-
sion of the conversation. He flipped to a blank page in his
notebook and wrote: *So sorry to hear about the untimely death
of your nephews . . . are you satisfied thus far with the progress
of the investigation?* Rudy reasoned that once Rasul made his
case, he could poke holes in it under the guise of thoroughness.
*Some have suggested that your nephews were tied to a group
allied with al-Qaeda . . . Have you yourself ever been allied with
Hizb-i-Islami? Earlier this year, the leader of Hizb-i-Islami
announced that it is incumbent upon every Afghan to engage in
jihad until all the occupation forces are driven out of
Afghanistan and an Islamic system is established. Have you
denounced this openly?*

The guards outside shouted to each other. Rudy looked up
from his notebook to see what all the commotion was about.
The iron gates opened. Rudy saw two vehicles idling on the
street outside the compound: Toyota 4x4s with blacked-out
windows. As the lead 4x4 turned into the driveway, a young
boy with a wheelbarrow ran alongside it. Judging from his
height and appearance, he was ten or eleven years old. The
boy's red football shirt caught Rudy's eye – Manchester
United – probably a knock-off made in China or Pakistan.

Suddenly, the windows of the waiting room imploded. Rudy's chair flipped backward, slamming him into the wall. Chunks of plaster rained down from the ceiling. They cracked into a million pieces on the hard marble, filling the room with white dust. Disoriented, Rudy pulled himself onto his hands and knees. He looked at his forearms. They were cut and bloodied. He sat back on his feet and checked his thighs. It was a miracle he hadn't been shredded to pieces by flying glass. He noticed the brocade curtains in tatters. They had caught the brunt of it.

Someone lifted Rudy to his feet.

'Are you OK, sir?' Haroon appeared traumatized. Rudy tried telling him he was fine, but he couldn't get the words in his head to come out of his mouth. 'My cousin,' Haroon cried. 'I must find my cousin.'

Haroon bolted out of the room, leaving Rudy on his own. He searched for his notebook. An eternity passed before he realized it was still in his hand. Dazed and confused, he stumbled out of the house and into the courtyard. Guards were running around in all directions. Their mouths were open but their voices were faint and distorted. It was then that Rudy noticed that his ears were throbbing, like they'd been boxed repeatedly. He focused on individual details of the scene around him. A giant hole had been blown into the driveway. The three-ton armoured 4x4 he'd seen pulling into it was crumpled down one side, like a piece of paper tossed into a bin. The heat of the blast had melted the bulletproof windows, turning them from tinted black to an opaque, deathly grey. The buckled, shrapnel-splattered passenger door had been prised open. Three bodies were stretched out on the driveway next to it. All of them were intact but none was moving. Rudy recognized one of the corpses. General Rasul.

Rudy skidded on the pavement. He regained his balance and lifted his foot. His sock was stained red and a piece of meat was clinging to it. It looked like a strip of gristle cut from a rare steak. Rudy looked around him. Bits of raw flesh were everywhere: in the fountain, on the ground, hanging from the razor wire. He wondered where it had all come from.

Haroon ran to him. 'Inshallah!' the Afghan cried. 'My cousin is safe. It was a suicide bomber. A boy. Many guard killed.'

Rudy looked at a charred lump lying beside him. It was covered in a strip of red polyester. He gagged. The piece of meat stuck to his foot was the suicide bomber.

Chapter 39

The Magnificent Seven stopped at a fork in the river. 'We must go left,' Ehsaan said through Haider. 'It will take us to a mountain. The Hizb-i-Islami camp is there.'

John looked down the tributary flowing left from the main stream. It disappeared between two foothills. 'How far?' he asked.

'Fifteen, twenty minute walk,' Ehsaan estimated.

John spoke to the brothers. 'From here on we need absolute silence,' he said. 'Do not speak unless spoken to. I don't want to hear a peep out of any of you. Not even a fart.' The group fell silent and followed the tributary through the foothills. The water tapered to a trickle as it opened onto a stretch of flat earth that ran straight into a mountain. John ordered everyone to take cover behind some bushes. Ehsaan pointed to a plateau three hundred feet up the mountain. There were buildings on top of it. It was the training camp.

John and Dusty took out their binos. A well-worn dirt track ran from the valley to the southern edge of the plateau. 'How did you get in and out of the camp when you were here?' John whispered to Ehsaan.

Ehsaan pointed to the track. 'There is only one way in,' he said through Haider.

'We'll see about that,' Dusty whispered. He pointed to the

cliff face leading to the western edge of the plateau. The incline was forgiving and there were ample notches and ledges to grab. 'I bet we could free-climb that.'

The northern and eastern sides of the camp were clearly inaccessible; the northern backed into the mountain; the eastern edge ended in a sheer three-hundred-foot drop. Having identified two possible access routes, John and Dusty searched for a suitable observation point where they could monitor the camp's activities from a safe distance. Six hundred metres north-west of the plateau, a small ledge of earth with a bushy ash tree growing on it would allow them to look down on the camp undetected. It was an ideal OP, provided they could reach it.

John spoke to the brothers. 'Ehsaan and Haider will come with me and Dusty. I want the rest of you to go back to the main river and find a place to camp for the night. When we're done with our recce, we'll come and get you. Whatever you do, do not come back here. If we do not come for you in two days, it means we've been discovered, in which case don't try to rescue us. Go home.'

The Magnificent Seven minus one headed back toward the main river. The two Scots, Haider and Ehsaan backtracked around the base of the western foothill to search for a way onto the OP. The hillside was covered in wild herbs and scrub. The remnants of an old track were still discernible in the overgrowth. They followed the trail up to a level area that connected to the ledge they'd identified from the valley. Piles of stones covered the flat ground. The mounds were man-made and plotted along symmetrical grids six deep and seven wide. Their OP turned out to be a graveyard. The burial places were simple stone monuments with the exception of three carved wooden coffins shaded by the ancient ash. 'Tombs of Maleks,' said Haider.

Shielded by the tree and coffins, John and Dusty studied the Hizb-i-Islami camp below. It was roughly the size of four football pitches. An obstacle course with crudely built log barriers, rope netting and swings occupied the western quadrant; the southern quadrant was home to a spring well and a makeshift firing range with targets overlooking the valley. The buildings, eight in total, were grouped in the northern and eastern portions of the camp. Those in the north seemed to be in good order. The ones to the east were in considerably worse repair. Three of the roofs had collapsed and the foundations were buckled into inverted Vs. Only one of the structures – a building sitting near the edge of the cliff – was standing. A wooden pen with goats, sheep and chickens was beside it. 'It looks like the Coalition got here before us,' said Dusty. 'I reckon they used a drone to whack a missile into the place.'

'The Coalition would have finished them off.' John studied the damage more closely. 'Look at the track leading up to the camp, the way the ground contours. This whole area is sat right on top of a fault line. I reckon it was an earthquake that brought those buildings down. The place was probably abandoned when the insurgents moved in.'

John and Dusty spent the rest of the day observing the camp and taking notes. They estimated there were around sixty militants in total. They appeared to be subdivided into three groups that rotated between physical training on the obstacle course, classroom instruction and weapons drills. The instructor on the obstacle course was a big brute of a man who slapped his students on the back of the head whenever they made a mistake. The classroom work was held outside and involved long lectures delivered by a man in a white skullcap. John and Dusty speculated that the lessons were more ideological than practical in nature.

Weapons' training was the camp's major strength. In addition to live-fire target practice on the range, the recruits were also put through dry drills such as stripping and reassembling rifles and learning how to discharge an RPG safely. Periodically, the weapon instructors would walk behind the one intact building in the eastern quadrant and reappear with some sort of goodies: boxes of live rounds, RPG grenades, explosives and their ancillaries. The building obviously housed the camp's munitions. John and Dusty were salivating.

The call to prayer marked the end of the training day. After a communal dinner of rice and meat, the insurgents retired to the buildings in the northern quadrant. A single sentry was posted along the southern perimeter. The two Scots thought they'd hit pay dirt. If only one side of the camp was patrolled, it would make a close target recce that much easier to achieve.

After two hours of near stillness, John and Dusty made their move. They took off their boots and asked Haider and Ehsaan to swap shoes with them. 'We don't want to leave boot tracks inside the camp,' John explained. 'It will look suspicious. Sandal prints will blend in.'

They put on the sandals and took them for a test drive around the graveyard. Having had their feet bound in hiking boots for weeks, walking in what were basically flip-flops took some getting used to. They could feel every pebble and their unsecured ankles kept wobbling. After a few laps, John and Dusty made their way down to the valley. Their plan was to free climb the western approach into the camp, away from the sentry's line of sight. A serious obstacle only discernible at close view soon dashed their plans. There was a fifteen foot vertical drop near the bottom of the approach. Climbing it in boots would be a tough proposition. In sandals, it was a non-starter.

They had no choice but to probe into the camp from the south, the patrolled area.

John and Dusty crouched in the brush, waiting for a chance to move. Shortly after midnight, the sentry's discipline cracked. He fell asleep. The Scots sprang into action. With their bellies low to the ground, they scuttled onto the track, moving swiftly up and along it. Then, just fifty yards short of the plateau edge, the sound of a motorbike revving sent them scrambling. They searched for whatever cover they could find. John dived behind a cluster of thyme bushes and flattened his body to the earth. The motorbike peeled out of the camp with its headlight blazing. As it passed, he took a calculated risk and looked up. The headlight revealed old tyre tracks as well as footprints and impressions of animal hoofs. The track was a bloody thoroughfare. They could sneak some weapons and ammo out along it, but a large haul would be impossible. Disappointed, John adjusted his ambitions.

The motorbike roused the guard from his sleep. Once again, John and Dusty were in a holding pattern until around 2.30 a.m., when the guard curled up in the foetal position. John and Dusty crawled past him and got to work. Sitting back to back in the western quadrant, the Scots observed the heart of the camp. The layout looked the same as it had from their perch underneath the ash tree. They kept their eyes peeled for movement and other clues that would offer insights into the insurgents' nocturnal routines. The dozing sentry spoke volumes about the camp's discipline and procedures. If guards felt comfortable enough to fall asleep twice on duty, odds were, no one ever checked on them.

Around three, a man stumbled out of a building in the northern quadrant and shuffled toward the eastern quadrant. He appeared to be half asleep and totally oblivious to his surroundings. The sheep and goats in the animal pen lifted their heads as the man neared. The animals were unperturbed. Clearly, they were used to night-time disturbances. The man disappeared behind the munitions building and reappeared a minute later. He returned – empty handed – to his sleeping quarters. Two more men performed the same ritual within the space of an hour. The trips had nothing to do with weapons and ammunition. They were all going to the toilet.

John checked his watch. In thirty minutes, the first call to prayer would wake up everyone in the camp. He gave a hand signal to Dusty. John wanted to move to the eastern quadrant to check out the munitions building.

The animals in the pen perked up as John and Dusty approached. They measured their movements but the sheep grew agitated. One started bleating. John lowered his hand inside the pen and allowed the animal to sniff his skin. As it grew accustomed to John's scent, the sheep engaged John physically, rubbing its head against his hand until the novelty wore off.

Having pacified the animal, John and Dusty crept to the far side of the building. As they rounded the corner, John felt like a kid sneaking into his parents' wardrobe to peek at Christmas presents. His excitement faded though when he saw the door. It was padlocked. 'If we bust it, they'll know someone's been here,' John whispered.

Dusty reached into his ankle pouch and pulled out a Leatherman pocket knife. 'I'll try picking it, but no promises. It's been a while.'

While Dusty fiddled with the padlock, John walked around to the side of the building to watch for insurgents. He noticed there were no proper toilets to speak of. The insurgents all relieved themselves over the edge of the cliff. The stench of piss and shit rising up from the valley below was incredibly strong. John figured the wind was circulating the odour back up. Suddenly, the sheep John had settled lifted its head. John's internal warning mechanism went into high alert. In the distance, he saw a man approaching. John walked back around to the far side of the building and put his hand on Dusty's shoulder. The younger Scot looked up from his work. John pressed his finger to his lips and pointed. Dusty knew what John was telling him. With nowhere to retreat, except into the path of the oncoming insurgent, they crouched beside the door and waited for the danger to pass.

The insurgent came around the corner. It was difficult to discern his exact features in the dark. His beard was long and bushy and he was carrying a water bottle in his right hand. The insurgent walked to the edge of the cliff, turned, dropped his trousers and squatted. John and Dusty didn't move a muscle. The insurgent was less than ten feet away, so close they could hear his shit hit the ground. When he'd finished, the insurgent wiped his arse with his left hand, cleaned it with water, pulled his trousers up and returned to his quarters.

Dusty whispered. 'Filthy bastard didn't even have the decency to hang his arse over the side.'

John looked to the spot where the insurgent had squatted, expecting to see a pile of steaming shit. But there was nothing there. Baffled, John walked to the edge of the cliff and peered over it. Instead of a sheer drop, he discovered a narrow staircase chiselled into the rock face. The top steps were covered in excrement. No wonder he and Dusty had heard crap hitting the ground. It had travelled less than a foot.

John showed Dusty his discovery. With the call to prayer imminent, they decided to explore the staircase. They followed it all the way down the cliff and into a cave with porous walls and a damp, sloping floor. They assumed the cave had been carved over centuries by water draining off the mountains. It would explain why the insurgents used the stairs as a latrine rather than a secondary route for moving in and out of the camp. During the spring thaw, the cave would be flooded

John and Dusty walked deeper and deeper into the cave. Rather than end in a wall of rock, it cut straight through the mountain. The other side opened onto undulating foothills leading down to the main river. John and Dusty found six of the Magnificent Seven sleeping soundly by the bank.

Chapter 40

'I have just the thing to cheer you up.'

Rudy cradled the phone in his neck and poured himself a Famous Grouse. 'Who says I need cheering, Lucinda?'

'Well you haven't had a terribly good run of late.' Rudy wondered which misfortune Lucinda was referring to: his brush with an eleven-year-old suicide bomber, or having his story about it bumped for an "exclusive" on a reality TV star entering rehab. 'But things are most definitely looking up,' she chirped. 'Harry got you an embed with British troops in Helmund. Isn't it exciting!'

It was indeed the news Rudy had been waiting for. But the anticipated enthusiasm failed to materialize. Instead, Rudy's heart started thumping and his breath grew short. Beads of sweat broke out across his forehead. He felt the walls of his office closing in on him. 'Hello.' Lucinda was still waiting for his response. 'Did you hear what I said?'

Rudy drank his glass dry. His hand shook as he poured himself another drink. 'I'm very busy with other stories right now.' He wished he could think of a better excuse but the room was spinning.

'Helmund is the only story that matters in Afghanistan right now,' said Lucinda. 'Remember what I told you: goodies and baddies – that's what readers want. Harry has all the details you need: what to bring, who to report to, how you'll get there and so forth. Best get packing . . .' Lucinda's voice trailed, like she was putting the receiver down.

'For Christ's sake, Lucinda. I was nearly blown up!' Rudy dabbed his forehead with a tissue. 'Maybe in a month or two I'll be ready for an embed, but not now. It's too soon.'

The line went silent. Rudy's breathing returned to normal. Lucinda was backing off. 'Stop whingeing and get a grip of yourself,' Lucinda blasted. Rudy's heart started racing again. 'What did you think you signed up for?' she scolded. 'No one forced you to take a posting in a war zone, Mr Lipkingard. You made a clear and informed commitment and if you refuse to honour it, neither this newspaper nor any other will require your services in future. Do I make myself clear?'

Rudy was flustered. He knew Lucinda could be unreasonable, but threatening to blackball him was a whole new level of sleaze. 'You can't force me to accept a dangerous assignment. It's unlawful. Not to mention, indecent.'

'You're not working for an American newspaper.' Lucinda cackled. 'No one is going to throw money at you simply for crying post-traumatic stress. You signed disclaimers stating that you fully understood the nature of the assignment you were undertaking. You met with Human Resources and believe me, young man, that department doesn't exist to serve you – it serves me. There is not an employment tribunal in this land that will find in your favour.' Lucinda allowed the threat to sink in before switching back to rallying mode. 'Besides, it would be irresponsible of me to allow you to even consider turning down this embed. I do have your best interests at heart, dear boy, surely you know that? Trust me, as soon as you're back in the saddle, you'll feel like your old self again.'

Rudy was cornered. If he didn't do as Lucinda asked, his career would be finished. 'What's Harry's number?'

Twenty-eight Afghans, twelve donkeys and two Scots; by SAS standards, it was a cast of thousands. And that didn't include the supporting players. Everyone in Dogrum was pressed into service to help John and Dusty pull off the seemingly impossible – steal Hizb-i-Islami's weapons cache.

John's plan was ambitious but straightforward. The raiding party would set up base near the river on the other side of the mountain, away from the camp. Once it was dark, he and Dusty would lead the way through the cave and up the staircase carved into the cliff face. The rest of the raiding party would fan out behind them to form a chain stretching from the top of the staircase all the way back to base. Dusty would keep watch for waking insurgents while John would break into the munitions building and assemble parcels of weapons and ammo to hand to Ehsaan – the point man on the top step. Ehsaan would pass the parcels down to the next fighter and so on and so forth until they were transported all the way down the line. Haider would be waiting by the river to coordinate the transfer of the parcels onto the donkeys. As soon as the beasts were loaded to capacity – or when there was nothing left to steal – the chain would wind up and return to base. John and Dusty would stay behind to blow the munitions building and cover their tracks. If all went according to plan, the big bang would look like an accident and the insurgents wouldn't have a clue they'd even been robbed.

John's chain idea was not entirely without precedent. Vietcong guerrillas were known to have attacked positions with only a vanguard of armed men. As their enemies fell, they would take weapons from the dead and pass them down the line until everyone was armed. There was, however, a major difference with John's plan: he did not want his men to fight. Period. Like the close-target recce, the idea was to get in and get out without firing a shot.

To secure the parcels to the donkeys, John devised a 'hook and eye' system using kilims and ropes. He drew designs of the various bits and pieces for Anvar. The Malek quickly set Dogrum's women and children to work. While they weaved and stitched, John, Dusty and Haider put the Magnificent Seven and the village fighters through their paces. They drilled the untrained force relentlessly for a week. The fighters had to master passing mock bundles of weapons and ammunition without dropping them. Inevitably, someone would get cheeky and start playing with a pretend grenade or rifle – a practice John was quick to rebuke. 'Under no circumstances are you to remove the gear from the bundles. If an RPG round or even a bullet falls on the ground, it can explode. And if that happens, you can forget about defending Dogrum because all of us – down to the last man – will be dead.' Curbing the fighters' appetite for engaging the enemy was also a challenge. 'Our aim is to steal as many weapons and as much ammunition as we can – nothing more,' John would say. 'Shooting will come later.' Most of the fighters accepted John's decree, but Daud, the glory-starved Majlis member, kept bringing up scenarios where it would be necessary to break open the parcels and take on the insurgents. The more Daud banged on about battling the enemy, the more John wanted him out, but doing so risked fracturing the group. So he assigned the loose cannon to donkey loading duties at the back of the line, where Haider could keep an eye on him.

The third and perhaps most crucial lesson John needed to instil in his fighters was silence. It could make or break the operation. Three times a day John would line them up and deliver the same directive. 'No talking, no laughing, no coughing, no farting; nothing that can give us away.' Haider would translate and John would have the fighters say it again in Kamviri.

The night before the operation, John asked the fighters to repeat the order one last time. But instead of using their native tongue, they recited the words verbatim in English. John was beaming.

Chapter 41

At ten minutes to midnight, Dusty gave the all-clear sign. John slipped off his Bergen and pulled out a torch which he'd pre-set to an infrared setting along with a pair of bolt croppers and his night-vision goggles. Using the croppers, he cut the padlock from the door of the munitions building and stuffed the severed lock in his bag to conceal any evidence of a break-in. The door creaked as he pushed it open. John stepped inside and switched on his torch and his night sight. The room lit up like a Christmas tree. The floor was stacked with crates containing everything he wanted and more: AKs, pistols, magazines, rounds, RPGs, grenades, Claymore-type mines, plastic explosives, detonator cord, electrical and non-electrical detonators, safety fuse, double twisted cable, fusee matches – even boxes of 5.56 rounds for Dusty's rifle. Hizb-i-Islami were kitted out better than most British army units.

John stepped out of the building, made a fist with his right hand and punched it down three times. Ehsaan, acting as point man at the top of the staircase, saw the movement and repeated it. With the 'stand to' signal set in motion, John got to work. He pulled a kilim from his Bergen and unfurled it. The thin rug had been modified to his specification. Pockets had been sewn into it – enough to hold six rifles and twelve magazines. John filled them quickly but carefully, lifting AKs and magazines one at a time from the crates. When the pockets were full, he rolled the kilim up and fastened it using two loops that joined together to create one master loop.

John carried the kilim outside and passed it to Ehsaan. The parcel changed hands down the steps and through the cave until it reached the far end where Haider was waiting for the final transfer to a donkey. He held the bundle in his arms while Daud searched for the master loop to hook on to an 'eye' attached to a strap around the donkey's middle. When the bundle was secure, Haider sent more kilims up the line for John to fill.

The bundles were moving fast and furious. Within twenty minutes they'd stolen enough AKs and magazines to supply Dogrum with spares to boot. The basics covered, John moved on to more advanced weaponry. He found a crate containing type 69 RPG launchers. The Chinese copies of the more famous Soviet made RPG-7s had a back-blast that could tear a man's shoulder off. But as general support weapons went, they were the best to hand. The launchers were an awkward fit for the kilims but John managed to squeeze them in.

John had just finished rolling a kilim when he heard movement outside. He walked to the door. Dusty was standing on the edge of the cliff. He was holding his right arm at a ninety degree angle to his body. His fist was clenched and his thumb was pointing down. It was the signal to freeze. Someone was coming.

John left the building and closed the door behind him. He joined Dusty and Ehsaan on the top step – out of sight of the oncoming insurgent. The three men crouched together and waited for the danger to pass. An arc of piss flew over their heads as the insurgent above relieved himself. The insurgent finished and walked away. But instead of trailing footsteps, John heard the squeak of the wooden door. The insurgent had gone inside the munitions building.

The two Scots nodded to each other. John pulled his knife from his waistcoat and sprang from the step onto the plateau. He bent his knees deeply as he landed to absorb the shock of his weight hitting the ground. The door to the munitions building was wide open. The insurgent was inside, studying a pistol in a beam of moonlight. The weapon wasn't John's main concern. Sooner or later, the man would realize that something wasn't right. One scream and he could wake the whole camp.

Moving stealthily, with his night sight on, John closed in on him. For the briefest moment, he felt sorry for the insurgent. The stupid bastard was so consumed with his shiny toy it hadn't occurred to him yet that an open door was cause for alarm. The error in judgement would cost him dearly.

John's body blocked the moonlight as he entered the building. By the time the insurgent realized he wasn't alone, John's knife was slicing through his throat. The insurgent thrashed and gurgled as the blood drained from him. Hooking his arms underneath the dying man John dragged him to the corner of the room. He was dead before John laid him down. As he studied the insurgent's still warm face, John felt no remorse. The dead man was a foreign fighter. It served him right for coming to Nuristan in the first place.

John went outside and re-initiated the 'stand to' signal. With perfect discipline, the chain kicked back into action. Dusty returned to his lookout post while John filled the remaining kilims with a strategic mix of assets: high explosive warheads for the RPG launchers, twenty pistols and magazines, a dozen Claymores, a few dozen grenades, four boxes of plastic explosives, det cord, detonators, safety fuse, six drums of double twisted cable and finally – the 5.56 rounds. Dusty would be chuffed.

John handed the last kilim to Ehsaan, folded his right hand into a fist and closed his left hand around it. The signal indicated that that portion of the operation was finished. Ehsaan looked at John as if he were a god.

The two Scots waited for the lads to clear the steps before attending to their last piece of business: blowing the munitions building. Dusty found some det cord, a non-electrical detonator and safety fuse. While he cut and knotted the cord, John broke open a box of plastic explosives and worked two sticks of the malleable material in his hands. The comforting scent of marzipan filled the room. John took the knotted det cord from Dusty and moulded the PE around it.

'Two metres of safety fuse should be just the ticket,' John whispered.

Dusty pulled the black fuse against his arm to measure it. 'Taking out the sleeping quarters in the north quadrant would be a piece of piss, you know. We could blow this whole camp back to the Stone Age.'

'Stick with the plan,' John ordered.

Dusty measured another length of fuse. 'If we don't level this place who will?'

'Think of the lads,' John hissed. 'What would happen to them if there was a cock-up and we got caught?'

'I am thinking about the lads,' Dusty shot back. 'Our lads, British soldiers fighting in Helmund.'

The reference shook John to his core. 'We're miles from Helmund.'

Dusty lifted his night sights and got up in John's face. 'You can't guarantee that the men training in this camp today won't be killing British soldiers tomorrow. We've got a chance here to help our troops. Let's take it.'

John grabbed a box of match fusee. 'It's not our fight.'

'Like hell it isn't.' Dusty knocked the matches out of John's hand.

John looked down. 'Shut up.'

'You shut up,' said Dusty.

John slapped his hand over Dusty's mouth. 'Shut up and listen.' The hum of a small aircraft engine was circling overhead. John let go of Dusty.

'We'd best get out of here,' said Dusty.

John fumbled around for the matches.

'– now!' said Dusty.

John found the box. 'Not until we blow this place.'

'The fucking Reaper over our heads will take care of that,' said Dusty.

'You don't know that for sure.' John found the matches and lit the fuse. They had several minutes until the black cord triggered the detonator and blew the munitions building sky high. They tore out of the building and ran down the steps. Thirty seconds later, the pilot-less drone fired two missiles into the Hizb-i-Islami camp. The ground shook as the plateau was engulfed in a fireball. John and Dusty clung to the steps for dear life. When the earth stopped trembling, they looked back up at the camp. It was wiped from the face of the earth.

'I hope the lads followed orders and didn't open the parcels,' Dusty panted.

John thought of his fighters. If even one bundle had been opened, the drone would see the weapons and target them. 'We've got to warn them!' John cried.

They ran through the cave and back to the river base. Haider and the fighters were waiting with the loaded donkeys. The Scots moved from animal to animal checking the parcels. 'Did anyone take the weapons out?' asked John.

'No,' said Haider.

'Are you sure?' asked Dusty.

'Of course,' said Haider.

'I'm not fucking around, mate,' said Dusty. 'If there's a weapon out in the open we're all dead.'

'Everything is on the donkeys as per John's orders,' said Haider. 'What is the problem?'

'Did you hear those explosions?' asked John.

'Kabul would have heard them. It was the munitions building, no?' asked Haider.

'It was the whole bloody camp,' said Dusty. 'A drone whacked it. And if the people flying that thing remotely see the arsenal we've got down here, they'll think we're insurgents and whack us too.'

John and Dusty finished inspecting the donkeys and moved on to the fighters. They wanted to be doubly certain no one had got their hands on an AK or RPG launcher. Everything was as Haider said. If the drone was searching for more targets, it would hopefully pass right over them.

'Tell the lads we'll lay up here until dawn,' said John. 'There's no point in risking a move with that drone hanging around.'

Haider circulated the command among the men. The Scots collapsed beside the river. John nudged Dusty. 'I told you it wasn't our fight.'

Dusty lay on his back. 'We got lucky,' he said. A single shot shattered the quiet night. 'What the fuck?' Dusty sat up and looked behind him. The fighters were grouped around Daud. The hot-headed Nuristani was holding a pistol in his hand. 'That little wanker.' Dusty turned to John. He was lying on the ground. 'This one really is your fight. Go teach Daud a lesson.'

John swallowed hard. 'I can't.'

'What are you on about? Rip into the little bastard,' said Dusty.

John placed his hand on his side. 'I can't,' he gasped. 'I've been shot.'

Dusty moved into emergency mode. 'I need my medical pack!' he cried. He lifted John's hand from the wound. 'Let's have a look at that, mate.' John winced as Dusty tore open his waistcoat and kameez. Two centimetres below John's ribcage, Dusty found a small hole. It was oozing blood. 'I see the entrance wound,' he said. 'I need to take a look at your back. Can you move?'

John nodded. With Dusty's help, he rolled onto his uninjured side. 'I can't believe this.' John's words were clipped, like he was struggling to get them out. 'We raid an al-Qaeda training camp without firing a round and that little fucker shoots me.'

'We should have left him in Dogrum with the women.' Dusty found another hole in John's back. It was three times the size of the one in front and ragged around the edges. 'I've found the exit wound. It looks like a clean shot.'

Haider ran to them with the medical pack. When he saw John covered in blood, he fell to his knees. 'Daud was playing with a pistol,' he said. 'I don't know how he got it. It went off accidentally. Oh merciful Allah!'

'Not now!' Dusty snapped. He grabbed a handful of field dressings from the medical pack, ripped them open with his teeth and pressed them against John's back.

'Is it bad?' John was now slurring his words. 'Be straight with me.'

Dusty slid an elastic bandage over the dressed wound and rolled John onto his back. 'The bullet sliced through your fatty tissue, you fat bastard.' He laid a gauze dressing over the entrance wound, looped the elastic bandage over it and ran it round John several times to apply pressure evenly from back to front. 'Maybe we should get Daud to shoot you on the other side, to get rid of your love handles.'

The corners of John's mouth turned up slightly.

Dusty spoke to Haider. 'Bring me a donkey – the one with the lightest load.' His tone was urgent. 'Tell the lads to stand to. We're leaving for Dogrum now. And disarm that twat Daud before he shoots someone else.'

At that moment, John grasped the gravity of the situation. Dusty would only risk moving at night if he felt there was no other way to keep him alive. 'We can't move,' John whispered. 'The drone . . .'

'You're out of action.' Dusty removed his shawl and wrapped it around John. 'I'm in charge, now.'

'. . . It's too dangerous,' said John.

'I wish we hadn't wasted all the morphine on Rafar so I could knock you out and shut you up.' Haider brought a donkey to the riverbank. Dusty cut down the kilims strapped to the beast. 'Grab his legs,' he said to Haider. They laid John across the donkey. 'Take his Bergen,' said Dusty. 'I'll take the weapons.' Dusty fastened the kilims to his own Bergen and shouldered the heavy load. 'Look what I'm doing for you,' he said to John. 'Carrying all the donkey's kit so you can ride in the lap of luxury.'

But Dusty's words fell on deaf ears. John was unconscious.

Chapter 42

Rudy's ears were blocked. His ill-fitting body armour dug into his thighs and his helmet obstructed his vision. He felt no pain though. The incessant rattling of the helicopter had shaken his body numb. Encased in a cocoon of fear, Rudy slid his helmet up. His fellow 'mixed-asscts' – that's how the flight manifest had referred to the passengers on the helicopter – were calm, focused, and professional – consummate military men.

The aircraft turned and dived. Rudy's heart palpitated. He clawed the sound insulation above his head. The soldiers found his reaction highly amusing. One lifted Rudy's round, orange ear defenders. 'Take it easy, mate. We're landing.' The gulf between military and civilian widened further when they disembarked. The soldiers left through the rear of the aircraft while the blades were still rotating. Rudy was strapped in long after they'd stopped.

An officer entered the fuselage and mouthed Rudy's name. He pointed to Rudy's ears. The bulbous ear defenders were still on. Rudy removed them.

'Rudy Lipkingard?'

'Yes.'

'Glad you made it. Welcome to Camp Bastion. I'm Captain Drake. How was your flight?'

Horrendous; nerve wracking; now I know how torture victims feel. 'Uneventful,' said Rudy.

'Excellent. That's how we like them,' said the captain. 'Please, collect your things and meet me outside.'

Rudy gathered up a backpack stuffed with clothing, a sleeping bag, power bars, a flashlight and toiletries. The tools of his trade – a laptop computer, a sat phone, stills camera and a small video recorder – were tucked safely inside a hard shell case. Rudy wished he could crawl inside it.

He took a deep breath and summoned all of his courage. Rudy was about to enter the place he'd been dreading most for days: Camp Bastion, the heart of British military operations in Helmund and the tip of the spear as far as he was concerned.

'So, are you ready to see the real war?' asked Captain Drake.

I've scraped the real war off the bottom of my foot, thank you. 'Can't wait to get stuck in,' said Rudy.

'You're a lucky chap. You should see my inbox. Every journalist in Britain wants an embed right now.' The captain waited for a reply; something suitably appreciative, no doubt. But gratitude was too great a stretch for Rudy. Feigning enthusiasm was the most he could muster in his fragile state of mind.

Rudy looked around the base he'd call home for the next week. It was spartan: a few dozen semicircular beige tents surrounded by blast walls. On the edge, a digger and bulldozer sat idle beside great mounds of earth. Beyond the perimeter, there was nothing – only desert. The wind howling over the flat, hot plains washed over Rudy like ocean waves, casting some of his anxiety adrift. Bastion was completely isolated. Not a single eleven-year-old suicide bomber in sight. It hardly made for enthralling copy, but Rudy couldn't give a toss. He had no problem fashioning stories from dust, as long as he was safe. He pointed to the bulldozer. 'What are you building over there?'

'A new runway,' said Captain Drake. 'We've retained some Afghan contractors for the job. Good chaps, actually. Hard workers.'

Rudy smelled a potential feature. 'Do you think I could interview them?'

The captain considered it. 'I'll see what I can arrange while you're in the field.'

Suddenly, Rudy was standing outside himself, looking in. Surely he hadn't heard the captain correctly. 'In the field?'

'We're sending you up country with the Paras, near Now Zad.' The captain nodded to the landing zone. 'You'll be inserted with that re-supply helicopter.'

Rudy looked over the captain's shoulder. A pallet of green cases was being wheeled into the aircraft that had just dropped him. His mouth turned as dry as the surrounding desert. 'What's the situation in Now Zad?'

The captain paused to choose his words. 'It's a bit of a mess.'

Rudy's anxieties flooded back. The captain had given him the worst answer imaginable. The English reserved that level of understatement for only the worst situations. 'Are you sure I won't be too much of a distraction for the troops? I mean, I would hate to be a burden. I'm sure there are plenty of stories I can do from here.'

'Nonsense,' said the captain. 'The troops are looking forward to your visit. The platoon commander, Captain McDermott, will brief you when you land. You're taking off in thirty minutes so stay close by. If you're hungry, help yourself to a box of rations in the waiting area. There's a brew in the tea urn and cold drinks in the refrigerator. Should we get rocketed or mortared, do go to cover in the hard shelter.' The captain smiled. 'I'm sure you've been through all of this before.'

*

The helicopter changed pitch and hovered. Rudy's mind raced. *It's not too late,* he thought. *They can't force me to do this. I'm going back to Bastion and there's nothing anyone can do about it.* A huge cloud of dust kicked up as the aircraft touched down. The rear door lowered and the crew whisked the supplies into the beige blur. A soldier screamed at Rudy. 'Out! Out! Out!' Rudy scooped up his gear and tried to stand, but his seat belt pulled him back. It was still fastened. The soldier flicked the restraint open with one hand. 'Get the fuck off the aircraft!' he screamed.

Rudy was practically hurled through the rear door. The dust outside was blinding. A member of the flight crew emerged like a spirit from the swirling dust. He grabbed Rudy and threw him down. The ground was hard and lumpy. 'Don't move until the lads tell you!' The soldier disappeared into the cloud. Rudy lifted his arms. He was lying on the supplies.

Thirty seconds and an eternity later, the helicopter took off. Rudy was terrified. *They've left me here. I've been abandoned on the front line!* The deafening click of rotor blades gave way to sputtering engines. The dust dispersed. A soldier hoisted Rudy up by the neck. The man's uniform bore the insignia of the Parachute Regiment. 'Get off the fucking gear. We're under fire,' said the Para. His voice was more annoyed than urgent.

A quad bike was waiting with an empty trailer. Two Paras jumped off and started loading the gear. Rudy stumbled after them, completely disoriented. 'Who the fuck are you?' asked one of the soldiers.

'I'm . . . I'm a journalist.' Rudy looked around. His eyes drifted back to the Para. 'Are you Captain McDermott?'

'You just missed him,' said the soldier. 'He went out on that heli.'

'He left!' Rudy's panic was laced with indignation. 'He was supposed to brief me!'

'He won't be briefing anyone for a while,' said the Para. 'Jump on and I'll take you to our new commander.'

The Paras finished loading the gear and the quad bike sped off. They turned into a compound fifty yards away. It was a typical Afghan set-up, modified for battle. The traditional mud-brick perimeter walls had been reinforced with Hesco baskets: steel mesh containers filled with dirt and debris. There was one single-storey building in the compound with a machine-gunner stationed on the roof. He was firing sporadic bursts. The soldiers below seemed immune to the noise.

The quad bike stopped and all hands pitched in to unload the gear. 'So, a journalist eh? Are you here to make us all famous?' asked the soldier who'd offered to introduce Rudy to the new commander.

Rudy shuddered with each discharge of the machine gun. 'I'm . . . I'm embedded with you for a . . . a week,' he said.

The Para laughed. 'The last journalist who said that got stuck here for three.'

'Three!' squealed Rudy.

'Don't worry. We'll look after you. Name's Jack by the way.'

Rudy wasn't comforted. Jack's face was covered in wispy hairs. He looked barely old enough to take care of himself. It was worse than Rudy's worst-case scenario: stuck on the front lines with a group of adolescents. 'Why did Captain McDermott leave?'

'Are you taking the piss?' said Jack.

The captain must have been wounded or killed. Rudy cursed his stupidity. He needed to make a good impression on these people, not alienate them by acting like an absolute tosser. 'I'm sorry.'

'Don't be,' Jack smiled. 'He's only a Rupert.' The black humour didn't suit the soldier's youth. 'I'll introduce you to the Sarge,' he said, hoisting one end of a green metal container. Rudy grabbed the other.

They carried the container into the compound's only building. Trails of footprints criss-crossed the silt-lacquered floors. It was as hot as an oven. Pervasive dirt and unbearable heat; Rudy really was in hell. They found a soldier off the corridor bent over a table, studying maps. His shirtless back was tanned and leathery. 'We have a visitor, sarge,' said Jack.

The Sarge looked up from his maps. He was older than Jack – maybe early thirties. His prematurely lined face was polluted with several days' growth. He appeared tired but in control of himself and his surroundings, a genuine, battle-hardened combat soldier. Rudy determined to stick to him like glue. 'I'm Rudy Lipkingard. I'm a journalist. I'm embedded with your platoon.'

'Name's Dougie,' said the Sarge. 'I'm platoon sergeant. Now acting platoon commander.'

'Did you know I was coming?' asked Rudy.

'No. But that's nothing new.' The Sarge was obviously not thrilled to have another unforeseen variable on his plate.

Rudy needed to ingratiate himself. 'Back in Bastion, they said you've been having a hard time here.'

The Sarge seemed to appreciate the acknowledgement. 'We just had a nine-hour firefight with the enemy. Three of our troops were wounded, including Captain McDermott.'

Rudy kept sucking up. 'I'm sorry about your men but congratulations on defeating the Taliban.'

The Sarge's face hardened. 'We're a long way from defeating them. The Taliban threw everything they had at us. Once we dropped a couple of thousand pounders on them, they left us alone. It's pretty quiet now.'

Rudy's eyes rolled up. The machine gun was still firing from the rooftop. 'This is quiet?'

The Sarge had grown impatient with the small talk. 'I don't mean to be rude but we're right in the middle of rehashing ourselves , , ,'

Rudy apologized. 'I didn't mean to get in your way . . .'

He raised his hand to shut Rudy up. 'Just give me an hour or so and I'll come and get you.' He turned to Jack. 'Make the journalist a brew and get him settled.'

Jack led Rudy into a back room. 'Just put it down here,' he said. They deposited the container on the floor next to a stretcher. Rudy watched while Jack unloaded medical supplies and added them to a depleted stack in the corner of the room. An empty box had been recycled as a bin. It was filled with old bandages stained with dried blood. 'Put your kit wherever you like,' said Jack.

Rudy laid down his backpack and hard shell case. 'This is where you treat the wounded?'

'Mind if I work while we talk?' said Jack. 'I'm not being ignorant. We're just really, really busy.'

'Don't mind me at all.' Rudy watched as Jack organized the supplies. 'Are you a medic?'

'Yeah,' said Jack.

Rudy knew it wouldn't hurt to have a medic in his corner either – especially if the unthinkable happened. He conducted an impromptu interview in the hopes of establishing a bond. 'Is that why you joined the Paras?'

'I joined the Paras because I wanted to be the best,' said Jack.

The jingoistic response should have sounded rehearsed. But Jack's delivery was entirely off the cuff. 'A nine-hour battle,' said Rudy. 'How did you manage to hold out for so long?'

'Nine hours is nothing,' said Jack. 'Our real issue here is

manpower. On paper a platoon's supposed to be thirty-one men. After last night, we've got twenty-two left including me and I'm a medic. Not an infantry soldier.'

After so much ISAF flannel, Jack's words were shocking. Rudy did the maths. 'My God. You've lost eight men!'

'Wounded,' Jack corrected. 'They all got out of here alive.' Jack was obviously proud of his achievement.

Despite ulterior motives, Rudy sensed a story taking shape: baby-faced Jack; front-line medic. 'Did you expect conditions to be this hard when you came to Helmund?'

Jack stopped what he was doing. 'Let me put it this way. To get into the Paras you have to jump out of an aeroplane. I'm not keen on heights, so when it came time for me to make my first jump, one of the older lads gave me a piece of advice. He said, if you're ever scared, Jack, just smile. I haven't stopped smiling since we got here.'

As the day wore on, Rudy discovered that Jack wasn't the only soldier with a black sense of humour. Every exchange between the men, no matter how minor, was riddled with it. It was the glue that bound them together. Every now and then, Rudy would emerge from his cocoon of fear to ask the men about themselves. The more the platoon liked him, he reasoned, the better they'd look after him.

The Sarge pointed to a satellite image. 'The Taliban are dug in here, here and here,' he explained. Rudy couldn't make head or tail of the grey blobs but it didn't matter. The Sarge thought he could and that was the important thing. 'My aim now,' the Sarge continued, 'is to keep the enemy pushed back from our location and keep my men alive.'

'Will you attempt to advance?' Rudy was trying to sound like he knew what he was talking about.

The Sarge shook his head. 'The Taliban have us spread like

butter all over Helmund. Until we're part of a bigger operation, the best we can do is sustain ourselves.'

By nightfall, the Paras were ready for the Taliban to make their move. Every soldier had his belt kit on and weapons ready. Rudy stood next to the Sarge, trying not to tremble. By 8 p.m., the majority of the platoon stepped down and sentries were posted on the walls.

'Do you think we'll be attacked?' asked Rudy.

'The Taliban never take the night off,' said the Sarge. 'You should get some sleep while you can.'

At 10 p.m. Rudy was jolted awake by a blitz of automatic fire. The soldiers were shouting. 'Stand to! Stand to!' Seconds later, the heavy machine gun on the rooftop opened up. The Taliban were attacking their position. Rudy's heart pounded. He grabbed his helmet and ran to find the Sarge.

He was outside, directing his troops. 'Stay on that wall. Those fuckers are gearing up I can feel it.' He briefly acknowledged Rudy. 'This is what you came to see, right?' Rudy looked at the tracer rounds screaming overhead. They were so close he dare not raise his hand for fear of having his fingers shot off. Rudy slipped further into his cocoon. He was in the middle of a pitched battle.

The Sarge spoke into a radio. 'Hello, zero. This is five-niner. Contact, over.' He moved toward the perimeter wall.

Rudy scuttled after him. 'Do you mind if I shadow you?'

'Do whatever you want, just don't get in the fuckin' way,' he replied. The battle escalated quickly. Rudy kept tabs on the action through the Sarge's radio dispatches. 'They're throwing everything they have at us . . . Artillery support is pointless . . . They're right on our position now . . . how close? We got lads throwing grenades over the walls to keep the enemy from climbing over them, that's how fucking close . . . we need air support, over.' He turned to Rudy. 'I'm heading up to the roof; get a better view of the action.'

Though terrified of moving, Rudy didn't dare stray far from his protector. 'I'm coming with you,' he said.

The Sarge was too busy to argue. 'OK, but keep your head down and do as you're told up there.' He stepped onto the ladder. Rudy nearly ran into him. 'One at a time,' he barked then bolted up the ladder and onto the roof. When it was clear, Rudy started climbing.

Just as he reached the rooftop, a giant explosion shook the compound. The ladder tipped backward with Rudy still on it, the words 'Mortar! Mortar!' circling him as he fell. A searing bolt of pain shot through Rudy's hips right before he hit the ground. He rolled to his side. A chunk of flesh was hanging out of his trousers.

Jack the baby-faced medic ran to him. 'I've been shot!' Rudy cried. 'I've been shot!'

'You took some shrapnel,' said Jack. 'Just take it easy and try to stay calm.'

Rudy thought again of the English penchant for understatement. 'Oh God!' he cried. 'Oh God! Oh God! Oh God!'

'Don't worry,' said Jack. 'I'll take care of you.'

The Sarge called down from the rooftop. 'How's the journalist?'

'He's been hit!' said Jack.

'How bad?'

'It could be fatal!'

Rudy's life flashed before his eyes. *Not here, not now!*

'He was hit in the arse!' said Jack. 'That's where journalists keep their brains, isn't it?'

The Paras howled with laughter.

Chapter 43

The sight of John slumped over the donkey reduced Anvar to tears. The old warrior was distraught. But his sorrow soon turned to anger when he learned how John was wounded. Anvar ordered Daud to the centre of Dogrum. There, before the entire village including women and children, he demanded his nephew explain why he had shot John Patterson – the man on whom Dogrum's future security depended. Daud sought refuge in the divine. 'I have no quarrel with this British man. I was holding the pistol and it went off in my hand. It was the will of Allah,' he insisted. 'Allah is displeased that the infidel is among us!'

Daud's lack of repentance enraged Anvar. He smacked the young man with the back of his hand. 'You are a weak and envious child who wants only for himself. I renounce you and all your offspring!' The irrevocable decree wasn't the end of the public flogging. Anvar called for an immediate referendum to decide whether Daud was fit to remain on the Majlis. The village men were unanimous in their vote. Daud was out. For endangering the life of John Patterson, Anvar had stripped his own nephew of power and patronage. But there was one final punishment remaining. As Malek of Dogrum, Anvar forbade Daud from ever touching a rifle or pistol again. For an Afghan male, it was the ultimate humiliation.

Anvar asked Haider to relay the day's events back to Dusty, along with his personal assurance that all of Dogrum was prepared to help nurse John back to health. The blow by blow of Daud's disgrace was cold comfort to Dusty. He'd never cared about the internal affairs of the backward little village before John was shot and he didn't care now. As for the offer to assist with John's recovery, there was no way in hell Dusty was letting anyone in Dogrum near him.

Dusty cut off John's dressing and sniffed the wound. It was infected. He took John's temperature. It was dangerously high. Dusty rifled through his medical kit. There was only one course of antibiotics. He started John on it immediately along with the last of the saline drips.

After three days of drugs and with no drips remaining, John was still delirious with fever and too weak to eat or drink. Dusty used enemas of cooled, boiled water to keep him hydrated but without intravenous lipids – fat – John was starving. He was literally wasting away before Dusty's eyes.

Consumed with worry, Dusty kept thinking about the days in Kabul before everything went to rat shit. Running a training programme; wagering pints of Guinness; taking the mick out of each other; trying to keep the ex-Rupert managers from pissing on their turf; he and John had never been closer. They had their work and they had each other. They didn't need anything else.

Dusty spent hours replaying their conversations, trying to pinpoint the moment when their good-natured joshing turned to sniping. Inevitably, he'd return to the same exchange: the KMTC, right after the run-in with the American security team. John had never asked Haider to weigh in on one of their arguments before. All that bullshit about 'my village' and 'honour'. The more Dusty thought about it, the more he was convinced that Haider had been playing them all along. He'd lied about the nephews to draw John and Dusty into his blood feud.

Five days into the antibiotics course, John's fever finally broke. He regained consciousness and attempted to sit up. He looked terrible. The rapid and sudden weight loss had doubled the creases in his face. Sprouts of white pushed up beneath his solid red beard. It was as if John had aged a year for each day.

John's appetite still hadn't returned two weeks later. He could barely tolerate broth let alone meat and rice. Fruit went right through him. His failing body sapped his spirits. Dusty decided John needed a project, something to distract him while his body healed.

Dusty kicked John's foot. 'Wake up you sad, skinny git. We've got men to train.'

John lifted his head and moaned. 'I can't hold a spoon. You expect me to hold a rifle?'

'One step at a time. We haven't even knocked up a firing range. But . . .' Dusty sat him up. '. . . if we start putting things in place now, the lads can hit the ground running come spring.'

'The lads won't take me seriously.' John looked at his sunken chest. 'I used to be a fighting cockerel. Now I'm just a feather duster.'

'Stop whingeing.' Dusty grabbed a pen and paper. 'We'll start by writing down our objectives, like we did with the CNPA. Then we can get to specifics like what the security cordon will look like.'

'Shouldn't Haider be here?' John asked.

Dusty didn't want to get into a big barney with John by sharing his suspicions about Haider. 'There're enough bloody germs in this place already,' said Dusty. 'We'll write everything down, I'll give it to Haider and he can tell it to the lads word for word.'

Despite his initial grumblings, John quickly became immersed in the work. After a few days, his defeatism retreated and his old can-do attitude returned. Whenever physical pain threatened to drag him under again, Dusty would pull him through it, usually by throwing up a dissenting opinion to rile him.

The therapy did wonders for John – and Dogrum. By the close of autumn, the village was transformed. John sat wrapped in a blanket on Anvar's balcony, admiring the new security cordon. Sangers – shallow holes surrounded by stone walls capable of withstanding RPG fire – were scattered throughout the terraced fields and inside the village. Stone ramparts had also been built, both to reinforce the wall surrounding Dogrum and provide additional cover for its fighters during battle.

With the physical defences in place, John asked the Majlis – which now consisted solely of Anvar and Baidullah – to gather every male in Dogrum over the age of sixteen along with the Magnificent Seven. John divided the men into groups of four. Each group, he explained, comprised a fighting unit. He then offered them a preview of the training programme he and Dusty had devised. First, every fighter would be taught how to use an AK and how to maintain it. Each unit would then receive instruction in defensive tactics and patrol techniques. Once they'd mastered contact drills with the enemy and wounded-man scenarios the fighters would engage in a full-blown combat exercise. Those fighters who demonstrated the greatest aptitude with rifles would be taught how to use pistols and RPGs. The most elite would receive explosives training.

John put the Majlis on notice that Dogrum would have to operate at limited capacity for at least two months while the training was under way. He also asked their permission to teach the children of Dogrum how to run re-supplies of ammunition during battle and administer basic first aid. John felt strongly that the village women should receive similar training but Haider advised against raising the issue. 'It is a step too far,' he cautioned.

The Majlis greeted John's plans with tremendous enthusiasm. But by mid-winter, with Dogrum snowed in by fifteen-foot drifts, everything threatened to unravel. John's wound became infected again. Dusty had no drugs left to treat him.

Chapter 44

Bullets ripped through a coffin lid, spraying splinters every-where. A dog barked; the sheep in the field bleated; a baby cried but the village of Dogrum remained, otherwise asleep. Twelve seconds later, another burst of rifle fire flew over the houses. Half a minute elapsed before a door finally swung open. Haider came tearing out of his house armed with his AK. He ran to the centre of the village and looked around anxiously. No one else was awake. He put his hand to his mouth and shouted. 'Stand to! Stand to! Stand to!'

Ehsaan and his brothers came running out of their house. Disoriented but excited, they called to the house above. 'Stand to! Stand to!' It started a chain reaction. Heavily accented cries of 'Stand to! Stand to!' echoed up the way as the fighters of Dogrum woke up and warned their neighbours. The village was under attack.

Men, both young and old, flew down the rooftops with their AKs at the ready. Some were shouting, others laughed – a few discharged their weapons into the air as they ran. They were all ready for a fight. One by one, the men slotted into position; a handful stayed up on the roofs while the rest jumped into sangers.

Dogrum's children, meanwhile, moved to their battle sta-tions. They ran to the village's newly designated munitions point. Daud barked orders as he distributed pre-marked satchels stuffed with magazines, grenades and RPG rounds. The youngsters slung the satchels over their shoulders and fanned out along the maze of newly built stone ramparts. The children darted in, out, and along the fortifications, keeping their heads low and out of sight as they moved re-supplies of ammunition out to the fighters.

Haider and the Magnificent Seven pepper-potted across the foot bridge. The sound of water rushing through the ravine below filled the valley. It was nearing the end of spring and the rivers of Nuristan were at their angriest. The men spread out, covering each other as they advanced. They hadn't yet determined the enemy's location. Haider jumped into his sanger at the far end of the bridge, one of three containing an RPG launcher and rounds. He found John and Dusty waiting inside.

The two Scots were the picture of calm: arms folded, their rifles propped against the wall with the safety catches on. 'What are you doing here?' Haider cried. 'This is not your station. Stand to! Stand to!'

John and Dusty started giggling. Haider's puzzled expression stoked their amusement. 'It's an exercise, you clown.' Dusty could barely get the words out for laughing.

John gathered the fighters together in the field. They all looked immensely proud of themselves. 'Firstly, I'd like to welcome you all to our exercise.' Haider repeated the words in Kamviri as John spoke. 'How many of you think it was successful?' The fighters exchanged approving glances. John met them with palpable disappointment. 'Well, you didn't succeed,' he declared. 'By my standards, this exercise was a complete failure. As soon as you hear gunfire you should be up and ready for action. It took two bursts of rifle fire and more than forty seconds before Haider initiated the "stand to" signal. If this had been a real attack by seasoned insurgents, Dogrum would have been overrun. I want you to think about what that would mean. You would be dead and your wives, daughters and sisters would be at the mercy of your enemies. I don't know about you lot but I haven't been working my arse off these past weeks to see you murdered in your sleep and your women kidnapped.'

John let the criticism sink in. 'Was I too hard on them?' he asked Dusty.

Dusty looked at the fighters. Their heads were bowed in shame. 'Nah. You might want to throw 'em a bone, though.'

John spoke to the fighters again. 'It takes nothing to roll out of bed, grab your AKs and get to your stand to positions,' he told them. 'But I will say this – once the signal was initiated, you lot performed admirably. You all knew exactly where to go.' John singled out Ehsaan. 'You and your brothers did a fine job covering each other as you moved into position.' The compliment lifted Ehsaan's spirits. John moved on to Daud. 'I was also pleased to see the children responding so efficiently.' John's praise was wasted on the disgraced villager. Daud eyed him with unveiled contempt. 'I'm putting all of you on notice,' John continued. 'Sometime soon, I won't say when, we'll have another exercise. It could be early morning or in the middle of the night. This time I want you up and responding in twenty seconds or less. Do you understand?' The fighters answered in the affirmative. 'Thank you again for your cooperation. Who's on sentry duty this morning?' Three of the fighters raised their hands. 'Get to your sangers then.'

The three men headed for their posts while the rest of the fighters lingered. Ehsaan pulled Haider aside. The oldest of the Magnificent Seven looked worried. Haider patted the young man's shoulder and went to speak with John and Dusty.

'The brothers are concerned you will not select them for explosives training,' said Haider.

'Tell them not to worry,' said Dusty. 'We'll start them on it ASAP.'

'Not yet,' said John. 'They're not ready.' He reached for his side and dropped his hand before it made contact with his old injury.

The gesture did not escape Dusty's notice. 'They're as ready as they'll ever be.'

John struggled to conceal his discomfort. 'We don't even have all the kit for an explosives course.'

'We'll make do with what we have,' Dusty countered.

John shook his head. 'We need a truck battery and some petrol.'

'We'll use the motorbike batteries.'

'The charge is too weak.' John called Ehsaan over and spoke to him through Haider. 'Do you and your brothers fancy learning how to use explosives?' Ehsaan nodded excitedly. 'Well, in that case, you're going to have to find a few things.' John looked at Dusty – then back at Ehsaan. 'Do you think you could get your hands on a truck battery and a few litres of petrol?'

'I know where we can obtain such items,' Ehsaan said confidently. 'It will take a few days – a week at most.'

'Forget it,' Dusty interrupted. 'A week's too long.'

John grew annoyed. 'I want to do this right.' He spoke to Ehsaan. 'No more than a week. You can take our motorbikes to use as barter.'

Ehsaan flashed a roguish grin. 'That will not be necessary. We shall not disappoint you.'

Back in their single-room dwelling, John removed his shirt and vest.

'When did it start hurting again?' asked Dusty.

'When did it stop?' said John.

Dusty examined John's side. An inflamed, red scar wrapped around it like a bite mark. The sight of it transported Dusty back to the terrible days of winter, when John lay dying on the bed. He'd given up all hope when one morning John called to him.

'The window,' John gurgled through fluid-filled lungs. 'Take me to the window.'

Dusty scooped up John in his arms. The fading Scot was so emaciated, the skin fell off his back. Dusty placed John's head in the crook of his shoulder and propped him up. It was still pitch-black outside.

'Not too long,' said Dusty, fearful that the draught would aggravate John's pneumonia. The glow of a hurricane lamp moved towards them and two figures came into view: a woman carrying a tray and a small girl. The woman's eyes were cast down. Dusty hadn't noticed her before.

For the briefest moment, John's eyes lit up. It was then that Dusty realized what John really needed. It wasn't work or even friendship that would keep him fighting. John needed the promise of a second chance. Every morning after that, Dusty rose before daybreak to get John to the window in time to see mother and child bringing them breakfast.

Dusty sniffed the swollen tissue. 'There's no necrosis,' he said, relieved. 'But I'd like to cut away some tissue to be on the safe side.'

John grew weary. 'Can't we give it a few days? See if it sorts itself out.'

Dusty put a pot of water on the wood-burning stove. 'You

know the drill. I'll make an incision, debrete the wound and suture.' Dusty pulled a scalpel from his medical pack and placed it in the pot.

John examined his chest, arms and abdomen. Six months ago his skin was taut. Now it hung off him. His pectorals and biceps had withered away and his ribs stuck out. 'Look at the state of me,' he said. 'You keep slicing pieces off and there won't be anything left.'

'You delay the training any more and I guarantee it.' Dusty laid a bivvy bag on John's bed and cleaned the surface with a damp cloth. He showed the dirty rag to John. 'We need to leave this place and get you to a proper medical facility.'

John lay down on the bed. 'A few good meals and some shuttle runs up and down these mountains and I'll be as good as new.'

'It'll take more than that. I've seen more meat on a butcher's pencil.' Dusty swabbed the scar with sterile water. 'As long as we're here that wound of yours will re-infect. We can be in Pakistan in a day; Islamabad in three.'

'Stop your yapping and get to it then,' said John.

Dusty grabbed the scalpel. 'If you're not entirely satisfied with my services you're welcome to take your custom elsewhere.'

There was a knock on the door. Haider burst into the room, breathless from running. 'A group of fighters are approaching the village,' he said.

John and Dusty looked alarmed. 'Hizb-i-Islami?' John asked.

'No,' said Haider. 'Americans.'

Chapter 45

The convoy of Hummers lurched towards the border with Pakistan. Rudy sat white-faced in the third vehicle from the rear, clutching the grab handle for dear life. The boxes of ammunition stacked to his left shifted precariously. If the vehicle rolled, Rudy would be crushed. His mouth filled with saliva, a precursor to vomiting. He tried to regain his equilibrium before his breakfast of dry toast and tea refunded all over the soldiers riding with him.

'You all right there, dude?' asked the soldier in the adjacent seat.

The American accent was reassuring. 'I'm afraid breakfast isn't agreeing with me,' said Rudy.

The soldier nodded. 'We call that Paktika belly. Give us a shout if you need something for it. We pop Imodium around here like candy.' Rudy's nerves steadied. There wasn't a trace of black humour in that answer. God bless the Yanks. It was bad enough in Helmund having a piece of shrapnel rip through his arse without the Paras having a laugh about it. Granted, the injury had been far from life-threatening but that didn't make it any less terrifying. Fuck the Sarge and Jack the bloody baby-faced medic. Rudy had sworn on the airlift out of Now Zad that he was finished with the Paras, embeds and Afghanistan for good.

And then the headline hit:

WOUNDED: OUR CORRESPONDENT'S HARROWING ACCOUNT

Lucinda milked the follow-up coverage for weeks.

'I'M NO HERO' SAYS INJURED JOURNALIST

THE ROAD TO RECOVERY; RUDY LIPKINGARD'S TOUGHEST BATTLE YET

'I OWE IT TO THE LADS': OUR CORRESPONDENT VOWS TO RETURN TO THE FRONTLINE

Rudy's wound had catapulted him to the highest degree of his craft. Instead of covering the story, he'd become it. The nightmare in Helmund had ushered in his dream. Rudy was the print world's John Simpson, a star bigger than the story itself.

Rival papers and TV news operations soon came courting with obscene pay packages, book deals and documentaries. Rudy turned them all away. 'I'm under contract and I doubt my editor would permit a buy-out,' he'd explain. But Rudy's coyness had nothing to do with legalities. None of the offers tempted him because every news organization wanted him for the same thing – war coverage.

No one seemed to realize that behind the headlines of heroism, Rudy was a quaking mess. During his prolonged convalescence in London, he assiduously avoided any discussion of Afghanistan, let alone the prospect of returning there. He couldn't bear to look at newspapers for fear of seeing an Afghan headline. So consuming was his anxiety, he would even turn his head away from news-stands. The same applied to television. Once he'd caught sight of a news story from an embedded reporter. The images transported him right back to the battle at Now Zad. From then on, if a pub had a news channel playing on the TV, Rudy would ask them to switch it off. If they refused, he'd leave.

The self-imposed information blackout worked a treat at first, but, inevitably, Rudy's traumatic memories found ways around it. The most innocuous things could trigger a flashback. During a dinner with friends Rudy found himself panic-stricken after the hostess presented a roast beef. The rare meat set against the red tablecloth reminded him of the suicide bomber's charred torso wrapped in the Manchester United jersey. Rudy narrowly avoided vomiting on his fellow guests before excusing himself. The episode convinced him to seek professional help.

A psychologist diagnosed Rudy with post-traumatic stress disorder and recommended he stay in the UK to undergo ther-apy. Lucinda baulked at the very suggestion. She had devoted too many column inches to building Rudy's legend. He was of no use to her in the UK. She needed him back in Afghanistan and the sooner the better. But even Lucinda realized that bul-lying the fragile journalist could backfire. So instead of a stick, she used a carrot to coax Rudy back into the lion's den. 'What about that whistle-blower chap you were so keen on?'

The mention of the story perked Rudy up. 'John Patterson,' he said. 'I can have the copy ready for tomorrow's edition.'

'You can't file that story unless you return to Afghanistan,' said Lucinda.

'Yes, I can,' Rudy chirped. 'I have all my notes here.'

'Your notes are not the issue,' said Lucinda. 'You're a per-sonality now. It's not *what* you write but *where* you write that counts. People expect Rudy Lipkingard to tell stories from the front line. They want you to report from dangerous places. Now if you want to throw everything you've worked for away and be just another plain vanilla correspondent then far be it from me to stand in your way. But if you choose obscurity, don't expect your stories to receive top priority. And don't expect your fans to remain loyal. No one loves a coward.'

Rudy was at a crossroads. He could return to Afghanistan as the newspaper's celebrated, fearless Kabul correspondent and guarantee his claim to the front page – or, he could stay in London, be labelled a coward and struggle to get his stories printed. 'If I return, do you promise to run the story?'

'Yes,' Lucinda assured him. 'Provided it checks out.'

The Patterson story was not Lucinda's priority, of course. As soon as Rudy stepped on the plane, she lined up another Helmund embed for him. This time, though, Rudy was ready to head her off. The unexpected offer of an embed with US forces had come through while he was still recuperating. It was the perfect time to take the Yanks up on it. Rudy was much less apprehensive about embedding with American troops. The US military had a bigger presence in Afghanistan. It was definitely better equipped. Most importantly, they weren't getting hammered like the British. If Rudy had to cover the war, then by God he was going to do it as safely as possible.

Rudy's eyes retracted along the column of Hummers. The square bodies were solid and armoured. He told himself he had nothing to fear. He was as safe as a baby in his mother's womb. He took out his notebook and searched for a blank page. As he flipped through it, a sentence written months earlier caught his eye. *Patterson's past? SOCA–ShieldGroup Smear Campaign?* The words drew Rudy back to the Jalalabad Road. At the time, Rudy had only thought of how the story could make him a star.

Now that he was one, it occurred to him that John Patterson could very well prove his salvation. Once the story was published, it would propel Rudy's career in a whole new direction. He could become a celebrated investigative reporter or even a top-flight political correspondent. Clearing Patterson and his team could free Rudy from the noose of war reporting.

An ear-splitting blast shattered the daydream. The ground shook. By the time Rudy processed there had been an explosion, another all-mighty bang rumbled him. It was the sound of the Hummer in front slamming back to earth after being blown off the road by an IED.

Soldiers poured out of their vehicles and shot into the dust. They shouted to each other between bursts: 'Forward, man, to the front, to the front!' Rudy crawled out of his undamaged Hummer and scrambled underneath it. The air was thick with smoke pouring off the vehicle that had been hit. The wind changed direction, revealing the full horror of the incident. The Hummer had flipped and landed in an embankment. It was on fire. There were soldiers trapped inside. The men were burning alive.

Rudy covered his ears to block their cries. He felt himself being pulled backward by the ankles. 'Are you OK!' shouted a soldier.

Rudy was too petrified to speak. The soldier lifted him to his feet and shoved him into the Hummer. 'Stay in the fucking vehicle!'

Chapter 46

A cramp curled around John's side, constricting his breathing. His legs burned and the skin on his face tingled. He tried working through the pain but the beast ravaging his body was too powerful to cage.

Dusty looked at him. 'You need to rest.'

'You sound like an old woman, you know that?' said John.

'Yeah, well, you look like one.' Dusty felt John's forehead. 'You're dehydrated. You keep pushing yourself like this and you'll pass out.'

'I'm fine,' John insisted.

'Bollocks. You're in worse shape than him.' Dusty nodded at Anvar. The old Malek was swaying back and forth on top of a donkey. Winter had been hard on Anvar. His eyes were sunken and his proud face had turned a troubling shade of grey. Dusty reached for a kilim bag slung around John's shoulder. Both Scots had switched their Bergens for local packs. 'If you won't stop and rest, at least let me carry your kit.' John shirked. 'Give it here or I'll start a drama,' said Dusty.

John knew Dusty would make good on the threat. The younger Scot had been dead set against the trip in the first place. But when American soldiers came to Dogrum looking for fighting-aged men to train for a local support militia, John knew something had to be done. He urged Anvar to go to the

American base near Kamdesh and tell the Yanks to stay away from Dogrum. Anvar agreed, but he wanted John to come with him.

Dusty stepped in front of John, blocking him. 'Give it here now,' he demanded.

Haider looked back at them. 'Why are you stopping?'

'We're not.' John slid the kilim from his shoulder and passed it to Dusty. 'I'm going to scout ahead.' Before Dusty could object, John ran past the group and up a ridge. The sprint compounded his already considerable pain. John's whole body was on pins and needles. He pushed himself over the ridge and collapsed.

By the time the others caught up with him, John was observing the valley below through his binos as if he were fighting fit. Dusty hurled John's bag at him. 'You pull another stunt like that and I'll carry you back to Dogrum.'

'You think I'm in bad shape?' John pointed to the head of the valley. 'Take a look at those sad bastards.'

Dusty looked through his binos. 'Poor laddies,' he said, astonished. 'Why didn't they just build an FOB in the middle of a bullseye and be done with it.'

They studied the US forward operating base in detail. Situated on a tiny sliver of land shoehorned between three immense mountains, the FOB was overlooked on all sides. The surrounding ridges provided ample cover for anyone wishing to attack: boulders, cedar trees, partially camouflaged re-entrants. Insurgents could hide in them for days studying the Americans, learning their routines, figuring out exactly when they were at their most vulnerable. The access routes on and off the base compromised its security further still. There were two: a main gate located at one end of a concrete bridge and an LZ – landing zone – on the other side. The barrier-less bridge traversed a T-junction where a tributary split from a fast-flowing river. The bridge could only be accessed via a slender dirt road running ten feet above the main river. Vehicles of any weight, let alone lightly armoured ones, would have to crawl along it or risk sliding into the water. Targeting them with an IED or RPG would be child's play. The LZ was even more defenceless. Helicopters had to drop hundreds of feet within spitting distance of the mountains to land on it. An insurgent could hit one blindfolded coming in or taking off.

A handful of local guards working in support of the Americans patrolled the area immediately around the base. Many of them looked like they were high on drugs. The only real deterrents to attack were inside the FOB: an 81mm mortar supported by a square, green LRAS – thermal imaging device for targeting heat signatures at night – and half a dozen Hummers mounted with Mk 19 grenade launchers or .50-calibre heavy machine guns. The rest of the camp's defensive measures were slapdash. Stone walls were under construction but a long way from completion. Burned carcasses of Soviet armoured personnel carriers and Hesco baskets served as temporary blast walls. The FOB looked more like a junkyard than an outpost for the most powerful, advanced military on earth.

'How do they sleep at night?' John wondered aloud. 'I'd be scared shitless if I was operating from there.'

'We'd better cache our weapons,' Dusty advised. 'The soldiers there are bound to be nervous.' He looked at John pointedly. 'And remember, not a word out of you. The last thing we need is to get mistaken for a pair of nutters and get shipped off to Guantánamo Bay.'

'I rather fancy those orange jumpsuits,' John joked.

'I'm serious,' Dusty warned. 'Have you looked in the mirror lately?'

Dusty's concerns were not without merit. He and John could

easily be mistaken for British radicals who'd come to
Afghanistan to fight for al-Qaeda. Their beards reached their
chests, Dusty's hair touched his shoulders and John's head was
shaved. Both wore sandals on their feet. The boots that had
once threatened to betray their Western origins hadn't survived
the winter.

The Scots, Haider and Anvar hid their rifles, magazines, pistols and knives behind a boulder and headed downhill. A pair
of outer cordon guards – locals – stopped them at the foot of
the concrete bridge. The locals patted them all down for
weapons and led them to the main gate where two American
soldiers were standing guard. The soldiers were dressed in full
body armour and armed with M4 carbines. Their eyes were
hidden behind mirrored sunglasses. One of the men's jaws was
disfigured by a wad of tobacco.

John whispered to Dusty. 'Tossers.'

Dusty's eyes narrowed with fury as he mouthed the words
shut the fuck up.

One of the locals spoke. 'These men from Dogrum village.
They come to meet commanding officer.'

The soldier with the tobacco turned his head and spat. The
hairs on John's neck stood up. 'Did they say what for?' asked
the soldier.

Haider spoke. 'We are here to discuss the security of our
village.'

The soldier hooked the tobacco in his cheek with his finger
and pulled it out. A brown, moist lump landed on the ground.
'Welcome to Camp Keating, sir,' he said, flashing a cheerful smile
speckled with bits of brown. He took off his sunglasses. With his
full face revealed, the young man was transformed from an
anonymous aggressor into a welcoming host. His eyes were wide
and friendly. 'I'm Corporal Rucker. Our commanding officer is

out visiting one of our development projects in the area. You and your friends are welcome to help yourselves to refreshments in our mess tent until he returns.'

The invitation was disarming. John had come to think of American troops as anonymous foreigners whose very presence threatened Dogrum's security. Corporal Rucker put a face on them. The young soldier couldn't have been more than twenty years old. Maybe he was like John, an off-the-street kid who joined the military because he had nowhere else to go. And now he was sat at the bottom of a valley in Nuristan, inviting any local who knocked on his door in for a brew and a chat. The poor laddie didn't have a clue.

John kept his head low, reacting neither positively nor negatively. He and the others were searched a second time and shown to the FOB's canteen. 'We're serving breakfast,' Corporal Rucker explained. 'We got pancakes, eggs, bacon, sausage . . .' he stopped himself mid-sentence. 'My apologies. I forgot you folks don't eat pork. Umm, coffee and tea are over there.' He pointed to pastries wrapped in plastic. 'Spunkmyer cakes. I'm pretty sure they're kosher or whatever.'

The familiar smells tugged at John's memory. He couldn't remember when he'd last tasted pork. The bacon and sausages made his mouth water, but he steered clear of the forbidden meat – if only to avoid offending Anvar.

As he sat at a table sipping tea and eating cake, John realized that bacon aside, the Western way of life had lost all appeal to him. The squeaky, American voices in the tent sounded more foreign than the Kamviri tongue he had yet to decipher. And after months of leathery, hardened Nuristani faces staring back at him, the smooth skin, perfect teeth and optimistic expressions of the US soldiers were like something out of a glossy magazine – perfect and unreal.

A soldier informed Corporal Rucker that the commanding officer was ready to meet 'the locals'. The corporal showed John and the others to a tent kitted out with white plastic chairs and a dry marker board with details of patrols written in English. It was the camp's briefing area. John couldn't believe the Yanks would allow non-authorized personnel inside it.

A few minutes later, the commanding officer arrived. He was accompanied by another man dressed in a tight, micro-fibre T-shirt and camouflage trousers. The CO's name and rank – Major – were written on the pocket of his uniform. The other man's role was anonymous. John didn't like the look of him.

'Welcome to our base, gentlemen.' The CO shook everyone's hand. 'One of you speaks English?'

Corporal Rucker pointed to Haider. 'That gentleman there, sir.'

'It's a pleasure to meet all of you. Please take a seat.' The CO waited for John and the others to sit down before pulling up a chair across from them. The anonymous man stayed at the back of the tent. 'So, how can we be of service?' asked the CO.

'We are from Dogrum,' said Haider. He pointed to Anvar. 'This is Anvar, Malek of Dogrum. Anvar has come to ask you as one leader to another to keep your soldiers away from our village.'

The CO bowed respectfully to Anvar. 'We are honoured to have you here, sir.' He examined the dry marker board. 'I don't believe we have a PRT in . . .' he looked at Haider, '. . . Dogrum was it?'

'You do not have a project in our village,' Haider confirmed. 'Your soldiers came to Dogrum last year. They offered to build us a micro-hydro station but we declined.'

The CO nodded as Haider spoke and continued doing it after he'd finished. The idea of anyone refusing American assistance seemed beyond his comprehension. 'You know, there are lots of other ways we can help you,' said the CO. 'We're building roads in Nuristan, schools, medical facilities. We're training local militias to work in support of the Afghan National Army and police. Tell us what you need. We're here for you. We're here to help.'

Haider held up his hand. 'You misunderstand. We do not want your help. All we want is to be left alone. Your visits to Dogrum have been very bad for our people. The insurgents watch your movements. They know where you go and who you talk to. Your soldiers visit one day, the next day the insurgents attack us as a warning not to cooperate with you.'

The CO regressed to his nodding posture. 'I apologize if our presence here has caused any problems for your village. Please know that if any of your people are injured as a result of our operations here, we will fly them to Bagram airbase where they will receive the best medical treatment the US Army has to offer. As I said, we're here to help.'

'We do not want your help.' Haider's voice was firm. 'If we accept it, the insurgents will attack us. They have already done so twice. If you return to Dogrum, they will attack us again.'

'What if the insurgents are already among you?' the anonymous man interrupted. The remark was like a red rag to a bull. John was furious.

The anonymous man nodded to the CO. 'Mind if I have a word with them?' He didn't wait for the CO to respond. 'I grew up on a small family farm.' He paced the room as he spoke. 'We grew crops, raised livestock – sheep, chickens. We didn't get rich from it but we managed to scratch out a good, honest living.'

John eyed the man suspiciously. Who was he? And why hadn't the CO introduced him to Haider? If he were a junior officer, his rank would be on his clothes. John recalled the few diplomatic operations he'd endured in the Regiment. Then it clicked. The fucker was anonymous for a reason. He was an intelligence officer – a spook.

'One day a wild dog slipped under our fence and headed straight for the chicken coop,' the intelligence officer continued. 'We chased it off before it ripped them all to pieces. Later, we found out that this dog wasn't actually wild. It was a pet – our neighbour's pet to be precise. Now our neighbours weren't bad people. They were farmers, just like us. All they wanted was to live peacefully and make a living from the land. When we told them how their dog had behaved, well, they promised us it wouldn't happen again. I guess I don't have to tell you – it did. The dog came back and threatened our chickens again. We told our neighbours to put the dog down, not just for our sakes, but for theirs too. After all, if our chickens were in danger, so were theirs. We asked and we asked and one day, sure enough, the dog slipped under our fence, got into the coop and killed all of our chickens. Then he went back home and killed all of the neighbour's chickens too. By the time we captured and killed that animal, every farm in the area had been attacked.' The intelligence officer shook his head. 'The crying shame is that none of it would have happened if our neighbours had just worked with us in the first place. Do you understand what I'm trying to say here?'

John looked at Corporal Rucker. The young soldier was lost. He eyed the CO. The major's head was bowed as if he wanted no part of the intelligence officer's agenda.

'I'm afraid I do not understand,' said Haider.

The intelligence officer sat down and put his feet up, exposing the bottom of his boots. John's anger escalated. Displaying the soles of the feet to another person was a huge insult in Afghanistan. For an intelligence officer, he certainly was a thick fucker. He may as well have dropped his trousers and waved his bare arse in their faces. 'The situation we got here is pretty much the same,' the officer explained. 'Now you people – you're like our neighbours. You just want to live peacefully and get on with your lives. The wild dog – he's al-Qaeda. And I guarantee you that just like that dog al-Qaeda will try to destroy your village as surely as they'll try to destroy us.' The intelligence officer dropped his feet and clasped his hands together. 'But we can stop them, if we work together.'

Haider considered the intelligence officer's argument. 'The situations are not the same. The insurgents never bothered us until you came here,' he said.

'Ah, but that's what they want you to think.' The intelligence officer tapped the side of his head with his finger. 'But if you really think about it, al-Qaeda was causing problems here way before we ever showed up. So why not help us help you get rid of them?'

John wanted to chin the smug bastard.

Haider kept his composure. 'Your desire to help us is admirable. But we do not want it. Again, we ask you respect-fully, please leave Dogrum alone.'

The intelligence officer stood again and folded his arms. His biceps were disproportionate to his frame – like they'd been grown with steroids. 'It's time you folks realized that there are two sides calling the shots in Nuristan right now: al-Qaeda . . .', he shoved his wide thumb in his chest, '. . . and us. Now if you don't work with us you may as well be working with them because you'll be giving the terrorists exactly what they want. They want to isolate you so they can control you. They'll do everything in their power to turn this country back into a ter-rorist haven. I sure as hell don't want that to happen and I'm sure you don't want it to either.' He stopped and took a deep breath. 'You're either with us or with al-Qaeda. There's no being neutral in Afghanistan.'

The veiled threat pushed John past breaking point. He exploded. 'Yank wanker!'

Dusty and Haider froze. The intelligence officer did a double take of John. 'I'm . . . I'm sorry. Is that English you're speaking?'

'Real English,' John thundered. 'Not that shite you're using.' The second sentence was an even greater shock to the Americans. John rose from his chair. 'Who's in charge here?' he demanded.

The intelligence officer and CO locked eyes, suggesting that a power struggle had been brewing long before John posed the question. 'I am,' said the CO. 'I'm the senior military officer in this sector.'

'Well then, I suggest you start acting the part.' John pointed to the intelligence officer. 'Because this knob isn't just putting innocent Nuristanis at risk – he's endangering every soldier under your command by turning the locals against you.'

'Hold on a goddamn minute.' The intelligence officer rose to John's challenge. 'People here welcome us with open arms. The United States is the best thing to happen to this place since . . .' he searched for a comparison, '. . . since . . . ever. Every village around here has taken up offers of aid.' The intelligence officer paused and looked at John suspiciously. '. . . that is until you arrived. But something tells me that's not a coincidence.'

'You're no different from any other country that's invaded Afghanistan,' said John. 'You didn't come here to help the people. You're here to help yourselves.'

'Oh really?' The intelligence officer gestured to Haider, Anvar and Dusty. 'How do you explain the roads we're building to your friends here? Or the schools?'

John spoke over him. 'Flannel. The lot.'

'. . . The Afghan people want a better life,' the intelligence officer continued. 'They want infrastructure, they want education. They want democracy. The only ones who don't are al-Qaeda and al-Qaeda sympathizers.'

John shot back. 'The only reason you're here is to prop up your puppet regime in Kabul and suck the country dry. You're not interested in empowering the Afghan people. Democracy my arse. Call it what it really is – mymocracy.'

The officer studied John from head to toe. 'What are you doing in Nuristan?'

John refused to deviate from the subject. 'I'm warning you, leave our village alone. There's no reason for you to come to Dogrum. There are no Taliban or al-Qaeda there. So why don't you take your tree-trunk arms and your tree-trunk head and fuck off back where you came from.'

The intelligence officer stuck his face in John's. 'Where are you from exactly?'

John raised his head and looked down his nose. 'Dogrum.'

'I mean where were you born?' The intelligence officer paced the room again. 'Because I've been racking my brain, trying to figure out what someone with an Australian accent is doing in Nuristan. You're not here with the Coalition, that's for sure.'

John laughed – hard. 'That just about sums it up. Australian? You can't even recognize an accent from your biggest NATO partner.'

The intelligence officer kept his eyes locked on John. 'Corporal!' he barked.

'Yes, sir.' The young soldier was more confused than eager.

'This man is now officially a person of interest to the United States government,' said the intelligence officer. 'Detain him immediately.'

The wide-eyed corporal looked to his CO for a counter-directive. The CO nodded, indicating the intelligence officer's orders would stand. The corporal raised his rifle and looked awkwardly at John. 'Sir, would you mind coming with me, please?'

John's lips curled into a sneer. He spoke to Haider. 'Tell Anvar we're finished here.'

Haider helped Anvar to his feet while John pushed his way past the corporal. The intelligence officer drew his pistol and took aim at John. 'Stop or I'll shoot!'

The entire room froze. Anvar raised his hand for peace. The old man spoke.

'Our Malek says if we have caused you offence, this was not our intention,' Haider translated. 'He asks that you let us leave as peacefully as we came.'

The intelligence officer held John in his sights. 'Tell your Malek we have business with your friend here. The rest of you are free to go.'

Haider explained the situation to Anvar. The old man spoke again. 'I am Anvar, Malek of Dogrum. This man is a trusted friend and an honoured guest of our village. He is here at my invitation. Should harm come to him, it would disgrace me and all of Dogrum. As sure as the sun will rise, I will sacrifice my own life and the lives of all of my people to defend this man's life and his honour.'

The intelligence officer wasn't moved. 'Listen up – Malek,' he spat the title, 'this is a US military base. The only law that matters here is Uncle Sam's.'

The CO intervened. 'Stand down,' he said to the intelligence officer.

The intelligence officer ignored the order. 'This matter is outside your jurisdiction.'

'Like hell it is,' said the CO. 'This is my base. What happens here is my responsibility. Now I'm not going to tell you again – stand down.'

The intelligence officer lowered his weapon. 'You're making a big mistake.'

'We'll see about that.' The CO addressed Haider. 'Tell your Malek all of you are free to go. As for visiting Dogrum, we will respect his wishes. My men will stay away from your village unless there is a specific security issue that requires our attention there.' The CO looked directly at Anvar. 'I'm taking you at your word that there's no other agenda here. But if I find out that Dogrum is providing aid or comfort to our enemies, be warned, we will take all necessary and appropriate action.'

Haider presented the offer to Anvar. 'Our Malek will accept this arrangement.'

'If you change your mind about accepting our help – our door is always open to you, Malek.' The CO singled out John. 'As for you, step foot on this base again, and I goddamn guarantee you, you will be detained.'

'Don't worry,' said John. 'I won't be back.'

The CO tilted his head and scrutinized John's face. 'Scottish, right?' He gestured to Corporal Rucker. 'Please escort these gentlemen off the base.'

Outside the tent, the young corporal worked up the courage to speak to John. 'Sorry about what happened back there. For what it's worth, everyone thinks that guy's an asshole. I'll be telling all my buddies tonight how you put him in his place.'

John kept walking. 'What is he? CIA? DIA? JSOC?'

The corporal fished some tobacco from a pouch and shoved it into his cheek. 'He ain't regular army and that's about all I can say.'

'You shouldn't put up with him or any other spook telling you what to do here,' said John. 'Real soldiers fight this war. Real soldiers should be calling the shots.'

'You'll get no argument from me on that one, sir.' The corporal said nothing more until they'd left the camp and crossed the concrete bridge. 'This is where we say goodbye. Y'all be careful. The hills have eyes, if you know what I mean.'

'You're a good lad,' said John. 'Look after yourself.'

'Um, sir?' The corporal fidgeted. 'It seems like you know the people here pretty good.'

'Some,' said John. 'Why?'

The corporal looked around. 'It's just that, well, it's kind of embarrassing to admit this, sir, but we're not always sure who we're fighting. I mean, the brass is telling us we're here to do humanitarian projects but we're getting attacked three nights a week. There's no way the insurgents are doing it all alone. They got to be getting some help from the locals.'

John considered how to respond. He felt no loyalty towards the young American – but he did feel sorry for him. 'If you know what's good for you, you'll stay out of all the villages here, not just Dogrum. Do you have soldiers stationed on the high ground?'

'There aren't enough of us here to mount regular patrols,' the corporal said. 'The CO put local guards on it.'

John shook his head. 'Do you want to survive in this valley?'

'Sure do, sir,' said the corporal.

'Then get your own men up there.'

John pulled the rifles from their hiding place. 'Haider, Anvar,' he said, handing them two AKs. He grabbed Dusty's 5.56. 'Here you go, mate,' he said, turning. Instead of an outstretched hand, John was met by a coiled arm and closed fist. Before he could duck, Dusty punched him in the jaw. The blow hit John like a gale. He spun round and crashed gracelessly to the ground.

Dusty glared down on him. 'Is your jaw broken?'

John cupped his aching face. 'Why'd you do that?'

Dusty grabbed his 5.56 and flipped it so the butt was pointing down. 'Because breaking your jaw is the only way to get you to shut the fuck up.' Dusty swung the rifle like a golf club. John rolled. The rifle butt clipped his shoulder.

John groaned. 'I think you fractured my collarbone!'

Dusty threw the rifle down. He grabbed John's waistcoat and lifted him to his feet like a rag doll. 'Then stand still because I'm not stopping until I've knocked every tooth out of that bloody big mouth of yours!'

A rifle round split the air. It was right on top of them. John and Dusty turned. Anvar was holding his AK. The old Malek had shot it into the air. His face was heavy with exhaustion. 'Why do you attack one another?' he asked through Haider. 'You are friends, are you not?'

Dusty gave John one last threatening look and dropped his waistcoat. 'Tell Anvar he wouldn't understand. It's a Scottish thing.'

The only words that passed between the two Scots the rest of the day were strictly operational. By the time they pitched camp for the night, John's anger over the sucker punch had subsided. After all, the battering wasn't undeserved. He had broken his word.

Dusty volunteered to take the first watch for the evening. John waited for Anvar and Haider to fall asleep before extending an olive branch to his fellow Scot. He sat down beside Dusty. The gesture didn't break the silence between them. John grabbed a stick and poked the dying fire. Red sparks flew from the smouldering embers into his face. John jumped up and patted his red and white beard frantically. Dusty laughed. 'Fuck off,' said John. Dusty grabbed the stick and shuffled the embers, releasing more sparks for John to snuff. John played along until they'd both laughed themselves out.

John looked at the stars. 'Clear night,' he said, still breathless from laughing. 'I do love it here.'

The light mood dissolved. Dusty looked at John. The glow from the fire cast deep shadows across the older Scot's face, making him appear almost skeletal. 'Do you want to get home in one piece?' Dusty asked.

John bowed his head. 'I know I shouldn't have done what I did today. You were right to have a go at me. I promised to keep my mouth shut and I didn't. I compromised my safety and yours and that was wrong. I'm sorry. Stay angry for as long as you need to.'

'I'm not angry,' said Dusty. 'And I went after you for your own good. What you did was just plain reckless.'

'Come on,' said John. 'That spook needed telling off. The way he was talking down to Anvar and threatening Dogrum . . .'.

'To hell with Anvar,' said Dusty. 'And to hell with Dogrum. Have you forgotten why we came to Nuristan in the first place? It wasn't to protect Anvar or train a bunch of locals. We came here to clear our names. We've done that. So what are we still doing here?'

'You know why,' said John. 'Dogrum can't defend itself yet.'

'It's the most battle-ready village in the whole fucking valley,' Dusty countered. 'Bloody hell, in all of Nuristan.'

'We need to finish what we started.' John appealed to Dusty. 'Let's just get through the explosives training. We'll start on it straight away. Once that's done, I give you my word, we'll head home.'

Dusty poked the fire again. 'Hate to break it to you, mate, but after today, your word is shite.'

'Not this time.' John grabbed Dusty's arm and looked at him. 'We will go home. I promise.'

Chapter 47

John flattened the green stalks with the palms of his hands. Haider and the Magnificent Seven surrounded him, observing. 'Make the area big enough to accommodate the explosive, but not so big as to announce it's there. You want to surprise the enemy,' John explained. While Haider relayed the instructions in Kamviri, John nodded to Dusty. The younger Scot passed him a petrol-filled plastic container painted grey and brown to blend in with the surrounding earth. John placed it in the small clearing and unwrapped a stick of plastic explosive. He worked the supple material into a ball as he spoke. 'Right now, that can of fuel is nothing more than a fire hazard.' John held up the finished ball. 'Add some PE and it becomes a highly effective weapon.' The Magnificent Seven were spellbound as they watched John assemble the rest of the explosive device.

'Can any of you lads tell us why a fuel bomb is such an effective defensive weapon?' Dusty quizzed.

Haider relayed the question to the students. Ehsaan answered. 'Because explosives can give thirty men the fighting strength of three hundred.'

'Correct,' said John. 'And do you attack your enemies with explosives?'

The brothers answered collectively. 'No. We only use them to defend ourselves against our enemies.'

'Do you talk about this with anyone?' Dusty added. 'Do you go bragging to your mates up and down the valley that you have bombs and they don't?'

'No,' Ehsaan answered in Kamviri. He finished the sentence in English. 'We keep our mouths shut.'

'That's right,' said Dusty. He looked at John. 'You could learn something from him, you know.'

'Just hand us the cable,' said John. Dusty gave John a drum of double-twisted electrical cable. The elder Scot loosened the end from the virgin drum, jumped to his feet and walked backwards as the cable unravelled. 'Ehsaan, I want you and your brothers to come back when we're finished and cover this cable over with dirt. Don't bury it. Just hide it.' John unwound the cable through the fields, along the side of the bridge and into the centre of Dogrum. He gathered the Magnificent Seven near the village's central sanger. 'From now on, this will be the explosive command sanger,' he said. 'This is where we'll keep the truck battery which you lads were good enough to find us.' John drove a wooden stake into the earth a metre from the stone fortification and tied a section of cable to it, leaving a metre and a half of slack to drop into the sanger. He pulled the cable taut and nodded to Dusty. The younger Scot took out his Leatherman knife and cut the cable from the drum, exposing the wires. John held them up. 'We initiate the bomb by attaching these wires to the battery. Only attach it when you're absolutely certain you're ready to initiate the explosion. There are no practice drills with this one, lads. You get one shot and one shot only so make sure it counts. Do you understand?' The Magnificent Seven acknowledged John's warning. 'Good. Now you can also detonate the fuel bombs with an improvised combination switch . . .'

Dusty threw his hand up. 'Hold on, mate. You're giving away too much.'

'You're right. Better we stick to basics,' said John, failing to grasp the true nature of Dusty's concerns. John carried on. 'The final step is to label the cable so we know which bomb it connects to. You lads know your numbers?' The brothers all nodded. 'Very well then, this is number one. We've got three more bombs to make.'

For the next two hours, John and Dusty walked the brothers through the process of planting the fuel containers, fixing charges and detonators and running the cables back to the command sanger. As always, the Magnificent Seven were fast learners, assembling the fourth and final device all on their own.

Ehsaan scribbled two successive dips with a left-handed tail, an Arabic number 4. He proudly displayed the paper to John and his brothers before taping it to the cable. For John, it was like watching a child take his first steps. 'I swear these lads were born to do this,' he said.

'They have been fortunate to study under the greatest warrior in all of Nuristan,' said Haider.

Dusty interrupted before the compliment took root. 'You ask me, we could learn a thing or two from them. God knows how they got their hands on a truck battery or all that other crap they brought back with them? Forget soldiering, these lads are natural-born businessmen.'

Haider tried to turn the conversation back to his agenda. 'The brothers did not want to let you down,' he said to John. 'They will do anything you ask of them; no matter how difficult. You are their leader.'

'Not for much longer,' said Dusty. He turned to John. 'They're ready to fly solo.'

John looked at Dusty as if to say *Not here. Not now.* Dusty ploughed ahead. 'It's time to kick them out of the nest, mate.'

The magnitude of the exchange was not lost on Haider.

Chapter 48

A mass of people descended on the convoy: screaming children, fathers holding toddlers, decrepit old men with walking sticks, women veiled from head to toe. The APC doors opened like dominoes and a dozen soldiers dismounted. Dirty hands poked out from jumper sleeves and beneath blue burkas, begging the foreigners for whatever they had to offer. Children swarmed around two female soldiers passing out soft toys. It was desperate. It was touching. It was exactly as Lieutenant Colonel Howard had planned.

A Western man in civilian clothing shouldered a video camera. Another Western man with dyed, shellacked hair and fake tan barked directions at him. 'I want to shoot my stand-up before the sun gets too high. Be sure to get some close shots of those kids. Get one hugging a teddy bear.' The cameraman dropped on one knee and moved his lens within inches of a girl's face. She screamed and ran away.

A young woman spoke to the man barking orders. 'They're setting up the clinic in that building.' She pointed to an empty concrete shell where the soldiers were corralling the villagers. Howard noticed that the shapely woman was generating a lot of interest among the local men. She was wearing a low-cut T-shirt and skin-tight denim – completely inappropriate for the environment. It didn't matter. She and the rest of the TV news crew would be out of there soon enough. That was the beauty of the Medical Civil Action Programme or MEDCAP. Journalists were in and out so quickly, they didn't have time to cause trouble.

'Do you think we can get some soundbites from you, lieutenant? asked the orange-faced correspondent.

Howard didn't correct the insulting demotion of his rank. TV journalists were his new best friends. 'May I suggest you get some b-roll of the clinic first?'

The correspondent was impressed by Howard's grasp of the industry lingo. 'You've worked with TV crews before, haven't you?'

'A few,' said Howard. 'Please, follow me.' Howard led the correspondent and his crew to the building. Soldiers with stethoscopes wrapped around their necks were depositing medicines on folding tables.

'The team here consists of two ISAF doctors,' Howard explained, 'one male, obviously, and the other female, supported by five military medics.'

The correspondent turned to his scantily clad producer. She was standing behind him like an obedient wife. 'I hope you're getting all this.'

The producer took out a notebook and started writing frantically. 'Do you always have a female doctor?' she asked.

'Yes,' said Howard. 'Afghan women wouldn't visit the clinic otherwise. One must always be mindful of the context in which one operates. Being sensitive to cultural concerns is imperative for a successful mission.'

'So what do you do here then?' asked the correspondent, as if the subject of women was a tedious box they were obliged to tick. 'Take us through the process, if you can.'

Howard launched into his well-rehearsed explanation. 'The

clinic is divided into five stations, each supported by an inter-
preter who liaises between patients and medical staff.' He
pointed to a medic unloading a box of pre-filled syringes. 'First,
patients are given de-worming medication. Most people in
Afghanistan have no access to clean water so parasites are a pervasive problem.' Howard continued with his tour. 'Station two
is for baseline medical evaluations. Station three is for one-on-
one consultations with a doctor. This is where patients can
discuss any particular ailments in more detail. Station four per-
forms the same function but behind a curtain. This is to give
female patients the necessary degree of privacy. And finally station five is where medicines are distributed along with
instructions on how to use them.'

'What kind of drugs do you prescribe typically?' asked the
producer.

'Ibuprofen, eye-drops, antihistamines, pre-natal vitamins,
that sort of thing,' said Howard.

'Sounds pretty basic,' said the correspondent.

'It is, but I would beg you to keep in mind that most Afghans
have never seen a doctor.' The correspondent pursed his lips and
nodded. 'Many of the conditions presented today can be treated
effectively with little intervention,' Howard continued. 'Skin
rashes, intestinal problems, headaches. That is why the primary
focus of the MEDCAP is preventative care. For example, preg-
nant women are given a full course of pre-natal vitamins to help
prevent birth defects. We also have a dental technician on hand.
He'll be passing out toothbrushes and demonstrating how to
use them correctly, which should make a nice visual for you.
We'll also be giving the children lessons on landmine awareness
safety.'

'Great,' said the correspondent. 'Let's get some b-roll now
and maybe later you can tell us all of that again on camera –

especially the part about being mindful of the culture and stuff.'

'It would be my pleasure,' said Howard. 'I'll leave you to it then.'

The clinic opened and the villagers piled in. The cameraman immediately zeroed in on an old man. Dropping his jaw for the latexed-gloved medic to squirt de-worming meds into his mouth, the ancient villager looked like a worshipper taking communion. The cameraman followed the old man through the rest of the MEDCAP loop: the baseline height, weight and blood pressure checks; the one-minute consultation with the doctor and the final pit stop at the mobile chemist.

'May I suggest you get some b-roll of a child as well? Afghan children are so very attractive,' said Howard.

The correspondent shouted to his cameraman. 'Don't forget the kids!' The cameraman found a suitably cute candidate and began again. The correspondent gave a cheesy thumbs-up to Howard. 'This is going to make a great story,' he said.

Howard relaxed a bit. The TV crew was swallowing the MEDCAP hook, line and sinker. They probably wouldn't ask him any sticky questions, such as what could be learned through such a rapid consultation or what kind of follow-up did patients diagnosed with chronic conditions receive. Like the PRTs they were covering, the journalists were looking for a quick impact story, heart-tugging photo-ops and spoon-fed facts to turn into video packages for the evening news. Print or TV, the press was all the same. If Howard took a junket on a tour of a girls' school under construction, no one ever asked him whether there were trained teachers to staff it. If it was a courthouse, no one enquired where the judges and lawyers – the backbone of a legal system – would come from or where convicted criminals would serve time. ISAF didn't build prisons. It wouldn't convey the right message.

The correspondent called over his cameraman. 'Roll on me with the lieutenant for a second. Be sure to get some patients in the background.'

The cameraman held the viewfinder to his eye. 'We have speed.'

The correspondent straightened his spine and sucked in his stomach. 'This village where we're standing' – his voice was loud and animated – 'it could be overrun by insurgents at any time. Couldn't it?'

Howard met the correspondent's gaze with equal gravity even though he knew the village had been fully vetted a week earlier and placed on a secure lockdown forty-eight hours prior to deployment. 'Building the new Afghanistan is a dangerous business,' said Howard. 'But we cannot allow the threat of violence to carry the day. ISAF's commitment is unwavering. The forces of terrorism shall not deter us from our mission.'

The correspondent turned to the cameraman. 'Did you get that?' The cameraman gave the thumbs-up. 'That was awesome,' he said to Howard.

'Would it be possible to get a copy of the finished story,' Howard asked, 'for clerical purposes?'

'No problem.' The correspondent turned to his producer. 'Get the lieutenant's address.'

The producer took down Howard's contact information. 'You're very good on camera, you know. Have you ever considered going into broadcasting?' she asked.

Howard acted flattered and surprised by her suggestion. 'It may be something to consider.'

'Well, I don't know if anyone's ever told you this, but you're a natural,' she said.

Howard had indeed heard it. And so had his superiors, hence why he was still in Afghanistan. His tour should have ended in the winter when a new general took over as ISAF commander. Then Musa Qala, a key town in Helmund where the British had negotiated a controversial truce with local elders, was overrun by the Taliban. The loss of Musa Qala was a public relations disaster for ISAF. Experienced public affairs officers, especially those familiar with the needs of broadcasters, were deemed too valuable to let go. Howard was asked to stay on at ISAF HQ for another tour under the auspices of Herrick – the codename for all British operations in Afghanistan. True to form, he couldn't bring himself to say no.

Spring was busy. In March, NATO launched Operation Achilles in Helmund, the biggest military operation since the start of the war. Though ostensibly aimed at clearing the province of Taliban, Achilles' immediate objective was the rebuilding of the Kajaki hydroelectric dam, something which was actually achievable. The Kajaki dam was captured by Coalition forces in under a month but the operation didn't grab as many headlines as ISAF had hoped. Civilian deaths kept overshadowing the message that all was going swimmingly in Afghanistan. The launch of Achilles was eclipsed by an attack on a Coalition post in Kabul that ended with nine civilians dead including three children. Days later, thousands of Afghans took to the streets of Jalalabad to protest over the killing of civilians by US Marines who had opened fire after their convoy was struck by an IED. Canadian troops were embroiled in controversies surrounding civilian fatalities in Kandahar and an operation in Herat stirred up a hornets' nest when more than fifty civilians were killed by airstrikes intended for the Taliban. By May, President Karzai was publicly condemning ISAF's tactics and NATO's myriad generals were bickering publicly over strategy. Orchestrating cuddly scenes of soldiers helping grateful Afghans was deemed more crucial than ever. ISAF needed to court public opinion. This time, however, Howard wasn't just pushing NATO's agenda, he was promoting his own.

Fed up with his complicity, Howard had determined to resign his commission at the end of his tour and embark on a career as a journalist, a television presenter to be exact. Why reach thousands when he could reach millions? If the press corps was too thick to tell the public what was really happening in Afghanistan, then by God, he'd do the job himself. Instead of a necessary evil, Howard now viewed his PAO work as an apprenticeship. Every junket taught him new aspects of his future trade and helped him lay the groundwork for his post-military calling. James Pilkington Howard Television Presenter would tell the world what Lieutenant Colonel Howard was duty-bound not to: the truth.

Outside the clinic, a group of children gathered around a female soldier. She was showing them a card with a red triangle.

'What is that?' asked the correspondent.

'It's the United Nations symbol for landmines,' Howard explained. He pointed to a pile of stones on a table. 'That's a common landmine marker used by locals.' An unescorted Humvee drove into the village. It had US military markings. Howard excused himself. 'I'll give you some space to film.'

The pointed tip of a cowboy boot dropped from the door of the Hummer, followed by the familiar hulking frame of Lieutenant Colonel Walter Raleigh. He was grinning so broadly his cheeks practically swallowed his eyes. 'Pinky!'

'Walter. What on earth are you doing here?' said Howard.

Raleigh sidled up to Howard, as if he were sharing a secret. 'I had something to tell you that just couldn't wait. Have you ever heard of a place called Dogrum?'

'No,' said Howard. 'Is it significant?'

'It is for you.' Raleigh could barely contain himself. 'I think I might have found one of your missing nationals.'

Chapter 49

It was after midnight when John was summoned. A boy came with a note bearing two lines written by Haider. *Anvar needs you immediately. Come alone.* Dusty didn't like the sound of it but John refused to stay and discuss the matter. Anvar had been growing weaker by the hour.

The room was stifling and stank of body fluids. Anvar was lying on the bed. The old man's face looked like a rotting melon against the red pillow. His pneumonia-ridden lungs bubbled with each laboured breath. Baidullah – the other half of Dogrum's diminished Majlis – was by his side, as was Haider. They were both reciting verses from the Koran.

Haider informed Anvar when John was present. The old man beckoned the Scot to his side. 'I do not have long, John Patterson,' Anvar said through Haider. 'Allah calls me to heaven.'

John knelt beside the dying Malek. 'Listen to me, old warrior. You have some life left in you yet.'

Anvar tried to swallow. John lifted the old man's head to stop him from choking on his own saliva. 'We are warriors,' Anvar coughed. 'We are the same. I have not known you long but I believe I know your heart.'

John took Anvar's hand. 'I have no secrets from you, Malek.'

Anvar squeezed with what little strength he had left. 'Then

tell me now, before I die: does your heart belong to the land of your fathers or does it reside here with us?'

Anvar's question tapped into John's deepest desires. He longed to stay in Dogrum; to lead his fighters and possibly regain all that he'd loved and lost. 'My heart is here, Malek.'

Anvar drew John's hand up and kissed it. 'You are like a son to me. But to be a true son of Dogrum, we must know your beliefs. I ask you now before these witnesses, do you believe in the oneness of God?'

John's thoughts spiralled back to a windswept mountaintop in the Brecon Beacons. *There is no God watching over us. He doesn't exist. God is a lie.* He looked at Anvar. The truth would destroy the dying Malek – and any hopes John had of building a new life in Dogrum. 'Yes,' John said softly. 'I believe in the oneness of God.'

Anvar's dimming eyes widened. He tried to sit up. John slid his arm beneath the old man's shoulders. 'Do you accept Muhammad as God's prophet?'

'Yes,' John lied again. 'I do.'

'*Al hamdu lilah!*' cried Haider. 'Praise be to God!'

Baidullah spoke through Haider. 'You must recite the Shahada before two Muslim witnesses. It is the most important of the five pillars of Islam. Repeat these words,' Baidullah commanded. '*laa ilaha illa allah, wa Muhammad ur rasul allah.*'

John repeated the Arabic declaration: *There is no God but Allah and Muhammad is the Prophet of Allah.* When he finished, Baidullah and Haider kissed John on both cheeks.

Anvar smiled contentedly. 'As a warrior, you have earned the right to lead men. And you have proven that you can lead them honourably. Now that you have declared your faith before us and God it is my dying wish that when I am gone, you, John Patterson, become Malek of Dogrum.'

John was overwhelmed. He hadn't expected his lie would lead to such a sacred responsibility. He felt like an impostor. 'I am not worthy of this honour, Malek.'

'You are the most worthy man in Dogrum,' Anvar insisted. 'Baidullah agrees. The Majlis has decided.' Baidullah collected Anvar's robe and gave it to John. 'This robe bears the sign of the Malek,' said Anvar. 'When I die, it shall be yours.'

John stroked the geometric pattern woven into the sleeve. 'And you must take a wife,' Anvar continued. 'I have selected the widow of Haider's brother for you.'

Anvar was offering John everything: community, status and, most importantly, Roshanak and Shams.

'We shall be brothers,' said Haider, tears streaming down his face.

Anvar's breath grew shallower. His body convulsed as he coughed uncontrollably. John held him until the fit passed. 'I must know before I die,' Anvar gasped, 'that I leave Dogrum in good hands. Say you will be Malek.'

John looked into the dying man's eyes. 'I will do as you command,' he said. 'I will become Malek of Dogrum.'

Chapter 50

Rudy ruffled the well-thumbed newspaper and threw it on the coffee table. The PA at the desk across from him deliberately ignored the display of impatience. 'Please call her,' said Rudy.

The PA's eyes didn't deviate from his computer screen. 'Mrs Jachin gave strict instructions not to be disturbed unless it was an emergency.'

'She'll make an exception,' Rudy huffed. 'I'm her most important correspondent.'

The PA stopped typing and looked up. His effeminate features suggested he was drunk with his tiny bit of power. 'Mrs Jachin's instructions were quite clear.'

Lucinda's door opened. Before the PA could object, Rudy squeezed past a departing minion into the office. He found Lucinda applying lipstick, a waxy matte orange that matched her hideous hair. 'I'm on my way out,' she said through contorted lips.

'We had an appointment,' said Rudy.

Lucinda clicked her compact like a castanet and dropped it in her handbag. She kissed her fingertips and placed them on Rudy's cheek as she swept past him. 'I'm running late. We'll reschedule for tomorrow.'

Rudy wiped the sticky residue from his face and ran after her. 'I leave for Afghanistan tonight.'

Lucinda called the lift. She stepped inside the empty space and looked at Rudy as if he were a complete idiot. 'Well, are you coming or not?' she said. Rudy jumped in as the doors were closing. 'Excellent story on the Americans, by the way. Four dead in one go. Your description of them burning to death was frightfully realistic.' She paused, as if she were experiencing an epiphany. 'We'll submit it for an award.'

'Thank you for that, Lucinda, but there's another story I'd like to discuss.' The bell sounded and the doors opened onto the lobby. Lucinda bolted through them, leaving Rudy to chase after her again. 'My story on John Patterson. You said you would print it if I returned to Afghanistan.'

Lucinda's stilettos clicked like a metronome on the black and white tiled floor. 'Well, you're not there yet, are you?' she said, pushing her way through a revolving door.

'We had a deal, Lucinda!' Rudy yelled through the glass barrier. He stumbled onto the street. 'You should have printed that story by now and you know it.'

'Good thing I didn't or I might never get you back to Kabul,' Lucinda cackled.

Rudy was furious. 'You can't recycle the same bargaining chip!'

'Oh relax,' said Lucinda. 'I haven't printed it yet because the copy needs work.'

'There's nothing wrong with my copy,' Rudy protested.

'Please,' said Lucinda. 'All those players and intrigue. I thought you understood by now that when it comes to international news, you have to keep things simple: goodies, baddies. If you can't dumb it down readers will skip right past it.'

'The war doesn't need dumbing down,' said Rudy.

'Oh really?' Lucinda waved a pair of gloves. 'Look around you. Most people haven't the slightest clue what's happening in

Afghanistan. Their interests are much closer to home. House prices, knife crime, immigration, buxom models baring their breasts – those are the stories people look for when they open a newspaper. Afghanistan is like veg, people only read about it because they think they should.'

'I think you're being too cynical,' Rudy argued. 'People care deeply when soldiers die in Afghanistan.'

Lucinda waved her gloves again. 'Only when they die en masse.' Rudy was visibly shocked. 'Oh grow up,' she said. 'When was the last time you saw a front-page headline about a lone soldier killed in action?'

Rudy had no comeback. It was true. So many soldiers had died in Afghanistan it now took an extraordinary loss of life to warrant a front-page mention. 'If I simplify the story, then will you run it?'

Lucinda hailed a cab. 'Once it reads better – and provided Harry signs off on it, then yes.' A black cab pulled over and the driver rolled down the window. 'St James,' she ordered.

Rudy blocked the cab door. 'Is it really necessary to involve him?'

'You're mucking about on Harry's patch.' Lucinda cleared her throat, her way of telling Rudy to move out of her way. She ducked into the cab. 'You really must learn how to get on with others. Which reminds me, Harry will be heading your way soon.'

Rudy poked his head in after her. 'Harry is coming to Afghanistan?'

'Some sort of MoD visit. These things are never announced in advance. Move away now or I'll be late.' Rudy stepped aside. 'Remember, play nice in the sandbox,' Lucinda ordered and shut the door.

Chapter 51

Though death was inevitable, Anvar refused to hand it an easy victory. Inch by inch: that's how the old warrior would meet his maker, a God whom John, in his desire to carve a new life for himself, had acknowledged falsely.

John took leave of the dying Malek at sunrise and only then to take a piss. He walked quickly to the village toilet, a wooden shack with a floor made of tree trunks dispersed horizontally. The gaps between them allowed any waste to fall hygienically into the valley below. John reached for his trouser strings. Suddenly, a loud CRUMP disturbed the tranquil morning. He bolted outside. Dusty had responded to the noise as well. He was standing outside their single-room dwelling.

John called to him. 'Where did it land?'

'To the south!' said Dusty.

John looked behind him. A ribbon of smoke was curling from the rocks above Dogrum. John knew immediately that it hadn't come from an RPG round or other direct-fire weapon. It had been fired indirectly, from somewhere behind the ridges overlooking the terraced fields. Dogrum was being attacked with mortars.

John cupped his hands and shouted to the houses. 'Stand to! Stand to!' The command was like a stick to a hive. Dogrum's fighters came charging out of their doors, repeating John's order. 'Stand to! Stand to!' The fighters jumped down the rooftops and into position. John and Dusty took up their places in the explosive command sanger. Dusty scanned the fields beyond the bridge with his binos. He was searching for a spotter, a fighter with eyes on Dogrum who was guiding the team manning the mortar base-plate from afar.

Another mortar round slammed into the hillside – this time to the north of Dogrum, near the waterfall. 'If they've got a spotter out there, they'll get it right soon enough,' said John.

'I'll find the fucker,' said Dusty. 'What if the mortars are a cover for a bigger assault?'

'The lads can handle it,' John said confidently.

Haider jumped into the sanger next to them. 'What are you doing?' said Dusty. 'This is not your position.'

Haider smiled knowingly. 'It is only an exercise.'

'Not this time, mate,' said Dusty.

An ear-splitting CRUMP sounded. Dogrum took a direct hit. The clunk and snap of thousands of wood fragments falling back to earth filled the air. The two Scots and Haider looked on in horror. The mortar round had obliterated the most important home in the village – Anvar's.

Haider screamed. 'Malek!' he crawled out of the sanger and ran towards the flattened building.

John ran after Haider and tackled him. 'Leave it! You must get into position.'

Haider stretched his hand toward the smouldering ruins. 'Malek!' he cried.

John seized Haider by the shoulders. The adrenalin of battle had renewed the Scot's strength. 'You disgrace your Malek by breaking discipline. Set an example for the lads. Get into position and fight. Dogrum must be defended!'

Haider's anguish retreated as the new order of the village

dawned on him. His eyes filled with a heightened reverence for John. 'Forgive me. I shall do as you command.'

Haider ran to the far side of the bridge while John scrambled back to the command sanger. Another mortar slammed into the village, demolishing a cluster of homes. Pieces of wood and fine debris fell like leaden rain.

John immediately thought of Roshanak and Shams. 'Where the fuck is that spotter!'

'I don't know!' said Dusty. 'But it looks like he's got company!'

A hail of small arms fire raked across the fields into the village. The Dogrum fighters responded with a barrage of their own. Children burdened with satchels of ammunition scrambled along the low ramparts, the crack of high-velocity rounds sounding over their heads.

'Can you ID their firing positions,' said John.

Dusty's binos were still glued to his eyes. 'Stand by with device 1,' he ordered.

John grabbed the cable marked one and poised the naked wires over the truck battery. 'On your command,' he said.

'Stand by . . . fire!' said Dusty.

John touched the wires to the battery. The electrical charge travelled up the cable to the petrol bomb planted in the fields. It detonated with an all-mighty bang. John could feel the heat from the explosion as the fireball shot sixty-feet into the air. The Dogrum fighters cheered wildly.

The bomb scorched everything within a thirty metre radius. Firing immediately ceased from the position. But the battle was far from over. Rifle rounds were still coming fast and furious from the untouched patches of green field. The charred area where the petrol bomb had detonated erupted again with live fire. The residual heat from the bomb was spontaneously exploding ammunition left by the dead insurgents. The Dogrum fighters opened up on the area. John crawled out of his sanger and waved to his men. 'Stop! Stop! Save your ammunition!' But the fighters didn't respond to the English language command. John slipped back into his stone fortification. His frustration was palpable. 'They're firing at ghosts.'

Another mortar round slammed into the village. 'I found the spotter!' said Dusty. 'South-west, top of the ridge.'

'Is he near device 3?' asked John.

'Close enough,' said Dusty

John grabbed the appropriate wires. 'You make the call, mate.'

'Stand by . . . fire!' said Dusty.

John initiated device 3. Another huge fireball exploded into the sky. Small arms fire continued unabated from the fields. 'Stay here,' said John. He leapt out of the sanger, weaved toward the bridge and waited for a cluster of children to pass before diving over a rampart. John was in a recovery roll when an RPG round screamed past his head and clipped the wall behind him. He heard the terrible cry of a child in pain. Despite his overwhelming desire to run back and help the injured child, John held his discipline and pressed on.

John joined Haider in the sanger on the far side of the bridge. Fighting side by side, the Nuristani and the Scot laid down fast, accurate fire. With the enemy on the back foot, the Magnificent Seven seized the initiative. They moved out from their sangers, covering each other as they took the fight to the enemy. The air was thick with rifle fire and war cries as the brothers forced the remaining insurgents to retreat over the ridge.

John ordered everyone to hold their positions. A few minutes passed with no small arms fire, RPG or mortar rounds. Suddenly, there was movement in the top terrace. A man crawled out from the green stalks onto a patch of burnt earth.

He was moving on his belly toward the ridge. Ehsaan shouldered his weapon and took aim at the slow-moving target. John put his hand on the stock of Ehsaan's rifle and shook his head, no. 'Allow him to retreat.'

With the battle won, John ordered the Magnificent Seven to search the locations where the enemy had fired from. Any bodies were to be lined up for burial and any abandoned weapons and ammunition recovered as booty. With the clean-up operation under way, John and Haider returned to the village to assess the damage.

Dogrum had been hit hard. A quarter of the village's housing was destroyed. The toilet was a pile of toothpicks and several of the ramparts had been damaged. A group of women were wailing over two motionless bodies. John thought of the child he'd heard crying. 'Where are the injured?' he asked.

Two wounded fighters stood as John entered the munitions building. He bade them through Haider to sit down. 'Save your strength, lads.' He saw Dusty hunched over a body, working furiously. The younger Scot reached for a cloth bandage, revealing the patient's face. John wasn't prepared for what he saw: blonde curls. Dusty was working on Shams.

John ran to the child and stood over her. Shams's injuries were severe. Her left arm was in shreds. Raw tendons were the only thing holding the tiny limb to her body. Dusty had applied clamps to the wound to keep the child from bleeding to death. The wee girl's face was also badly hit. Her eyes were bandaged and slivers of shrapnel marred her delicate white skin. Her blood-soaked blonde curls opened the floodgates to John's darkest memory. 'Will she . . .' John could barely bring himself to ask. 'Will she live?'

Dusty kept working on the child. 'She's in bad shape,' he said. 'There's no saving that arm. I'll have to amputate.'

'What about her eyes?' John's voice was uncharacteristically faint. 'Will she be blind?'

The question shattered Dusty's objectivity. 'Hell if I know. I can keep her alive for a day or so. But she has no chance if she stays here.' Dusty took a deep breath and regained his composure. 'I'd best get that arm sorted before she wakes up.' He grabbed a scalpel and held it over the child. 'Medieval barbers had better working conditions.'

The door opened while Dusty was operating. Roshanak walked in behind a group of women, her red veil partially obscuring her face. She screamed when she realized Dusty was cutting into her child. Roshanak dived for the younger Scot but Haider caught her. Dusty carried on with the operation. 'Get her under control or get her out of here,' he barked. Roshanak thrashed about, screaming and tearing her clothes. Haider lost his grip and the distraught mother lunged for Dusty again. This time John swooped in to restrain her. The touch of a strange man fed Roshanak's maternal rage. She bit John's face, puncturing a hole in his cheek. He yelped as blood poured from the wound into his red and white beard. Haider wrapped his arms firmly around Roshanak's waist and pulled her away.

Dusty bandaged Shams's stump and wrapped the amputated limb in a cloth to spare the mother from having to look at it. 'There's nothing else I can do for her,' he said to John. 'I best see to the lads now.'

Haider relayed Dusty's words to Roshanak. The distraught mother, drained of spirit and energy, collapsed beside her daughter. John lingered nearby. He wanted to comfort them both.

'Come,' said Haider. 'She will be all right.'

'No,' said John. 'They shouldn't be alone.'

'There are others in Dogrum who need you – Malek.'

It took several hours for John and Haider to sift through the debris of Anvar's decimated home. Baidullah was recovered; cut, bruised and traumatized but otherwise alive. The gentle scholar had been loyal to his Malek to the end. He was still holding Anvar's robe when they found him. He passed it, reverently, to John.

John lifted Anvar's corpse from the ruins. It was feather light. The old man's lifeless eyes were still open. John lowered the lids and carried Anvar to the centre of the village where everyone could pay their last respects to the dead Malek.

Dusty pulled John away from the mourners. The elder Scot motioned to Haider to join them. 'The lads recovered ten bodies, nine AKs, an RPG launcher and this.' Dusty produced a dagger with a carved bronze handle.

John had no interest in the weapon. 'Is Shams strong enough to be moved?'

Dusty was still focused on the dagger. 'Doesn't this look familiar?'

'I don't care about the bloody dagger,' said John. 'I've decided to take Shams to the Yanks. It's her best chance for survival. I want you to stay here and look after Dogrum while I'm gone.' He turned to Haider. 'You stay here with Dusty. I'll take Daud with me.'

'Are you off your head?' said Dusty. 'You're not going anywhere without me. And there's no fucking way either of us is going back to Camp Keating.'

'The CO said if any of our people were injured he'd fly them to Bagram for medical treatment,' John insisted.

'Injured as a result of their operations.' Dusty shoved the dagger in John's face. 'This had nothing to do with the Yanks, mate.'

'It has everything to do with them!' John thundered. The

outburst disturbed the mourners. All eyes converged on the two Scots. 'Dogrum was peaceful before the Yanks came here.'

Dusty gave John a moment to calm down. 'Come with me,' he said. 'There's something you need to see.'

John and Haider followed Dusty to the fields where the bodies of the attackers were laid out side by side. Two of the corpses were badly charred from the fuel bombs. The rest were largely intact save the fatal wounds caused by bullets and shrapnel. 'Look at them,' said Dusty. 'Not one of them is foreign. They're all Nuristani.'

'The foreigners must have retreated,' said Haider. He gestured contemptuously at the corpses. 'These dogs have the face of Kshto. We were attacked by Hizb-i-Islami.'

'Is that right?' Dusty singled out a body. 'Then how do you explain him?'

John inspected the corpse more closely. The dead man had a patch over one eye. Dusty held up the bronze dagger. 'This was found on him.' He laid the knife on the dead man's stomach. The identity of the corpse was indisputable: the one-eyed Rasul clan representative who'd called for their heads at the *jirga*. 'This attack had fuck-all to do with the Yanks,' said Dusty. 'Bloody hell, it had fuck-all to do with the war. It's a tribal pissing match.'

'That is not true,' said Haider. 'They are insurgents.'

'You're a filthy liar!' Dusty exploded. 'All that crap about the *jirga*'s decision being final. Honest and incorruptible my arse; the *jirga* didn't give them our heads so they came here to finish the job.'

'How dare you accuse me of lying!' cried Haider.

John could take no more. He arched his back and screamed, 'Enough!' The outburst ripped his sutures apart. He fell forward in agony.

Dusty and Haider both reached for him. 'Let go,' Dusty hissed. He helped John to the ground. 'Tell me what's happening, mate?'

John grabbed his side. 'It's nothing. I've busted a few stitches, that's all.'

'You need bed rest,' said Dusty. 'Three days minimum. You need to get your strength back so we can get the hell out of this shithole.'

John gritted his teeth. 'No,' he insisted. 'I'm taking Shams to the Americans – tonight.'

Chapter 52

The armoured personnel carrier pulled up to the front gate. The officer in the passenger seat called to the guards. 'Andiamo, Andiamo!' The Italian looked over his shoulder. 'We go to PX. You come?'

Lieutenant Colonel Howard declined graciously. 'Thank you, but someone's expecting me.'

The Italian tried to entice him. 'It is like America. Big! Is . . .' he consulted with his driver.

'Superstore,' said the driver.

'Si! Superstore!' said the Italian.

Howard didn't begrudge the Italians their bit of fun but he hadn't come to Bagram to shop. 'Thank you, but I can't.'

Inside the gate, Walter Raleigh was waiting with a Jeep. Howard transferred himself and his Bergen to the vehicle and nodded. 'Good to see you, Walter.'

'Who are your buddies?' asked Raleigh.

'Italians,' said Howard.

'Do you trust them?' asked Raleigh.

'I looked at the ISAF departure manifest and hitched a ride with them as they were leaving HQ,' said Howard. 'They have no idea who I am. I'm still in Kabul as far as ISAF is concerned.'

Raleigh hit the accelerator. 'Let's hope it stays that way.'

The runway at Bagram was going full tilt: transport, attack and logistical aircraft taxied, landed and departed while forklifts ferried gear on and off C-130s. Raleigh pulled up outside a hanger. 'Wait here,' he instructed. He disappeared inside and reappeared a few minutes later. 'I got you on the next flight out.' He pointed to a Chinook being refuelled. 'It'll make one stop in Kunar Province before landing in Kamdesh. Sorry I couldn't get you there direct. Choppers are like rocking-horse shit around here.'

Howard gathered up his Bergen. 'No worries, Walter. You've been incredibly generous already.'

'The CO in Kamdesh knows someone is coming, but he doesn't know who or why,' said Raleigh.

Howard paused. 'And if he asks questions?'

'He won't,' Raleigh assured him. 'As far as he's concerned, it's all classified. Remember, once you're dropped you'll have an hour on the ground max before the chopper returns. I'm not sure how much you can accomplish in that time.'

'Probably nothing,' said Howard. 'But I must try.'

Raleigh took Howard's hand. 'Anyone gets word of this and we'll both be court-martialled.'

Howard felt as if the moment required a grander gesture, an embrace. The strapping American beat him to it. Raleigh pulled Howard to his chest and slapped him on the back. 'Good luck, Pinky. And God bless.'

Howard broke free. 'If there is a God, Walter, consider your good deed in Afghanistan done.'

'Hold up a minute.' Dusty pulled out his binos. John stroked Shams's hair. The little girl was cradled in a litter tied to the top of a donkey. 'The Yanks didn't take your advice.' Dusty passed his binos to John. 'They still have local guards stationed around the base.'

John gave the area a cursory look. 'They didn't give us any trouble before,' he said, handing the binos back. He tugged on the donkey's reins.

Dusty stopped him. 'You can't just go charging in there. You have no idea where those guards' loyalties lie. They could be working for the Rasuls – bloody hell, they could be Rasuls.'

John huffed. Dusty hadn't stopped spewing conspiracy theories since they'd left Dogrum. 'You're losing the plot, mate.'

'Me?' Dusty gave John the once-over. 'You're the one wearing a dead man's coat.'

John cast his eyes down. Dusty was still operating under the belief that they would both return home soon. 'Anvar gave it to me before he died.'

'You haven't been right in the head since Dogrum was attacked,' said Dusty. 'First you want to leave me behind and take Daud with you . . .'

'Daud wouldn't have been missed,' said John. 'He's useless. You're not.'

'Daud tried to kill you,' said Dusty. 'He'd have slit your throat while you were sleeping.'

'For the last time, he didn't mean to shoot me. It was an accident.' John pulled the reins again.

'Wait.' Dusty changed tack. 'Let me take the girl to the Yanks. You stay behind and cover me.'

'I promised Roshanak I'd put Shams on a helicopter myself,' John insisted.

'Roshanak can't understand a bloody word you say,' Dusty argued.

John ignored him and carried on. Dusty had no choice but to fall back into a covering position.

The local guards eyed John as he dropped onto the dirt track leading to Camp Keating. As soon as they saw the geometric insignia on his sleeve, their demeanour turned from suspicion to reverence. The locals knew they were in the presence of a Malek.

One of the soldiers manning the front gate came out to meet John. 'Stop right there, sir.' It was Corporal Rucker.

John scooped Shams up from the litter. 'I have a wounded child.'

Corporal Rucker called back to his fellow guard. 'We got local wounded!'

John cradled Shams in his arms. 'She's critical,' he explained. 'She needs to be flown out for treatment immediately.'

'Give her here, sir,' the corporal said.

John resisted. 'I want to stay with her.'

'I have orders to detain you if you step foot on this base. Please,' said the corporal. 'I promise I'll take care of her.'

John passed the wounded child to the young soldier. Corporal Rucker checked under the child's blanket for hidden explosives. 'We got a re-supply chopper coming today. We can fly her out on that.' The corporal shook his head when he saw Shams's bandaged stump. 'It busts me up to see kids like this. Was it a landmine, sir?'

'No,' said John. He wanted to elaborate – to explain how the US presence in Nuristan had visited death and destruction on Dogrum. But the young corporal's humanity curbed John's tongue.

'If you like, sir, I'll stay with her while she's getting prepped for transport. I'll put her on the chopper myself,' said the corporal.

It tore John up to leave Shams in another person's care. But he had no choice. He kissed her on the forehead. 'Thank you.'

The corporal hesitated, as if he couldn't decide what to do. 'Some folks around here, I don't need to tell you who, think of you as the enemy. I would advise you strongly not to hang around.'

John was unmoved. 'I know I'm tearing the arse out of it, but I'm not leaving until I know she's on her way to Bagram.'

Chapter 53

Howard looked past the tail-gunner and out of the rear door of the Chinook. An Apache was overtaking them from the rear. The agile, four-bladed attack helicopter was an escort for the larger 1960s-era workhorse. Chinooks in Afghanistan were always falling out of the sky, brought down by unforeseen mechanical failures or enemy fire. Howard checked to see if his fellow passengers were aware of what was happening outside the fuselage. Some had settled in for a kip. Others were listening to iPods; the telltale white wires ran from their breast pockets up to their ears. Howard wondered what John Patterson would make of them.

The Apache peeled off and disappeared over a ridge. The Chinook wedged itself between two mountain peaks and dropped like a stone. Howard's stomach slammed into his throat. He looked through the tailgate. The rear blades were rotating just feet from the rock face. One nick and the aircraft would explode.

The Chinook touched down on the LZ. The blades kept rotating as soldiers rushed on to help unload supplies. It was clear the pilot had no intention of hanging around any longer than necessary. Howard gathered his Bergen and left by the rear ramp. A stretcher passed him as he disembarked. He paused to look at the tiny victim on it. The child's head was wrapped in clean, white gauze; an IV line ran from a saline bag on her stomach to her left arm. The right one was missing.

Corporal Rucker shouted to the flight crew. 'We radioed ahead to Bagram. They're expecting her.'

Howard grabbed the corporal as he jumped off the aircraft. 'Where's your CO?'

Corporal Rucker looked at Howard's insignia and saluted. 'Sir.'

The press corps descended on the Defence Secretary. Print journalists shoved tiny tape-recorders in his face while the broadcasters aimed video cameras and waved microphones wrapped in bushy grey wind sleeves under his chin. A handler moved the Secretary in front of a line of freshly washed Viking Armoured vehicles. The gleaming APCs made a better backdrop than the depressing concrete blast walls surrounding Bastion.

The Secretary called for quiet and launched into what was meant to appear like an off-the-cuff speech. 'This is where the future of world security will play out . . .' he began. The journalists listened intently, even though printed copies of the carefully crafted statement had been given to them in advance. Rudy stood at the edge of the crowd, listening half-heartedly. He hadn't come to Bastion to cover the staged event. That job fell to Harry and the rest of the correspondents who'd parachuted in with the Secretary. Rudy was there as Harry's backup – 'someone to pass the baton to just in case,' as Harry put it, 'because in a war zone, one never knows when one may encounter a spot of trouble.'

Maybe, but in Bastion, one could be fairly certain nothing would happen during a highly secured visit by a cabinet minister. The eight-square-mile camp was sited well away from populated areas. As long as you didn't go out on patrol with the soldiers, you could be fairly confident of leaving alive and unharmed.

The press conference wrapped and the Secretary was shown to the cookhouse where pre-screened soldiers were waiting to greet him with rehearsed lines and pose for photo-ops. Harry broke from the pack to have a word with Rudy. The newspaper's resident spook had traded his customary three-piece suit and briefcase for a bespoke khaki trousers and vest combo and a leather satchel.

'Going on safari?' asked Rudy.

Harry was sweating profusely. He reached into the satchel and produced a starched white monogrammed handkerchief. The half-dozen pockets on his vest were apparently decorative. He dabbed his face with the pristine linen. 'This heat is unbearable,' he moaned. An Afghan walked past them, a local employed by the base. Harry followed him with his eyes. 'It's bad enough being at the sharp end without the spectre of heat stroke looming over our heads.'

Rudy didn't know whether to laugh or lash out. What the fuck did a pampered spook like Harry know about the sharp end? 'You'll be flying out with the Secretary in twenty minutes,' Rudy noted. 'I, on the other hand, am stuck here until tomorrow morning, thanks to you.'

Harry offered a pained expression. 'I did try to get you on the Secretary's helicopter, old chap. But the MoD just wouldn't allow it.'

'Well, *I* don't work for them now, do I?' said Rudy. Harry arched an eyebrow. 'Cut the crap, Harry. You know as well as I do that you didn't need me here. There are half a dozen agencies covering this thing. You're up to something, so why don't you just spit it out.'

Harry sighed like a man accustomed to being misunderstood.

'I do admire your pluck, Rudy.' He reached into his leather bag and pulled out a folder. 'But if I could be so bold as to offer you a bit of advice. A story is only as credible as its source. Next time, be sure you know exactly who it is you are dealing with.' Rudy took the folder and opened it. The documents inside were personnel files. The name on the dossier hit Rudy like a sledge-hammer. 'I would advise you to review that away from prying eyes,' said Harry. 'Do be a good man and destroy it when you're done.'

The Chinook rose up between the mountain peaks. The accom-panying Apache buzzed the valley floor and swooped up and over a ridge. John ran up onto a small ridge, willing whatever energy he had left to Shams. He stood motionless long after the aircraft had disappeared over the horizon.

John heard footsteps approaching from behind. He turned, expecting to see a local guard. He wasn't prepared for what he found. It was Corporal Rucker. And the young soldier wasn't alone.

Rudy sat cross-legged on a cot in a sweltering tent, sweat drip-ping from his chin and nose. He took a long drink of bottled water and opened the confidential personnel file on one Mr John Patterson.

The first few pages offered a brief sketch of Patterson's life prior to the SAS. Born in Arbroath, Scotland, to working-class parents, his primary school teachers described him as 'bright but undisciplined'; a 'disruptive child' who 'cared more about sport than academic achievement'. The files picked up some years later when Patterson joined the Parachute Regiment. The military rec-ognized something in the youth his teachers hadn't. Patterson's commanding officer had written a letter recommending him for

SAS selection. John joined the SAS when he was barely out of his teens. According to the file, he was the youngest person at the time to be accepted into the elite force.

Patterson excelled in the Regiment, participating in every major SAS operation of the late twentieth century. His service record was flawless, though he had ruffled a few feathers along the way. Comments from rotating superiors ran the gambit from glowing to restrained admonishment. Some felt John Patterson didn't show enough deference to authority. But even his detractors didn't question his commitment, ability or leadership. There were even memos recommending John Patterson for an officer's commission.

Then it all unravelled. Patterson was eighteen years into his Regiment career – two years shy of retiring – when he was pulled from an operation in Bosnia and sent home to Hereford for 'compassionate reasons'. Two weeks later, John Patterson resigned from the SAS. The final paper in the file offered a clue as to why. The memo written by the regimental sergeant major contained notes of an incident relayed by John Patterson's squadron sergeant major: Peter Mitchell. The memo concluded with a recommendation that John Patterson be referred to a specialist military doctor for psychological monitoring and treatment.

Lieutenant Colonel Howard didn't recognize the frail figure with the wild eyes, long beard and bald head. Was it really his old mentor? 'John?' he said. 'John Patterson?'

John looked as if he'd seen a ghost. 'James?'

Howard tried to connect the familiar voice with the stranger in front of him. He walked up to John and embraced him. Rather than conjure the familiar, the gesture seemed to emphasize how far apart they'd grown. 'I thought you were dead,' said

Howard. 'I came here hoping to get a message to you. When this young man told me you were here, I could scarcely believe it.'

Corporal Rucker smiled at John. 'I reckon you're the most popular man in Nuristan, sir.'

'The wee lassie?' John said anxiously.

'I put her on the chopper myself,' Corporal Rucker assured him, 'just like I promised.'

John nodded. 'You're a man of your word.' He turned to Howard. 'Unlike some men I know,' he said, pushing past him.

Howard was confounded by John's actions. He ran after him. 'Where . . . where are you going?'

'Like I'd tell you,' John sneered.

Howard had been so consumed with finding John, he'd forgotten how he'd left things with his old mentor. 'If this is about the meeting with ShieldGroup and SOCA, I can explain.'

'There's nothing to explain.' John turned to confront him. 'You sold me and my team out.'

'I never would have allowed General Rasul to harm you and Dusty,' Howard insisted. A sickening thought suddenly occurred to him. Howard looked around. 'Oh my God, where is he? Is he alive?'

'I'm alive, you toff!' Dusty ran up onto the ridge and flung his arms around James. The two men tumbled over. 'I never thought I'd be so happy to see a Rupert!'

Howard revelled in the proper reunion. 'You look well, Dusty. Remarkably well.' He stood up and drank in the sight of his lost colleagues. 'When I heard there was a Scot causing trouble in Nuristan, I knew it had to be one of you. What on earth are you doing here?'

Dusty's exuberance did nothing to allay John's suspicions. 'Causing trouble, eh? Well, if you came here hoping to drag us back to Kabul you've wasted your time. Rasul can't touch us now.'

'So you've heard?' said Howard.

'Heard what?' asked Dusty.

'About General Rasul.' Howard searched their eyes for a spark of recognition. They didn't know. 'He's dead,' Howard said gleefully. 'General Rasul is dead.'

'Are you sure?' said Dusty.

Howard was grinning from ear to ear. 'The old bastard was murdered by a suicide bomber. Suitable end for a warlord, don't you think?'

'Is it safe to go back to Kabul?' asked Dusty. 'Rasul had a lot of mates. Some of them paid us a visit the other day.'

John glared at Dusty. Howard failed to pick up on the enmity between the two Scots. 'No one is going to squander political capital to service the vendetta of a dead warlord,' he said. 'The game is over for Rasul.'

'Is that all this is to you?' John's voice dripped contempt. 'Some sort of political game?'

Howard felt wounded by the accusation. 'Of course not, John.'

'What about your mates at SOCA and ShieldGroup?' John pressed. 'I don't think they'd be best pleased to see us.'

Howard looked at John in earnest. 'They never were nor will they ever be my mates. Trust me. It's in their interest to act like the whole thing never happened. In fact I wouldn't be surprised if they wrote you two glowing recommendations.'

Dusty nudged John. 'Or a year's back pay.'

'So is that how it's going to be then?' John's tone grew more disdainful. 'You and your mates sell us out, and now that Rasul's dead you want to sweep the whole thing under the rug.'

'I never sold you out,' said Howard. 'And I would never deny what's happened to you.'

'Really? So what are you going to do about it, James? Are you going to stand outside the Houses of Parliament and tell them what really happened with Rasul's nephews? Will you hell. You're no better than SOCA or ShieldGroup. All you care about is covering your own arse.'

John's level of vitriol was a complete shock to Howard. 'I risked everything to come and find you, both of you. Do you know what would happen if my superiors found out what I was doing?'

John spat. 'Go rescue someone else.'

'Don't be so hard on young James,' said Dusty. 'He's here for us now. That's all that matters.'

'A heli will be back soon to collect me,' said Howard. 'Come with me and I give you both my word – you'll be back on British soil in seventy-two hours.'

John started walking away. Dusty grabbed him by the robe. 'I know you're angry with James but enough's enough. It's time to go home.'

John stroked the insignia on his sleeve. 'I am home.'

Chapter 54

The memo was written in the sterile language of a military professional. As he read, Rudy recalled the details relayed to him over coffee in the dungeon of the King's Road McDonald's. Pete Mitchell's words flew from his memory and onto the page, breathing narrative life into the brief and damning account of John Patterson's attempted suicide.

John was away on an SAS operation when his family was taken from him. A white van ran down his wife and daughter at a zebra crossing. His wife was killed instantly, his daughter was air-ambulanced to hospital where she died a few hours later. The driver of the van was charged with DUI and involuntary manslaughter.

John didn't shed a tear during the closed coffin funerals. His mates put it down to years of military discipline. But when he disappeared into his house for a week, people started to question how well John was coping with the devastating loss.

Pete Mitchell was John's squadron sergeant major and longtime friend. He found John sitting on a settee in the front room, red-eyed, unshaven, holding a can of warm Guinness. Mitchell recalled going to the kitchen to fix John a brew. There were no teabags and the milk in the fridge had gone over.

Mitchell returned to John empty-handed. 'You can't stay in this house for ever,' he said. 'Sooner or later, you'll have to go out.'

John rolled the can of stout between his hands. 'I'm getting my Bergen together for few days tabbing in the Beacons.'

The Welsh mountain range was like a second home to the Regiment. But Mitchell didn't think John should go. 'Are you sure that's wise?'

John didn't respond kindly to the suggestion. 'What do you mean by that?'

'I'm worried about you, mate.' Mitchell took the can from John. 'I know you're hurting – bad. If you need to go to the Beacons to ball your eyes out, let me come with you and we'll do it together.'

They planned to do the 'Fan Dance', a twenty-five-kilometre march/run up and over the mountains and back again. Many aspiring SAS soldiers failed selection attempting it.

Mitchell and John parked across from the Storey Arms Mountain Rescue Centre and headed up Pen-y-Fan, the tallest mountain in the Brecon Beacons. Mitchell stuck close to John as they passed by the area of Tommy Jones's obelisk, a memorial to a Welsh boy who'd lost his way in the Beacons and died. The landmark had acquired a special resonance in the wake of John's tragedy.

On the return leg of the Fan Dance, a storm front rolled in. Despite near zero visibility, the pair pressed on with a compass and map. But when driving rain and 80 mile an hour cross-winds threatened to blow them off the mountain, Mitchell insisted they stop for the night.

They tabbed east and set up camp on the lee side of Cribyn, the next mountain over from Pen-y-Fan. Mitchell positioned his bivvy bag to form an inverted V with John's. He wanted to be able to talk to his friend without having to scream over the howling winds.

That night, Mitchell tried to engage John in conversation. He pointed to the summit of Cribyn. 'Imagine being a Roman up there, freezing your arse off in an OP.'

'Imagine falling off it,' said John. The rest of their banter was the same – flat and humourless. John just wasn't himself. He didn't bring up his wife and daughter and Mitchell didn't press him.

The next morning Mitchell awoke to an empty bivvy bag. John was missing. He stood up and shouted: 'John! John!' When he didn't get an answer, Mitchell immediately assumed the worst. He pulled on his boots and ran to the top of Cribyn.

The sky was overcast and the air was damp and peaty. On the far side of the cairn marking the summit, Mitchell saw John teetering on the edge of the precipice, one step away from certain death.

Mitchell wanted to grab John and wrestle him back. But he feared the sudden movement would send his friend over the edge. He approached him cautiously. 'What do you say we have a brew and talk about this?'

John stared blankly into the distance. 'There's nothing to talk about.'

'There's everything to talk about,' Mitchell pleaded. 'I know at least forty men not far from here who would be distraught if they knew what you're thinking of doing.'

'Those forty men don't need me.' All the pain John had bottled up was rising to the surface, threatening to explode. 'My wife and daughter did. I should have been home. I should have been watching out for them.'

At that moment, Mitchell knew John had every intention of throwing himself off the mountain. 'You can't blame yourself for what happened. It was an accident.' John took no comfort from the words. Desperate, Mitchell invoked the threat of eternal damnation to talk him down. 'God is watching over your family now. Just like he's watching over you.'

'There is no God watching over us,' John hissed. 'He doesn't exist. God is a lie.' John's voice erupted with pain and rage. 'My family was murdered!' He turned to Mitchell. 'The bastard that hit them was high on heroin. A fucking drug addict murdered my family. I should have been there! I should have been there to protect them!'

Mitchell's voice trembled as he tried to talk John down. 'It's not your fault, John. There's nothing you could have done. You can't blame yourself.'

John fell to his knees and wept uncontrollably. 'Her skull was crushed, Pete. Her beautiful face—' John choked on his words. 'My wee girl died surrounded by strangers. She died scared and alone.' John's entire body heaved with grief. He grabbed his head with his fists and hurled his body forward towards the edge of the cliff. Mitchell swooped down and grabbed him around the chest.

John's body went limp and Mitchell cradled him away from the precipice. 'Don't do it. You must carry on,' Mitchell urged. 'Too many people depend on you.'

'It's too late,' John whimpered. 'It's too late. They're gone.' Another wave of grief washed over John. He rose to his knees and threw his body toward the cliff edge again.

Mitchell dug in his heels. 'Think of the Regiment. The lads need you!' John thrashed around but Mitchell held tight. Slowly, John's energy drained. He sobbed and sobbed until he had no more tears to cry.

It seemed like hours had passed before Mitchell felt confident enough to loosen his grip. They returned to the bivvies, gathered their things and tabbed down the mountain. Back in Hereford, Mitchell begged John to stay at his house.

'I know I gave you a fright up there but I'm over it,' John insisted. 'I'll never try anything like that again. I promise.'

Despite John's assurances, Mitchell was worried he might try to harm himself again. The next day, Mitchell went to see the regimental sergeant major and told him, in strictest confidence, what had happened on the summit of Cribyn. Mitchell wanted the RSM to reassign John to a training task – where he could keep an eye on him.

Two days later John was summoned by the RSM, squadron OC and CO of the Regiment. They told him they knew about his attempted suicide and ordered him to submit to psychological testing.

John left them to confront Pete Mitchell. 'How could you sell me out to a gang of Ruperts?'

Mitchell was gutted. He'd never imagined the RSM would breach his confidence. 'I swear I didn't do it to stitch you up. I thought you needed time to sort your head out, that's all. You know what the RSM's like. He would have had you back on operations straightaway. I swear to you, John, on my life and the life of my kids, I never thought it would go any further than squadron level.'

'You've ruined me.' John's voice was hollow and bitter. 'Once something like this gets out, it never goes away. The lads will never trust me again.'

'You're wrong,' said Mitchell. 'Nothing has changed. They'll all still look up to you.'

'Would you trust a man who tried to kill himself?' John countered. Mitchell bowed his head. 'I've lost everything,' said John, 'my wife, my daughter and now my reputation. There really is nothing left to live for.'

'That's not true, mate,' said Mitchell. 'Fuck the RSM. You still have the Regiment.'

'Not any more,' said John. 'I resigned.'

Chapter 55

John shook his arm free and continued on. Dusty called after him. 'This is not your bloody home.' John collected the donkey and headed down the path away from Camp Keating. 'Do you hear me!' Dusty cried. 'Home is a million fucking miles from here!'

Howard remained with Dusty on the hillside. 'What does he mean, he's home?'

'I don't know.' Dusty shook his head, trying to explain. 'There's this woman back in Dogrum. He's got this whole fantasy in his head about her.'

Howard's eyes oscillated between the two Scots. Dusty was as he remembered; a bit more beaten-up perhaps, but still strong, defiant and full of life. But the thin old man with the bushy beard and ethnic robe ambling down the path was just an echo of the mentor he'd once revered. Howard had come to Nuristan hoping to save both John and Dusty. He never imagined that only one of them would want to be rescued. 'What happened to him, Dusty?'

'What hasn't?' Dusty looked at the empty LZ on the edge of Camp Keating. 'When are you out of here, James?'

Howard checked his watch. 'Less than thirty minutes, assuming the heli hasn't been redirected or shot down.' He gazed at the surrounding mountains. Howard had never been so far from his comfort zone, so completely separated from everything familiar. A premonition crept over him like a chill. At that moment Howard knew that one of them would die. He spoke to Dusty in earnest. 'Let him go.'

Dusty whipped around. 'What?'

Howard's intuition urged him on. 'I'm begging you. Let John go his own way.'

'Are you off your head,' said Dusty. 'He'll die if we leave him here.'

Howard pointed to Corporal Rucker. The young infantry man was hovering nearby. 'Do you see that soldier? I didn't ask him to come with me. His CO ordered him to. Do you know why?' Howard didn't wait for Dusty to answer. 'Because he refused to let me see *The Scot from Dogrum* alone.'

'Now you really do sound like a Rupert,' said Dusty. 'This is Nuristan, not Kabul, James. No one's allowed outside those gates without an escort.'

'Listen to me!' Howard grabbed Dusty by the shoulders. 'The CO described John as *a person of interest*. Do you know what that means? The only reason they haven't detained him yet is because they don't want to alienate Dogrum as a potential ally. But I promise you, sooner or later, they will come after John. Do you really want to be standing next to him when that happens?'

'Well, did you tell them they have nothing to worry about?' Dusty shot back. 'Did you tell them John isn't al-Qaeda?'

'Of course I did,' said Howard. 'I told them I'd trust John Patterson with my life. But now . . .' Howard looked down the path, 'now I'm not so sure. The John Patterson I knew is gone.'

Dusty leapt to John's defence. 'He's the same man who pulled your green arse through the Regiment.'

'I understand your loyalty,' said Howard. 'But even you can't deny that John has changed.'

'So he's grown his beard long and lost a few stone,' Dusty argued. 'That doesn't make him bin Laden's wingman, for fuck's sake.'

'I'm not accusing him of being al-Qaeda,' said Howard. 'But can you tell me, honestly, that he's still one of us? *I am home*; those were his words.' Dusty had nothing to counter. 'If he wants to be with this woman and live his life in Nuristan then let him go, Dusty. He doesn't want to be saved. But it's not too late to save yourself. Come with me.'

Dusty searched for John. He was winding his way through the foothills leading to Kamdesh village. 'He's not as far gone as you think.' Dusty turned to Howard. 'Can you give us a week?'

Howard wanted to see the situation through Dusty's eyes; he wanted to give John the benefit of the doubt. But he couldn't. 'A week won't change anything—'

'Can you send a heli for us in a week?' Dusty pressed.

Howard paused. 'I suppose it's possible but . . .'

'Send a heli for us and I promise John will be on it,' said Dusty.

Howard's premonition grew more intense. 'Please. I implore you, Dusty. Come with me now. You may not get another chance.'

Dusty was already running after John. 'One week,' he called back to Howard. 'One week and we'll be on our way home.'

Dusty caught up with John. 'Were you trying to wind me up back there?' he asked, breathless from exertion. John kept his eyes trained forward. The unresponsiveness only hardened Dusty's resolve. 'So now you're not talking to me? All right then, I'll talk for both of us. I'll talk so much your ears will bleed.'

'You should leave with James.' John still refused to make eye contact with Dusty. 'You don't belong here.'

'Neither do you,' said Dusty.

John turned to face him. 'You're wrong. Dogrum is the only place I do belong.'

'It's Roshanak.' Dusty said her name as if it were illegal. John looked away. 'There's no point denying it,' said Dusty. 'It's been obvious for months. You want to stay here to be with her.'

'It's not just Roshanak,' said John. 'Things have changed.'

Dusty tapped his temple. 'That bitch is fucking with your head, mate.'

John grabbed Dusty by the collar. 'Don't ever talk about her like that.'

Dusty met John's challenge. 'You want a fight, then let's fight because I'll beat you senseless if that's what it takes for you to face facts. There's nothing between you and Roshanak. You're not going to marry her and live happily ever after. She can't replace your dead wife and that poor wee girl of hers can't replace your dead daughter. Your family is dead, John. They're dead.'

Dusty's bluntness brought all the horrible memories flooding back to John. He fought back tears. 'Leave them out of this,' he warned.

'Admit it,' said Dusty. 'You think you can replace them. You think you can recreate in Dogrum what you had back home. There's nothing else in this shithole worth hanging around for.' John cast his eyes down and let go of Dusty. 'Wait a minute,' said Dusty. 'You're holding something else back from me, aren't you? What is it?'

John raised his arm. The insignia on his sleeve unfurled like a flag. 'I'm Malek of Dogrum,' he said solemnly.

Dusty's eyes darted back and forth between the insignia and John's face. 'You're fucking what?'

'I'm Malek of Dogrum,' John repeated. 'Anvar asked me to take his place before he died. I accepted. So you see, mate, I do belong here.'

Dusty's expression morphed from distress to disbelief. He started to laugh. Soon, his whole body was shaking. 'So that's why . . .' Dusty spat the words between belly howls, '. . . that's why you've been wearing that manky coat.'

John wasn't laughing with him. 'It's a Malek's robe.'

'Oh, get over yourself!' Dusty's howls turned scornful. 'You grew up on a council estate. There's no fucking Malek of Arbroath.'

'That's where I started,' said John. 'But this is where I was meant to end up. It took me a while to realize it but now I see that everything that's happened since we've been in Afghanistan has been leading up to this: the CNPA task, the contact on the Jalalabad Road, the *jirga*, all of it. I am the Malek of Dogrum, Dusty. It's my destiny.'

'Your destiny? Now you're really taking the piss,' said Dusty.

John raised his chin. 'I wouldn't expect you to understand. What would you know about taking care of other people? The only person you've ever cared about is yourself.'

'At least I know who I am!' Dusty shoved his finger in John's chest. 'And I do care about someone. I care about you, John. People are full of shite. Hell, I'm full of shite. But not you; you're honest and you're decent and you're the only person I've ever trusted. Why do you think I left the Regiment right after you? Why do you think I followed you to the ends of the bloody earth? Don't you dare accuse me of not caring. I have fought like hell to keep you alive and I'll be damned if I leave you here to die.'

John reflected on all that Dusty had done for him since leaving Kabul. 'Without you, I would be dead right now. And for that I'll always be grateful to you. But it's time for us to go our separate ways. Go home with James. My people are waiting for me.'

John kissed Dusty on both cheeks. The foreign gesture made Dusty cringe. '*Your* people my arse. You can't even talk to them without Haider translating for you.'

'Haider doesn't mind,' said John. The sound of helicopters approaching filled the valley. An Apache flew over a ridge. A Chinook followed on its heels. 'That'll be for James. You better get moving if you want to catch him.'

Dusty looked at the Chinook and back at John. 'Haider is using you. Can't you see that?' The Chinook manoeuvred into position and dropped onto the LZ.

'You're wrong,' said John. 'Haider thinks of me as a brother. And we will be soon enough. I'm going to marry Roshanak.'

'You're not marrying her,' said Dusty.

'Roshanak will be my wife and Shams will be my daughter,' John insisted. 'It's already been decided.'

'By who?' Dusty grabbed John's jaw and turned it. 'That bitch tore a lump off you. You think she's going to lie back and spread her legs for you now? Or will you just order her to do it – Malek.'

John was indignant. 'I would never force Roshanak to do anything. Haider said she wants to marry me.'

Dusty shouted above the din of the helicopter. 'Wake up, mate. Haider will say and do anything to keep you in Dogrum. He's a fucking liar.'

'He's never done anything to make me doubt him.' John collected the donkey's reins. 'Which is more than I can say for you.'

'I've always had your back. Always,' said Dusty.

'Really.' The Chinook lifted off from the LZ. 'Then tell me, how is it that Rasul's nephews knew exactly when and where to find us that morning?'

Dusty stiffened. 'Rasul knew we were scheduled to be there. He had us wiped from the board. Remember?'

'We checked in an hour and a half before our slot,' said John. 'The nephews didn't know our routine.'

'They must have triggered us from the car park,' said Dusty.

The Chinook finished its ascent and turned south-east; over John and Dusty's heads. John shouted over the noise. 'I didn't put it together until I saw that bag of beads. The nephews had a tout inside the KMTC, someone who knew exactly when we would be there. That bloke I saw hanging around outside Range Control – he's the one who triggered us, isn't he?' Dusty looked guilty as hell. 'I hope it was worth it,' said John. 'I hope you made bags of money doing business with the nephews' tout.'

Dusty wiped his face with his hands. 'I admit I fucked up big style with that one. But I swear . . .' A burst of small arms fire erupted from the foothills east of their position. They both turned. A trail of smoke from an RPG round was streaking up from the ground. The missile was heading right for the Chinook.

The RPG round sliced through the back rotor disc of the great helicopter. Thick smoke poured from the fuselage as the Chinook spiralled out of control. The pilot struggled to salvage the aircraft, but the momentum was too great to overcome. It slammed into a mountain and burst into a black and orange fireball.

John dropped the reins. 'We need to get out of here. Now!'

Dusty stood motionless. 'James!' he cried.

John pulled Dusty along with him. 'There'll be hell on for this! That Apache's coming back and it'll take out anything that moves!' The Apache returned just as they cleared the ridge. The war bird strafed the foothills with a 40mm cannon and unleashed a hellfire missile into the area where the RPG had come from. Everything within forty metres of the impact was blown to pieces.

When the Apache cleared off, Dusty insisted on searching the crash site. He surveyed the wreckage through his binos. Burning debris and small electrical explosions were strewn over a widespread area. No one on the helicopter could have survived. 'James is dead,' he said.

John bowed his head. 'He should have stayed in Kabul where he belonged.'

Dusty grabbed John by the collar. 'Don't you get it?' he hissed. 'James died trying to save us. That Rupert is a fucking hero.'

Chapter 56

Rudy couldn't face returning to his bureau and staring at an empty computer screen. The last of his fading passion for his craft had been castrated by the dossier on John Patterson. Rudy's primary source had a history of mental instability; no one would print the story now.

Rudy needed to numb his pain. He asked the driver to take him to the only place in Kabul where a shattered man could drown his sorrows in like-minded company – the Elbow Room.

The assembled clientele hadn't changed since Rudy's first visit a year earlier: fellow journalists, dishevelled aid workers, and security contractors. He found an empty stool at the bar and ordered a Scotch. Rudy downed it in one go and immediately asked for another.

A fat belly invaded his space. 'I suggest you finish that quickly and be on your way.'

Rudy looked up. Simon Hampson was sneering down at him. 'Piss off,' said Rudy.

'Remember who you're talking to,' Simon warned. 'All I need to do is snap my fingers and you'll be out of here on your arse.'

'That's right.' Rudy sipped his refreshed drink. 'You have friends in Kabul,' he said sarcastically. Rudy looked around. 'Where's your jailbait girlfriend?'

'Jailbait?' said Simon. 'All my female companions are of

consenting age, thank you very much. There are documents to prove it, so if you've come here to stir the shit, you little turd, forget it. Haven't you learned by now? I'm untouchable.'

'Don't flatter yourself,' said Rudy. 'You're not interesting enough to write about.'

Simon motioned to the barman. 'Lager.' He turned to Rudy. 'So what are you doing here then?'

Rudy drank his Scotch. 'What does it look like?'

'Don't take me for a fool,' said Simon. 'You're up to something.'

'I know what you're thinking.' Rudy raised his drink and addressed Simon as he would an audience. 'You're wondering what I'm doing in this fair establishment when I should be out covering stories, aren't you? Well, allow me to enlighten you, Mr Hampson. I'm here because I've surrendered to the will of the British people.'

'You're drunk,' said Simon.

'On the contrary,' said Rudy. 'I've never been more lucid. When the British people open a newspaper, what do you think they want to read about? A failing military campaign thousands of miles away? Government waste? Corporate corruption? Child brides scalding their genitals? Do they hell. Property prices, ASBOs, glamour models getting their tits out – that's what the British care about. So I ask you – why should I risk life and limb covering stories that no one will read? Provided, of course, my sage editor in London runs them, which most of the time, she doesn't.'

Simon shook his head distastefully, took his lager and sat down at a table where a young Chinese prostitute was waiting to stroke his neck. Rudy reckoned she was even younger than the last one. He pulled out his notebook and made a note: *Sex-slave/ Mercenary pimp. Goodies/ Baddies.*

Chapter 57

A cockerel crowed. The shrill cry was followed by another and another until the entire valley was engulfed by the swell and ebb of nature's chorus. Dusty sprang from his bed, his heart pounding with anticipation. This was not just another morning in Dogrum. It was his last.

John was already up and dressed. The breakfast tray lay untouched on the table before him. He picked up a pomegranate and studied it.

Dusty sat down across from him and smiled at the fruit. 'I didn't think those were in season yet.'

'I asked the Magnificent Seven to go find you one.' John handed the fruit to Dusty. 'You won't get anything near this nice in Britain.'

Dusty bashed the red orb on the table. He picked the plump seeds from the broken fruit one at a time and savoured the sweet juices as they burst in his mouth. 'These are almost worth staying here for.'

'I'll give you an orchard, then.' John flourished his hand. 'I am Malek, after all.'

Dusty smiled. 'I said almost.' A feeling of melancholy descended on them both. 'You know when we reach the border, I'm dragging you over it,' said Dusty.

John tore a piece of flatbread. 'The Magnificent Seven would never let me go.'

The melancholy dissolved. 'You're a fool to trust them, you know.'

'Oh don't go on,' John moaned.

'No,' said Dusty. 'They're no different from Haider. They're cunning little bastards.' He held up the pomegranate. 'Where the hell did they get this? Or all the other shite? They're from a poor village, remember? I'm telling you, they're not who you think they are.'

John threw his bread down on the tray. 'We've got a full day's walk ahead of us. Let's just agree to disagree and drop the subject.' John lowered his eyes, his way of signalling that the discussion was over.

They finished their breakfast in silence and prepared to leave. Dusty closed the top flap of his Bergen. 'I hope you don't mind but I helped myself to a couple of Claymores. Things might get hairy once I'm on my own.'

'No worries,' said John. 'Take whatever you need.'

John and Dusty shouldered their packs and emerged from their single room dwelling, the last time they'd do so together. The buzz of a small aircraft engine sounded high overhead. John searched the sky. A storm front was rolling in. A drone was circling ahead of it.

'That's two days on the trot now,' said Dusty. 'What do you think they're looking for?'

'The insurgents who attacked us,' said John. He cast a protective eye over his fiefdom. The women were tending the fields. Roshanak was among them. Her scarlet veil had lost much of its vibrancy without Shams's blonde curls at her knee. How John longed for them all to be reunited as a family. He scanned the hills and peaks beyond Dogrum. The wall of grey was closing in. A terrifying thought suddenly gripped him: what if Roshanak was taken from him too? He turned to Dusty. 'That storm looks pretty angry. Maybe we should hold off a day or two.'

'We've both seen worse in the Beacons.' Dusty headed toward the bridge. 'You'll say anything to keep me here, won't you?'

'Then we must all hold our tongues.' Haider smiled as he joined the two Scots.

'Come to see us off then?' said Dusty.

Haider opened his arms and embraced Dusty. 'I know we have not always seen eye to eye. But you have done much to help my people . . .' he nodded to John, 'and my Malek. You have given Dogrum a future. For that, you shall always be as dear to me as family.'

Dusty prised himself free. 'So you think of me as a brother?'

Haider tilted his head. 'Maybe a sister.'

The Magnificent Seven were assembled at the bridge. The brothers had three donkeys in tow laden with cloth satchels. 'You lot don't pack light,' said Dusty. 'What do you have there?'

Ehsaan spoke. 'Goods from their village,' Haider translated. 'They hope to trade with the Pakistanis.'

Dusty spoke to Haider. 'Do these lads definitely know where they're going? I don't want to end up in Iran.'

'The route to Pakistan is an ancient one,' Haider assured him. 'All of Nuristan knows it.'

Dusty and the brothers headed out while John lingered to have a quiet word with Haider. 'You'll talk to Roshanak while I'm away?'

'Do not worry,' said Haider. 'She will do as she is told.'

The answer did not sit well with John. 'I don't want her feeling pressurized.'

Haider dismissed the idea. 'What greater honour is there for a woman than to be the bride of a Malek? We will have the wedding upon your return.'

John embraced Haider. His feelings of foreboding returned. 'Look after her while I'm gone and remember, don't hesitate to give the "stand to" order if you think you're being attacked. Better safe than sorry.'

Haider kissed John on both cheeks. 'I shall not let you down, Malek.'

John detected the faint chop of helicopter blades. He ran to catch Dusty and the others. 'Do you hear that?'

'What's the matter now?' asked Dusty.

John looked at the mountain they were about to climb. The waterfall tumbled off it, feeding the river that ran beneath Dogrum. 'There's a helicopter up there. First a drone and now a heli; it's got to be an operation. We should hold off until we know it's clear.'

'There's a war on,' said Dusty. 'It could be years before the skies are clear.'

'It's too risky.' John grabbed Ehsaan. 'Stop,' he commanded. Ehsaan looked confused.

'What do you think you're doing?' asked Dusty.

'I won't endanger the lives of my people,' said John.

'I'm not one of your people.' Dusty's old frustrations returned. 'If you want to stay here, then stay here. But I'm going to Pakistan today.' Dusty pushed past John.

John called after him. 'Wait. Come back.' Dusty ignored him and kept walking. John faced a terrible decision: he could follow his instincts and let Dusty brave the journey alone or ignore them and ensure his friend's safety. He let go of Ehsaan and motioned forward.

*

The Magnificent Seven whipped the donkeys into a fast trot up the rocky incline. Again, John found himself struggling to keep up. He cursed his cramping side and aching legs. The clouds rolled in, shrouding their ascent in thick dense fog. By the time John stepped onto the mountaintop, he was soaked through with sweat and mist. A cold wind swept over the flat peak, slapping his emaciated frame. John's hands felt like they'd been stabbed with hot pokers. He fanned his arthritic fingers on his rifle to try and confuse the pain.

The head of the waterfall was broad and frothy. The brothers followed the riverbank upstream until the churning waters cleared and calmed. Ehsaan handed off the reins of his donkey, held his rifle aloft and waded into the river. It reached no higher than his shins. It was a natural ford.

The rest of the brothers gathered up the donkeys and followed him in. John and Dusty brought up the rear. The rocks beneath their feet were slick with moss, forcing them to take cautious, measured steps. The fog descended again and the Magnificent Seven vanished behind it. John and Dusty instinctively drew closer together.

The Scots stepped on the far bank. The mist was so thick they couldn't see more than five feet in any direction. There was no sign of Ehsaan or his brothers. John searched the ground for tracks. He gestured upriver. 'They went this way.'

John and Dusty followed the trail left by the brothers and their beasts. The earth sloped gently upward. The river disappeared from their field of vision, though they could tell it was near from the sound of the water rushing beneath them. The visual deprivation heightened John's awareness. He sharpened his ears and reasserted his grip on his rifle.

A sound rang out from behind the curtain of fog – the clunk of metal slamming into metal. John and Dusty stopped dead in their tracks. They both recognized the sound instantly: the working parts of a general purpose machine gun moving forward and failing to pick up a round. The noise had been programmed into their minds over countless drills and exercises. *Never initiate an ambush with a general purpose machine gun.*

The botched ambush attempt was confirmed by the voice that followed. 'Shit, man.'

John spun around right and fired at the voice. 'Contact right!' he yelled above the short, automatic bursts. Dusty sprayed the area with his 5.56. John ran backwards and jumped down onto the riverbank. Behind the fog, the ambush party opened up with a barrage of high-velocity rounds. Bullets were flying everywhere. John switched his rifle to single shot, aimed it over the escarpment and fired quick double taps while Dusty fell back.

The ambush party shouted directions to each other. 'Target on the move! Target on the move!' Dusty joined John in cover and the pair rolled onto their bellies. Their faces were just inches apart. Another torrent of bullets flew at them; they were being targeted from downriver, from the area they'd just walked through.

'Fuck me,' Dusty panted. 'We walked right past the killer group.'

John pulled out his binos and looked over the escarpment. A pocket opened in the fog, offering a glimpse of a rifle: an M4 Carbine with an M203 grenade launcher attached to the barrel. John dropped down. 'We are really in the shit. They're US Special Forces. Fuck, I knew there was an operation up here. That drone must have been tracking insurgents.'

Dusty's eyes widened, as if the pieces of a complex puzzle had suddenly fallen into place. 'Fuck me,' he whispered.

'We need to let them know this is a blue on blue,' said John.

Dusty rolled on top of him and grabbed him by the collar. 'Don't you get it!' he yelled. 'The drone was tracking *us*.'

'That's crazy,' said John.

'The Yanks think you're al-Qaeda,' said Dusty. 'James told me they would come after you. Fuck, they probably think it was you who shot down his heli.' Two bullets slammed into the Bergen bulging from Dusty's back. He rolled off John, slipped off the pack and unzipped it. He pulled out the Claymores and inspected them. The horseshoe-shaped mines were undamaged.

A soldier shouted downriver. 'They've come through your position! Move up the track! Move up the track!'

'We stay here and we're dead,' said John. 'We need to get back to Dogrum.'

Dusty stuffed the mines back in his Bergen. 'Fuck Dogrum. We need to get to Pakistan.'

An HE bomb screamed over their heads. The high-explosive round hit a rock jutting up from the river. The water exploded into a deadly fountain riddled with fragments. The voices of the soldiers drew closer. 'Up the track! Up the track!'

John slid off his Bergen and laid his rifle and pistol across it. 'I must protect my people!' he said, wading into the river. Dusty followed him. Using their packs as floatation devices, the Scots swam towards the far bank. A powerful current caught them by the legs and whipped them around. The water tossed them about, slamming them into rocks and spinning them in circles until it spat them out at the edge of the ford.

Ehsaan and two of his brothers ran into the water to help John out. They too were wet and badly beaten up. On the far bank, John and Dusty took stock of their remaining defences. The brothers had managed to salvage their rifles, one donkey and a few loose satchels. Dusty inspected his 5.56mm. It was still dry. He looked at the brothers' AKs. 'Their weapons are soaked,' he said to John. 'We can't count on them.' The ambush party were still shouting to each other upstream. The fog was starting to dissipate. 'We need to move light and we need to move now,' said Dusty.

John spoke to Ehsaan. 'Where are the rest of your brothers?' The Nuristani couldn't understand what John was asking him. John pointed west. 'Dogrum,' he said to Ehsaan. 'We go back to Dogrum.' Ehsaan nodded to his brothers. The two Nuristanis shouldered their rifles and gathered up the satchels to put on the donkey.

'Leave them,' said Dusty. The brothers ignored the unintelligible command. Dusty grabbed one of the satchels and threw it down. 'I said leave it. Leave it all. We need to go now.'

Ehsaan scooped up the satchel and clung to it like a life raft. 'What have you got there, you little bastard?' Dusty pulled his knife from his waistcoat. John looked on in horror as Dusty raised the weapon above Ehsaan's head and thrust it down. The blade passed within millimetres of Ehsaan's chest before plunging into the satchel. Dusty pulled out the knife and examined it. The blade was covered in sticky, brown residue. Dusty's face erupted with rage. He turned his back to Ehsaan and held the knife up for John. 'That's raw opium!' Dusty declared. 'These bastards are running drugs right under our noses!'

The blood drained from John's face. Images of his dead wife and daughter flashed through his mind: a sheet pulled over a tiny body, the double-coffined funeral. John's original motive for coming to Afghanistan came back to haunt him. He'd come to fight drugs traffickers. He'd come to stop heroin from destroying another British family.

'The Rasuls didn't attack Dogrum because they were after us,' said Dusty. 'These little fuckers were cutting in on their drugs trade.'

John looked at his star pupil. Ehsaan's face was defiant and
unrepentant. John felt sick. How could he have been so blind?
The Magnificent Seven were never interested in fighting insurgents. They wanted to take over the Rasuls' opium smuggling
business. When Hizb-i-Islami failed to give the brothers the
training they needed, they found John: the ex-SAS soldier stupid
enough to do it.

Ehsaan dropped the satchel and aimed his AK at Dusty's
back. John leapt forward and pushed Dusty to the ground. 'Get
down, mate!'

Ehsaan pulled the trigger. His soaking-wet rifle erupted in an
orange flash. A bang sounded and Ehsaan dropped to the
ground, his face burnt and bloodied. The rifle breech had
exploded in his face. In his haste to take revenge on Dusty,
Ehsaan had killed himself with his own weapon.

The last two brothers reached for their AKs. But their youthful agility was no match for John and Dusty's experience. The
Scots un-holstered their pistols, aimed and fired. The brothers
dropped where they stood. John looked at the blood seeping
from the tightly grouped holes in their heads. He'd taught these
men everything he knew; he'd treated them like sons and they
betrayed him in the worst possible way. John spat on the
corpses. 'Go to hell!'

The crack and thump of high-velocity rounds rumbled the air
again. Voices sounded from the far bank. 'Across the river!
Across the river!' Dusty grabbed John and shook him. 'The
Yanks are coming for us.' John snapped back while Dusty
retrieved the Claymores. He gave one to John and together they
forked the fragmentation mines into the ground. Dusty cracked
the trigger on the grip switch of his Claymore, twisted it and
plunged it back in. John waited fifteen seconds and did the same
to his.

The Scots quickly cached their Bergens behind a mass of boulders and ran like hell towards Dogrum. They managed to put a few hundred yards between themselves and the riverbank when they heard the first Claymore explode. The ambush party screamed as seven hundred ball bearings tore into their vanguard. Howls of pain followed by cries of 'Man down! Man Down!' reverberated across the mountaintop. A quarter of a minute later, the second Claymore detonated – unleashing another fatal barrage.

John and Dusty jumped down onto the path leading back to Dogrum. They flew down the jagged mountain, dropping and sliding as they hurled themselves toward safety. A group of soldiers pursued them to the head of the waterfall and stopped. One soldier yelled into a radio while the others took aim.

Bullets gouged the ground all around the fleeing Scots. An HE round landed thirty yards ahead of them. John dropped and rolled behind a boulder to escape the fallout from the blast. Dusty dived in after him.

With their faces cut and chests heaving, they huddled together, rounds ricocheting around them. Beyond the sounds of battle, the distant chop of helicopter blades threatened more trouble.

'That's coming for us,' Dusty panted. 'If we break for Dogrum, the heli will follow us right in there.'

John drew up his weapon. 'I've got two magazines left. You get yourself over the ridge and away from here. I'll cover you.'

'All morning you've been hounding me to stay. And now you want to get rid of me? Make up your fucking mind.'

John turned to Dusty, his blue eyes begging forgiveness. 'You wouldn't be in this mess if it weren't for me. I'll cover you. Please, mate.'

'Go to hell,' said Dusty. 'We're in this together.'

Cries of 'Stand to! Stand to!' rang out from Dogrum. John's face filled with alarm and dread. The men of Dogrum – his people – were moving over the rooftops and into position. 'Haider thinks Dogrum's under attack. I have to warn them to stand down before it's too late!'

John tore down the mountain with no thought for his own safety. His only concern was Roshanak and the village he'd sworn to protect. The ambush party converged on John's position. Just as they were about to let loose with a fatal volley, Dusty jumped out from behind the boulder and waved his rifle conspicuously. The soldiers re-aimed their M4s. Dusty hit them with fast and accurate double-taps and rolled just in time to dodge the return fire. The soldiers fell back. Dusty had driven them into cover.

John saw Haider running toward the bridge. His loyal friend was doing exactly as he'd been taught. He was heading for the sanger on the other side. John cupped one hand to his mouth and shouted. 'Stand down! Stand down!' But the order was swamped by an Apache swooping down over the terraced fields. John kept screaming 'Stand down! Stand down!' but his cries were no match for the advancing gunship. The Apache opened up its 30mm chain gun. Haider took a direct hit. A round tore through his body, exploding his flesh into pink mist. John dropped to his knees. When the firing stopped, all that remained of Haider was a red stain.

The smoke from the chain gun licked the Apache's belly. An RPG round flew out of Dogrum and screamed past the helicopter. John's fighters were trying to shoot it down. John screamed at the top of his lungs: 'Stand down! Stand down!' But the battle was now unstoppable. The Apache circled around for another hit.

John rose and stumbled helplessly toward Dogrum. Dusty tackled him at the foot of the bridge. 'Take cover!' he screamed, dragging John into Haider's empty sanger. The Apache hovered as it shot two hellfire missiles into the village. The rockets slammed into the houses and exploded. Dogrum erupted in a ghostly cloud. The Apache circled around once to inspect its target. The war bird had been devastatingly efficient; Dogrum was annihilated.

John and Dusty waited for the Apache to fly off before leaving the safety of the sanger. John looked on helplessly at his village. Not a single building was left standing. Body parts of men, women and children lay everywhere in the debris. John's will to live drained away as he replayed the milestones that had brought him to this terrible moment: the body tumbling out of the nephews' Toyota, the landslide sweeping the Kutchi to their deaths, the drone destroying the Hizb-i-Islami camp, the mortar landing on Anvar's house. Another memory surfaced from the catalogue of destruction: the first visit to Camp Keating and his confrontation with the intelligence officer. John collapsed as the awful truth descended on him. His temper had brought Dogrum to ruins.

John's face contorted with agony. He opened his mouth to cry out, but the scream was silent. Suddenly, a man rose from the ashes of the village. He was shocked and disoriented, a pistol dangling from his fingertips. It was Daud.

More survivors surfaced from the rubble: five men, two children – a woman. Her face and clothes were indistinguishable beneath the layers of dust. John's eyes welled with tears when he realized who she was – Roshanak!

Some invisible hand had kept her alive. John vowed to the God he had forsaken that he would never again let her out of his sight. Roshanak stumbled forward and threw herself on the spot where Haider had been slain. She wailed as she clawed the bloody earth. John ran across the bridge to comfort her. She stopped him with an icy, unforgiving stare.

Roshanak's eyes flooded with hatred as she searched the ground around her. She picked up a stone and hurled it with all her might. It flew through the air and struck John's forehead. He fell to his knees, dazed.

Daud joined Roshanak and stood over her. He waved his pistol at John and screamed. 'Kafir! Kafir! Kafir!'

Roshanak added her voice to Daud's. 'Kafir! Kafir!' she howled, rocking back and forth. The rest of the Dogrum's survivors joined the frenzy until the valley was alive with the cry: 'Kafir! Kafir! Kafir!'

Dusty ran to John's side, his rifle at the ready. The elder Scot was stunned and bleeding from Roshanak's blow. 'What's happening? Are the Yanks behind us?' he asked frantically.

Dusty stepped in front of John to shield him. 'It's a mutiny, mate.'

John didn't believe it. Certain that the cries of 'Kafir!' were intended for the American ambush party. He turned and scanned the fields. There was no one there. He looked to the path leading up the mountain; it too was empty. The villagers were still chanting: 'Kafir! Kafir! Kafir!' There was no escaping it; he was the infidel.

Daud waved his pistol wildly. Dusty walked backwards, covering John as he warned off the vengeful Nuristani. 'Easy there, mate. We've all had a rough morning. Just lower your weapon and we'll be on our way now.'

Daud aimed the pistol at John and fired. Dusty responded with a single shot from his 5.56. The bullet from the pistol missed John and caught Dusty's hand just as the rifle round slammed into Daud's skull. The Nuristani's head exploded.

Dusty dropped his rifle and grabbed his wounded hand. There was a bloody gap between his index and little finger.

John stepped into the role of defender. He aimed his AK at his mutinous subjects. The villagers armed themselves with stones and advanced on the two Scots, chanting: 'Kafir! Kafir! Kafir!'

John kept his rifle trained on them. 'Run,' he said to Dusty.

Dusty stuck by his side. 'We'll see this through together.'

'I'm the one they want; not you.' John urged his friend to save himself. 'I was a fool to think I ever belonged here. But you knew better, Dusty. You knew me better than I knew myself.' The villagers raised the stones above their heads. 'Never forget who you are, because you and me, we're the same, mate. We're the fucking same.' John aimed his AK at the rabid villagers and squeezed the trigger. 'We're Scotsmen!'

Chapter 58

KABUL 2008 . . .

The crippled fugitive shook violently as he raised the tumbler of Scotch to his mouth. Rudy looked at the clock; his copy was hours overdue. He took Dusty's mangled hand in his. 'What happened next, Mr Miller? What became of John Patterson?'

Dusty forced the whisky past the lump in his throat. 'John didn't have it in him to kill those people,' he said, 'even though they'd all turned on him. He unloaded his magazine right at their feet. *Run*, he screamed at me. *Run*. And I did; as fast as my legs would take me, across the bridge and up through the fields. I thought John would try and make a break for it too but when I looked back, he was still in Dogrum. The villagers had him by the arms and legs. He didn't struggle, mind. John was too dignified for that. They raised him up over their heads, walked him to the middle of the bridge and threw him over the side like a bag of rubbish. They kept repeating as he fell: Kafir . . . Kafir . . . Kafir . . .' Dusty's voice trailed away as the words pulled him back to the horrible moment. 'And that's what became of John Patterson,' he said softly. 'SAS soldier, last Malek of Dogrum, true son of Scotland.'

Dusty rocked back and forth in his chair, weeping bitterly.

Rudy allowed him to cry unhindered until the tears had run their course.

'And what about you?' said Rudy. 'How did you survive?'

Dusty held out his empty glass. Rudy obliged him with a refill. 'I climbed back up the mountain – back to where the Yanks had ambushed us. I found my Bergen and put some dressings on my hand. I stayed on that mountaintop for two days, observing the villagers, waiting for them to clear off. I wanted to recover John's body, you see. I wanted to give him a proper burial. I know he would have done the same for me. But by the time I made my way down to the valley, John was gone. The river must have carried his body away; that or the animals got to him.'

Dusty turned his face towards the wood-burning stove. The shadows from the grate looked like prison bars against his hollow cheeks. Rudy couldn't believe the withered wreck sitting across from him was the same strapping ex-SAS soldier he'd left on the Jalalabad Road. 'What about after that? Did you try and make it to the border? To Pakistan?'

Dusty smiled. It wasn't an expression of joy. The grin was maniacal. 'And get whacked by the Yanks? Are you off your head? I had no ammo left; nothing to defend myself with except my knife. And bandits soon stole that – after they beat me near to death.' Dusty looked down on his bent, twisted torso. 'That's the thing about this country,' he said. 'When you're strong, Afghans respect you. They'll invite you into their homes and villages. They'll be your best fucking mate. But show even a hint of weakness and you're on your own. There's no love or mercy for the weak here. Compassion gets you killed in Afghanistan. The only way to survive is to look after yourself.' Dusty stared into his past, his eyes recalling horrors and hardships Rudy couldn't begin to imagine. 'I would have died where the bandits left me if it weren't for John.'

'But . . .' Rudy was taken aback. 'I thought the villagers killed him.'

'Of course they bloody killed him. Haven't you been listening to a word I've said?' Dusty grumbled. 'I couldn't let John's story die with me. I knew I had to make it back here, to Kabul. I had to find you and let you know what happened to him. And now John's story is yours, you lucky bastard.'

The wind rattled the windows of Rudy's office. Dusty rose to leave. The frail Scot didn't look fit enough to survive the cold. 'It's terribly bitter out there. You're welcome to stay until morning,' said Rudy. 'I'd be honoured to have you as my guest.'

Dusty grabbed the bottle of Famous Grouse from Rudy's desk. 'This will see me through just fine. Fair trade for the camera,' he said and hobbled off into the Kabul night.

Rudy stared at the pictures on the computer screen long after Dusty had gone. The disillusioned journalist was now the custodian of an incredible tale. Who were the goodies and who were the baddies? ISAF, US Forces, Kom, Kshto? None of them had a monopoly on decency – not even John Patterson. Like Rudy, they all had selfless aspirations and selfish agendas. But was a public weaned on stories of black and white conflict prepared to read the messy truth?

Rudy poured himself another Cragganmore, lifted the glass, studied it and put it down without taking a drink. He highlighted the pictures on the screen and poised his finger over the delete key . . .